FROM THE
VOID

BRYAN SMITH

Grindhouse Press #108
ISBN-13: 978-1-957504-21-6

Other Grindhouse Press titles by Bryan Smith

PROLOGUE

THE FIRST THING—AND, REALLY, one of the very few things—you'll need to know about me is that I survived the End Times. This should be obvious. Otherwise I wouldn't be here to put pen to paper. Of course it's questionable whether anyone will ever read what I have to say within these pages, but I think it's important to at least attempt to establish some record of what happened.

There are precious few of us left, we humans. Whether those of us who remain can repopulate and renew this decimated world remains to be seen. I frankly wouldn't bet money on it. Not that money means anything anymore. On the off chance I'm wrong, however, my hope is this manuscript might serve as a cautionary tale. It is my intent to be as honest as possible in this account. Therefore I'll be adopting the role of third person narrator for the rest of these pages. If I do the job I've assigned myself properly, you shouldn't be able to guess which of the players in this tale is me. At least not until very close to the end of my story.

What follows is the truth as I know it. I was privy enough to the thoughts and feelings of my compatriots to feel confident I can accurately portray events from their points of view. Here and there will be bits one might interpret as "fiction", though I prefer to think of them as artistic license. These are included to convey the grand scale of

1

what happened during those first calamitous End Time days. In these instances the specific event might not have occurred, but many things like them certainly did.

Once upon a time we lived in a fairy tale world in which the only monsters we had to worry about were of the human variety. Madmen and terrorists. Crooked politicians and corporate greedheads. An ordinary world inhabited by billions of ordinary human beings. A flesh and blood, concrete world built upon an unquestioned foundation of solid, non-malleable reality. This was our world, earth, and anything beyond it was unknowable and purely the theoretical province of theologians and spiritualists.

Until, that is, that unbridgeable gap between our reality and the unknowable began to decay. Until the denizens of that dark place came howling into our world, bringing with them a storm of death and destruction, and planting a seed of rot that would infect each of the intermingling alien worlds.

This is my story.

This is everyone's story.

This is how the world died . . .

1

FROM OUT OF THE BLACKNESS, a shape emerges and hides in shadow.

It is a formless, amorphous thing. A shifting, slithering mass of a substance resembling raw petroleum. It looks like nothing that has ever drawn breath in this world, like nothing that could possibly be alive, but alive it is and within it resides an awful consciousness, a black-tinged, malevolent intelligence that pulsates with hate and a gnawing need to destroy all that is alien.

All that is of this strange new world it has invaded.

But to do this it must adapt.

It begins to discern the shape of the world beyond these shadows and what it detects sickens it. So strong is this initial repulsion it nearly attempts to retreat to the world from which it has come, a realm it subjugated and made its own long ago. So long ago this new world may not have existed then. But it is an ancient thing and time is a concept so small, so abstract, that it attaches no significance to it.

All that matters is beginning anew the process of conquest and annihilation.

To that end, it casts a net with its mind, searching for a place to begin . . .

Searching for a suitable Host.

FROM THE VOID

Then . . . here.

Yes, this will do.

~

The day the world watched the president of the United States of America die on live television began for most as uneventfully as any other.

For most, but not for all.

~

Nashville, TN
September 25
6:00 a.m.

Emma Singleton awoke to the not-quite-dulcet tones of the morning zoo crew on one of the local Top 40 stations. She groaned and slapped the radio alarm clock, knocking it off the nightstand in the process. The clock landed on the floor with a *thunk*, but the zoo crew babbled on, the tinny, snickering voices drilling into her sleep-befuddled brain like a thousand tiny needles.

Gritting her teeth, she reached over the side of the bed, gripped the clock's electrical cord in a shaking hand, and ripped it free of the outlet. She relinquished the cord and fell back into bed. She stared at the ceiling, just barely visible now in the dawning light of the new day, and tried to think of a good reason to get out of bed. She was unemployed, having been fired from her bartending job at the Villager Pub a week earlier. Rick McAllister, her boyfriend of the last year and a half, had dumped her the week before that.

Thinking about it now, as she lay half-awake in bed at the ungodly hour of 6 a.m., it seemed pretty obvious she had nothing to live for and so getting out of bed to face the day was really quite pointless. Except . . .

Except she'd made a promise to her mom during an excruciatingly endless long-distance phone conversation the previous night. A vow she wouldn't allow herself to sink into depths of intractable depression. She wouldn't sit around in her apartment moping all day. She wouldn't keep drinking vodka until she passed out. Because, as her mother had so sternly reminded her, she'd gone down that path once before in her life and it hadn't turned out so well, now had it?

Mom's guilt-tripping worked its predictable efficient magic. Emma had gone to bed the night before fully intending to get up bright and early and go hit all the top temporary employment agencies

4

in town.

But something had changed within her between the moment she turned out the light and closed her eyes the previous night and now. The sense of motivation instilled by her mother's words had deserted her utterly.

Her gaze flicked to the right, where she'd laid out the clothes selected the night before for her temp interviews. Prim and proper dress clothes. The sort of buttoned-down, conservative outfit she could never comfortably wear. The blouse and skirt were cleaned and pressed. They were the clothes of a conscientious, careful woman. No wonder they looked swiped from a stranger's wardrobe.

Emma's normal clothes lay in a rumpled heap on the floor. Her cropped black T-shirt with the fishnet sleeves and her black, low-slung hip-hugger jeans. And the studded black vinyl belt she wore with nearly every outfit. Her rock 'n' roller clothes. The *real* Emma's clothes. Emma the songwriter and musician. For maybe the millionth time this week she lamented the fact that creative people couldn't go out and apply for jobs in their chosen fields the way, say, a junior executive or customer service rep could. It seemed colossally unfair, but it was the way of the world. There was no temp service for out-of-work novelists or singers. A deeper darkness tinged her thoughts now, the way they always did when she allowed herself to contemplate the steep odds against "making it" in any of the creative fields. It depressed her to think of all the genuinely gifted people who every year resigned themselves to a life spent working as automatons in factories, their talents left to wither while they did what they had to do in order to collect those meager paychecks, a bit of money that kept the lights on and kept food in the fridge. The hand-to-mouth life.

Emma sighed.

"Fuck it. I ain't doin' it."

She rolled onto her side and lifted the cordless phone from her nightstand cradle. She punched in Phil Parker's number and listened to the pulse of the ringing phone.

Phil picked up on the fifth ring. "You better have a good fucking reason for calling me at this hour, Emma Singleton."

Emma winced. "I'm sorry. I know it's early."

"You're fuckin' A right it's early. Christ . . ." There was a pause. "Holy shit, it's six in the goddamned morning."

"I'm sorry, really. It's just that . . . can I please have my job back?

5

Look, I know I freaked out when Rick dumped me, but that's all over now. I've got my shit back together and I want to go back to work." The pleading tone in her voice made Emma cringe, but she couldn't help it—there was just no way to mask this level of desperation. "Look, I'll do whatever you want to make up for not calling those times I skipped work. Double shifts for a while. Anything."

Phil sighed. "I don't know. I already took on another girl part-time . . ."

"So fire her."

Phil laughed. "You're really something, you know that? I can't fire a girl I just hired for no good reason."

"Can't you? You're the boss."

A heavier sigh emanated from Phil's end this time. He didn't say anything for several moments. Then he chuckled. "You said you'd do anything, right?"

Emma's grip tightened on the phone. She bit her lip, steeling herself for what she knew was coming. She managed one word: "Yeah."

Phil cleared his throat. He at least had the courtesy to sound nervous when he said it: "Will you . . . have sex with me?"

Emma hesitated only a moment, then said, "Once. I'm not gonna be anyone's whore." She quickly switched to a sultrier tone: "But I'll make that one time memorable, I promise."

Phil chuckled again, but he still sounded nervous, like he couldn't quite believe he'd had the nerve to propose something like this. With his wife still asleep next to him in their bed, at that. "You've got a deal. Show up an hour before time to open. That way we'll have the place to ourselves long enough to . . . do it. Got it?"

"Got it."

Emma put the phone back in its cradle.

Then she pulled the sheets up over her eyes and went back to sleep.

~

Kent Gowran emerged from Fido's coffee shop on 21st Avenue at five minutes after noon. He took a seat at one of the sidewalk tables, set his steaming Styrofoam coffee mug on the table, and flipped open that day's edition of *USA TODAY*. He scanned the headlines but found little of interest in either the national or international news. Same old empty rhetoric and bluster from the leaders of both political parties

He flipped through the sections until he reached the Life section and was just digging into a story on filmmaker Michael Moore's latest documentary when something at the edge of his peripheral vision tugged his gaze away from the newsprint.

A sense of something approaching. What—and from where—he couldn't immediately discern. An object roughly the size of a football entered the upper range of his field of vision, an indeterminate brown blob plummeting from out of the sky. It hit the sidewalk in front of him with a wet *SPLOOSH!* Someone, a woman from the sound of it, let out a startled yelp. Droplets of moisture splashed the cuff of his slacks and his shoes. The paper slipped from his fingers, hit the edge of the table, and slid into his lap. Numbly, he messily folded the section and put it away, then leaned forward to examine the bloody mess on the sidewalk.

Other people drew near the fallen creature—which he saw now was a bird, a big black one—and there was a babble of excited voices. None of the words registered. He was too busy trying to figure out what had happened to the fallen creature. It didn't look as if it had been shot (and he couldn't imagine anyone would be shooting birds out of the sky on a busy city street, anyway). But it stank. Bad. Like something that had been dead long enough to begin decomposing.

He shook his head. "What the fuck?"

Just then a louder, booming voice intruded, and the crowd of rubberneckers began to disperse as a big shadow fell over Kent's shoulder. He looked around to see a big man—in all senses; the man was well over six feet tall and weighed in at probably 300 pounds—in a chef's apron standing over him.

"Sorry 'bout that, mister. We'll comp your meal, of course."

Kent could do nothing but blink and nod. "Uh . . ."

The big man put his fingers in his mouth, sucked in a lungful of air, and let out a whistle loud enough to pierce eardrums in the next hemisphere. "Yo, Jimmy! Get your ass out here! We got another bird on the fuckin' sidewalk!"

The man looked at Kent, smiled, and spoke again in a milder tone. "Sorry 'bout that. That's the third of those bastards to land on my sidewalk this week." He sighed and shook his head. "Bad for business. Real bad." He smiled again. "Listen, why don't you take a nicer table inside? We'll even give you some more freebies."

Kent shook his head. "No . . . no, that's okay. I'm fine, really." He glanced down at his pants and shoes. Only a very few drops of blood had touched him. No real harm had been done. But the whole

7

episode was creepy as hell. He looked again at the big man, who he assumed was either the cafe owner or manager. "Why do you think birds are dropping out of the sky here?"

The big man shrugged. "Wish I knew. Lot of weird shit happening lately. It's not just here. One of my neighbors had a bird, way bigger than this one here, land on the windshield of his Hummer. Smashed right through it. Bunch more dropped outta the sky over a highway outside of Memphis. Caused a bunch of wrecks, a big tractor truck jackknifed. Some people got killed. Poor bastards didn't know what hit them. Like I said, man, some weird shit."

Kent shook his head again. "Jesus. This is the first I've heard of it. What do they think it is? Some kind of airborne disease?"

Yet another head shake from the big man. "Nobody knows. And it ain't just birds it's happening to. And not just animals. People are droppin' dead for no reason. And I don't mean like they normally do. It's some kinda epidemic or somethin'. Only nobody can identify a cause."

Kent's brow furrowed deeply. "What? But—"

The big man clapped him on the shoulder. "Listen, I ain't got time to talk. All kinds of crises brewing in the shop." He nodded at Kent's *USA TODAY*. "There's an article in that front section you should check out. Second page."

The man left without another word, disappearing through the cafe's front door. A kid of about nineteen—also wearing a white chef's apron—came bustling out with a fistful of cleanup tools. Kent got up with a sigh and moved to the next table over while the kid snatched the bird up with gloved hands and dropped it into a heavy black garbage bag.

He was settling into his new chair when he happened to glance at the shopfront directly across the street. A fat man in a Hawaiian shirt was looking over a table of bargain books outside the Book-man/Bookwoman used books store. But it wasn't the man (or his loud shirt) that had drawn his attention. At the moment, Kent was unsure precisely what he'd seen. He frowned. There'd been . . . something. Whatever it was had unsettled him on a primal level. He became aware of a crawling sensation along his spine, a tactile feeling so intense he was briefly certain a snake had crawled up under his shirt.

"Jesus . . ." he muttered to himself. "Way too much weirdness to-day."

The physical sensation faded, but the sense of disturbance remained. Something indefinable, he had no clue what, was wrong. His gaze flicked to the left, where he saw Vandy students and businessmen filing into Bosco's brewpub for lunch. Then to the right and the dark door of the closed Villager Pub. He stared at the closed sign on the bar's door and wondered whether it was that darkness that had attracted him.

No. He didn't think so.

Kent sighed.

He watched the people walking up and down the busy Hillsboro Village sidewalks and tried to shake off the bad feeling. The Village was what passed for a "hip" neighborhood in Nashville. Vanderbilt Hospital was a couple blocks down 21st, and the Vanderbilt University campus was just beyond that. Vandy had a well-earned rep as a rich kid's school. So the neighborhood reflected a certain amount of affluence. It was also a great neighborhood for girl-watching. Sleek businesswomen and young Vanderbilt students in fashionable clothes strutted by. It was a bright day. The beginning of fall, but the weather still felt like mid-summer and the women were still wearing outfits displaying a lot of tantalizing flesh.

He surreptitiously observed a young blonde girl moving down the sidewalk in his direction. She couldn't be any more than nineteen, but she was stunning. Sleek, toned, and tanned, with a face that looked like it ought to be on the cover of Cosmopolitan. She was wearing a pleated tennis-style skirt that was short and showed off exquisitely shapely legs, as well as a tight halter top that just as temptingly showed off her other assets.

The girl was Vandy material, no doubt about it. Probably had some rich or nauseatingly handsome boyfriend. Not that it mattered. Kent was just looking. He was married and happy to be that way. Still, he continued to watch the girl as she paused at the sidewalk directly in front of him. She was staring across the street at Bookman/Bookwoman. Kent gave up the pretense of reading the paper and studied the puzzled expression on her face.

Then it hit him—she'd seen it, too.

Whatever it was.

He opened his mouth to say something to her, but then she was in motion again, crossing the street, weaving easily through the jammed traffic on 21st. She reached the other side of the street within moments and stood on the sidewalk outside the bookstore. Kent saw her frown deepen as she appeared to study something on the white concrete.

Kent set the paper aside and stood up. He'd forgotten completely about his cooling mug of coffee. He moved to the sidewalk's edge but paused there because the traffic was moving again. His heart raced as he stood there watching the girl. This had nothing to do with his initial attraction to her. Some part of him, for reasons he couldn't quite identify, believed the girl was in danger.

But that was crazy. What could happen to her in broad daylight in Hillsboro Village? Aside from being knocked sideways into traffic by falling birds, that is. But surely the shop owner had exaggerated that problem. Kent was sure he would have heard about it before now if something really significant was going on. He felt a little ridiculous to realize he was really and truly worried for this girl's safety. There was no one who looked even remotely threatening anywhere near her. Regardless, the feeling wouldn't go away. If anything, it intensified.

Traffic began to slow again. In a few moments, he would step off the sidewalk and hurry to join her on the other side of the street. But in the next moment something happened that forced him to act sooner.

The girl disappeared. She didn't blink out of existence like a ghost in a movie or anything like that. What happened was a thousand times more alarming. She dropped abruptly, like a woman falling through an open manhole. But Kent knew there was nothing like that in front of Bookman/Bookwoman.

Instinct pushed him off the sidewalk and in front of an oncoming powder blue BMW. The car's front bumper struck him in the knee and sent him stumbling across the street. He crossed the center lane and fell backward. He heard screams and a screeching of brakes as he landed flat on his back on the other side of the street. He knew he should be concerned only with his own safety at this point, but instinct snapped his gaze toward the stretch of sidewalk where the girl had been standing.

There was nothing there.

Then, for just a fraction of a second, there was something.

A jagged black slash in the flesh of the world. And that horrible, deep, deep darkness was the last thing he saw in the instant before the squealing wheel of a Ford Explorer rolled over his head, sending Kent Gowran spiraling down into a different kind of darkness.

~

Venture News Channel Headquarters
Atlanta, Georgia
1:01 p.m.

Zeke Johnson sat behind the anchor desk and tried not to freak out as the usual whirlwind of between-commercials activity took place around him. He stared into the lens of the camera in front of him and tried to convince himself he hadn't seen what he believed he'd seen in that last surreal moment before the break.

There was a voice squawking in his earpiece, demanding his attention.

He ignored it.

He was still staring at the lens. It was just a lens, nothing more. Just a piece of precision-ground glass through which his smiling, perfectly-coiffed image was captured and sent into the homes of millions of people around the world. It certainly was not a portal into a dark and terrifying other realm. He was tired. Very tired. The long hours and stresses of cable TV news were finally getting to him. So it wasn't that surprising he'd experienced a momentary . . . well, *hallucination*.

The voice was still squawking in his ear. His producer, Tony Dawkins, was pitching a fit. "Zeke! Dammit! We're back live in less than thirty. Are you okay?"

Zeke drew in a breath and summoned his brightest plastic news guy smile. "Yes. I'm fine."

"Are you sure? We've got Maria on stand-by."

Zeke maintained his frozen smile and gave his head a barely perceptible shake. "I'm fine. Really."

Tony sighed. "Okay, if you're sure you're all right."

"I'm fine. Trust me."

The break ended. Zeke opened his mouth to begin the next news segment, but the only sound that emerged was a strangled groan of terror. Tony was screaming in his ear again, but Zeke didn't hear the producer's frantic cries.

He was hallucinating again. Only it sure didn't seem like a hallucination. Something was moving inside the camera lens. A swirling, ghostly apparition. It had to be a hallucination. Otherwise the guys and gals in the control room would have seen it, or at least would have known something out of the ordinary was happening.

Zeke's jaw dropped as he watched the center of the lens push outward, distending like a slowly growing air bubble. Something seemed to be reaching for him from the other side of the lens. Which was just crazy. There couldn't be something *alive* behind that piece of glass. And glass wasn't that malleable. It wouldn't move like that—it would just shatter.

Something in his brain had misfired. There could be no other explanation. He wasn't perceiving reality as it actually was. And that scared the hell out of him. He knew his career as a television newsman would be finished if he allowed others to know what was happening to him. He was aware of Tony talking in his ear again, but he wasn't getting the sense of the words. He couldn't focus. He looked at the teleprompter, seized on the first sentence there and actually managed to speak it. He sounded stiff to his own ears, like an awkward high school drama student taking the stage for the first time. But at least he was talking. There was no dead air. Tony wasn't cutting him off. Not yet. Zeke gained confidence as each ensuing sentence rolled off his tongue. He kept his gaze trained just below the level of the camera lens.

He'd be okay if he could get through this segment. Pleading exhaustion, he'd accept Tony's offer to have Maria substitute for him after that. The segment shifted to a videotaped report that would last nearly a minute, and Zeke blew out a big sigh of relief.

Tony said, "That's it. You're coming out after this segment."

Zeke nodded. "Okay. I'm more tired than I thought, I guess."

He risked another glance at the lens and heaved another heavy sigh.

It was just a lens again. Not a haunted portal. Not a living, pulsing, breathing inexplicable synthesis of technology and living organism. He cleared his throat, took a sip of water, and waited for the video report to end.

~

Newark, New Jersey
Near Rutgers University

Warren Hatcher awoke to a familiar buzzing in his head at 1:15 p.m. A subtle crackling, he recognized it as the sub-aural sound of untold thousands of brain cells dying as a result of last night's overindulgence at Mulligan's Irish Pub.

He sighed and turned on to his side, meaning to go back to sleep for another few minutes. Or another hour. Whatever. Like it made a difference at this point. A month into his fall classes at Rutgers and already he was well on his way to failing every one of them. He'd slept through his schedule of classes again today, taking one more shaky step down that slippery slope toward academic doom. Not a smart thing to be doing under any circumstances, but especially so this time, considering he'd entered the fall session already on academic probation.

He groaned and willed his eyes to shut.

He didn't want to think about it. He wanted to sleep. Sleep would take it all away. But sleep didn't seem possible now. The swirling thoughts in his head had ignited the morning-after panic with which he was becoming all too familiar.

Sighing, he surrendered to the inevitable and sat up. He swung his legs over the side of his bed and rubbed at his bleary eyes. He blinked and saw only a blurred, distorted version of his cramped studio apartment. Then his vision cleared and he saw the note on the nightstand. He recognized Amanda's handwriting at once, saw the squiggly tail-end of her signature on the nearest side of the paper, which stood in a tented upside-down V next to the phone.

He grimaced and snatched the note off the nightstand. He smoothed it open and read:

> *Last night was fun. You are always fun, sweet Warren. But enough is enough. It's obvious where you're going—downhill— and I just can't walk that road with you. School is important to me, believe it or not. So last night was the end, baby. Please don't call, write, or come sniffing around. I don't want to hurt you any more than I have to, and believe me, if you fail to heed this advice you will get hurt.*

The word "hurt" was underlined three times. Warren thought that was overkill. How dense did she think he was?

The note continued:

> *I wish you luck with whatever life brings you, sweetheart. Though I never want to hear from you again, you'll always be important to me. I know it sounds strange, but you reached places within me (haha!) few ever have. You're a special boy. I hope you find a way to turn yourself around, but I have no confidence you can do so. I'd stay if I thought there was any chance you could get better, but I don't. At all.*

13

FROM THE VOID

Best to be done with this now and forever.
I love you.
I'll miss you.
Have a nice life.
Hugs 'n' kisses,
Amanda

Warren read the note three times before crumpling it into a ball and tossing it aside. The little wad of paper knocked a picture of his mother and father off the top of his dresser. The picture frame landed with a flat crack of breaking glass.

Warren closed his eyes. "Shit."

This was clearly going to be one of those relentlessly crappy days. The kind that starts bad and stays bad (and maybe gets a hell of a lot worse). Thinking about Amanda's note filled him with anger. The tone of it was so insulting, condescension couched in a lot of phony affection. "Sweet Warren", she'd called him. And "sweetheart". There should be a law. Any use of the word "sweet" in a breakup note ought to be a capital offense.

On the other hand, it was hard to refute anything she'd said.

Warren got to his feet and shuffled over to the mirror. He frowned at the image that looked back at him. The heavy, bruise-colored bags under his bloodshot eyes made him look a decade older than he really was. And his unwashed, bed-rumpled hair and scraggly week-and-a-half old beard made him look like a bum.

Unable to bear looking at himself any longer, Warren's gaze went to the fallen picture frame. He picked it up and carried it into the kitchen, where he peeled back the cardboard backing, extracted the picture of his parents, and dropped the now useless frame into the trash basket. He felt something slide away from his fingertips, then looked down and saw whatever it was fluttering to the floor.

He realized what he was seeing an instant before it landed face-up on the floor. He heaved his heaviest sigh of the morning, leaned back against the kitchen counter, and slid slowly down until his butt met cold linoleum. He put a hand over his face and tried to stifle the snif-fle that wanted to come. He couldn't do it, of course, and soon his eyes were welling with moisture. But he forced himself to look at the old photo he'd hidden behind the picture of his parents three years prior.

When it came right down to it, everything that had gone wrong for him these last three years all stemmed from an all-consuming need to forget the girl in the picture. The image showed her smiling on a couch, cradling the guitar he'd given her for Valentine's Day.

He cupped the picture in two trembling hands.

The tears began in earnest then, and the last thing he saw before they blinded him was a single drop of moisture landing on the image of Emma Singleton, Warren's great lost love.

~

Harrisburg, Pennsylvania
1:15 p.m.

There was something wrong with the flower.

Jasmine Holtz poured more sweet tea from the yellow pitcher into her mug. She set the mug on the table and leaned back in her chair to study the little patch of flowers next to her patio. There were snapdragons and daisies, and green shoots of various sizes growing here and there in the brown patches of dirt. She'd neglected to do the weeding this week and it was starting to show. She meant to do it after having a bit more tea, but the tea and the task were forgotten as she narrowed her eyes and studied the defective flower closely.

The daisy's center, normally a cheerful bright yellow, had darkened considerably, become almost black. But that wasn't the most disturbing aspect of what she was seeing. The dark button in the middle throbbed subtly, the way the flesh around an infected open wound might if left untreated too long.

She picked up her mug and took a sip of tea. She frowned. She could swear she'd just seen a tiny blip of purple light at the center of the button. She set the mug down and got to her feet with a sigh. She saw the purple blip again as she walked to the edge of the patio. She shuddered. It looked like a demon eye winking at her. But she banished the thought and lifted the hem of her yellow sundress to kneel in the dirt of her little garden. She knew there had to be a rational explanation for this odd phenomenon. The purple blip was just a trick of the bright midday light. And the blackening of the flower's center was likely the result of a plant disease she knew nothing about. She'd have to do some research online. She hoped she wouldn't have to rip up the whole garden and start over.

From this vantage point, however, it was clear the intermittent purple blip could not be attributed to anything as mundane as a trick of the light. There was an intimation of motion every time she glimpsed the little speck of purple, just the faintest ripple in that black center, like the displacement of water that occurs when an air bubble emerges from the lungs of a person swimming underwater.

Odd. Very, very odd.

For the first time, Jasmine began to feel truly unsettled by what she was seeing. Against her better judgment (not that she truly possessed such a thing as good judgment; she was notoriously impetuous), she knelt closer to the strange flower. The purple blip flashed faster. When her face was less than a foot away from the daisy, the flashing blip changed colors, shifting from a calm purple to an angry red. Which was a funnily apt way of thinking about it, Jasmine decided, because she sensed the color change was wired to some sort of emotional center.

She also sensed the flower was a threat to her life. She wasted no time wallowing in denial. Her rational mind would be the death of her, so she shut it down. She gripped the flower by the stem and ripped it out of the ground. A sound like a scream emerged from the daisy's dark center and she flung the uprooted flower aside. It landed on the pebbled concrete next to the table.

Jasmine got to her feet and ran through the open patio door and into the house. She dashed into the kitchen, opened a drawer, and rifled through a mound of odds and ends until she found what she was looking for. Then, heart slamming in her chest, Jasmine returned to the patio and again knelt over the diseased flower, the pebbled concrete pushing painfully into her bare knees. She opened the box of matches with shaking hands and promptly dropped it, spilling matches everywhere. She snatched the empty box up, found one of the matches, and struck it against the flint pad on the side of the box.

The match flared to life and Jasmine allowed herself a moment to steady her nerves before applying the little flame to the daisy. The flower ignited and the screaming she'd heard before burst forth once again, this time so loudly it caused her to tumble backward and clap her hands over her ears. Anxious to put some space between herself and the inexplicable thing on her patio, she scooted backward through the open patio door into her living room. She gripped the edge of the door and threw it shut, mercifully muffling the screams of . . . whatever it was.

On her hands and knees now—and panting like a dog playing in the sun—she moved to the door and peered through one of the glass panes at the twisted, blackened, horrible thing that had once been a seemingly ordinary flower.

She stared at it for a long time, waiting for any hint of further plant shenanigans. But nothing happened. In a while she got up and went straight to the liquor cabinet. She then returned to the kitchen and prepared the first of several very stiff drinks.

~

Washington, D.C.
1:29 p.m.

The president of the United States took a small sip of single-malt scotch then put the glass down and again read through the careful speech prepared for him by a team of the best writers money could buy.

He sighed.

He'd read this latest draft some two dozen times already. Though the information it was meant to convey was couched in very cautious, non-hyperbolic language, there was no getting around the fantastical core facts he was set to reveal to the nation on live television in just a few hours.

Something was wrong. Something potentially terrible. Something beyond the understanding of even the finest scientific minds in the country. A troublesome thing the governments of the world had kept under wraps until now, out of fear of inciting a global panic. But now the issue had to be addressed. The problem was getting worse. It was spreading. Before too much longer, the nature of the problem would be evident to everyone. So now it was imperative the public be made aware of the evolving situation before things got out of hand. It wouldn't do to face a relentless barrage of accusations while the administration did nothing but sit on its hands and fret while the world came unraveled.

Then again, the president's gut was telling him concerns of a political nature might not matter much longer. He felt a wave of helpless fear coming over him—a feeling he'd not been much familiar with in his adult life until lately—and reached again for his glass of scotch. He sipped a bit more of the expensive hooch, taking care to strictly limit his intake. It wouldn't do to be drunk on live national television.

After, though . . .

The president loosened his tie and undid the top two buttons of his heavily starched white shirt. He ran a hand through hair streaked with gray and breathed a sigh so weary it might have sent the stock market tumbling had he made the sound on live television. He straightened the small stack of papers in his hands and again read through the first lines of the most important speech of his life:

"My fellow Americans, greetings. I have come before you tonight to tell you things you frankly may not believe . . ."

~

Nashville, TN
1:35 p.m.

Emma gritted her teeth and gripped the edge of the foosball table tightly as Phil Parker pounded into her from behind. The bar's interior was dimly lit and a shade was drawn over the glass front door. The otherwise empty room was alive with the trace scents of beer and cigarettes, ingrained smells that were marginally nicer than the momentarily more prominent odors of sweat and KY jelly.

She watched the plastic foosball men jiggle on the metal bars and tried to blank her mind. She didn't want to have to think about what was happening. Doing it from behind had been her idea. At least this way she didn't have to look at him. But Phil wasn't making it easy to descend into a state of detachment. His Trojan-sheathed cock pistoned in and out of her with manic intensity. She'd been bent over this goddamned silly game table for maybe five minutes, but it felt more like five hours.

As per Phil's instructions, she'd arrived early to fulfill her end of their verbal agreement. It was a demeaning, degrading thing she was allowing to happen here, no doubt about it. But she also knew she wasn't up to doing all the hard things necessary to significantly change her station in life. So she considered a few minutes of utter humiliation a worthwhile exchange for restoring the status quo.

One of Phil's big hands moved from her slim waist to paw at her breasts. A spark of anger made her grunt, a sound Phil of course mistook for genuine sexual excitement. She wanted to knock the groping hand away, but refrained, hoping the miserable bastard's extra bit of sensual pleasure would hasten his orgasm and thus end this nightmare. But he went on for another torturously long few minutes, grunting, grinding, and groping for all he was worth (not much, in Emma's informed opinion), until at last he exploded inside her and thrust her forward so hard her grip slipped off the edge of the foosball table and sent her crashing into it.

Emma shrieked. "Goddammit!"

Phil laughed. He gave her one last thrust with his still partially engorged penis before pulling the slippery shaft out of her sore vagina. He kissed the back of her neck and gave her a light, open-handed tap on the ass. Emma squirmed away from him and retrieved her folded-up jeans from a nearby bar stool. She shook them out and pulled them on, then stepped into her Doc Martens, glaring at Phil all the while.

But the toothy, shit-eating grin spread across Phil's face never wavered. Emma wished she could take a chainsaw to it. Phil was a big man, well over six feet tall and more than a few dozen pounds overweight. But despite his slovenliness, Phil wasn't a bad-looking man. He was even sort of handsome from certain angles, and in favorable lighting. Which was one of the reasons the aging sleazeball was able to bed the occasional dim coed. There were other reasons, of course, including a not-insubstantial net worth and a (somewhat faded) level of fame the two hit country and western singles he'd had in the '70s still afforded him.

He dropped the condom in a nearby trash can and winked at Emma. "Gotta say, I've banged a lot of fine women over the years, but you're right up there with the best of them."

Emma rolled her eyes. She tapped a cigarette out of a fresh pack of Marlboros. "Gee, thanks. You have no idea how proud that makes me."

Phil chuckled. "You should be proud." He eyed her up and down, shaking his head and whistling in admiration. "You are one fine lady. Sure you don't want to make this more than a one-time thing? I could make it worth your while."

Emma lit her cigarette, inhaled, and blew out a cloud of smoke. "Right. I fuck you. You give me money. You go back to your clueless wife at the end of the night. How did you know I've always wanted to be a whore?"

Phil laughed and shook his head again. "You fuck better than any whore I ever knew."

"Lovely." Emma grimaced. "We had a deal. Please stop this line of talk right now."

Phil held up his hands and said, "Whoa, whoa, whoa. I'm not going back on our deal. I'm just letting you know you have options in case you ever . . . need help with the rent, or whatever."

Emma didn't say anything. She stubbed out her cigarette and picked up her purse. Then she hurried past Phil before he could give her another of those obnoxious taps on the ass, moving quickly through the game room en route to the bathroom. She threw the door shut, turned the lock, and dropped to her knees in front of the toilet. The smell of unflushed urine made her gulp as she felt the first surge of bile at the back of her throat. Then the partially digested remains of her lunch came out in a burning spew that brought tears to her eyes. An ensuing series of painful dry heaves left her a tearful, shaking wreck on the floor. At last she was able to reach for the flush handle and send the foul mixture of piss and vomit swirling away.

She got to her feet and wobbled over to the sink, where she turned on a tap and splashed water onto her face. She patted her face with a paper towel and peered into the mirror above the sink.

She made her lips stretch into a falsely cheerful grin. The practiced tip-garnering grin that had the subtlest hint of come-hither to it. "Smile, Emma," she told her reflection. "After all, the day can only get better from here."

She washed her hands and left the bathroom.

Her last day of work was about to begin.

~

A good crowd of regulars and random walk-in customers had gathered at the Villager Pub by 7 p.m. The Villager wasn't big, just a bar area and a game room dominated by a row of dart boards. There was a jukebox in the corner, but nobody had put on any tunes yet. The half-dozen or so people sitting at the bar alternately talked boozily to each other and watched the television mounted on the wall behind the bar. One very drunk Vandy girl kept loudly requesting a channel change. She wanted to see *The Simpsons*. But she was outvoted by regulars who wanted to hear what the president had to say. His speech was set to commence in fifteen or twenty minutes and all the major networks had granted him a block of premium air time.

Something was up, that was the consensus among the bar's patrons. Something big. But there was no consensus as to the nature of the "something big". Some had their money on news of a developing international crisis, of imminent war perhaps. Others anticipated word of an enormous medical breakthrough, maybe a cure for AIDS or cancer. The Simpsons girl said the president would be announcing proof of the existence of extraterrestrial life. She was joking, but some took her seriously, insisting such a thing was entirely within the realm of possibility. This led to the inevitable wild speculation about what the government was *really* hiding out there at Area 51.

The talking heads on the television were engaged in speculations of their own, though none of their ideas were as fanciful as anything discussed that night at the Villager Pub. They touched on a number of currently hot geopolitical topics. And each possibility they broached was as far removed from the extraordinary truth as the bizarre theories bandied about by the drunks at the bar.

Probably more so, in fact, given what we know now.

~

Aaron Harris entered the Villager Pub at 7:15, five minutes before the president's speech. He slid onto a bar stool vacated by a drunken patron who'd staggered off in search of the bathroom. The man sitting to his right scowled and looked ready to say something. Probably he was supposed to be saving the seat for the just-departed man. Whatever he'd been about to say remained unsaid, however, when he got a glimpse of Aaron's intense gaze.

Aaron grinned and the man turned away, choosing to shift his attention to the dwindling head of his latest beer. People often wilted this way the moment they perceived the great potential for violence lurking just beneath the facade of his male model-level good looks. He had great hair, high cheekbones, and a square jaw with a slightly cleft chin. He looked like a hero from some old pulp tale, and he liked to occasionally sport a five o'clock shadow to enhance the impression.

Girls liked him. He was one of those fortunate guys who had never had any genuine angst in that department. Throughout his life he'd been able to win over and seduce practically any woman he'd ever desired.

Emma Singleton was one of the rare exceptions to the rule. She consistently rejected his repeated advances and it infuriated him. But he never let the frustration show. That would be too much of a blow to his ego and image. He just kept showing up at the pub, knowing that eventually Emma would succumb to the inevitable and give in to the lust she must privately feel for him.

He knew what the problem was. Emma was too self-consciously "alternative," an annoying catch-all code term Aaron despised; it meant "cool", "hip", and indicated general tastes in music, movies, and clothes, all non-mainstream of course. Those who embraced the label also had a loathsome tendency toward leftist politics. A girl like Emma couldn't allow herself to go for a guy like Aaron. It would blow her image.

FROM THE VOID

But one day, he knew, she would recognize how silly the trappings of her carefully crafted lifestyle were. That day always came for girls like her. They got tired of being poor and their tastes in men shifted from leather-jacketed bad boys to hotshot businessmen—men like Aaron.

He just had to be patient.

He caught her eye and raised a finger. She nodded without smiling and knelt to retrieve a fresh pint glass from the cooler under the bar. She filled the glass with amber-colored beer from the Shiner Bock tap. Shiner had become his usual by default. His real drink of choice was scotch over ice, but the Villager was a beer-only joint and he'd settled on Shiner as a marginally acceptable substitute. Emma set the glass on a coaster in front of him, then turned to move back to the other end of the bar.

"Emma!"

Emma sighed and faced him. A faint smirk touched a corner of her mouth. Seeing it pissed him off. He was aware of equally intense desires warring within him—an aching need to kiss those lush, pouting red lips of hers, and a newly-born wish to drive a fist right into the center of that pretty face. Yeah, he thought, let's see you smirk when that happens. And it will, bitch, it will.

She was wearing her usual rocker clothes. A tight black T-shirt with pink fishnet sleeves, black jeans, and a studded dog collar around her neck. Her hair was shaggy and dyed black. There was a ring in her eyebrow and another in her nostril. He could see tattoos showing through rips in the fishnets. She looked ridiculous. Except that she was scorchingly hot. Right now, in fact, she seemed like the most imminently fuckable girl in all of Nashville.

She widened her eyes in an exaggerated way and held up her hands. "*What*, Aaron? I've got drinks to pour."

He realized he'd been staring at her for several moments. He grinned. "Sorry, spaced out there a moment." He ignored the snickers of those sitting within earshot. "Listen, I heard the Belcourt's showing a couple of those Jap horror flicks you like next weekend. I thought maybe—"

"No."

And then she was gone, back now behind the row of taps, pouring beers for assholes. His hands curled into tight fists as anger burned within him, an emotion that boiled over a moment later when the man sitting to his right finally found the courage to address him:

"Don't you think it's time you gave it up, boy? Can't you see she sees right through you?"

Aaron shoved the man off his stool. The old bastard fell to the floor with a startled yelp. Aaron resisted an impulse to drop to his knees and use the man's flushed-red face as a punching bag. He didn't want to go to jail. That wouldn't go over well at work, another place he had a carefully crafted image to maintain. Ignoring the angry shouts of the other customers, Aaron dropped a couple of bills on the bar to pay for his untouched beer and hurried out of the Villager.

He ducked down an alley and ran to his car, where he sat behind the steering wheel for several minutes and replayed in his head the humiliatingly dismissive way Emma had rebuffed his latest invitation.

That cunt!

She didn't know what she was missing, that was for fucking sure. For the first time, it dawned on Aaron he really might not have a chance with her. And that was so completely wrong he could hardly comprehend it.

He gripped the steering wheel hard enough to make the bones in his hands ache. He imagined Emma walking down this same alley at three in the morning, after the Villager had closed. He saw himself leaping out of the car, seizing her, and dragging her behind a dumpster. He could almost feel his hands closing around her narrow neck, could see her eyes bulging out as he squeezed the life out of her.

Aaron finally began to relax. He rubbed the bulge at his crotch.

He knew what he had to do now.

~

Emma poured a free pint of Shiner Bock for Mickey Shepherd. He accepted it with a smile and a wink. Emma returned the smile. Mickey was a good guy. A hardcore alcoholic, but absolutely harmless to anyone but himself. He was sixty-five years old and painfully thin, almost frail. That creepy yuppie bastard could have done real damage to him knocking him off his stool that way.

Sometimes Emma hated being a girl. Every reasonably attractive chick she'd ever known had to deal with obsessive jerks like Aaron Harris at some point. Sociopathic assholes whose good looks gave them a ridiculous sense of entitlement. Some of them were harmless, but others posed a genuine threat. She had a feeling Aaron could well fall into the latter category. She'd have to be careful walking home at night for a while.

She was in the midst of pouring a Miller Lite when cries went up from several of the patrons to turn the volume on the TV up. She put the beer down and aimed the remote control at the television, holding the button down until the yellow volume bar zoomed past the half-way mark.

Then she stepped back and listened to the president along with everyone else.

The presidential seal was shown against a blue background. Then that was gone and the president was shown sitting behind his desk in the oval office. Sitting there in his dark blue suit, crisp white shirt, and straight black tie, the man elected under dubious circumstances had never looked quite so . . . well, presidential.

In that last moment before he spoke, Emma realized she'd almost forgotten to breathe. She sensed it too, now. Something was up.

Something big.

The president cleared his throat and said, "My fellow Americans, greetings. I have come before you tonight to tell you things you frankly may not believe—"

The president continued speaking for several more moments, but the meaning of the words was lost on the Villager's patrons. Their attention (and that of everyone watching around the world) was captured by an odd sight behind the so-called leader of the free world—a widening black fissure in the wall. The strangest thing about it at this point was that there was no sound of destruction, no crackling rending of drywall and lumber. The dark slash opened so quietly some at first thought what they were seeing was the result of some defect in their television sets—a notion forgotten an instant later when a long, black tentacle emerged from the deeper blackness and wrapped itself around the president's neck.

The look of surprised terror on the president's face was matched by the expressions of countless millions watching the bizarre scene unfold on their television screens. The president grabbed at the tentacle and was yanked out of his chair. The tentacle appeared to flex and then retract, pulling the president backward and slamming him against the wall. Secret Service agents appeared on-camera, rushing to the president's aid. There was a lot of frantic shouting as the camera pulled backward for a wider shot of what was happening. The Secret Service agents grabbed hold of the president's arms and legs and tried to pull him free of the tentacle. One agent aimed a gun through the dark fissure and fired several times. The president flinched at the sound of each report, but his expression changed to pure agony as the tentacle began to pull him through the fissure, which was still too narrow to accommodate his size.

Emma put a hand to her mouth and backed away from the television when she heard a sound like the snapping of a toothpick. "Oh . . . God . . ."

The people around the president were screaming now. His body abruptly folded in at the middle as the dark fissure widened a bit. Then, along with two Secret Service agents still desperately clinging to him, he was pulled backward into the darkness. The remaining agents stood around looking stunned.

There was a shout from someone off-camera and the screen went blank. The network then went to a shot of a stunned, slack-jawed correspondent, a man who clearly didn't know what to say. "We seem to have . . . to have . . ."

With the exception of one still-in-progress darts game in the other room, the Villager's interior was perfectly quiet for several long moments.

Until Mickey Shepherd said, "It's a trick."

Emma turned to look at him. She felt numb all over, as if she'd been pumped full of anesthetic or some powerfully narcotic drug. She blinked slowly at Mickey. "What?"

He nodded. "A trick. Special effects." He looked up and down the bar, searching the frightened faces there for signs of agreement. Then he looked at Emma again. "A goddamn practical joke, that's what that was."

A Vandy student who'd taken the seat vacated by Aaron said, "No way. That was real." There was a look of hopeless terror on his barely post-adolescent face. "Oh, Jesus, what the hell was that?"

Emma shook her head. She still felt numb. She wanted to believe Mickey. "I don't know. I . . . don't know."

She glanced again at the television. The image of the fumbling reporter was gone.

In its place was a test pattern.

She flipped through the channels. All of them. Except for some cable channels, the same pattern was in place on most. On others was the symbol of the Emergency Alert System.

Somebody said, "Holy shit. It's the end of the goddamn world."

Emma felt woozy.

She scanned the horrified, disbelieving faces arrayed around the other side of the bar. "This is an open bar now." Her voice sounded distant to her own ears, like the dimly perceived sound of a neighbor's television. "Help yourselves. I need to sit down."

She eased herself to the floor behind the bar and folded her legs beneath her. A conversational din arose as the Villager's patrons argued about what they'd seen. Emma tuned it out, reduced it to a wave of incoherent babble. She thought of the vial of Valium at the bottom of her purse and decided she'd take one of them in a little while. Then the image of the thick, dark tentacle emerging through the black fissure in that wall filled her mind and she decided two Valiums might be an even better idea.

~

Harrisburg, Pennsylvania
7:45 p.m.

The 911 operator was still squawking in her ear, but Jasmine Holtz wasn't hearing him anymore. She returned the phone to its cradle and walked back to where the very still body of her husband lay sprawled in front of the television. She knelt beside him and stroked his graying brown hair. A tear emerged from the corner of one eye and slid slowly down her cheek.

She sniffled and wiped the tear away.

"Oh, Gary." Another sniffle, this one just a hair's breadth away from becoming a wrenching sob. "I always told you to watch your goddamn cholesterol better . . ."

She grimaced.

What a stupid thing to say to her dead husband. High cholesterol wasn't the real culprit here. Perhaps it played a minor, contributing role, but the real truth was that Gary Holtz had died of fright.

He'd been standing in front of the living room television, watching in horror as the president's speech was interrupted by something inexplicable. Then, at the same moment the president's spine snapped, Gary said something that sounded like, "Oh," and pitched head-first to the floor. Jasmine then lost her mind for a little while, screaming, wailing, shaking Gary's still body, begging him to get up. But he was already gone. She managed to get herself together and call 911. Paramedics would be arriving soon. But she knew with cold certainty there was nothing they could do.

Her sweet husband was gone, and she was alone in the world. She reflected briefly on how cruel and unfair life was, then ceased thinking about it, at least for now. It was something she already knew too well.

She stroked Gary's hair some more. "Why you, sweetie? Why not me?"

But she thought she knew the answer to that question.

Gary had been terrified by what he'd seen, so completely overwhelmed that a crucial part of his body revolted. Jasmine had been frightened too, of course, but she had not been surprised. Not so soon after the episode with the diseased flower. She hadn't told him about that. How could she? It would've sounded like the ravings of a crazy person. But now she wished she'd opened her stupid mouth and talked about it.

Maybe this wouldn't have happened.

How could she not blame herself? Yet Gary would tell her she was being stupid, that she was doing that reflexive second-guessing thing all people in mourning do. Oh, what a good man he'd been. He would so hate to know she was feeling any guilt at all.

She lay down beside him, wrapped her arms around him, kissed his still warm forehead, his mouth, and his cheek. "My sweet, sweet man. Oh, Gary."

She cried some more.

When the paramedics hammered on the front door a few minutes later, she disengaged herself from that final, bittersweet embrace and got up to let them in.

2

SOMEWHERE IN THE USA . . .

LAURA BRANDNER EMERGED FROM THE front entrance of the coffee shop where she'd worked as a barista for going on three years. She immediately fired up a cigarette and sucked in a deep lungful of death. Yes, she knew full well the smoke filling her lungs was laced with all sorts of dreadful poisons. She also knew she didn't care. Not too much anyway. She was still young at twenty-four. Things like cancer and emphysema were things she associated with old age. And the way things were going these days it didn't look like anybody was gonna be getting much older.

She'd smoked her first post-work cigarette almost down to the filter by the time she became aware of the little girl watching her from the street curb. She smiled as she lit a second cigarette, and the little girl smiled back and waved shyly, a winningly demure look crossing her delicate features. Her hair was a lustrous sheath of finely combed brown that hung halfway down her back, and she was dressed in a schoolgirl's uniform.

Laura blew a cloud of smoke at the dark sky and smiled again. "What's your name, sweetie?"

The girl giggled. She clasped her hands behind her back and kicked at an invisible pebble on the sidewalk. "I'm Abby."

Laura nodded, as if affirming something she'd known all along—

but she'd never seen the little girl before. "Pleased to meet you, Abby. I'm Laura." She gave a sideways nod at the coffee shop. "Are you waiting on your Mommy? Is she inside here?"

Abby shook her head. "Nope."

Laura frowned. "There someone else you're waiting for?"

Abby smiled. "Yes. You."

Laura's frown deepened. "I'm . . . sorry. I don't understand."

The girl moved away from the curb now, coming toward her in an unhurried way, with her hands still clasped behind her back. Her smile was still in place, but it seemed somehow less sweet and innocent. But that was absurd. She was just a little girl, and as completely non-threatening as any normal child.

Abby laughed. "I've been waiting for you." Her brow furrowed slightly and she pursed her lip. And her eyes rolled briefly upward as she appeared to think something over. Then her gaze fixed on Laura again. "Yes. I'm your . . . niece."

Laura's first instinct was to scoff at the girl's patently false statement. This was a joke. Had to be. The girl just had a lively imagination and was playing a game of make-believe while she waited for . . . well, whoever. And she meant to say something to that effect. But something happened.

She blinked hard and stared in confusion at the girl for a moment.

Then she smiled tentatively. "You're my niece."

Laura almost laughed. What a silly thing to say.

Of course Abby was her niece.

She frowned again. "What were we talking about?"

Abby giggled. "You were saying how tired you were from working all day." She yawned and stretched her arms wide. "You should take me home now." The girl leaned closer to her, stared into her eyes with an intensity that should have been disconcerting but wasn't. And Abby suddenly smiled brightly again. "Kelly will worry if we don't get home soon. Besides, you've been wanting to fuck her all day. It's all you've been able to think about."

Laura gaped at the girl. "Abby, that's not . . ."

She blinked again and everything went fuzzy for a moment. She felt something hot burning her fingers and saw that her second cigarette had burned down nearly to the filter. She flicked the filter and attached length of unsmoked ash away, jammed her fingers into her mouth, and looked at Abby. Abby, who was still smiling at her in an oddly disconnected way, like a scientist studying a specimen.

She eased her hand away from her mouth. "Wha-what happened?"

Abby shrugged. "Nothing. You're just tired."

Laura nodded. "Yeah."

Abby extended a slim, pale hand and Laura numbly, automatically took it. The girl gave her a gentle squeeze and the pain departed her singed fingers in an instant, and so completely it was as if they'd never been burned in the first place.

Abby locked gazes with her again. "Home."

Laura swallowed a thick lump in her throat. She felt unaccountably nervous. Which didn't make sense. They were on a brightly lit street in a nice part of town with lots of people around. There was nothing to be afraid of.

Abby nodded. "Nothing at all."

Laura managed a weak, uncertain smile. "Nothing."

Abby giggled.

Then, still clasping hands, they set off in the direction of Laura's apartment.

3

THE DAY AFTER THE PRESIDENT died was a day of chaos. The secret protected so fervently by those in power was a secret no longer. Though the American government's initial, panicked instinct was to clamp down, this proved impossible. An effort was made to shut down all normal modes of disseminating information, especially television. The suddenly ascendant vice president didn't want horrific images of the president's demise playing endlessly on every channel. In the ensuing hours and days, the word "Orwellian" was thrown around a good bit.

However, the power of the internet quickly rendered the vice president's efforts meaningless. Video files of the president's death were posted online within minutes and were downloaded by the millions. The nation's internet service providers took over the role normally played by networks and cable news channels, posting "live" updates with furious frequency. Recognizing at last the futility of attempting to suppress all media in the digital age, the government's iron-fisted tactics were abandoned. And so the flurry of furious speculation began in earnest. Concepts such as alternate dimensions and rips in the time-space continuum, once strictly the province of science fiction, were discussed seriously by men and women whose knowledge of things scientific wasn't much broader than that of the average tapeworm.

Word soon went out that the vice president, due to be sworn in as president within moments, would speak to the nation before the night was out. It was said he would speak of the things the late president had been set to reveal earlier in the evening. It was a long night for most of the country. The vice president's speech aired at 12:45 a.m., Central Standard Time. The man was a good decade and a half younger than the late president, and he looked as bewildered by events as the hundreds of millions of people watching him around the world.

It should come as no surprise to hear that nothing the man said reassured or comforted anyone.

~

Newark, NJ
September 26
10:07 a.m.

Warren's eyes fluttered open. He looked at the bedside clock and was astonished to see he had a remote chance of making it to his Contemporary European Literature class. It was entirely within the realm of possibility that he could get up, throw some clothes on, drive to school, and dash across campus fast enough to arrive in class right at 10:30.

But it wasn't going to happen. Warren sighed. Just thinking about running made him tired. The actual physical act would probably kill him.

He groaned into his pillow and said, "I am so pathetic it fucking hurts."

A true statement, Warren had to admit. And he doubted anyone he knew would argue with it. It was depressing. Here he had a chance to turn around his life. Showing up for this one class could be just the thing to snap him out of this near-terminal state of melancholy. It could be the beginning of a chain reaction of good fortune, the first necessary baby step in leaving the past and all its baggage behind forever.

But he just wasn't up to it.

Which, come to think of it, made for a pretty apt metaphor for his whole life.

He didn't want to think about it anymore, not now anyway, and so he closed his eyes and tried to go back to sleep. The world and its unpleasant realities began to slip away and he entered a dream realm far more pleasant than his drab life in Newark. He sat shirtless on a beautiful, flower-covered hill in some shiny, faraway place. It reminded him vaguely of the countryside in Tennessee. He smiled and turned his eyes up to the sun. He felt good. He felt clean. His body finally purged of the toxins he'd fed it for so long. This was a glimpse of a better future. A healthier, happier time than the present. Then he heard a familiar voice calling to him.

He frowned and said, "Emma?"

Then there was a louder, more insistent sound and his eyes snapped open. The beautiful, idyllic hill was gone and he was once more face-down on his bed in Newark. The jarring sound came again and he realized someone was pounding on his door.

"All right, already!" He sighed heavily. "Jesus."

He got out of bed, stepped into his jeans, and pulled on a Ramones T-shirt. He shuffled over to the door and pulled it open.

He grunted. "What are you doing here?"

Amanda Lawrence pushed past him into the apartment. She was thin and naturally blonde, her hair cut in a longish pageboy style. She was wearing a purple v-neck T-shirt and red corduroy pants. In one hand she held a rolled-up newspaper. Warren was wary of the newspaper. She was in a state of high agitation. He wouldn't put it past her to start whipping him about the head with it.

She looked livid as she stepped closer to him. "Where the fuck have you been?"

Warren threw the door shut and moved over to the refrigerator. "What's it to you? You broke up with me yesterday. By the way, fuck you."

"Don't walk away from me, asshole. And don't talk to me like that."

Warren grabbed a bottle of Yoo-hoo from the fridge and closed it. He showed Amanda a disbelieving scowl. "You're too much. Really. You break up with me via a gag-inducing cutesy letter and you're giving me attitude?" He shook his head. "Jesus."

Some of the fight went out of her then. Her shoulders sagged. But she didn't avert her gaze. She unfolded the newspaper and held it up so Warren could see the huge headline that took up most of the front page: PRESIDENT DEAD.

Warren dropped his Yoo-hoo. "Holy shit."

Amanda shook her head. "You didn't know." A statement, not a

33

question. "The leader of the freaking free world dies on live television and you're oblivious as usual."

Warren blinked. He didn't say anything for a few moments. Then he took the newspaper from Amanda and walked over to the bed. He sat down and read the first paragraphs of the most surreal news story he'd ever seen. He stopped reading midway through the story and looked up at Amanda, who stood over him with her arms folded beneath her breasts, looking as stern as any out-of-patience school marm or prison warden.

"Is this a gag? Is this a joke newspaper you had a friend print up?"

Amanda rolled her eyes. "You paranoid freak." She walked over to the small television propped atop a stack of plastic milk crates and turned it on. A fuzzy image of VNC anchor Zeke Johnson appeared. "Watch."

Warren's gaze settled on the screen. He forgot his anger at Amanda for a moment and focused on what the talking heads were saying. After a while Amanda switched the channel to Fox News and then to CNN. Everywhere it was more of the same. She switched stations again, then again, enough times to get her point across. Even fluffball channels like MTV and ESPN had essentially changed formats, becoming twenty-four-hour news outlets.

Finally he could watch no more of it. He went to the television and turned it off. "I feel like I must be dreaming. This is insane."

Amanda smirked. "Join the club."

He rubbed his eyes, then blinked hard and focused on Amanda. "So I missed the story of the ages. Okay. I still don't know why you're here."

"Where else would I go?" Her expression hardened and she seized a handful of his T-shirt. "My family's a thousand miles away. I haven't been here long enough to make any other friends. You're all I've got."

"But you broke up with me."

"Consider us reconciled."

Warren laughed. "That's crazy."

Amanda relinquished her hold on his T-shirt and sat down on the bed. He opened his mouth intending to tell her off some more but saw her shoulders shaking and his feelings toward her began to soften. He sighed and sat down next to her, draping an arm around her shoulders in time to hold her steady as the first of many powerful sobs wracked her body. He held her close, stroked her hair, and made shushing noises, uttered words of reassurance that bordered on nonsensical.

By the time she was calm enough to talk to him again the front of his T-shirt was soaked with her tears. He grabbed a Kleenex from a box on the nightstand and handed it to her. She sniffled and blew her nose with shaking hands. She looked at him and managed a weak smile. "Thank you."

Warren shrugged. "Listen, if you need me with you for this, I can go along with that. It's not like there's anything else worth salvaging in my life." He laughed humorlessly. "Hell, I finally have a legit reason to ditch school."

Amanda made a sour sound somewhere between a laugh and a sniffle. "Thank you. You don't know how much this means to me." She snuggled closer to him and planted a lingering kiss on his mouth. "I never should've written that note anyway. I wasn't thinking straight. I'm so sorry."

Warren didn't reply to that. His opinion was there'd been nothing at all wrong with her thinking during the composition of that note. Yeah, she'd been a little meaner, not to mention a little more condescending, than she'd needed to be. But she'd done the right thing. She was new to Rutgers and it was clear he'd been dragging her down, putting her in danger of washing out of school in her first semester.

"I'll be damned."

Amanda frowned. "What?"

Warren grunted, shook his head. "I'm an asshole." He smiled at the puzzled look that dawned on Amada's face and said, "Sorry, that was the mother of all non-sequiturs, wasn't it?"

Amanda smiled. "For what it's worth, I don't think you're an asshole. Just confused." She hesitated a moment, then added. "And brokenhearted."

"You're being kind," Warren said, choosing to ignore the latter part of her statement. "There's something I don't understand, though—why don't you just get on a plane and fly down to Florida? Surely your parents would buy you a ticket."

An exasperated groan seemed to propel Amanda off the bed. She began to pace around the tiny apartment, stopping now and then to glance out the window. "I can't do that. The government's suspended commercial air flights indefinitely. Seems they think it's too dangerous, what with the universe busy trying to turn itself inside out, or whatever the fuck it is that's happening."

She stopped pacing and looked straight at him. "I want you to drive me to Florida."

So that's what this boils down to, Warren thought.

"But—"

"But nothing." She strode over to the bed and placed a hand on his chest, pushing him backward until he was flat on his back. She sat astride him and pulled off her shirt. Her bra came off next and Warren instinctively reached for her breasts.

Amanda seized his wrist and held it tight. "We're leaving tomorrow. Time enough to get everything figured out. And we have a lot to figure out, baby. What route we need to take. How much money we'll need to get to Miami, and how we're gonna raise that much cash inside of a fucking day." She gave his wrist a hard squeeze. "Okay?"

Warren sighed. He closed his eyes a moment. She didn't need to manipulate him this way. Or any other way, for that matter. It all came back to what he'd told her earlier—he didn't have anything else in his life worth hanging on to.

He opened his eyes. "Okay."

She smiled. "Groovy."

Then she kissed him and they both forgot about the madness overtaking their world for a little while.

~

Nashville, TN
11:00 a.m.

Emma awoke to find herself sprawled across the small, uncomfortable vinyl-covered couch in Phil Parker's small office. Someone had covered her with a trench coat. She swept away the makeshift blanket and sat up, groaning at the pounding ache in her head. Her mouth felt dry the way it did after a binge. It occurred to her the amount of drinking she'd done after watching that freaky thing that happened to the president certainly fit the definition of a "binge".

She groaned again, wrapped her arms about her midsection, and rocked herself gently on the edge of the couch. "Oh, God."

The door to the office swung open and Phil Parker came bustling in, his hand at his ear, his mouth flapping as he spewed invective at the mouthpiece of his cell phone. He winked at Emma and plopped into the chair behind his desk. "I don't care about what's happening in Pakistan, you sorry, lazy-ass sack of shit."

Emma rolled her eyes.

Mr. Charming in action.

With his free hand Phil mimed a squawking motormouth. "Yeah, yeah, yeah. What the fuck ever, Jacob. The sky is falling and all the little chickenshits are running around like their goddamn heads have been cut off. But that don't mean shit to me, okay? All's I know is you don't have your ass here by six, you're out of a job."

Emma's boss listened to Jacob Dunham's reply as he rocked agitatedly in his chair, eliciting a series of rapid-fire, ear-piercing squeaks from the overworked casters. "Uh-huh," he said, nodding. "Uh-huh, well, Jake, I appreciate the suggestion, but I don't think I can stick the whole goddamned bar up my ass, you smartass son of a bitch."

He snapped the phone shut and made a sound of frustration.

Emma tried not to smile. "Jacob's quitting?"

Now it was Phil's turn to roll his eyes. "Yeah. That fuckin' fruitcake. And now I'm short-handed again." He fixed Emma with a serious expression. "You're gonna have to work a double shift again."

Emma sighed. "No."

Phil exploded. "What!? Oh, come on!" He slapped the surface of his desk hard enough to send a loose stack of papers sliding over the edge. "I can't fucking believe this! I really fucking can't! How ungrateful can you be? Out of the goodness of my motherfucking heart, I give you a second chance and this is the thanks I get? Unbelievable."

Emma felt a brief surge of anger then, but she was too weary to indulge the emotion. She got to her feet and moved toward the door. "I'm going home. I need to sleep."

She banged through the office door before Phil could say another word. She sped through the bar's darkened interior and out the front door, then stood blinking on the sidewalk, shocked at the sight of what appeared to be a perfectly ordinary day on 21st Avenue. The traffic was as congested as ever. People were sitting in chairs outside coffee and pastry shops. She studied the faces of passing strangers, searching for hints of trauma in a series of largely nondescript faces. After a short while, it became apparent there *was* an undercurrent of tension, of anxiety, but it wasn't a crippling thing and that surprised her. The world around these people was unraveling, decaying in some strange, unfathomable way, and yet they were all going about their usual business.

Emma wanted to scream at them. She wanted to seize them by the throat and break through that barrier of denial propping them up, that kept them going through the motions like so many mindless automatons.

But it would be no use. They'd only think she was a lunatic. She sighed and moved away from the bar's entrance, turning to her right and threading her way through the stream of people as she walked briskly in the direction of her apartment building, The Mayflower, which was only five blocks away. Five blocks later, she crossed Fairfax and walked through the tiny rear parking lot of her building. She slipped between a Volvo and an old Mercedes station wagon and started down the stretch of sidewalk that ran parallel to the rear of the building. But she came to an abrupt stop at the sight of a dog lying dead some six feet in front of her.

"Oh, no."

The depression she'd been feeling since waking threatened to spiral out of control. The animal, a sweet Basset Hound named Henry, had belonged to a young Vandy student. Some pretty blonde girl whose name she didn't know. Emma would chat briefly with her when their paths crossed out back or in the nearby park, and she'd seemed like a very sweet young woman. She wondered where the woman was, and if she knew her pet was dead. That didn't seem likely. She wouldn't leave Henry lying here like this.

What had happened to him anyway? Henry was a young dog, playful and full of energy. Though her stomach fluttered at the thought of getting closer to the dead animal, she did so anyway, kneeling next to its carcass and peering closely, looking for any obvious signs of trauma. But there was nothing. Except for the fact he clearly wasn't breathing, he looked fine, as if he might merely be sleeping. But just to be extra sure, she put a hand on his belly and leaned closer still, striving to detect even the faintest hint of a pulse or weak breath. But again, nothing. Just a whiff of some foul odor. A death smell. If she'd believed there'd been the remotest chance of bringing Henry back from the brink, she would've scooped him up and driven at high speed to an emergency veterinarian hospital.

She shook her head and sniffled. "Oh, Henry . . . what happened to you buddy?"

Henry, of course, didn't answer. Emma, not knowing what else to do, scooped the little body up in her arms and carried him up to her apartment. Once she was inside, she located a blanket and wrapped him up in it. She knew the Vandy student, who lived in the opposite wing of the U-shaped building, wouldn't be home for a few more hours. In that time, Emma would try to think of a way to break the news gently to her.

She didn't turn on any of the apartment's lights, preferring the semi-gloom to a harsh artificial glare. The light wouldn't do her hangover any favors, and the near darkness better suited her grim mood anyway. She spied her acoustic guitar, an old Ovation, sitting propped in a corner, and picked it up. Then she sat on the edge of her sofa and began to pick out a few melancholy notes, humming a melody that was at once haunting and familiar. It was a lovely piece, something she'd begun playing without thinking. The words came to her and she sang a few lines.

When she realized what the song was, she struck a sour note and stopped playing. The sorrowful tune was "Warren's Song". She'd written it years ago, near the end of her troubled and heartbreaking relationship with Warren Hatcher.

Damn his sweet, beautiful soul. Wherever the hell he was now.

She put the guitar aside, suddenly unable to find solace even in music, her life's truest remaining passion. After sitting there silently on the edge of the sofa for a while—her mind lost in thoughts of a different time—she got up with a weary sigh and trudged off to bed.

~

Phil Parker failed to take notice of the frisbee-sized black hole in the floor beneath his desk. Something resembling a thick, hair-covered pink worm emerged from the hole and began to ooze slowly toward the polished brown loafer covering his left foot.

He thought of Emma bent over the foosball table and rubbed absentmindedly at his crotch. He unzipped his trousers and reached across the desk to draw a box of tissues closer. The slithering, worm-like appendage of the creature from the hole oozed across the top of his shoe as he was taking his cock in hand. Thinking about Emma had gotten him all worked up. He needed to unload some jizz or he'd be distracted the rest of the afternoon. The pink tentacle started to curl around his ankle.

Then a big, discordant noise from outside the office made him jerk in his chair. Some fool knocking on the door, demanding entrance long before the bar was due to open. The tentacle retracted, disappearing back into the hole so quickly Phil never saw it. He did, however, finally see the black circle on the floor. He also saw a very faint flicker of movement within the blackness. He leaned closer, his brow furrowing deeply as he tried to make out a shape. A sound emerged from the hole, a high, piercing screech that made his teeth hurt. And now he had an impression of more frantic movement within the hole, followed by a sense of something hurtling toward him, like a just-launched nuclear missile leaping out of a silo. By the time it occurred to Phil he ought to be scared out of his wits, it was too late.

The hole widened abruptly and a thing much larger than the original tentacle burst forth, upending the desk and driving Phil back against the wall. Phil screamed and called for help, but there was no one to help him. The pounding on the front door resounded again and Phil opened his mouth to issue one final screeching plea. But then the mouth of the creature opened wide and punched hundreds of needle-like teeth into his abdomen. Every nerve ending in his body sizzled with unbearable agony as some form of otherworldly venom was pumped into his veins.

Then he was thrown to the floor, where he remained conscious for several awful moments as he watched the thing slurp his intestines like strands of spaghetti. He died thinking of Emma, his wife, and whether he was going to hell.

~

An Underground Bunker
Noon

The new president sat at the head of a conference table. Also seated at the table were the highest-ranking members of the cabinet he'd inherited from the deceased president. He studied their grim faces, searching for any hint of something hopeful. But there was nothing. Just that same sense of a grave, impossible dilemma. They looked like a bunch of men (and one woman) about to be marched off to the death chamber.

The president struck the table with the base of a fist, making lukewarm coffee slosh over the edge of his mug. "This is insane. We're the richest country in the world. We have access to the most brilliant minds in the world. We're surrounded by technology so advanced it boggles the mind. There should be a solution to this problem. We should be able to think of *something* . . ."

The cabinet members exchanged expressions of weary exasperation. Some shifted uncomfortably in their chairs.

The president sighed. "There's a black fucking hole where Pakistan used to be. Every recon drone we send in disappears without a trace. And we sit here doing nothing. What's wrong with this picture?"

Jack Campbell snorted. "There's nothing to be done about that situation. Sir."

The president shot Campbell a withering glare. He didn't like the man. And he'd been furious when the late president had named him Chairman of the Joint Chiefs of Staff. But he was right. Goddamn him. Still, he couldn't keep the helpless anger out of his voice. "So we're just going to throw up our hands and surrender, is that it?" He laughed, but the sound became a wheeze as his throat constricted with emotion. Christ, he was on the verge of a breakdown. This was no way for a president to behave. Especially in the presence of so many hardened old bastards.

He cleared his throat. Then he looked each of them in the eye in turn. "It's incredible. Isn't it? Here we are, deep underground, insulated, safe from the worst weapons our earthly enemies can throw at us. And yet we're as vulnerable as any ordinary man or woman walking unprotected on the streets."

He leapt out of his chair and jumped up on the table, taking satisfaction from the startled yelps the action elicited from his cabinet members. He watched their eyes go wide with fright as they scooted backward in their chairs, and he felt a kind of wild exhilaration, a feeling he hadn't experienced in decades, since before he embarked on his career in politics. He pointed a finger at the ceiling and screamed, "There! Look up there! What do you see? Just a ceiling, right?"

He looked down at them and saw pity in their eyes. They thought he'd lost it, that he'd cracked under the strain. Well, fuck them. Maybe he had. And how could any sane person blame him? "That ceiling is a solid thing. Above it are other chambers, other places where the elite among us might seek refuge in the face of Armageddon. And above all of these secret places are layer upon layer of reinforced steel and concrete. Above that a mountain. This is an impenetrable fucking fortress!"

Campbell cleared his throat. "Mr. President—"

The president leveled a forefinger at him—it shook with the fury of his passion. "Shut up, you fat fuck!" He looked again at the ceiling. A note of strange serenity entered his voice when he spoke next. "Despite our most elaborate efforts to construct a place where we are absolutely safe, we are helpless. We are sitting ducks. At any moment a hole might open in that ceiling and something beyond our understanding might come screaming into this room. Something horrible beyond any previous conception of horror."

Campbell stood up. "Mr. President, you are not fit to lead this country. I suggest you tender your resignation at once and spare yourself and your family the embarrassment of an open revolt among the members of your administration."

The president looked at him. "The fabric of reality is decaying. The universe is unraveling. There is another place. A black realm beyond this one. Its inhabitants are eating their way into our world. They may devour us entirely. Do you deny this, General?"

Campbell shook his head, but his stern expression never wavered. "No, sir."

The president stepped off the table. He straightened his tie and smoothed back his hair. A part of him wanted to fight this. His political self, that portion of his personality that had taken him this far up the ladder of power. But the politician in him was dying, and he was relieved to realize he didn't have the will to rally that aspect of himself one last time. He began to feel a sense of liberation. No, that wasn't precisely it. The word "liberation" implied a degree of empowerment and he didn't feel anything like that. The opposite, in fact. But he did feel free. The immense burden was off his shoulders. He also felt free of his previous ambition. His former aspirations seemed like the incomprehensible desires of a stranger now.

He looked Campbell in the eye. "You're right. I am not the right person to lead the nation at this time."

The general heaved a big sigh. "I'm sorry it has to be this way, sir."

The president nodded. "I believe you. But I think you'll come around to my way of thinking soon enough." He smiled at the general's raised eyebrow. "I mean that. Carry on as best you can as long as you can. I expect nothing less from a man like you. It's admirable. But I think you'll know my despair soon enough. That's what I'm sorry about, General."

And with that he left the conference room. The sound of the door snicking shut behind him had a note of melancholy finality about it.

~

VNC Headquarters
Atlanta, GA
1:45 p.m.

Zeke caught fleeting glimpses of two of his colleagues through the thin vertical spaces to the left and right of the door in the bathroom stall. Matt Lewis, a producer, was examining his reflection in the bathroom mirror while he washed his hands. Dean Clark, who had moments ago finished unloading a dump of epic proportions in a stall next to Zeke, leaned against the wall with his massive forearms folded beneath his disturbingly perky man-teats and nodded as Matt repeatedly (and viciously) stabbed Zeke in the back.

Dean was VNC's newest weather reporter. He'd been hired for his personality as much as for his knowledge of meteorology. Dean was a Big Funny Guy in the vein of John Belushi or Chris Farley. Audiences loved him. Which meant the suits upstairs loved him, too. As a fledging news outfit operating in CNN's hallowed home territory, VNC needed every ratings edge it could get. But his appeal was a mystery to Zeke, and right now he'd give anything to drive a fist straight into the middle of his blubbery face. His hands curled into fists as he thought of the way Dean had so aggressively buddied up to him since the day he was hired. They'd gone out for drinks together several times. Jesus. Of course, duplicity in the world of television news was nothing new, but Zeke was certain he'd never encountered anyone so baldly two-faced as Dean fucking Clark.

Matt Lewis cranked a handful of paper towels out of the wall-mounted dispenser and briskly dried his hands. "I'm telling you, the guy is a nothing. A zero. A cipher. You ever just look at him when he's not paying attention to you, when he's off in his own little world? Man, it's creepy. There's nothing going on there, I swear to you. He's a total blank slate. And he's so perfectly handsome it's almost like he's a pod person, like he can't possibly be real."

Dean chortled. "Yeah, I know what you mean, buddy. It's like he rolled off some anchorman assembly line. He's Plastic Zeke, model number six-hundred and fucking sixty-six."

Matt Lewis almost doubled over with laughter. He braced one hand against the edge of the sink basin and held the other over his belly until he recovered. "Oh, shit. That's funny. Yeah, I bet if you shaved the hair at the back of his neck there'd be one of those barcode symbols."

Dean held his arms straight out and paced about the bathroom, doing an impression of a fat Frankenstein's monster. "I am Zeke Johnson. I am your anchorman." He said the words in an archly stilted, exaggerated way, like a robot from a '50s b-movie. "Welcome to New World Order News. I mean Venture World News."

That set Matt off on another ludicrous laughing fit. Zeke ached to leap out of the stall and pummel both the snide bastards. His face flushed red and his teeth were on the verge of puncturing the bit of lip pinched between them.

"And what was with that near meltdown of his yesterday?" Matt's tone shifted now, became more serious. "Guy freezes up on air like some jittery grade-school boy at his first school play."

Zeke flinched, recalling that he'd made a similar analogy at the time. Hearing this echo of his thoughts tumble out of Matt's mealy mouth was depressing. It gave the man's other negative comments extra weight. Maybe it was all true. Maybe he was nothing more than a pretty shell, just a glorified prop with a voicebox and a pulse.

NO!

That was pure bullshit. He was smart. He had the grades and IQ to prove it. And he was nowhere near as shallow as these jerks were making him out to be.

But Dean Clark saw things another way: "Yeah, that was weird, dude." Zeke rolled his eyes. A grown man, a professional, using the word "dude" like some stoner or surfer? Pathetic. "Hell, I'd almost feel sorry for him—if he wasn't so fucking full of himself."

Zeke's eyes went wide.

That son of a bitch!

"Uh-huh." Through the vertical slit to his left, Zeke could see Matt nodding. "Ain't that the truth. He's conceited as hell. A stuck-up, pompous, arrogant asshole."

Zeke seethed.

The two-charter member of the I-Hate-Zeke anti-fan club fell silent for a few moments. But Zeke was too enraged to notice at first. Then one of the men made a loud, throat-clearing noise and said, "Ah . . . is that you in there, Grant?"

Zeke frowned.

Grant?

Who the fuck was that?

He wracked his memory for a face to match the name, but it wouldn't come. Panic started creeping in. He didn't want these guys to find out the object of their derision had been listening the whole time.

So he decided to wing it. He cleared his throat and pitched his voice deeper than usual. "No. It's Tom. Tom . . . Grunick."

Zeke wanted to slap himself. Hard. Tom Grunick was the name

of the character played by William Hurt in *Broadcast News*. His favorite movie. Out of all the names he could have picked, why that one? Jesus jumping Christ on a motherfucking pogo stick! He'd have been better off telling them he was Ronald Reagan. He prayed his adversaries wouldn't make the connection.

"Sorry to bother you, Tom." Matt. The sleaze. "Thought you might be our buddy."

Zeke cleared his throat again and kept his voice pitched low. "No problem."

Matt clapped a hand on one of Dean's mountainous shoulders and said, "Let's go grab a bite to eat."

"Wooooo-doggie!" Dean Clark made an exaggerated sound of licking his chops. "That's the best idea you've had all day. Feel like I could eat me a horse!"

Zeke thought, *You look like you already did, you fat prick.*

Then they were gone, the door gliding shut behind them. Zeke drew in and expelled a deep, calming breath. He counted to ten. Some of the volcanic rage swirling within him subsided. He hitched his pants up, washed his hands at the basin, and opened the bathroom door. He searched the corridor for signs of Dean and Matt before proceeding. They were nowhere in sight. The profound degree of relief he felt then made him feel like a coward. It wasn't like him to avoid confrontation.

He stepped into the hallway and turned left, moving quickly toward a bank of elevators. He punched the down button and waited for one of the doors to open. While he waited, he wondered how anyone could be as petty as those two, given the momentous things happening in the world today. It was as if they were utterly oblivious to the possibility the world was ending. He replayed their conversation in his head, marveling at how very goofy much of their banter had been. They were like a couple of frat boy buffoons shooting the shit around a keg. Amazing. And to think they'd called him the shallow one.

A bell dinged and a set of doors slid open to his left. He hurried in that direction and ran straight into Angie McDowell, one of the makeup technicians, striking her with enough force to send her tumbling back into the elevator car.

"Aw, shit!"

Zeke rushed to her aid, proffering a hand to help her back to her feet. "Jeeze, I'm so sorry. I was in a hurry and didn't see you there."

She swatted his hand away and scrambled to her feet unassisted. "Fuck you. Watch where you're going, you absent-minded jerk."

Then she slipped past him and hurried out of the car. He watched her slim figure zip down the corridor, enjoying the way her shapely butt moved in those tight khaki slacks. Then the elevator door closed. He punched a button marked "L" for Lobby and the car began its descent.

It occurred to him he didn't know where he was going or what he was doing. He was supposed to be heading to the studio. But he appeared to be in the process of leaving the building. He knew he should feel alarmed by this apparently unconscious (and foolhardy) decision, but he felt no such thing. He still had no clue what he had in mind beyond exiting the building, but that was okay. He'd figure something out. All that mattered was that he would not be returning to the studio. Not now. Not ever.

He shook his head, wondering how he could have progressed so quickly from worrying about his job to walking away from it forever. Angie McDowell had displayed a previously well-masked disgust for him. Coupled with the overheard bathroom conversation, it implied a disturbing pattern. How many people at VNC thought Zeke Johnson was self-centered scum?

Some of them? Most of them?

It made Zeke sick to think about it.

After stopping numerous times to admit and carry several people to various floors, the elevator at last arrived at the lobby.

Zeke hesitated a moment longer. It wasn't too late to turn around and put a stop to this madness. Maybe he did have some personality flaws. It was remotely possible, he supposed. He could work on some things, make people like him better. Then he sighed and joined the flow of people entering the lobby.

A little later he was in his car and moving away from VNC Headquarters. He thumbed a button and the Thunderbird convertible's top began to retract. He lowered the windows and moved a hand roughly through his heavily moussed hair. He loosened his tie and enjoyed the feel of the wind against his face. When his beeper chirped a few minutes later, he chucked it out the window.

~

Harrisburg, Pennsylvania
5:02 p.m.

"Can you believe that!?" Rose Horton shook her head and stared in wide-eyed disbelief at the television screen. "He's resigning! Who's going to be president now?"

Rose was a heavy-set woman in late middle age. She favored clothes with bright floral patterns and had a big helmet of frosted hair that made her look like a time-traveling refugee from the early 1960s. She lived alone in the house across from Jasmine. Her husband had died more than a decade ago, just a few months before Jasmine and Gary had moved into the neighborhood. The way she talked about Jim Horton—constantly, and frequently in the present tense—was sometimes creepy. You'd think the man had passed away only months ago.

She sighed. "I don't remember the order of succession, Rose. I'm not thinking so clearly right now."

Rose's demeanor shifted at once. The news was forgotten as the whole of her attention zoomed in on Jasmine. She patted Jasmine's hand and her face took on a look of intense concern. "You poor dear. No one expects you to be thinking clearly." She made a clucking sound and shook her head. "So don't you go worrying what other people think. You listen to me, because I've been through it, okay? Your folks will be here soon. And your brother. Let them handle the arrangements and whatnot."

Jasmine sniffed. "You know what's funny?" She smiled even as she choked back another sob. "I was just thinking about how you talk about Jim as if he's still here sometimes. I don't think I'll be doing that ten years from now. Because I don't believe there'll be any world left by then. Hell, there may be no world by next week."

Rose passed a tissue to Jasmine, who accepted it gratefully and blew her nose. Rose clasped hands with her and looked at her even more intently now. "Don't you worry about what you can't control, sweetie. You can make yourself sick with worry and it does no damn good at all. This thing that's going on, I know it's scary, but I have faith everything will be okay in the end. The best minds in the world are working around the clock to stop whatever's making this crazy stuff happen. I truly believe they will succeed. But I've made peace with the idea they might not and I'll tell you why. This may be the end of our world, but there's another world beyond this one. I don't mean other planets, but another realm of existence. The afterlife. Heaven. The silver lining here is that failure only means I'll be reunited with my Jimbo that much sooner in that better place. Just as you'll be with your Gary again."

Jasmine didn't say anything. She didn't know whether she believed in an afterlife. She hoped like hell there was one. The notion of Gary not continuing on somewhere else in some new, unfathomable form hurt too much. Yet when she looked deep within her heart and tried to be honest—at least with herself—about what she truly believed, she always failed to achieve that level of inner peace she imagined people of pure faith possessed. She had too much trouble wrapping her mind around the idea of a soul separating itself from a body at the instant of death and ascending elsewhere. It seemed like too much of an old-world, archaic concept. A grand lie conceived by ancient tribal elders to comfort the peasants in the face of perpetual famine, pestilence, and war. In the final analysis, she'd always considered herself too smart to fall for what amounted to nothing more than a bunch of creaky old supernatural hokum.

Except that things were different now. There was a startling new paradigm to take into account, one that, on the surface at least, forced even the most militant atheist to allow for the possibility of alternate planes of existence. Hell, that was a given at this point. What was even more intriguing, from Jasmine's point of view anyway, was what seemed like a real chance that some supernatural force was at work here, laboring to rip asunder the fabric of reality. A fact that suddenly made all that old-world hokum no longer seem quite so . . . hokey.

Jasmine balled up the tissue and dabbed moisture from the corners of her eyes. She felt a little better now. Rose, as kooky as she sometimes seemed, had a point. Maybe there was a silver lining. Hell, maybe she should embrace The End. Maybe she should be on her knees right now, praying to God, just in case.

Her gaze went to the television, where the focus had shifted from the president and the developing international crisis. The Headline News anchorwoman, a sleek, young Hispanic woman named Maria Delgado, was talking about one of her colleagues. The man's picture was shown in a corner of the screen. Zeke Johnson. Apparently, the man had gone missing and a search was underway.

Rose patted her hand again and stood up. "I'm going across the street a minute, okay? Poor little Phoebe's been cooped up all day." Phoebe was Rose's yappy Pomeranian. "I'll let her out to do her business and be right back over."

Jasmine waved vaguely at her. "Oh, go on and stay home for a while. I know you must be tired of sitting with me. Go rest up some."

"Nonsense." Rose's brow furrowed deeply. "I don't want to hear any more such silliness out of you, young lady. I am your neighbor and your friend, and I will be here for you as much as you need me."

Jasmine sighed. "I didn't mean to offend you. I just . . . I wouldn't mind being alone for a while. Come back later tonight. I'd like the company, really. I just . . ."

Rose nodded. Her expression had softened somewhat. "I understand. Believe me, dear, I understand. It was ten years ago, but sometimes it seems like yesterday. I'll leave you alone for now. But you call me the instant you feel like you need somebody here, you got that?"

Jasmine nodded. "I do." She managed a weak smile. "And thanks for calling me a 'young lady'. It warms my forty-two-year-old heart."

Rose smiled. "Why, you're just a sapling still." She touched the other woman's cheek. "I'll be off now. You call me!"

Then she was gone, leaving through an archway that led into the foyer. A moment later came the sound of the front door slamming. Jasmine flinched. Then she sighed, relieved to at last have a bit of time to herself. She hadn't been alone since the moment the paramedics had arrived and performed their futile attempts at resuscitation on her dead husband. The intervening hours had been filled with an unending stream of personal visits and phone calls from friends and neighbors, and from Gary's business associates and family.

Jasmine got out of her chair and walked around the house, still feeling a tad sluggish from the pills she'd been taking to calm her nerves. She turned out each light she encountered, allowing an early evening darkness to envelop her. She imagined most people were doing the exact opposite today. Today humanity existed in a world in which awful, unfathomable horrors were quite likely to emerge out of dark spaces at any given moment. It was a scary thing, of course, but for the time being Jasmine was numb to the horror of it all.

For now, at least for this moment and probably the next, she welcomed the darkness.

~

Rose Horton stumbled over something as she began to cross the street. She managed not to fall flat on her face, but when she turned around to scan the road for the impediment, she saw nothing. So she stood there, hands on her protruding hips, and shook her head. "Huh. That's the damnedest thing. I could've sworn—"

Then she frowned.

Because now there was something in the road—and in the

approximate vicinity of where she had expected to see the rock. Something about the size of a cockroach. It was moving. Twitching, actually. Sort of flicking up and down without getting anywhere.

Rose scowled. She hated bugs. Filthy, nasty, disgusting things. She moved closer and raised her foot to crush the offending creature. But then she saw that whatever it was was actually protruding from a very tiny hole in the asphalt and was clearly just the tip of something much larger.

The wiggling thing surged through the hole, sending up a shower of asphalt and releasing a cloud of steam that smelled awful, like a battlefield trench filled with sunbaked corpses. Rose flew backward and landed flat on her back in her front yard. Something that looked like a winged serpent fluttered in the air in the street. Its mouth full of needle teeth made an awful chittering sound. The thing's bulbous head twitched and its glowing red eyes extended on thick black stalks.

Rose, praying she might reach the sanctuary of her home before the thing could focus its attention on her, began scooting backward over her lawn. Then she stopped and screamed as the thing dove out of the sky directly at her. Its mouth opened wide and the needle teeth drilled into her neck. She remained alive for a time as the creature's venom flooded her veins. The pain was exquisitely terrible.

The last thing she saw was the blood-red eyes of the serpent as they jerked about atop their dancing stalks.

4

DARKNESS UNLEASHED

TWO DAYS AFTER THE PRESIDENT died, and one day after his successor's abrupt resignation, the world as those of us living then had known it came to an end.

~

Early morning,
Somewhere in the U.S.A. . . . .

It sits on a couch in a human dwelling, the one shared by its first slave and her lover. It is still getting used to this form, the tiny body of its host, and is still figuring out all it can do. Its physical capabilities seem limited compared to those of the larger women, and it has considered abandoning the Abby-shell and taking up residence in Laura. Or her lover, Kelly.

But this diminutive form is not without its advantages. The larger creatures make certain accommodations for Abby-shell, treating her with a degree of deference, as if she is special somehow. The creature residing within the Abby-shell knows this is not a result of its myriad mental manipulations of the women. It has looked into the knowledge recesses of Abby's dormant mind and knows this is typical "adult" treatment of "children".

So it is content to sit here and use the remote control to watch images on the television while Laura prepares for "work". It pushes the channel-up button again and again, flipping rapidly through the full range of images, then repeating the cycle again and again. At first this seemed to annoy the larger women. The one called Kelly even demanded she stop and settle on one channel. It silenced her by reaching into her brain and destroying a small piece of it.

The images make it happy. Scenes of confused and frightened humans. They are powerless to do anything about the decay eating away at their world. The Abby-shell's facial muscles stretch and do that strange thing called a "smile". Smiling, as near as it could determine, is a uniquely human thing, something they do in moments of pleasure or happiness.

Once it looked into a mirror and made Abby-shell smile just to see what the expression looks like.

Fresh disgust roils within its soul at the memory.

It looks forward to destroying all of humanity, if only so it never again has to gaze upon something so hideous.

The Abby-shell's smile nonetheless grows broader.

For the time is nearly at hand.

Its pets are coming soon to do its bidding.

~

Nashville, TN
6:45 a.m.

Jeff Wheeler poured a cup of coffee from a dispenser in the break room. He dropped a couple of sugar cubes into the swirling black liquid, watched them fizz a moment, then added a dollop of cream. He tasted the concoction, shuddered at the sharp sizzle of hot liquid, and snatched up his clipboard from the counter.

He left the break room, walked through a hallway and out to the Ford dealership's service area. He approached the nearest service desk and nodded at the man across the counter. "Hey, Dave."

Dave Lucas gave a tired nod in response. He had a bristly, clean-cut appearance, with sandy blond hair cut down to a length of less than a quarter. But the hair stood straight-up. Why a man who cut his hair that short would use any kind of gel was a mystery to Jeff. Dave's hair looked like something you could scour a dish with—an insight he chose not to share.

Jeff took another sip of his coffee. "What have you got for me this morning?"

Dave sighed and rubbed bloodshot eyes. He drank a little too much sometimes, and so often showed up for work with eyes that looked like pink gumballs. He chuckled. "A weird one. Old dude out there wants you to look at his Taurus."

Jeff frowned. "What's weird about him?"

Now it was Dave's turn to frown. "I don't know. He's just . . . weird." He chuckled again and shook his head. "Well, you'll see. He's waiting for you now."

Jeff shrugged. "A buck's a buck."

Another tired chuckle from Dave. "I heard that."

Jeff turned away from the service desk and walked outside to greet the weirdo. It was still semi-dark out here as the sun continued its lazy ascent. There was only one other person in the lot at this early hour and Jeff at first assumed he was some strange homeless person who'd wandered off the street. The dealership was in the very heart of the city, so it happened sometimes.

But the guy was leaning against the only Taurus parked in the row of spaces reserved for service department visitors. Then it came to him. This was the weirdo Dave was talking about. Jeff regarded the man with a growing degree of apprehension. Something about the man made him unaccountably nervous. Jeff felt a sudden desire to retreat back into the service department. To maybe even go hide somewhere deeper within the dealership.

Instead, he gave himself a mental slap. The man might be an oddball, but he was also a paying customer. *A buck's a buck*, he reminded himself. So what if the dude was carrying a big wooden staff and wore flowing robes that made him look like some biblical figure out of an old Cecil B. DeMille epic. The bizarre choice of attire didn't necessarily mean there was anything wrong with him. Maybe he was dressed for a costume party. The excuse struck him as lame even as he thought of it—who the hell went to a costume party at seven in the morning?—but he decided it likely made as much sense as whatever the truth actually was.

He cleared his throat, pasted a big false smile across his face, and approached his customer. "Howdy there, friend. I'm—"

The man at last turned to face him. The grim expression he leveled at Jeff made him forget whatever else he'd been about to say. Then he spoke in a quiet but somehow stentorian voice, "You are Captain Flash Wheeler. You are the One True God."

Jeff blinked rapidly. "Uh . . ."

"Shut up and listen." The man's voice crackled with a strange energy. Jeff felt helpless to do anything but obey his every word. Inside, he was panicking, his guts shriveling, his brain turning to mush.

"Calm yourself, Wheeler."

Jeff relaxed immediately. His gut unclenched and his senses sharpened. He peered at the old man intently, suddenly hanging on his every word.

The old man nodded. "Good. Now listen to me. You are the savior of the new age. You have only been waiting for this moment to arrive." A disgusted expression momentarily flickered across the man's face. "My God, I sound like motherfucking Bono. But nevermind. Soon awareness will dawn within you. Until then you must keep yourself safe during the coming storm. I will return to guide you later. Until then, you will internalize what I've told you on an unconscious level."

Jeff nodded numbly. "On an unconscious level. Sure. Got it."

The old man almost smiled. "Yes. That you do, Captain Wheeler."

Jeff's brow creased slightly, a lazy, semi-conscious frown. "I'm a captain."

"You are now." The old man smirked. "Don't worry, it'll make sense later. Of a sort. And now I'm going to perform a cheap parlor trick. I'm going to snap my fingers and the conscious level of your mind will forget this encounter. For now."

The man snapped his fingers.

Jeff blinked and stared at empty air. He grunted. "Huh. Weird, man. What am I even doing out here?"

He shook his head and told himself he needed to start getting to bed at an earlier hour on work nights. He sighed and walked back into the service department.

~

The governments of the world held their collective breath for more than two days after the American president's televised demise. During that time, they kept a nervous eye on the vast black patch of nothing formerly occupied by the nation of Pakistan. A number of radical plans of action were discussed, including a massive use of nuclear weapons. The reasoning put forth by the advocates of this option was based on the assumption that the black space was an opening into another plane of existence. Therefore, any warheads detonated in that other world would have no deleterious effect on earth.

Maybe it even would have worked.

But the governments, led of course by Russia and the U.S., both of whom still possessed the largest nuclear arsenals in the world, waited too long to pull the trigger. And so early in the morning on that day of terrible reckoning, the world was left virtually defenseless when wave upon wave of winged, screeching nightmares came gushing out of all that blackness. Hundreds of thousands of them. Millions, perhaps.

And they were just the advance guard.

~

Other creatures emerged individually, and by twos and threes, from smaller rents in the fabric of reality. These smaller waves of attackers seemed to emerge everywhere at once, as if coming forth on some hidden signal.

~

It's early morning somewhere in the heart of America. A group of schoolchildren stand at a rural street corner, awaiting a bus that will take them off to another dreary day of school. One kid, a blond boy, grows weary of the heavy bookbag strapped to his back. He unslings his burden and lets it fall to the ground.

He frowns. Why was there no thump of the overstuffed bag hitting the sidewalk?

That's when he glances down and sees the dark hole next to his feet, a ragged patch of blackness where there should be a white concrete slab. He immediately thinks of all the scary things he's been seeing on television lately and so isn't terribly surprised when the monster's head leaps through the hole. The other kids are screaming and running away. He wishes he could go with them, but the monster has taken one of his legs in its mouth and all of a sudden it feels like a thousand gazillion hypodermic needles have been stabbed into him by some crazy, sadistic doctor.

His suffering in these next moments is more than I need to tell you about. Millions of children like this little boy will soon experience the same pain.

~

In Atlanta, Georgia, in the Venture News studio, a creature emerged from a black slash in the air and bit off the head of anchorwoman Maria Delgado. The camera angle shifted as the thing turned its conical head and gave millions of viewers a close-up view of something most of them would be encountering in the flesh very soon. I'm sure some people dropped dead at the sight of it.

They were the lucky ones.

~

The American government scrambled every piece of fighter aircraft at its disposal, sending thousands of pilots on suicide missions. The skies above America and much of Europe and the Middle East resounded with the sounds of bone-rattling explosions. Tons of shrapnel rained down, killing many of those watching the show on the ground.

The fighter planes actually managed to wipe out scores of the swooping creatures. But they were vastly outnumbered. The creatures themselves varied wildly in size. Some were the size of birds. Others were twice as large as the planes attempting to destroy them. Often the larger ones would swat the planes out of the sky, as if they were no more threat than a buzzing gnat.

By the time the acting American president finally decided to launch nuclear warheads, it was too late. The military was in a state of disarray. However, a number of missile silos actually did send their nuclear payloads into the air. Inevitably, some of these went off target and missed the space formerly occupied by Pakistan altogether. Many thousands of human beings died in an instant with each errant detonation.

~

Throughout the early part of that day, there was still sporadic television news coverage of the rapidly unfolding worldwide disaster.

First came word that the missing nation of Pakistan was no longer the lone great, gaping hole in the world's topography. Similarly massive patches of blackness swallowed Brazil, Hong Kong, Paris, Ukraine, and a big chunk of the northwestern portion of the United States. There were more. Many likely went unreported by the news agencies, most of which ceased to function after a few hours. Fresh waves of winged attackers swarmed out of each new rip in our reality's decaying fabric.

In Rome, a patch of blue sky above the Vatican turned black, as if someone had punched a hole through a painting. More screeching creatures came zooming out of that blackness and soon the streets around that holy center ran red with the blood of thousands of tourists and religious pilgrims.

In Times Square in Manhattan, one of the winged things emerged from an opening in one of the massive television screens ringing the square—which itself had been displaying images of the carnage from other parts of the world—and impaled a young couple with one of its enormous talons. Then it lifted them into the air—with their limbs still twitching—and devoured them like a restaurant patron gnawing food straight off a skewer.

A missile launched from North Korea exploded in the air above Los Angeles. The atomic weapon was not as powerful as the U.S.-manufactured nuclear warheads, but knowing that wouldn't have mattered to those vaporized by the blast. A big section of the city was flattened. Many more thousands of lives extinguished in the time it takes to draw a single breath. A retaliatory strike was launched from U.S. nuclear subs patrolling the waters in that part of the world. Any other time these events would have set off a third world war, but thereafter the governments of the world effectively ceased to function. There were a few more nuclear launches, but it's believed these were either accidental or the last, defiant acts of a few mad zealots.

The cataclysmic changes in the shape of the world inevitably triggered enormous natural repercussions. Dramatic atmospheric shifts caused typhoons that wiped out several island nations and significantly reduced the above-water land mass of many others. The numerous nuclear detonations sent a vast amount of ash and debris into the air and set great, roiling black clouds adrift. A degree of nuclear winter would eventually affect much of the globe. The strangest aspect of it all was that the earth kept spinning on its axis, that it didn't implode or go hurtling into the sun. Perhaps the hand of God Himself kept the world in place throughout these wrenching changes. But I am not a scientist. Nor am I a religious scholar. These things are beyond my ken.

Of course . . . these natural and man-made catastrophes would later seem as nothing compared to the effects of the creeping rot that would soon infect this Deadworld.

But we didn't know that yet.

~

By about noon of that day the few still functioning television sets were picking up nothing other than sporadic EAS signals.

Then those stopped as well, displaced by a ceaseless static buzz.

~

When this time of hell on earth came to an end, a development occurred that seemed to indicate the worst was over. The small pockets of survivors would soon gain a degree of false confidence, which would encourage them to emerge from their various hiding places and attempt to pick up the pieces of their shattered world. I wish I could journey back in time to warn my fellow survivors, to tell them that this period of relative quiet was but a lull.

Alas, of course, I cannot.

57

5

NASHVILLE, TN
September 27
4:20 p.m.

Something heavy struck the roof of the car and rolled off, hitting the ground with a dead-weight sound. The jarring impact made Aaron Harris squeal with terror and curl into an even tighter fetal ball in the trunk of the Lexus, where he'd been hiding from the relentless onslaught of the flying demons most of the day.

He'd chosen the trunk as a hiding place out of pure necessity. He'd been examining the contents of the trunk as he stood in the gray, early morning light. In it were several lengths of rope, a box of large black garbage bags, a roll of duct tape, a hunting knife, and a nail gun, all purchased while shopping at the neighborhood hardware store the night before. And all of which he'd planned to put to good use soon after breaking into Emma Singleton's apartment.

Finding out where she lived hadn't been difficult. In fact, it'd been ridiculously easy. He knew she walked to work, and he'd heard her tell more than a few people at the bar that she lived on Fairfax, which was just a few blocks west of the Villager Pub. So he'd simply walked up and down Fairfax, pretending to be another Joe scouting the densely populated neighborhood for a new apartment. He knew he'd found the right building because she'd helpfully placed a strip of masking tape on her mailbox, upon which she'd written in ink, "E. Singleton."

But his plans for Emma were forgotten soon after he filled a burlap bag with his new toys. The sky above him darkened and the air filled with a high, hideous sound, a sound prehistoric beasts might have made millions of years ago. He looked up and saw a black mass of nightmare creatures. Great, winged things with glowing red eyes, thick, snake-like bodies, and talons the size of machetes. When the things dropped en masse toward the city, instinct made Aaron hop into the trunk and pull it shut.

And there he'd remained for hours, listening to the soundtrack of a seemingly endless horror film play out around him. The awful screeches grew almost unbearably loud as the creatures neared the ground. Then came the first screams of human beings caught out in the open. He heard cars crashing into each other. Then the wail of sirens. Then gunfire. But the human resistance didn't last long. Soon the gunfire ended and all Aaron heard was more screeching and screaming.

It went on for an eternity.

Or so it felt closed up in that tight, dark space all those hours.

Gradually, he began to realize the screaming of humans had ended. And the screeches of the demon-things were only occasional disruptions in an otherwise oppressive silence. He knew he wouldn't be able to stand it much longer in the trunk. As much as he loathed the idea of leaving his safe place and moving around outside, where he'd be exposed and defenseless, he knew he couldn't remain here forever.

Still—he thought maybe he'd hold tight a little longer.

For the first time in a good while, his thoughts turned back to Emma. He wondered where she'd been during the attack. Given the early hour, she'd probably been asleep in her bed. Would she have been safe by staying inside? Maybe. But maybe not. He remembered the oft-replayed tape of the president's death. Obviously, if the president was vulnerable in the Oval Office, then no one was safe anywhere.

Not even here, in the trunk of this car.

The thought triggered a new surge of claustrophobia and for a moment he reached out in the darkness, meaning to push the seat forward and climb into the back seat of the car. Then he heard another impact, something that dropped out of the air and landed with a dead thump somewhere in the street nearby. He heard a sound somewhere between a hiss and a wail. He knew at once it was not a human sound. But it was a sick sound. The sound of something dying.

He listened more intently and soon heard more big impacts. Some nearby, loud crashes. Still others were dim thuds in the distance. When ten minutes passed without hearing another of the impacts, he drew a deep breath and pushed the seat forward. He climbed into the car, then crawled down to the floorboard. Until he had an at least marginally better sense of things outside the enclosed environment of his car, he wanted to stay hunkered down, out of sight.

He glanced up and saw that whatever had struck the car had been heavy enough to crumple the front end of the roof. Miraculously, the rear windshield was still intact. He peered through it and glimpsed a huge fire burning in the distance. After a while, he gathered his courage and climbed up to the level of the blown-out back door windows. He glanced through the space where the window on the driver's side had been and got his first glimpse of the thing that had hit his car.

One of those winged things.

It was dead.

He stared at it a moment longer, then thought, Oh, fuck it.

He climbed out of the car, then stood on the sidewalk, legs still stiff from the hours spent curled up in the trunk. He glanced again at the dead demon, then did a slow turn and surveyed his surroundings. He saw more dead demons. One was sprawled across the roof of an apartment building on the opposite side of the street. Another was impaled on a spiked fence. There were others in the streets. They were all dead. He knew because he didn't hear that eerie wailing sound anymore.

What the hell?

He couldn't fathom this new development. He was glad to see the things were dying, of course, but what was the reason? Had the government unleashed some sort of poisonous gas into the air? But that made no sense. Surely something deadly enough to destroy these creatures would have killed him just as effectively. Or maybe they simply had severely limited life spans. Like flies.

Like deadly, bloodthirsty demonic flies. From hell.

Aaron giggled.

A mad sound. A lunatic sound. He flashed back to his vivid

fantasies of the night before, the things he'd imagined he would do to Emma once she was under his control.

And he giggled again.

A mad sound. Yes, that was appropriate, wasn't it? After all, madness had come to this world, had overtaken it, in fact. From where he stood, he could see human limbs that had been tossed aside like toothpicks. Dozens of them. He saw torsos without limbs. He saw the head of an elderly woman perched atop the hood of a car. He saw wet organs glistening on gray asphalt, saw strands of intestine dangling from tree limbs like Christmas tinsel. He giggled yet again. How horrible. How delightfully, wonderfully horrible it all was.

He glanced again at the thing that had struck his car. His curiosity piqued, he knelt next to it for a closer look. It was like an unholy synthesis of dragon, serpent, and super-sized bat. He'd thought they were demons from the beginning, that they'd literally come pouring out of hell, Satan's legions come forth to wage war on humanity. Maybe that was true. It made as much sense as anything else he could think of. But maybe they were from somewhere else. Maybe what those wackos had been saying on TV was true, that they had come from some alternate dimension, emerging through holes in the decaying fabric of reality. He'd been so obsessed with his plans for Emma he'd only half paid attention to any of that babble.

And speaking of that lovely lady . . .

She was probably dead now, but he wanted to verify that before moving on.

He moved to the rear of his Lexus and smiled when he saw the keys on the ground, still where they'd fallen when he'd leaped into the trunk. He picked them up, opened the trunk with the keyless entry button on the electronic fob, and retrieved the burlap bag of dark goodies.

Then, whistling a sunny tune, he set off in the direction of Emma's apartment.

~

Emma scurried back under her bed when she heard the footsteps. Someone was entering her apartment through the place where the front door had been. Earlier in the day she'd been awakened by the commotion outside. Upon parting the curtains covering her bedroom window to get a glimpse of what was going on, she was unable at first to accept what she was seeing. It was too much like a scene from some wild disaster or fantasy movie. The huge black things with wings couldn't possibly be real. But that sense of numb detachment only lasted until one of the flying things came hurtling out of the sky on what looked like a direct path to her apartment.

So she dove for the nearest cover available, which turned out to be the underside of her bed. And there she'd remained most of the time. She listened as more of the things crashed into the building, their bodies punching holes through brick and mortar with distressing ease. She heard the heart-rending, soul-freezing screams of some of her neighbors as they were plucked from their own bedrooms and living rooms.

Twice before, she'd gathered the courage to leave behind the dubious shelter the bed afforded. These were during relative lulls in the destruction. She'd still heard screams, still heard the leathery flapping sound of huge wings, but these sounds had been distant, far enough away that she should be safe. Relatively speaking. But each time she got lucky, catching glimpses of nearby creatures before they could see her. They were patrolling the sky above the city at this point, groups of them turning in lazy circular patterns. The frenzy of before was not in evidence, but that didn't mean they weren't still a threat. But when she spied one perched atop a power line—and saw another gliding some thirty feet above the ground over Fairfax—she retreated to her bedroom sanctuary.

The next time she ventured forth was hours later, well after the last time she'd heard any sounds whatsoever from outside. She got as far as the living room, where she saw pieces of the shattered front door scattered across the floor. Also, the window overlooking the parking lot had been blown out, as had a big segment of the adjoining wall. The sofa was turned over and the coffee table was in splinters. But none of the damage to the furniture meant anything to her. Nor did seeing the mangled remains of Henry, who'd been dead already anyway. The thing that stole her breath and brought her to the brink of passing out was seeing what remained of Michelle Anderson.

Pieces of Michelle's legs were on the floor. After gnawing them down to the bone, something had tossed them aside like discarded chicken wings. The woman's head lay near the demolished section of wall. A piece of the spinal column was visible. It looked like a large, segmented yellow worm.

Emma wondered why the woman had been killed here rather than in her own apartment, or out in the hallway. Not that it mattered now. She was dead and the thing that had killed her was gone. It disturbed her that something so hideous had occurred so close to her hiding place.

She was consumed then with a need to be away from what was left of Michelle's ruined body and so stagger-stepped toward the door. But she stopped cold when she heard a new sound. She listened to footsteps ascending the staircase outside and experienced a burst of something that may or may not have been precognition. This new presence wasn't otherworldly. It was human. It moved with stealth and deliberation. Emma knew she should be eager for human company, for someone to commiserate with, but she felt suddenly sure she didn't want to be seen by the stranger.

So here she was again, hiding under the bed, listening to the creak of the floorboards beneath the man's shoes, and straining hard not to make the slightest sound. She kept her breath tightly regulated, allowing it to ease slowly in and out. She prayed she wouldn't suddenly hiccup or cough.

The man was moving around the living room. She heard him kicking aside bits of broken furniture. At one point she thought she heard him make a sound. It took her a moment to identify what she was hearing because it was so incongruous given the day's events and the presence of Michelle's mutilated body in the living room.

Then she heard it again and now there could be no mistake.

He was giggling.

She drew in a sharp breath and felt a chill spread through her body. Whoever he was, the man was a complete nutbar. The unfairness of it made Emma's head ache. Christ, it wasn't enough that she had to figure out a way to survive in a world ravaged by demons from another dimension—now she had a garden variety human psycho to contend with as well.

The footsteps grew louder, then she saw the man's shoes appear in the doorway. He whistled as he entered the bedroom, some cheerful, off-key tune that made her cringe and want to cover her ears. The man turned to the right and moved over to her dresser, where he pulled open drawers and rifled through her clothes. She saw tops and T-shirts fall to the floor. Another drawer opened and the man breathed a sigh of deep contentment and pleasure. She heard him draw in a deep breath and knew the perv was sniffing her panties.

Emma suppressed a groan. This violation coupled with the still-fresh images of Michelle's bloody death was too much. Fighting back a tide of nausea required a fierce determination of will. In that moment Emma figured she had a pretty good idea what it was like to have to lie absolutely still in a trench and pretend to be dead while a platoon of enemy soldiers goes marching by.

The man dropped her undergarments and moved to the opposite side of the room, where he yanked her closet open and swept back all the clothes on hangers. She turned her head and saw him squatting there as he dug into the recesses of her closet, tossing old shoes and boxes aside in the process.

For the first time, it occurred to her to wonder who he was. She could tell by the body type—and expensive shoes—that it wasn't Rick. Who did she know who was this creepy?

Phil.

But her boss had been missing since yesterday. Besides, this man was buff and athletic. Phil was heavyset.

It came to her in a flash.

That belligerent yuppie, the one who'd been hitting on her for months at the pub. She'd last seen him the night the president died. He'd hit on her, as usual, and she'd rejected him more brusquely than usual, probably because the memory of her humiliation at the hands of another arrogant male was still so fresh in her mind. That, and she'd been tired of the guy's bullheaded persistence.

He'd found out where she lived—not a difficult thing to do, she knew—and now here he was, probably thinking he'd take advantage of the mass chaos to take by force what she refused to give up willingly. The thought made Emma shudder with fear. She had no weapon, nothing with which to defend herself against a man so much bigger and stronger than she. She could scream and call for help, screech herself hoarse even, and no one would come. Anyone within earshot would be too concerned for their own safety to come running to her aid.

The man, Aaron, ceased tossing the contents of her closet all over the room. He sat cross-legged on the floor, stroking a red vinyl go-go boot with a platform heel. She'd last worn the things the previous Halloween. She'd dressed as a sexy devil. The outfit had been quite the hit with the boys at the pub. But now, as she watched Aaron push the sole of the shoe against his crotch, she knew she'd never wear the boots again.

Christ, what a sick, sick bastard.

Once he found her—as he surely would—what would he do with her with no one around to intervene? She had a feeling a man like this one wouldn't be satisfied with raping and beating her. He would need to do something to put her in her place, to make her really regret all the times she'd turned him down and bruised his ego.

He'll torture me, she thought. *Maybe for a long, long time.*

Then he'll kill me.

She thought of that old adage about cockroaches and lawyers being the only creatures hardy enough to survive all-out global nuclear war. She figured the list should now be amended to include Ted Bundy wannabes like this asshole.

Aaron groaned and rocked on the floor, rubbing the sole of the boot harder against his crotch. It struck Emma as ridiculous. The big, bad psycho getting himself off with a piece of her footwear. But thinking that failed to make what she was seeing any less frightening. The man was preoccupied, but soon he'd be done with this exercise in weirdness. Then he'd be looking for her again. And it would only be a matter of time before he thought to check under the bed.

So she had to make a move while she still could.

She drew in a breath and held it. She laid her hands flat on the floor and, with exquisite care, moved very slowly to the left. The edge of the bed was still a few feet away. When she reached the open space beyond it, she would move into a crouch, get her feet firmly planted beneath her, then bolt out of the room like an Olympic sprinter. With any luck, she'd catch him by surprise and get enough of a head start to get out of the building and duck down an alley before he could catch up to her.

First, though, she needed to get there. So she flexed the muscles in her shoulders and slid again to the left. Then again. Flex and slide. Flex and slide. Then she was at the edge of the bed, about to emerge into the open. Aaron was still at the closet. She heard him groaning. She heard him say her name. He was working himself into a frenzy. Wouldn't be much longer before he was done.

Emma readied herself to slide to the left one last time.

Then she heard something.

More footsteps. But not Aaron's. He was still on the floor in front of the closet, still engaged in his tawdry intimacy with her go-go boot. But clearly he'd heard the footsteps, too. She heard him draw in a sharp breath. Then there was a small thump. The boot being tossed aside. She turned her head in that direction and saw him get to his feet.

The footsteps from the living room moved closer.

Then there was another sound. A voice: "Emma? Are you here?"
Jake Dunham!

She heard a soft scraping sound, something moving against fabric.
Aaron removing something from a pocket? She moved into the open
and jumped up as Jake came into the room.

"Jake!"

Her exclamation elicited a surprised shriek from Aaron, who
whirled in her direction. She saw the gleaming serrated hunting knife
in his hand and felt a chill finger of fear reach into her heart. Then
Jake came rushing into the room and swept Emma into an embrace.
She looked over his shoulder as the lanky stoner boy crushed her
against him in relieved exuberance. He wasn't yet aware someone else
was in the room. She looked at Aaron's eyes, saw the malevolence
glittering there as he glared at Jake's back. The fingers of his hand
turned red as his grip tightened around the knife handle.

He moved one careful step in their direction. Emma braced her
hands on Jake's shoulders and pushed with all her might, breaking the
embrace then spinning him around to face the other man.

Jake said, "Whoa."

Aaron froze. His gaze flicked from Jake to Emma and back again.
He licked his lips, then his mouth hung open. He looked like a coyote
contemplating prey.

Jake loudly cleared his throat. "Listen, dude, I don't know what
you've got in mind with that knife, but I'd think twice about it if I
were you. It might wind up in your ass, y'know?"

Aaron sneered. "Yeah, right. Why are you two looking at me that
way anyway?" A smile lifted the corners of his face, an expression
that did nothing to diminish the feral, predatory gleam in his eyes.
"The world is coming to an end, or haven't you noticed? We're under
assault by legions of flying demons, for Christ's sake. I'd be crazy to
be out without some kind of weapon. So knock off the paranoia,
okay?" He made a show of putting the knife away. "There. You
happy?"

Jake shook his head. He glanced at Emma, read her opinion of
the knife-wielding intruder in an instant, and stepped in front of her.
"No. I'd say we're pretty fucking unhappy, actually. What are you doing in my friend's apartment?"

Aaron opened his mouth to say something, but Emma pushed
Jake aside and took a defiant step forward. "You came here to rape
me didn't you, Aaron?" She grunted, a sound that articulated her

disdain for the man better than mere words could. She turned to Jake. "You know what I saw this creep doing while hiding under the bed?"

Aaron's face flushed red and the tight line of his mouth quivered slightly as he ground his teeth.

Jake draped a protective arm over her shoulders. "Tell me."

Emma made the same sound of utter disdain. "He was pleasuring himself with my go-go boot." She nodded at the spot on the floor where the boot had landed upright. "That one right there."

Jake scowled. "Aw, man, you fucking pervert."

Emma nodded. "He sat on the floor grinding it against his crotch and groaning."

Aaron's face was so red now he appeared to be on the verge of a stroke. "You shut up, bitch."

Now Emma smiled, a small one that just lifted the corners of her mouth. "I've never seen anything so disgusting."

Jake chuckled. "I bet."

Aaron knelt and grabbed a burlap bag off the floor. "Go to hell, cunt."

Emma arched an eyebrow. "What's in the bag?"

Aaron managed a mad grin. "Like I said, go to hell. Cunt."

"Come *oooon*." She adopted a mocking little girl pout now. "Show us what's in the bag, 'kay?"

His wild grin still in place, Aaron slung the bag over his shoulder and moved toward the door. "Maybe some other time, slut."

And then he was gone. They listened to his footsteps as he moved through the living room then out into the hallway beyond.

Jake breathed a big sigh. "Jesus." He looked at Emma with concern. "You okay?"

Only then did she realize how weak she felt. Her legs buckled and she let herself pitch backward onto the bed. Jake sat at the edge of the bed and held out his arms. She crawled into his embrace and clung tightly to him while the tears flowed.

~

Aaron thundered down the stairs, kicked open the building's back door, and rushed into the early evening gloom. He marched toward Fairfax. He quaked with fury. Much of his rage was directed at Emma, but a significant portion of it was channeled inward.

He'd never in his life known such humiliation. No one, especially no *woman*, had talked to him like that. He should've kept the knife out, should've gutted the both of them like the stinking hippie pigs they were.

He stopped in the middle of Fairfax and glanced back at the building. He pulled the knife from his jacket pocket and considered going back to do what he should have done in the first place.

Then he sighed and put the knife away.

No.

They'd be expecting him, would be watching for him. He smiled as a new course of action came to him.

Something that might be more fun.

He crossed the street, stepped through a break in a small hedge, and hunkered down. While he watched the rear door of the apartment building, he rubbed the flat of the blade against his crotch and remembered that go-go boot.

6

ON THE GARDEN STATE PARKWAY
September 27
6:10 p.m.

"It's quiet out there."

Warren felt Amanda's warm breath on his ear. It was reassuring, that warmth. It meant life. Survival. As long as they were drawing breath, they still had a chance. He reached for her hand in the darkness, held it tight, and was pleased to find it only shook slightly in his grasp.

His other hand tested the smooth metal of the closed trailer door. They'd been safe here in the dark throughout the day, but Warren had a feeling that had as much to do with luck as anything else.

Amanda sighed. "I think we can go out there now."

Warren frowned. "I don't know. We're all right here. I think we should still wait a while. Until . . ."

Amanda waited a beat, then said, "Until what? Until help comes?" She breathed an exasperated sigh. "Help's not coming."

"You don't know that."

But, thing was, somehow he did know that. Felt it deep down in his gut. Help wasn't coming. Ever. Which scared the shit out of him.

He wanted to be strong for both of them, wanted to protect Amanda and somehow safely steer her through this nightmare. It was silly, this macho desire to play the chivalrous hero, some kind of knight errant. Especially considering how little faith he had in his ability to shield either of them against the dangers awaiting them.

They hadn't glimpsed the outside world in many hours. They'd abandoned their car after one of those flying things had picked it up and heaved it across four lanes of traffic. They should be dead. But they'd been saved by a combination of buckled seatbelts and properly deployed airbags. Warren believed the ballooning white bags had confused the screeching creatures and sent them off in search of other prey. They managed to fight free of the bags and extract themselves from the ruined car.

The sky above them was full of the flying things. When one of them started screeching in a particularly manic way, Warren gripped Amanda by the hand and dashed a jackknifed tractor trailer, which sat astride two and a half lanes of dead highway. No cars moved now. The stretch of asphalt between them and the trailer was an obstacle course of twisted wreckage and broken bodies. Here and there the road was dotted with splashes of dark crimson.

The trailer door stood open, beckoning to them the way a lonely church in the middle of nowhere calls to a wayward pilgrim. They managed to get inside and pull the door shut before one of the flying beasts could pounce on them. Any one of those things could have pulled the door off the trailer with ease. So Warren figured they hadn't been spotted after all. Which, as best he could tell, meant they'd only delayed certain horrible death.

It was Armageddon out there.

"I can't stand it in here any longer." Amanda's voice had a plaintive note now, was just a breath away from a whine—not that he could condemn the impulse to whine, given the circumstances. "It's worse this way. This waiting. It's so quiet. I don't think they're out there anymore."

Warren grunted. "So you're psychic now?"

Amanda's grip tightened on his hand, a signal that a burst of temper was imminent. "I can do without the sarcasm. If you want, I'll leave by myself and we'll go our separate ways. You can go back to fucking Newark, or Nashville, or wherever the hell, and I'll make it to Florida on my own."

Warren breathed a weary sigh. "Please chill, okay? I'm sorry. I said

I'd get you home and I meant it."

He gave the door a shove and it swung open with a loud squeal that made them both cringe. They stood at the edge of the trailer and stared at a sky nearly overtaken by the full dark of evening. Except for a mass of dark clouds, the sky was empty, devoid of careening winged demons. Ahead of them, the fading light made the assemblage of trashed and abandoned cars look like a spooky automotive graveyard.

Warren jumped to the ground. Then he offered a hand to Amanda and helped her down. She hugged herself tight and shivered. She pressed herself against Warren and he wrapped an arm around her.

"What do we do now?"

She sounded lost and afraid, almost like a child. It made Warren further regret his snappishness a moment ago. Protect her, he thought. Do whatever it takes.

He coughed. "I . . . I'm not sure. I guess we should start by looking for a car that'll still run."

She groaned. "In this mess? We're doomed."

Warren surveyed the discouraging array of wrecks, dismissing each of them without a second glance—until his gaze settled on a tan Ford Escort hunched against the far guardrail. Its rear and passenger side windows were blown out, and it had a flat rear tire on the driver's side.

Warren said, "Let's check that one out."

Amanda frowned. "It's got a flat."

"That might not be a problem."

They crossed the street carefully, stepping over mounds of debris and, one time, the corpse of a demon. Looking at it reminded Warren strongly of pictures he'd seen of victims of poison gas attacks. Its strange limbs were contorted and its mouth was stretched wide in an expression of obvious agony.

Amanda said, "Look, there's another one."

Warren saw it. This one was much smaller than the other, with wings that were a sickly pale gray rather than the coal-black of most of its brethren. Its dead red eyes looked like billiard balls. "I wonder what happened to them?"

"Maybe they can't survive long in our world." Amanda sounded hopeful, almost excited. "Maybe something in our atmosphere kills them if they breathe it too long."

Warren shrugged. "Could be."

He hoped she was right. More than anything else, he wanted the world to revert to some semblance of normality. The angst that had possessed him for so long seemed ridiculous now. He'd give anything if he could jump back in time a few years and force his younger self to get over Emma quicker and move on in a more positive direction in his life.

Might as well wish on a shooting star, you whimsical fool . . .

"Oh, Warren." Amanda put a hand over her mouth.

They were close to the Escort now. Warren saw immediately what had so disturbed Amanda. The car was full of dead people. A dead woman behind the wheel. A dead child in the passenger seat. He felt weak in the knees as they came to a stop alongside the car—a car that was essentially a family's mangled coffin.

Amanda shivered again. And there was a note of pleading in her voice when she said, "Let's look for another car, okay? There's got to be another one."

Warren gripped her firmly by the shoulders and looked into her eyes. "They're all gonna be like this. I don't think we should waste time looking for something else." He nodded at the larger of the dead demons. "We can't be sure these things are all dead. Remember how many of them there were? And we only see two dead ones. Fact is, we don't know what the hell's going on. Same as before."

Amanda frowned. "So . . . what? We're just gonna haul those poor people out of their car and dump them in the road?"

Warren closed his eyes a moment.

God, but he felt so tired.

He looked at Amanda. "Yeah," he said, sounding solemn but steadfast. "That's exactly what we're gonna do. Only I'll do the dirty work. You won't have to touch them."

Amanda gagged when Warren opened the passenger side door and the woman's corpse fell out. "Oh. This is so vile. So wrong."

Warren hooked his hands under the dead woman's armpits. He swallowed hard to suppress his rising tide of nausea. "I won't argue that point."

He planted his feet and pulled hard, and stumbled backward when he failed to encounter the expected degree of resistance. He landed flat on his back amid a pile of another victim's entrails. Amanda shrieked. Jagged bolts of pain shot down each of his splayed limbs. He opened his eyes and saw Amanda kneeling over him. She was saying "Ohmygodohmygod" over and over, like a stuck record. He

72

blinked his eyes to clear his vision and groaned as he painfully pushed himself into a sitting position.

The top half of the dead woman's body lay on the street next to the car. The bottom half of her body—from approximately the waist down—was still positioned behind the steering wheel. Well, that accounted for his miscalculation. He'd figured on having to haul out a good deal more dead weight.

He got to his feet and moved forward on legs still wobbly from the fall.

Amanda laid a hand on his shoulder. "What do you think you're doing?"

He looked at her. "Finishing what I started."

Amanda shook her head vehemently. "No. Fuck that. No way we're riding in that bloody mess of a car. Look at you." She indicated his soiled clothes with a wave. "You already look like you stepped out of a slaughterhouse. Nuh-uh. I'd rather take my chances on foot."

Warren sighed. "You sure about that? Even though there's no guarantee there won't be more of those flying things?"

She nodded. "I'm fucking positive, pal."

Warren's shoulders sagged. "Well, then." His gaze drifted back to the Escort. "I bet there's a spare tire in that trunk. I bet that car would take us a long ways. Gonna be a shame to leave it behind."

"We'll survive."

Warren wasn't so sure. He believed their odds of long-term survival hovered somewhere between slim and nonexistent. But he wasn't about to lie down in the road and wait for death to come screeching out of the sky either.

"Fine. So what's our next move?"

Her gaze followed the twisting stretch of dark highway. "Start walking, I guess."

"Should we see if anything's salvageable from your car first? Our bags, at least?"

She shrugged. "Sure."

Determining the approximate location of Amanda's car was a simple matter of following an almost straight line backward from the trailer. They picked their way through the debris again and arrived at the mangled green Taurus. A shudder of retroactive terror swept through Warren at the sight of it. It was totaled. Not even a salvage yard would take it now. He muttered a silent prayer to the God of Airbags and leaned through the blown-out driver's side window.

FROM THE VOID

The keys were still in the ignition. He pulled them out and moved to the rear of the car. He slid the key in the trunk lock and gave it a twist. He tugged at the trunk lid, but it wouldn't budge.

Amanda said, "What's wrong?"

"It's stuck. The crash did something to it, I guess."

Amanda pushed him aside. Her right foot shot out and the heel of her black boot clanged against metal. The trunk lid popped open.

Warren gave her a sheepish look. "I loosened it for you."

She smirked. "Sure."

They hauled their bags out. Warren had just one. A light traveling bag with a shoulder strap. Amanda had several bags and suitcases. She opened the suitcases and began rooting through them.

Warren frowned. "What are you doing?"

She spoke without looking up or pausing in her work. "Obviously we can't carry all this stuff. So I'm consolidating."

Warren left her to it for the moment, returning to the car to retrieve a couple more useful items—a tire iron from the trunk and the Maglite flashlight from the glove compartment.

Amanda's gaze flicked to the tire iron. "Good idea."

Warren shrugged. "I don't imagine it'd be much protection against one of those things. But I've got a feeling they're not the only danger out there now."

Amanda grunted. "Yeah."

She zipped up a bag similar to Warren's and slung it over her shoulder. She stood up and said, "Let's get our asses in gear, boy. It's a long fuckin' way to Florida."

Warren almost smiled. "I'm sure we won't have to walk all that way. We'll find a car we can use. Or hitch a ride. Something."

She patted his shoulder. "Sure. We can hope for that. Now let's go."

They turned south and took their first steps down that long road.

7

HUNSTVILLE, AL
September 27
6:30 p.m.

Zeke finally decided to leave the bathroom of his Days Inn motel room for a simple reason—he was bored. Also, he was hungry. And thirsty. The sink's faucet would only yield a thin trickle of brown-tinted water. There was a curiosity factor at work, too—he wanted to know what was going on in the world outside this tiny room.

He moved to the door and gripped the brass doorknob.

And he hesitated.

Hours had passed since he'd last heard anything like the chaotic sounds of mass destruction that had dominated the earlier part of the day. Instinct told him it was now safe to venture beyond the confines of this room, which wasn't exactly a fortified bunker anyway. He knew well enough that his survival was a product of sheer luck. Did he really want to push that luck now, regardless of what his instincts told him?

The answer, apparently, was yes.

The same caution-damning impulse that caused him to walk away from his job at VNC was at work again, making him turn the doorknob and pull the door open. He felt the fine hairs on the back of his neck tingle when he got a look at the hole in the middle of the room. The front end of the small bed had fallen into it, partially plugging it. But there were still glimpses of that horrible deep darkness around the edge.

He had a brief but strong impulse to shut the door and retreat again to his seat on the toilet. Instead, he edged slowly into the room, scanning every corner for signs of lurking monsters.

Nothing.

He breathed a sigh of relief and moved farther into the room. He stayed close to the walls, giving the collapsed bed a wide berth. He was contemplating his next move when he spied a glimpse of something shiny on the floor.

He groaned. "Damn."

His keys had fallen off the nightstand and now lay on the floor perhaps an inch away from the edge of the hole. With great reluctance, he dropped to his hands and knees and began to inch toward the hole. On the off-chance something else from that strange dark realm might emerge, he wanted to present as small a target as possible. When he was a foot away from the keys, he glanced at the largest section of visible blackness—about the size of an open manhole — and saw something pale flickering there.

Something like a coiled, segmented whip—with eyes.

Zeke gulped.

He snatched the keys off the floor and scurried backward. The stalk with eyes emerged from the hole and stared at him as he got to his feet. It made a sound like squealing brakes. He cringed and stumbled backward. The sound was a sharp blade plunging through the middle of his skull. The visible part of the creature convulsed, the stalk shaking so hard it became a pale blur. Seeing this made him think of a rattlesnake about to strike.

The association made him turn and dash out of the room. He heard a rumbling behind him. Then a groaning, splintering sound and a crash. Zeke didn't glance back to see for himself, but he had a feeling the hole was blocked no longer. He ran flat-out for the far end of the parking lot, where his powder blue Thunderbird convertible was parked. There was evidence of carnage all around—bodies, distant fires, and ruined buildings—but he couldn't afford to be distracted by the nightmarishness of it all. An instant's hesitation could be all that separated him from survival and death.

As he neared the car, he fumbled for the electronic fob and the keys nearly slipped from his hands. He cried out and seized them tighter before they could fall. He found the unlock button and pushed it twice. The car's lights blinked. A moment later he yanked the driver's side door open and fell in behind the wheel. He jammed the key in the ignition, twisted it, and the engine roared. He put the car in gear and mashed the gas pedal to the floor. The car shot forward, bouncing twice as it hopped over the concrete slab between parking spaces. The jouncing motion threw the door shut and the car peeled out of the lot.

The rumbling sound receded as he turned left and rocketed through the middle of town. The posted speed limit here was forty, but the needle on his speedometer was edging up close to ninety. Judging from the war zone look of his surroundings, he doubted he needed to worry about violating traffic laws. The needle hit the one-hundred MPH mark and kept moving. Such was his terror of the thing he'd barely glimpsed. He wasn't sure if he *could* stop. But then he saw a looming 3-way T intersection, which required him to slow and turn either left or right.

He tapped the brake pedal a few times, slowing enough to whip the wheel to the right, peel out, and keep going. He'd reached the outskirts of the small city by the time he finally felt able to risk a glance at his rearview mirror.

He sighed.

Whatever that thing was, he'd left it behind. So he was safe again. For now. But he knew that might not be the case for long. This was a new world, one no longer ruled by men. There were other strange creatures out here; more of the things with the jittery stalks, and more of the flying demons, and more of who knew what the hell else. A hole could open in the road ahead of him and swallow the Thunderbird whole.

The thought made him gulp.

He switched on the Thunderbird's high beams and slowed down, tapping the brake until he was moving at a rate slightly below the posted speed limit. He leaned forward and studied the road ahead. He saw right away it was a good thing he'd abandoned his NASCAR-driver-gone-psycho impression. The road was littered with stalled cars and pieces of cars ripped apart by the winged invaders. There were bodies and parts of bodies, both human and non-human. He steered carefully through the grisly obstacle course, at one point driving several dozen yards along the road's shoulder to skirt an especially congested stretch of asphalt. He glanced at one burned-out metal hulk and shuddered at the sight of the charred skeleton still ensconced behind the wheel. Then he was on the road again and the way ahead was relatively clear.

He did see more bodies, but most of them looked to be dead demons. He wondered what possibly could have killed them all. Maybe something in the earth's atmosphere was incompatible with their alien biology. A spark of hope flared within him at the thought, but he refused to allow it to grow into a flame. This remained a world that had come undone. There was danger all about. His close encounter with the stalk-thing at the motel was proof enough of that. This new development only meant the chances of surviving to see another day had improved to a small degree.

It occurred to him to wonder exactly where the hell he should be going. Maybe there were shelters and relief stations set up somewhere. It could be that new centers of authority were being set up even now.

He turned on the radio and winced at the burst of static. He lowered the volume and pushed the seek button. The digital dial hit every frequency on the FM band and returned nothing but more static. So he switched to the AM band and got the same thing until it landed on an EAS recording on the 1510 frequency. The message instructed citizens to remain indoors and seek a safe place, a closet or a cellar. It further advised listeners to remain tuned for further instructions. That was it. Short and not very sweet, in Zeke's estimation. It played on an endless loop, that same maddening, monotone voice, a snippet of phony calm. He nonetheless felt compelled to listen to it several dozen times, hoping against hope that a live broadcast would begin, that some wondrous voice of salvation would come forth from the ether.

But it never happened.

At last, unable to bear more, he turned the radio off and was soon consumed by the oppressive silence of this dying world. He drove for miles without seeing much of anything, save for the occasional dead demon. The road began to hypnotize him and he almost nodded off a few times. He began to think he should find a place to pull over and sleep for the night. What was the point of this aimless driving anyway? He didn't have a destination in mind—not even a vague one—and he had a notion no single part of the country was any safer than another.

Then he saw something in the road ahead, a small, pale figure staggering slowly down the center line. He slowed down, and as the figure drew closer he experienced a mixture of shock and excitement. It was a woman. She was nude and disheveled. A mass of tangled blonde hair hung to the center of her tapered back. She stopped dead in the road and turned to face the approaching car.

He stopped the car and got out. "Lady, are you all right? Do you need help?"

She stared blankly at him a moment, then dropped to her knees.

Zeke rushed to her aid, kneeling next to her and placing a tentative hand on one slim shoulder. She was shaking, but not making a sound. Zeke figured she was fighting back tears of relief—so he was stunned when she lifted her face and revealed a wide, almost manic grin.

Zeke frowned. "Um . . . is something wrong?"

A loud internal alarm went off then. Every instinct in him urged him to return to his car, to speed away from this crazy woman at once. But he just couldn't do it. Surely her odd demeanor was a product of the trauma she'd endured today. Hell, he felt close to cracking himself. Besides, he was alone. And afraid. He craved the comfort of human company, a warm body to cling to in the dark night ahead. It dawned on him that she wasn't unattractive, albeit in a redneck, trailer-trash kind of way.

She laughed. "That's a nice car, mister."

Zeke's frown deepened. "Um . . . yeah. I suppose it is."

"I was hopin' we'd get one like that."

Zeke started to say something, but jerked his head to the left at the sound of a snapping branch. A big, beefy man in dirty overalls and a green John Deere hat emerged from the line of trees beyond the road's shoulder. Zeke's heart skipped a beat at the sight of him. The man's imposing size was scary enough, but what really made his insides curdle was the sight of the big shotgun propped over his shoulder.

The woman's gaze went to the man as he reached the road, the grin on her face becoming sly. "Hey, Billy. Thought you was never comin'."

Billy spit a wad of tobacco juice on the street. "Was takin' a leak." He glanced at the Thunderbird and grinned, displaying a mouth mostly devoid of teeth. "Well, looka that. That's a mighty fine automobile, mister."

Zeke cleared his throat. "You can't take my car."

The woman sprang out of her crouch and drilled a fist into the middle of his face, sending him tumbling backward. Before he could even attempt to stand, the woman pounced, kicking again and again at his crotch and midsection. He initially tried to ward off the blows, but she was so relentless he finally curled into a ball and waited for her to be done.

She kept it up much longer than necessary, cursing and screaming at him all the while. "NOBODY TELLS MARY LOU CRAWFORD WHAT TO DO, YOU SORRY SACK OF SHIT! YOU HEAR ME, YOU GODDAMNED COCKSUCKING SONOFAWHORE? I SAID DO YOU FUCKING HEAR ME!?"

Just when he thought she'd at last decided to have mercy on him, she rolled him over, straddled him, and worked his face over like Muhammad Ali practicing on a punching bag. He felt blood burst from his lips and nose, felt the salty tang of it fill his mouth. He finally figured out the woman meant to beat him to death, and he could either lie here and take it or fight back. So he grabbed her wrists, gathered all his remaining strength, and shoved her backward.

She fell flat on her butt in the road and loosed a scream of pure fury.

Zeke scooted backward and prepared to defend himself against a fresh assault.

Then there was a loud CLACK, the sound of a shotgun shell being jacked into the chamber. "That's enough, Mary Lou."

Zeke's bleary gaze went to Billy. He was unsurprised to see the shotgun barrel pointing straight at his head. "Okay, fine. Take the car, you want it that bad."

Billy's brown eyes were flat and unwavering. "I reckon I ought to shoot you, boy. Can't have you reporting that fine ride stolen."

Zeke couldn't help it. He laughed. "That's absurd. Who would I report it to?"

Mary Lou was on her feet again. She stood with her fists clenched, glowering down at him. "Shoot him. Shoot the son of a bitch in the goddamn head."

Billy grunted. "Nah. Man's got a point. There ain't no more law left. Least not for the time bein'. And I ain't one for killin' a man 'less I got to."

Mary Lou glared at the big redneck. "You fuckin' pussy. Gimme that gun. I'll do it myself."

Billy shook his head. "Can't let you do that. Wouldn't be right."

Mary Lou's demeanor shifted then. The tension went out of her body and she slinked closer to the big man. Zeke saw that Billy's gaze was riveted to her big, melon-like tits. She went up on her toes and hooked her hands around his neck. She pressed a bare thigh against his crotch. "Don't you love me?" she cooed.

Zeke figured his only chance might be a dash into the woods. Of course, he likely wouldn't get far before a shotgun blast punched a hole through his back and sent his guts flying across the road, but he had to try. So he started to push himself up. In a moment he would leap to his feet and run like hell.

But it was then the situation took a turn he wasn't expecting.

Mary Lou tore the shotgun from Billy's hands, jammed the barrel deep into the cushion of his big belly, and pulled the trigger. This all happened too fast for Billy to do anything but blink in surprise. Then he staggered backward, cupping his hands over the gaping red hole in his stomach. Mary Lou jacked another shell into the chamber and dropped him with one more blast, one that tore away the top part of his skull. The big man hit the ground with a thud and Zeke settled back on the road, all thoughts of flight temporarily forgotten.

He felt sick.

Mary Lou came over and placed the hot barrel against his forehead. "That's what happens when a man don't do what I tell him. He gets hisself shot." She prodded his head with the barrel. "You ain't gonna be that dumb, are ya?"

Zeke's mouth flapped silently for a moment, then he managed to say, "No."

Mary Lou smirked. "Tell ya what. I won't kill ya after all, so long's you do what I say. How's that sound, boy?"

Zeke swallowed hard. "Good?"

"Good as it's gonna get for you, leastways." She tapped the top of his head with the shotgun barrel. "Here's the first order I'm givin' you. This here's a test, boy. Pass and you get to live. Fail . . ." She jerked her head in the direction of the dead man. "Well, I reckon you know what happens then."

Zeke was shaking. He managed a nod.

"Get on your knees."

Zeke did as she instructed.

She licked her lips. "Now beg. Beg for your fuckin' life, boy."

The barrel of the shotgun touched the middle of his forehead again. He saw her finger slip through the trigger guard and curl around the trigger. A vivid memory of what the shotgun blast did to Billy's head flashed through his mind like a scene from a gruesome splatter movie. He imagined his head blown apart like that, and thus did not have to fake the note of abject pleading in his voice when he said, "Please don't kill me."

Mary Lou snickered. "That's a good start, boy. But it ain't good enough. I wanna hear you mewl like a fuckin' baby."

Zeke's eyes misted over. He thought of himself dead. A piece of rotting meat on the ground. Just another piece of doomsday detritus to be ignored by any other survivors who might happen by. Now the tears came. And the sobs. He tried to say the words he thought the woman wanted to hear, but they were rendered incoherent by the force of his emotion. Then she was laughing at him and it was worse. He couldn't fathom how anyone could be so devoid of humanity.

Mary Lou's voice softened. "Okay. You passed the test, fucker."

Zeke's only answer was another sob.

Mary Lou chuckled. "Man, I'm gettin' a kick out of this whole deal. I don't ever have to work at fuckin' Wal-Mart again. I can do whatever I want. I can kill your ass and nobody'll ever do a fuckin' thing about it." She laughed again, this time at the look of horror that passed over Zeke's face. "Don't worry, boy. I ain't gonna. Like I said, you passed the test."

Zeke sniffled. "Th-thank you."

Mary Lou moved back a few steps "Whatever. Get the hell up."

Zeke needed a moment to reconnect with his body, to feel capable of movement. Then he braced his hands on the pavement and pushed himself up. He got to his feet and stood on legs so shaky he felt like he might keel over at any moment.

Mary Lou waved the shotgun in the direction of his car. "Thataway. Let's go for a ride."

Zeke looked at the Thunderbird. Though it had only been a matter of minutes, it felt like years had passed since he'd first spied the naked woman staggering down the middle of the road. He wished now that he'd driven on by. Of course, he couldn't have done that. All he'd seen then was a woman in apparent need, and he wasn't the kind of person whose conscience would allow him to ignore that. In that moment, Zeke wished he'd been born a sociopath. Or even an out and out fucking loon, like Mary Lou.

The woman poked at the small of his back with the shotgun barrel and he at last began to move toward the car. He blinked against the glare of the Thunderbird's lights. The keys were still in the ignition and the engine was running. He briefly considered whether he might be able to jump behind the wheel, put the car in gear, and speed away without getting himself killed.

Mary Lou seemed to read his thoughts. "I'm gonna let you drive, boy, but don't you dare try anything funny. I'll start blastin' the second I think you're gonna act the fool." She poked his back with the shotgun again. "Ya hear me?"

Zeke sighed. "I hear you."

He moved around the open driver's side door and slid in behind the wheel. Mary Lou kept the shotgun leveled at him as she moved to the other side of the car. Then she yanked the door open and dropped into the passenger seat. She slammed the door shut and laid the barrel of the shotgun in his lap.

She grinned at Zeke's look of distress. "I wouldn't make any sudden movements if I were you." She giggled like a schoolgirl. Then her expression hardened once again. "Now let's get this fuckin' show on the road."

Zeke—very carefully—pulled his door shut.

Then he put the car in gear, and he and his captor moved deeper into that silent night.

8

HARRISBURG, PA
September 27
6:45 p.m.

Jasmine Holtz remained where she'd been throughout that long day—slouched in Gary's favorite chair in the living room of the house she and her husband had shared for the last decade. The only light in the otherwise dark room emanated from the television set, which showed only a rippling field of black-and-white static.

She'd made no attempt to hide when the legions of hell (or whatever) had come forth to decimate the world. Still consumed with grief over losing Gary, she hadn't mustered much fear of the screeching flying things she'd seen on television. She'd spent much of the day anticipating—perhaps even hoping for—imminent death, expecting one of the creatures to come crashing through the living room window at any moment.

But it never happened.

So she at last stirred from her spot in the living room for the simplest of biological reasons—she needed to pee. She got up and shuffled off to the nearest bathroom, which required her to move through the living room, through the kitchen, and into the bedroom. Though she still felt most comfortable in the dark, the darkness now was such she had to turn on lights to move through her house. It amazed her the power was still on. The outside world seemed dead, but that world's technology—for the time being, at least—continued to function. She wondered in an absent way whether she ought to get on the phone and try calling some people. Or maybe power up her computer and see if she could talk to anyone on the internet. These were vaguely intriguing possibilities, but she did not feel up to pursuing them at the moment.

She opened the bathroom door, blinked at what she saw there, and pulled the door shut at the same instant the thing perched on the edge of the sink launched itself in her direction. It struck the door and rebounded, landing on the tiled floor with a soft thump.

Then she heard it scrabbling at the door, its tiny talons gouging grooves in the painted wood. Jasmine stood frozen there for a time with her hand clenched tightly around the door knob. The thing in her bathroom was a miniature version of the flying demons she'd seen on television. It was no bigger than the average housecat. But it had those same leathery black wings, those same dead red eyes, and those same razor-sharp talons and teeth. Despite its diminutive size, she had no doubt the thing could kill her.

How did it get in there? she wondered.

The bathroom had been closed. And she was sure she would've heard anything forcing its way into the house. One of those strange holes in the world must have opened on the other side of this door. A small one perhaps, but large enough to allow her uninvited guest entry. The realization had the effect of swiping away the hazy gauze of disconnection that had hovered between herself and the dramatic events in the outside world.

She grimaced as the thing threw itself against the door, making it rattle in its frame. Her breathing came in quicker bursts and for a moment she was on the verge of hyperventilating. Then she mentally berated herself for acting the shrinking violet. She was right to be afraid, but if she wanted to survive beyond this moment—as her instincts surprisingly indicated she did—she would need to think and act on a calmer, more rational level.

Get your stuff together and think this through, Jaz, she thought.

The thing in her bathroom, she decided, might well be as deadly as she imagined. But it was tiny. And she doubted it possessed the intelligence to figure out how to work the doorknob. It could either bash its way through the wood or kill itself trying. Either way, it would take time.

So you have a head start, she thought. *Maybe a few minutes. Maybe only seconds.*

Get moving.

She let go of the doorknob and hurried out of the bedroom. She was in the kitchen when she heard the bathroom door splinter. The crackling sound of wood yielding to the creature's furious assault grew louder, and Jasmine paused at the kitchen counter long enough to select a large carving knife from a wooden block. She heard a flapping of wings and whirled about in time to see the tiny demon come hurtling through the air at her. Instinct caused her to raise the knife, and the blade punched through the creature's midsection. The thing screeched and flapped away from her. It remained airborne a few moments longer, fluttering weakly to the opposite side of the kitchen, where it struck the refrigerator, uttered a faint, almost pitiable screech, and dropped to the floor.

Jasmine let out a big breath and put a hand to her chest. "Oh my God."

She crossed the kitchen and stared down at the creature. It lay on its side with its tiny talons curled against the blade. It looked so pathetic—so much like an impaled baby—that she experienced a fleeting moment of pity for it. A thick yellow substance oozed from its wound and spilled down the length of the blade. An odor like spoiled food emanated from it.

She was pretty sure it was dead. But she was just as certain her house was no longer a safe haven—if it had ever been one. In all likelihood there was a black space somewhere in the bathroom, a portal through which the dead thing at her feet had come. It stood to reason it was only a matter of time until something else—perhaps something much larger—came through as well.

She would have to leave her home.

Probably forever.

The thought made her eyes fill with moisture for a moment. But she refused to succumb to emotion. There would be time for tears later. Maybe. She steeled herself and returned to the bedroom, affording the ruined bathroom door only the briefest of glimpses. She snatched her purse off her nightstand and hurried out of the room.

Back in the kitchen, she dropped the purse on the counter, grabbed a canvas bag from a hook in the pantry, and filled it with canned goods. She added a can opener and a few utensils from a drawer. Next she climbed a step stool and took a Styrofoam cooler down from the pantry's top shelf. She filled this with ice from the freezer, then packed it with a few perishables from the fridge.

Packing the food felt a bit absurd—a little like preparing for a weekend getaway—but she didn't know what kind of world was waiting for her out there. She didn't want to have to go foraging for sustenance her first night away from home.

Next she returned to the bedroom and quickly filled a bag with several changes of clothes. She glanced one last time at the bathroom on her way out. Through the shattered lower half of the door, she could see only white tile and the sink. She was tempted to pull the remnant of the door away from the frame and give the room a closer inspection. But the impulse was fleeting. Her common sense took over and carried her back to the kitchen.

She returned to the living room where she removed a small photo album from a shelf and placed it in her handbag. Then she walked out of her home for the last time. In the garage, she placed the Styrofoam cooler in the trunk of her BMW. Everything else went up front with her.

Before she could leave there was one last bit of business to attend to. She lowered her panties and squatted at the rear of the garage. Peeing on the cool concrete made her feel like a savage. She suspected, though, that this particular indignity would soon rank among the least distasteful she would have to endure. When she was done, she returned to the car and drove away from her home without a single glance back. Looking back would hurt too much, maybe more than she could handle.

Instead, she kept her gaze on the road ahead and didn't glance at the rearview mirror until she was several miles down the road. She scanned the yards of houses she passed, searching for signs of other survivors. But there was no indication anyone else remained alive in the neighborhood. She saw abandoned cars and houses in ruins. Other houses appeared essentially intact, but they somehow conveyed an emptiness as depressing as the ruins. And the overall impression of utter desolation failed to improve as she moved out of the neighborhood and drove toward town. To the contrary, the ruin of Harrisburg was nearly as depressing as the violation of her home.

In the end, it was more than she could take.

She drove out of town and headed out to the highway.

9

September 27
10:05 p.m.

Jake Dunham stood shirtless at Emma Singleton's bedroom window. He was watching the street below, scanning it for signs of Aaron Harris. Emma watched him from the bed, where she lay naked beneath a single sheet.

He was a tall man. Maybe not quite NBA-level tall, but certainly tall enough to be a star player on most college basketball squads. But he was scrawny, the kind of skinny where he might disappear altogether if glimpsed from a side angle. He was a good guy. Sweet and adorable. He was no Rick McAllister in the looks department, but he was cute in his own gawky way.

Still, she couldn't believe she'd fucked him. The sex had been imbued with a sense of desperation, an unarticulated hope they might reach a center of pleasure within each other so pure it would somehow overwhelm the death and darkness surrounding them.

But when it was over there'd been no sense of transcendence. For Emma, there'd only been more tears, an inevitable crash. Jake had been mostly silent in the aftermath of that desperate passion. He'd

88

even slept for a time after Emma rebuffed his attempt to console her. After he woke up, he seemed to have gone to a dark place within himself, a deeply contemplative state that took his mind away and left only a physical shell here. She'd looked into his eyes at one point and realized he wasn't seeing her at all.

So she slept some herself. Sleep that was fitful and filled with dreams of death and chaos. In one of them Aaron returned to her room. He grinned a demon's grin. His eyes were red and bulbous. In one hand, he held Michelle's severed head, the length of spinal column depending from the stump of her neck like the limp corpse of a snake. In his other hand was the hunting knife. He hissed at her. His mouth opened and a black, forked tongue rolled out. Michelle's mouth formed a crooked grin and opened slightly to emit a wheeze of something that might have been laughter.

Emma awoke then with a cry.

The sound triggered Jake's return from the dark place. She was so relieved when he took her in his arms again. Seeing Jake so gloomy—even in these circumstances—had frightened her nearly as much as her encounter with Aaron. That darkness was so out of character for the normally affable Jacob Dunham.

Emma sighed. "Do you think he'll stay away?"

"I don't know. Maybe." Jake's gaze went back to the window. "No. That's not what I think at all." He laughed, but there was no trace of humor in the sound. "I have this typical guy impulse to tell you what you want to hear, what I think will make you feel better. But I can't do that. Not anymore."

Emma frowned. "So . . . you think he *will* be back?"

Jake shrugged. "It's hard to know what a headcase like that will do, but I have a hunch he's not gonna stay away just because we told him to."

"Dammit."

"Yeah, it sucks. But we have to face some hard facts. There's nothing to keep him away. We can't file a report with the police. There's no official authority of any kind to keep him at bay." Jake's expression darkened again, and seeing it sent Emma's own mood spiraling downward. "I hate to say it, but I have a feeling guys like Mr. Harris are gonna thrive in the days ahead. It's their world now."

Hearing Jake say this made Emma feel like crying again, but her eyes remained dry. Despite her fear, there was a center of numbness inside her and it was growing outward by the moment. Soon, she supposed, she would feel nothing at all. Part of her thought that might be a good thing, but the rest of her was terrified by the notion.

But she knew Jake was right. They'd tried calling the police numerous times. In the beginning there'd still been a faint level of hope. A glance out the window revealed that the power was still on in many parts of the city. And the phone was on. Surely if these things were working some semblance of the former power structure must still exist. But the calls to the police station and 911 went unanswered. They called other people. Friends. Relatives. And the result was always the same. Nothing.

She threw the sheet aside and climbed out of bed. She retrieved her clothes from a pile on the floor and hurriedly put them on. She grabbed her boots, plopped down in a chair, and pulled them on.

Jake frowned. "What are you doing?"

"Getting dressed."

"I can see that." Jake, perhaps feeling compelled to emulate Emma, found his T-shirt and pulled it on. "Are we going somewhere?"

Emma walked over to the window. She peered out at the same dark and empty street Jake had studied so intently earlier. She saw lights in the distance, but not as many as before. Most of the lights that were on were concentrated in one area. They appeared to be somewhere in the vicinity of the Vanderbilt campus. Another, smaller grouping of lights farther away emanated from the downtown area.

She looked at Jake. "We can't stay here. Not with that creep maybe lurking around. Not with pieces of my neighbor strewn all over the living room." She moved away from the window, strode across the room toward the closet. "We've stayed too long as it is."

Jake sat now at the foot of his bed, one leg propped over the other while he tied a shoestring. "I don't know if leaving now is such a good idea."

Emma came out of the closet with a traveling bag. She opened it and laid it on the bed. "I'm not staying here. I can't. It's not just the possibility of Aaron coming back. This place feels . . . tainted. It's not a place where people live anymore. It's a mausoleum."

"The whole fucking world is a mausoleum."

Emma glared at Jake. "I know that," she snapped. Then she sighed and her expression softened a bit. "I'm sorry. It's just that this particular mausoleum was my home for the last two years. And I just can't stand to be here any longer."

Jake nodded. "I can understand that. And I'll go wherever you want to go, I guess." A corner of his mouth twitched. "But I think we shouldn't leave yet."

Emma shoved clothes into the bag. "Why not?"

Jake stood and, in a moment, resumed his previous position at the window. "Because it's dark. Because there's no telling what's going on out there. There could be more of those things around. Even if they're all dead, which I doubt, there's those openings between their world and ours. I've been out there. There's a lot of them. It's like the world itself is coming unraveled. In the dark you could walk right into one and not realize it until it's too late."

Emma felt a mounting frustration as she listened to Jake. She knew he was only telling her the truth as he saw it, but that made it no less maddening. The core of it was the continuing disintegration of the world, of reality itself, and that remained a concept she had great difficulty wrapping her head around. She wanted back the world she'd known. Solid, unmalleable reality. This new world, this twisted bizarro realm where the very air before you could turn black and loose hideous monsters from another dimension, this was unacceptable. A world in which the substance of reality could be shredded like the pages of a book was not one she wanted to inhabit. The bitch of it was she felt no real eagerness to die, either.

She zipped the bag shut and looked at Jake. "I'm aware of the dangers. But I mean to walk out of here within the next few minutes. I wanna see if anyone else is alive out there. Unless you've got a better idea. One that doesn't involve staying in this apartment."

Jake's brow creased as he thought about it a moment. "Maybe I do have an idea."

Emma folded her arms beneath her breasts. "Let's hear it."

"Like I said, my main worry is the dark. Going out there now would be tantamount to a kamikaze mission. And I don't know about you, but I don't particularly want to die."

Emma sighed. "Yeah. Me, either."

Jake moved away from the window and stood directly beneath the ceiling light. The way the light struck his shaggy light brown hair and ragged goatee made him look almost angelic. His pale blue eyes twinkled in a way she might have interpreted as mischievous, or even seductive, under other circumstances. Emma thought again of their frantic coupling and wondered whether there might be a potential for something greater between them beyond the desperation of the moment. The thought brought forth another wave of depression. Because what good could something as fragile as love possibly be in a doomed world?

Jake said, "I agree with you. We should leave." Then his tone became firmer, more emphatic. "But we should wait for morning." He raised his voice and pushed ahead when he sensed she was about to protest. "Now, hold on. Hear me out. There's a compromise to be made."

"There is?"

Jake nodded. "We'll leave this apartment. Right now, if you want to. We'll spend the night in one of the other apartments in this building, then head out after the sun comes out."

Emma's frown deepened. "What if we break into an apartment that's still occupied? I know some of these people. More than one of them would shoot an intruder under normal circumstances. Now . . ."

Jake sighed. "I think your neighbors are either all dead or are gone and not coming back any time soon. Think about it. We've been here all night. We haven't heard a thing. No voices. No creaking floors or stairs. I'm willing to bet we've got the whole building to ourselves. And if I'm wrong, hell, we'll knock first and announce our presence. If we find anyone that way, I don't think they're gonna shoot us. Shit, they'll probably welcome us with open arms. Just think how happy we'd be if we looked out the window and saw other living humans walking down the street."

Emma pursed her lips as she thought about it. Jake's proposal made a certain amount of sense. A significant part of her still ached to be gone from this dead place, but a new voice of reason was speaking within her now—and she found she was willing to listen to it.

She smiled. "Okay. We'll do it your way. This time."

The relief that filled Jake's face then almost made Emma laugh. He smiled broadly. "Great!" He grabbed her bag and slung it over his shoulder. "Let's get moving, then."

They left the bedroom. On their way out to the living room, Jake detoured into the kitchen alcove and opened a drawer. Emma heard a clink of silverware as he sorted through its contents. He tossed a couple of steak knives onto the counter and threw the drawer shut.

"You don't have a big carving knife, do you?"

Emma shook her head. "Nope."

"Damn." Jake sighed. "I guess these'll have to do."

He shoved one of the steak knives into a front pocket of his jeans and passed the other to Emma, who took it but regarded it with a skeptical frown. "I doubt I could stop a charging poodle with this thing, much less Aaron Harris."

Jake shrugged. "I'm sure we'll have a chance to better arm ourselves before long. There's a world of weaponry out there for the taking." A shadow seemed to fall across his face. "That's another thing, we've got to acquire firepower before our nemesis does. You know damn well Mr. Sleazebag will lift a Glock off the first dead cop he sees."

The notion made Emma more anxious than ever to leave her apartment. "Let's get out of here. Now."

Jake nodded. "Yeah."

Emma caught a quick glimpse of Michelle's remains as they moved through the living room, then averted her gaze. They stepped through the space formerly occupied by Emma's front door and stood in the dark hallway. One glance at Michelle Anderson's apartment was enough to rule it out as a possible destination. Its door was missing as well, and the darkness beyond that opening was of a quality more disturbing than ordinary darkness. Something was there. Aaron, perhaps, or a reality rift, or some otherworldly presence with a newly acquired hunger for human flesh.

A turn to the left would take them down a staircase leading to four more apartments on the floors below. They descended the staircase to the second floor, where they paused at the door of apartment 3A. Jake tried the closed door, but it was locked. He looked at Emma. "What do you want to do?"

Emma remained uncomfortable with the idea of breaking and entering. Someone could be lurking silently on the other side of that door. Someone no doubt as terrified as she'd been during all those hours under her bed. She didn't know all her neighbors and wasn't sure who lived in this apartment. It would be better to try the door of someone she knew, a person whose reaction she could possibly predict. She crossed to the other side of the landing and tried the door to 4A.

It, too, was locked.

She took a deep breath and slowly expelled it. She knew these people. Laura and Kelly. Two twenty-something lesbians who occasionally stopped in at the Villager for a pitcher of Shiner Bock. She rapped softly on the inlaid glass window and said, "Kel? Laura? It's Emma. Are you in there?"

She waited. Jake stepped up beside her. "You can't be timid about this. If they're in there, they probably didn't even hear you."

Emma sighed. He had a point. She didn't want to make a lot of noise, but she didn't see how there was any alternative. She banged the base of a fist against the window. "Kelly! Laura! Come on, guys, open up. It's just me and Jake out here."

Again, they waited. They stood perfectly still, barely breathing, straining to detect any hint of movement from within the apartment. The interior of the apartment was obscured by a piece of plywood nailed to the other side of the door. This was to deter potential smash-and-enter burglars. All the apartments in the building were similarly protected. Emma had always thought it was a sensible measure for the building's owner to take, but now it was another source of frustration.

Jake said, "I think we ought to try getting in here. They know us. If they were in there, they'd let us in."

Emma frowned. She loathed the idea of forcing her way into a friend's apartment. But Jake was right. Damn him. They could, right now, enter an apartment likely to be unoccupied, or they could waste who knew how much of the rest of the evening searching for a more easily accessible place to crash.

She sighed. "Yeah. Okay. Let's get in there."

Jake handed her the bag and she took it by the shoulder strap. "Step back."

Emma shuffled backward and watched as Jake braced himself squarely in front of the door, then surged forward, driving the flat of his right foot forward with every ounce of strength he could muster. There was a cracking sound, but the door held. Jake braced himself and kicked again. Then again. Each time the cracking sound was louder. Then, after maybe a dozen kicks, the door came away from the frame.

Jake grinned. "After you, my lady."

Emma peered into the dark kitchen. The emptiness and shadows unsettled her. Beyond the kitchen was a small dining room. A small table and chairs occupied the middle of the room. Except for an empty napkin holder at its center, the table was bare. And aside from the piece of plywood on the kitchen floor, there was no evidence of destruction. Nor was there a death smell.

Still . . . some instinct held her back. She looked at Jake. "Could you go first? It's not that I'm scared or anything—"

Jake laughed. "Well, personally, I'm scared shitless. But your wish is my command."

Before she could reply, he strode into the apartment and flipped a switch. Light filled the kitchen and made the shadows in the dining room recede. Emma let out a sigh and followed him into the apartment. She closed the door behind her, although it almost seemed a pointless gesture—anyone who wanted in now could easily gain entry.

Jake met her nervous gaze and seemed to read her thoughts. "I'll figure out a way to secure the door. Maybe jam that table between the door and stove."

Emma smiled. "Thank you."

"If nothing else, I think we can at least safely assume we're alone here." Emma noted the deep sadness in Jake's voice. He'd dated Kelly prior to her coming out a couple years later and had always remained close to her. "What a fucking shame this all is."

Emma didn't say anything to that. What *was* there to say? A tragedy of unparalleled proportions had occurred. She'd missed the news coverage in the earlier part of the day, but Jake had told her enough to know that millions of people had died. Perhaps billions. She tried to conceptualize the possibility of that many people dead and just couldn't do it. It was too much. She decided that for the time being she would only concern herself with her own safety and her own small patch of the world.

And Jake, of course.

Jake moved into the dining room and flipped another switch. Light gleamed against the inlaid glass panels of the dining room cabinets. Emma opened the refrigerator and was pleased to see a supply of adult beverages. One six-pack of hard cider, another of Guinness Extra Stout, and a bottle of Korbel. She removed two of the brown Guinness bottles from the six-pack and looked for an opener.

Then Jake called out to her: "Emma! Come here."

There was an urgency in his voice that caused her to abandon her search. She hurried through the dining room and into the living room, the still unopened bottles clanging together in her hand. "What's—"

She'd been about to ask him what was wrong, but there was no need—she saw at once the cause of his outburst. A little girl of about eight or nine huddled in a corner of the living room. She wore the uniform of a schoolgirl, a pleated skirt and a navy-blue sweater with a crest. She had long light-brown hair in pigtails. An expression of terror made her pale and vulnerable features resemble those of a fragile doll.

Emma glanced at Jake. He no longer seemed quite so self-assured and able. He was visibly baffled by how to deal with the frightened girl. Emma wasn't so sure, either, but she had a hunch the girl might respond better to a female entreaty. So she set the beer bottles on an end table next to the sofa and moved into the center of the living room. The girl's eyes widened and she pressed her back against the wall.

Emma forced a smile. "It's okay, sweetie. We're not going to hurt you."

The girl gave her head an adamant shake. "You broke in. You're burglars."

Emma laughed softly. "We're not burglars, silly. We're friends of Laura and Kelly. Do you know them?"

The girl nodded. "Laura is my Auntie. I come here sometimes. I've never seen you before." She lifted a finger and pointed over Emma's shoulder. "Or that man."

Emma shrugged. "I'll tell you the truth, okay? I'm friends with your Auntie, but not real good friends. I'm not over here much. But that man there." She indicated Jake with a jerk of her head. "He's real good friends with Kelly. Maybe you've heard Kelly talk about him. His name's Jake."

The girl's expression changed then. A mistrustful glint remained in her eyes, but it was clear she'd relaxed some. Her gaze went to Jake. "You were Kelly's boyfriend?"

Emma glanced backward and saw Jake shuffle farther into the living room. His hands were shoved into his pockets. She guessed this was a subject he'd prefer not to discuss with a girl so young, thus the obvious discomfort. "Yeah," he said, standing beside Emma now. "I was."

"What's your last name, then?"

"Dunham."

The girl nodded. "And what was Kelly's middle name?"

Jake laughed. "You ought to consider a career in law enforcement when you grow up. And Kelly's middle name was . . . is . . . Kelly. That's a trick question, you sneaky devil. She goes by her middle name. Her first name is Lynn. Usually it's the other way around. Kel used to pretend to be mad at her parents about it."

And now the girl smiled. "Yes. You pass."

Seeing the girl smile did wonders for Emma's mood. It was so good to see another living person at the end of this dark day. And not just any person. A young, smart girl with a vibrant personality. It was disturbing she'd been left to crouch in darkness all day. She hoped like hell Kelly and Laura were safe elsewhere, but the girl's presence here all by herself didn't bode well for that. Emma decided she would look after the girl if no rightful guardian came forth to claim her. It would be a big responsibility, but she wouldn't leave the girl to fend for herself.

The girl extended a hand. "My name is Abigail. But you can call me Abby."

Emma smiled and accepted the girl's hand. "Pleased to meet you, Abby." Her smile receded. "You don't happen to know where your Aunt Laura and Kelly are, do you?"

The girl pulled her hand away and her expression darkened. She tugged on one of her pigtails and chewed her lower lip. Emma felt awful for asking Abby a question with such dreadful implications, but she had to know the answer. The girl lifted her face and Emma saw barely restrained tears glimmering in her eyes.

Abby's voice emerged as a stammer: "I-I . . ."

Emma scooted closer and pulled the girl into her arms. Abby buried her face in the older woman's bosom and unleashed a torrent of sobs that shook her frail slip of a body. Emma stroked her hair and made gentle cooing noises. She glanced back and saw a grim expression on Jake's face, a look that was equal measures concern and fear. She knew how he felt. Neither of them were at all experienced in the care of a child. And now it fell to them to care for one in a dangerous new world. She hoped they would be up to it.

Abby put her hands on Emma's shoulders and pushed out of the embrace. She stared at Emma through eyes that were puffy and red-rimmed. She sniffled and said, "Kelly left early this morning to go to her job. She makes sandwiches at Provence."

Emma nodded. Provence was a shop on 21st Avenue.

Abby wiped tears from her face with the back of a hand. "Laura walked to Provence with her. She was supposed to come right back." Fresh tears leaked from the corners of her eyes. "And n-n-n . . . now she's n-never coming back."

Emma pulled Abby into her arms again and glanced again at Jake, who'd just returned from the kitchen with a bottle opener. He popped the top off one of the Guinness bottles and drank deeply from it. He picked up the other bottle and asked her the question with a look.

Emma nodded.

Jake popped the cap off the second bottle and set it on the end table. Emma left it there for the moment, content for now to allow little Abby to cling to her as long as she needed.

~

The green dumpster behind Provence sat as still as the cars parked in its rear lot. A dog sniffed the ground around it. The dog had the coloring of a collie but its fur was short and it was lean of body like a greyhound. Something shifted inside the dumpster and the dog's floppy ears perked up. Then there was a scraping sound as the dumpster's sliding door was opened from the inside. The dog grinned and wagged its tail happily. It recognized this scent. This was someone it knew, a friendly human who lived in the same building as its master.

Laura Brandner eased her head through the opening and cautiously surveyed her surroundings. She saw cars. She saw what was left of her lover, Kelly. The broken body was still on the ground near the store's rear entrance. Laura's breath hitched at the sight of it. One of those flying things had snapped Kelly like a toothpick and she lay now at a hideous angle, her dead eyes open and staring at dirty asphalt. Laura's stomach convulsed and she averted her eyes from the sickening sight.

She saw the dog looking up at her with an expectant grin. "Hi, Maggie."

The dog wagged its tail.

Laura reached down to stroke the top of Maggie's head. "Yes, Maggie's a good girl. Oh, what a good girl."

A single tear etched a path down her cheek. "Oh, good girl. Oh, Kelly."

Laura pulled herself through the dumpster's opening and dropped to the ground. She felt stiff and sore from a day spent huddled in the dumpster. More than that, she was filthy. The stench of all that tossed-out food had made her sick. She'd thrown up and the smell of her stomach's regurgitated contents had only made things worse. She longed to take a long, hot shower.

And she needed to be away from this place. She walked over to where Kelly's body lay and knelt next to her. She planted a kiss on a cold forehead and muttered her last respects. She hoped somewhere some trace of Kelly's special essence could hear these words.

Maggie sniffed at her ear.

Laura scratched the dog behind the ear and stood up.

"Let's go."

The dog followed her out to 21st Avenue. Much of what remaining energy she possessed went out of her as she took in the carnage. There was a lot of blood. A lot of death. She had witnessed some of the destruction from inside Provence. She and Kelly had holed up in there with other store employees during the initial onslaught of screeching death. A few hours later, during a perceived lull, Laura convinced Kelly they should try to make it back to their apartment. Kelly had thought it a dumb idea, but Laura had been adamant. They had to go back for Abby. The emotional urgency eventually wore Kelly's resistance down and so, along with three other Provence employees, they had ventured outside.

They were attacked at once. Kelly was killed instantly.

Laura took the only refuge available, the dumpster. Where she remained the rest of the day, listening while people around her were slaughtered. Now, from this vantage point, it looked as if the entire world must be dead. Other than the dog at her side, there was no evidence at all of any life. That this horror had occurred at all was awful enough, but having to face it alone, without Kelly, depressed and sickened her.

Her top priority now was to find out if Abby was still safe at the apartment. Emotionally, she wasn't ready to concede the possibility that her niece might be dead, too. But, as she took in the sight of the shattered storefronts and cars with their tops ripped off like the lids of cans, a more pragmatic part of her accepted the likelihood that sweet little Abby was no more.

She would cling to hope, however, until she discovered definitive proof of the girl's death. So she turned to her right and started down the sidewalk along 21st, with Maggie trotting at her heel. She moved slowly, stepping over bodies and debris with care. The street lamps were on, which made the going easier than it should have been at night, but the path was treacherous and she slid one time when her left foot came down on something wet and squishy. She regained her balance and glanced down, wincing when she saw she'd stepped in a pile of body parts.

Grateful she'd already purged the contents of her stomach, she quickened her pace and soon moved beyond the section of 21st dominated by shops and restaurants. The apartment where she'd lived with Kelly was only two more blocks away. As she neared the building, she began to perceive a couple of dim, shadowy figures a few blocks further down. Her heart gave a lurch and she came to a sudden halt. But Maggie barked and sprinted ahead.

She saw one of the dim figures turn in her direction and immediately let out a big breath. She'd at first thought she might be seeing more of those creatures, but this was not the case.

She heard a voice call out: "Maggie!"

The dog barked excitedly.

Laura smiled.

At least someone in this world was having a happy reunion tonight. She didn't know Maggie's owners well, but she was thrilled they were here. It would be nice not to go through this horror alone.

She took a step in their direction.

But then something clamped over her mouth and pulled her into an alley between buildings. A jolt of terror burned through her. Some man had a hold of her. He was big and strong and she could feel his erect penis pushing against the seat of her jeans. She tried to scream, but his hand muffled the sound. She kicked and flailed, but the man pinned one arm behind her back and wrestled her to the ground. He rolled her over, sat astride her, and drove a fist into her jaw that rendered another scream stillborn.

Laura's vision went fuzzy. Her assailant was just a black blob, a shifting shadow within the deeper darkness of the night. The man drove another punch into her jaw and she felt pain beyond anything she'd experienced before. She thought her jaw might be broken. Forget screaming now. She could only whimper. And the man silenced even that by clamping his hand over her mouth again.

At last her vision cleared and she saw the man's face.

She recognized him.

Aaron Something-or-other.

A young businessman who was a fixture in the shops and bars of 21st Avenue.

He meant to rape her.

Maybe even kill her.

And there was nothing she could do about it. He was just too overpowering. And he looked crazed. The manic gleam in his eyes made her think of Charlie Manson. Then he showed her the hunting knife and she closed her eyes.

No need to bear witness to the coming atrocity.

She thought of Kelly, and hoped she'd soon be seeing her in a better place.

And she thought of Abby and prayed for the little girl.

~

Aaron dragged the unconscious lesbo deeper into the alley, pulled her behind a dumpster and sat with his back flat against a building's wall. He'd heard footsteps approaching and so had thought it prudent to get himself and his victim out of sight.

The footsteps paused.

Then he heard a woman's voice: "I could swear I saw her right about here."

And now a man's voice: "And you're sure it was that girl from Provence?"

The woman said, "I don't know. I thought . . . maybe. I looked this way and saw her, then Maggie came running up. When I looked up again, she was gone."

"Well, she doesn't appear to be around now. Let's keep moving."

Then they were gone.

Aaron let out a breath and returned his attention to the girl. He sat astride her and grinned. She was young, maybe in her mid-twenties. And she wasn't bad-looking for a carpet-muncher. He'd seen the bitch holding hands and making googly eyes at her girlfriend several times at the Villager Pub, so he knew what her orientation was. Which was why he wanted her awake for this. He wanted her to know what was happening to her at the hands of a man. He slapped her face several times, but she never stirred. It occurred to him maybe she was faking, but it was a passing thought. He knew he'd nearly knocked her head off with that last blow.

He sighed. "Fuck."

Oh, well.

He cut her clothes off, shed his own clothes, and violated her. He was done barely a minute later. And she was still unconscious. He put his clothes back on and sat astride her again.

He placed the knife at her throat.

His nostrils flared at the sight of her breath moving in and out. He imagined Emma in this cunt's place and felt some fresh stirrings at his crotch. The image clarified before him, as vivid as a picture on a high-definition television screen. Here was Emma. There was that delectable mouth. That delicate chin. Those pretty, pretty eyes. And her throat, so slim and tender, an Audrey Hepburn throat.

FROM THE VOID

He growled and punched the knife through flesh.

The body beneath him jerked.

And Aaron giggled as he watched the beautiful red river flow out of the dead woman's throat.

10

NEAR HALETHORPE, MD
September 29
9:40 a.m.

Jasmine Holtz decided it was time to get back on the road. The eerie emptiness of the motel she'd been holed up in for the last day was getting to her. There'd only been one other car in the lot when she arrived. A dinky old red Chevette with a pale blue right fender. It had that cobbled-together look of a junker. Jasmine had searched the motel for signs of its owner—to no avail.

When she peeked outside after waking up this morning, the Chevette was gone. Weird, and not a little bit creepy. She was surprised she hadn't heard the car's owner skulking about in the night. She was even more surprised she hadn't been awakened by the sound of the car's engine as it started and drove away from the motel.

Later, when she was on the road again, she wondered why the Chevette's owner hadn't disturbed her much nicer vehicle. She expected to encounter a degree of lawlessness in this drastically altered new world. There were no rules now, at least no enforceable ones. The owner of the Chevette, stealthy as he/she evidently was, might have come into her room and taken the keys to her BMW. Or worse.

A predatory male might have raped her and killed her first.

She obsessed over the mystery for a while as she drove. Mostly because she needed something to occupy her mind other than the relentlessly bleak unfurling vista of destruction that was I-83. The Chevette's owner had to have been aware of her presence. The sleek and shiny BMW would've been impossible to miss, parked so conspicuously right in front of the motel. The mystery person had obviously been lurking somewhere out of sight the whole time. She just couldn't figure out why that person hadn't come forward at some point. Even the most casual observer would have seen that she was no threat, just a slim, unimposing woman in her early 40s.

But, for reasons she couldn't imagine, the motel's phantom guest chose to stay out of view and then steal away in the night. The mystery didn't just baffle her—it infuriated her. She wished whoever it was had come forward. She needed company. The quality of the company almost didn't matter. The presence of any other human being—psychos obviously excepted—would make her feel so much better.

She passed the city of Baltimore. She did consider entering the city to see if she could find some people there. But instinct told her to circumvent the dark metropolis as I-93 joined 695. The city's skyscrapers rose like giant tombstones against the sky. A precognitive feeling of dread grew within her as the outlines of the tall buildings became clearer. There was nary a light on anywhere amidst all that gray. She sensed nothing but death in that direction, and so she kept to 695 until she was south of the city, where she steered the BMW onto I-95.

Maybe her fear of the city had something to do with its proximity to Washington, D.C., which, after all, was where the president had been killed. Lots of people had been killed all over the world, of course, and she didn't have any realistic expectations of finding an oasis of normality farther south. But that image of the president's death was so vivid, and so ingrained in the forefront of her consciousness, that it was enough to keep her heading toward a part of the country with which she was mostly unfamiliar. She also had an idea it might be a good idea to get to a more temperate climate for the coming winter. Always assuming, of course, she was still alive by then.

Traversing the long, winding stretches of interstate wasn't as problematic as she'd imagined it might be. Doom had come screaming out of the sky so suddenly—and so overwhelmingly—on that day of death and chaos there'd been little time for a panicked exodus from the cities. There were stalled cars and trucks here and there, even occasional large clusters of them, but she had yet to encounter one she couldn't get around. She hoped her luck would hold up in that regard. She didn't much fancy the idea of having to abandon her car and find a new one somewhere farther along the road.

A glance at the BMW's fuel gauge showed that its tank was half full. She could get a good ways farther along on that, but when she saw the exit for Halethorpe she decided to pull off the interstate and see if she could find a working gas station. She still had most of the day ahead of her and would feel much better about spending so many long hours on the road with a full tank. She only hoped she'd be able to find a gas station with still-working pumps.

She came off the exit and saw a small grouping of convenience stores and fast food restaurants looming just ahead of her. The closest was a large Exxon, on the left side of the street at the approaching intersection. She pulled into the store's parking lot and steered her car toward the nearest pump.

She turned the engine off and got out of the car.

~

Halethorpe
10:27 a.m.

"There's somebody at that Exxon across the street."

Warren hopped over the counter and moved to the front of the Wendy's restaurant, where Amanda stood staring through a window. He followed her gaze and saw a woman of about forty get out of a car. A nice one, too. He couldn't tell for sure from this distance, but he thought it might be a BMW or Porsche.

Warren said, "Holy shit. Let's get over there."

Amanda looked at him. The expression on her face was wary. And resolute. She shook her head. "No. I think we should stay out of sight until she's gone."

Warren frowned.

The woman was the first living person they'd seen since early in the previous day, when they'd encountered an elderly man sitting on a bus stop bench in downtown Baltimore. The man was physically frail and their conversation with him hinted at an early stage of senility. He talked about his wife as if she were sitting there next to him, but he'd been alone on the bench. Otherwise he was lucid, and he talked about the destruction of his city with the cool detachment of a veteran combat correspondent. Until, that is, he grew unaccountably belligerent and chased them off by swinging at their heads with his cane.

As far as Warren and Amanda had been able to tell, the man was the only human being left alive in a city of millions. Warren couldn't fathom it. There should have been other people in a place so big. But there were only corpses. Thousands upon thousands of them. Human and demon. Many of the human casualties were obvious victims of demon attacks. But a significant percentage appeared physically unharmed. Something else—some invisible gas perhaps—had killed them. Warren could imagine the government utilizing chemical weapons in a desperate, last-ditch attempt to defeat the swarming creatures. The potential huge loss of human life would have been seen as an acceptable risk. But the chemical weapons theory didn't explain the survival of that one feeble old man. Or their own survival, for that matter.

Thinking about it frustrated Warren. Whatever had happened, there was no explanation forthcoming from whatever remained of the government (if anything). Maybe they'd all offed themselves after seeing the horror wrought by their final solution.

Baltimore was a ghost town, invested with the atmosphere of an ancient and crumbling place, a once-vital metropolis fallen to ruin long ago. Warren had sensed a formless malevolence, a nameless taint that infected the empty buildings and the air itself. It wasn't a feeling of being watched, or at least not just that. It was a creeping dread, a growing certainty the physical substance of the city had acquired a kind of quiet and feral life of its own. Warren felt this most acutely when passing beneath a traffic light. It was still functioning, but the color of the light never changed, remaining a bright, unblinking red that made him think of the bulbous crimson eyes of the winged demons.

So rather than making camp in the city as they'd planned, they got the hell out of there and spent the night here in Halethorpe. But the smaller town was as empty of life as Baltimore. There were bodies everywhere. Dead people. Dead demons. After a full day of baking in the sun, the ripening corpses gave off a stink that permeated the cool air.

After encountering so much death and desolation, Warren was thrilled to see the woman across the street. A growing voice of paranoia had been whispering the opinion that he and Amanda might be the only two surviving humans in the entire world. A more rational part of him didn't find the notion plausible, but these days he was inclined to lend thoughts tinged with paranoia a greater degree of credence. It was a depressing thing. He didn't much relish the idea of adopting the role of Adam to Amanda's Eve. But here was proof he'd been wrong.

He couldn't understand why Amanda didn't share his excitement. "You mind explaining that? Because I have to tell you, that's crazy. She sure doesn't look dangerous."

Her gaze still riveted on the woman, Amanda made a pensive noise and shook her head. "Looks can be deceiving."

Warren groaned. "Oh, come on. Look, I'm going over there. Otherwise she'll be gone and we'll still be here arguing."

He turned away from Amanda, but she grabbed him by the elbow and spun him around. Her eyes were wide and flashing with anger. "You're not going anywhere." Her grip tightened on his elbow and she pulled him closer. "We're doing fine on our own. We don't need anyone else."

Warren held her gaze a moment, then closed his eyes and sighed. "Jesus . . ." A sharp pain between his eyes made his brow crease. He opened his eyes. "No."

He tugged his arm free of her grip and walked out of the restaurant. He strode rapidly across the restaurant's parking lot and kept his gaze straight ahead, willing himself not to glance back to see if Amanda was following. He knew there might be hell to pay later for defying her, but right now he didn't care. He couldn't allow her paranoia to kill this opportunity.

The BMW's owner turned at the sound of his footsteps when he reached the middle of the street. There was obvious apprehension in her eyes, and she took an unconscious step backward. He smiled and waved to show her he wasn't a psychopath. She moved another step backward and might have kept moving, but the gas pump blocked her path. He increased the wattage of his smile, hoping it didn't make him look like a grinning maniac.

He could see now he'd been right about her approximate age. And she was slender and attractive, with a striking face that would garner her second looks from men for many years to come. He couldn't help thinking of Anne Bancroft in *The Graduate*, but with blonde hair. She was attired all in black, like a person in mourning.

He called out to her as he reached the other side of the street.

"Hello, there! I'm harmless, I promise. You have no idea how happy I am to see you. Other than one crazy old man in Baltimore, you're the first living person we've seen since . . . that day."

The woman still seemed wary of him. He guessed he couldn't blame her for that. You'd have to be a fool to trust a stranger in this environment. On the other hand, she didn't seem about to bolt, so Warren guessed he didn't strike her as particularly scary-looking.

Warren stopped walking when he reached the rear of her car, sensing he shouldn't get too close just yet. "I hope I didn't scare you." He dialed down the wattage of his smile. "My name's Warren Hatcher."

The woman's smile was less tentative now. "Jasmine Holtz." She moved away from the pump and extended a hand, which Warren shook. Her skin was soft against his. It would feel good to be caressed by that hand. Which was a strange thing to think at a time like this. Warren thought of Amanda and felt a brief surge of shame.

Jasmine's gaze was frank. One could almost call it "probing". Warren felt heat touch his cheeks and couldn't believe it. He was blushing. He felt like a kid in this woman's presence. She was so refined, so evidently sophisticated.

But if the woman sensed his awkwardness, she showed no sign of it. She said, "Is someone with you?"

"Um . . ."

Her gaze flicked to the Wendy's building. "You said I was the first living person 'we've' seen." She looked him in the eye again, and he had to fight the impulse to fidget beneath that unwavering gaze. "Or did you misspeak?"

Warren glanced over his shoulder at the restaurant. The glare of the morning sun made it impossible to see into the building, but he supposed Amanda was still inside, glaring at him from the other side of that window. The silver Mazda they'd driven down from New Jersey was still parked in front of the building, and seeing it made him feel marginally better. He'd half-expected her to drive off in a fit of pique, leaving him to stew here for hours until coming back for him.

He looked at Jasmine, shrugged. "My, uh . . . girlfriend is in there. We were foraging for food. I was trying to figure out how to work the equipment, maybe cook up some burgers and fries."

Jasmine pursed her lips. Her gaze went again to the restaurant. "What's your girlfriend's name?"

"Amanda."

Jasmine smiled. "Pretty name. Are you in love with her?"

"Um . . ."

Warren cursed inwardly. He wished she'd asked him anything but that. He liked Amanda. But he wasn't "in love" with her. At least not the way he'd been in love with Emma Singleton. But judging her against Emma wasn't fair. The all-consuming passion he'd felt for Emma was one of those once-in-a-lifetime kind of deals. That was something he'd never experience again, and it was high time he accepted that.

Warren nodded, deciding then to tell the petty lie.

"Yeah." He coughed. "I guess I am."

Jasmine sighed. "Well, that's wonderful. You're lucky to have someone to love. I . . ." Jasmine's voice drifted off. She arched an eyebrow and nodded at something over Warren's shoulder. "Here comes your lady love now."

Warren turned and watched Amanda cross the street. He studied her face, tried to discern some hint of consolation there, but her blank expression was hard to read. Only her eyes, hard and focused, gave any indication of her feelings. He'd felt a spark of hope at Jasmine's words, but now that tiny flame snuffed out.

Amanda reached the pump. She stood apart from them, with her arms folded under her breasts. She glanced once at Warren—those hard eyes stinging him—and fixed a gaze on Jasmine that was nakedly mistrustful. "I'm gonna lay it out for you, lady. We're not going to bond with you. We're not joining forces. I don't even want to know what your fucking name is."

And now she looked at Warren. "This is how it's gonna be. You've got a choice to make. You can either do the honorable thing and stick with me, or you can hook up with this old hag. But before you decide, you remember this—you made a promise. You said you'd get me home. You said you'd protect me."

Warren gritted his teeth and seethed. He looked at the ground and shoved his hands into his pockets (to hide that they were curling into tight fists). He refrained from saying anything for several moments, knowing that to speak from anger was to invite disaster. Regardless, he was definitely angry. Beyond angry. He was pissed off. Big time. Amanda had no right to be issuing ultimatums.

He let out a big breath, pulled his hands from his pockets, and rubbed his eyes. When he looked at Amanda again, her expression was the same—resolute, unyielding. Though her attitude infuriated him, he knew he would ultimately do what she wanted. He didn't want to, of course, but he would not break his promise. Giving in to her selfish wishes would taint their relationship, maybe even irreparably harm it, but he planned to stick by Amanda's side until she told him she no longer wanted him there.

In a frosty tone he said, "I don't break promises. But—"

Whatever he'd been about to say was forgotten in the next moment—because that was when he was shown the relative peace of the last few days had only been a lull, a pause in the unraveling of the world.

Amanda dropped like a dead weight, her knees hitting the asphalt with a crunch that made his stomach lurch. Warren went to her, knelt in front of her. She covered her face and wailed. He tried to pry her hands from her face, but they wouldn't budge and he only succeeded in eliciting another pitiful wail. He felt a shadow pass over him, then saw Jasmine kneeling next to Amanda. The look on his face then was the beseeching expression of a helpless child. The older woman's eyes shone with empathy, but she looked as clueless as Warren felt.

Warren laid a trembling hand on Amanda's shoulder. "Amanda, honey . . . please, tell me what's wrong . . . please . . ."

Her body convulsed, and she swayed on her knees. A low, muffled moan issued from behind her hands, which were beginning to slide down her face.

Warren looked at Jasmine. "Jesus Christ, what's *wrong* with her?"

Jasmine shook her head. "I'm sorry, I don't know."

"Is she having a stroke? What's going on?"

Jasmine again said, "I don't know."

Amanda leaped to her feet so suddenly it caused Warren to fall backward. The back of his head thumped against the BMW's rear bumper, sending a jolt of pain down his body. Amanda screamed. Warren blinked hard and staggered to his feet. He stumbled a step or two forward before he could see clearly again—and then stopped dead in his tracks. A helpless horror swept through him, making his legs go weak.

Her hands no longer covered her face. But there was nothing there. Just a black space. Her body shook like that of a person gripping a live electrical wire. Warren moved a tentative step in her direction, extended a trembling hand toward her. Jasmine gripped him by the arm, holding him back.

Her body stopped shaking and she dropped to the ground.

Warren loosed a scream of anguish: "NOOOOOOO!"

The black space widened and consumed her body. Warren couldn't believe it. Only moments ago she'd been fine. Healthy. Whole. The enormity of the loss hit him like a medicine ball to the gut. Amanda was gone. He could never get her back. Could never talk to her again. Never kiss her again.

Something moved within the blackness. A fuzzy brown stalk with a single red eye atop it emerged and twitched when it saw them. Jasmine pulled Warren toward her car. He stumbled backward on legs rendered numb from shock. He heard her open a door, heard her say something, but the words were lost to him—the whole of his attention was focused on the thing crawling out of the black space once occupied by Amanda. More stalks emerged, but these had no eyes. When they reached for the ground, he began to get a sense of something like a spider.

A big one.

Jasmine pushed him into the BMW and he fell across the front seat. She shoved him over to the passenger seat and fell in behind the wheel. Then she started the car, put it in gear, and sped away from the convenience store.

Warren sat up straight. He couldn't accept what he'd seen. Amanda couldn't be dead. It just wasn't possible a woman he'd had sex with only hours earlier no longer existed. It didn't compute. Nor did the manner of her death. He saw that black space in the center of her face again and touched a finger to his own nose. The tip of his finger was cold, like the touch of an icicle. He pulled his hand away from his face and held it palm out. He squinted, studying the intersecting lines of the soft flesh there. He knew if he took a knife to that flesh, if he opened it, a line of red would gush forth. And there would be pain from the slit nerve-endings. He was made of solid materials and liquid, bone and water and blood. Strands of DNA, atoms, molecules, electrons.

It'd been odd enough—and disturbing enough—to know these rips in the fabric of reality could occur at all. He'd seen black spaces in roads, in buildings, even in the sky, and seeing them had frightened him every time. But now that he knew he wasn't even safe in his own skin . . . well, hell, what was the point in even continuing?

The BMW hit the exit ramp at a high rate of speed and Warren was thrown against the door as Jasmine cranked the steering wheel. Then he was tossed to the left as Jasmine spun the wheel back the other way when they reached the interstate. Warren's face was buried briefly in Jasmine's hair, which smelled faintly of lavender. He settled back in his seat and groaned.

"Ugh . . . I'm gonna be sick. Pull over."

Jasmine glanced at her rearview mirror. She looked tense. Scared shitless, actually. But she relaxed after staring at the mirror for several moments. She let out a sigh and guided the car to a stop at the road's shoulder. Warren had the door open before the car came to a complete stop. He leaned over and vomited on concrete. Then he wiped his mouth and sat back up before the puke smell could make him sick all over again.

He pulled the door shut and looked at Jasmine. "Okay."

Jasmine nodded.

She put the car in gear again and drove on down the road.

Warren sighed. "Do you have a gun?"

Jasmine looked at him. "Forget that. I won't let you kill yourself over this."

Warren grunted. "And why the hell not? What the fuck is the point of living anymore? You saw what happened to Amanda. That could happen to me. Or you. At any goddamn minute."

Jasmine's gaze went back to the road. "The point," she said, "is I don't want to be alone." Her voice thickened with some emotion. "Okay?"

Warren's brow furrowed.

He didn't know what to say to that.

Not yet anyway.

11

The apartment was in a complex in a suburb of Nashville called Antioch. Mountain High Apartments. Funny name, because there didn't seem to be any mountains in the vicinity. Antioch was as desolate as any of the other communities they'd passed through on the way up from Alabama. And as tainted by the evidence of decay as those other communities. The sky above them was as cloudless, but there was something not quite right about it. The brilliant blue Zeke knew they should be seeing wasn't there. The daytime sky had a washed-out look, as if they were viewing it through a vast and filthy expanse of gauze. He'd initially attributed this to fallout from the nuclear exchanges, but now he wasn't so sure.

He had a theory. He believed the sky's dull hue was a fresh wrinkle in an ongoing process, another way in which the fabric of reality was changing. And, yes, decaying. A rot of some sort had set in, some infection brought into this world by the inhabitants of that other place. The evidence of that rot was all around them. In the countryside, where verdant stretches of forest seemed to wither before their eyes, the leaves of trees turning black even as ripe and sturdy limbs sagged and turned bone-dry. And in the cities, those empty amalgamations of concrete and steel and glittering glass, where buildings that must have been very new were nonetheless beginning to crumble, towering monuments to capitalism that suddenly were looking as shabby as rickety backwater shacks.

And then there were the dead people. Not just the ones killed by the flying demons on that nightmarish day, but others, people who had dropped dead in the intervening time. Old people, sure, but also young, apparently healthy people. Zeke was certain something in the shifting nature of existence was killing them, some poison from that other place. He could only assume he and Mary Lou were immune to whatever it was. That, or they had yet to come into contact with the gas or germ responsible. If some percentage of the world's human population truly was immune to the effects of the rot, Zeke reckoned it must be a very tiny number. One percent, maybe. Or less.

But there'd been one family living at Mountain High when they arrived, a young mother and father and a boy of about ten. Zeke's spirits soared at the sight of them. They'd come running up to his Lexus when—at Mary Lou's direction—he'd driven into the complex. He remembered the way their eyes had glimmered with relief, an emotion that mirrored his own feelings.

That relief was short-lived.

Because Mary Lou, still as stark naked as she'd been when Zeke first laid eyes on her, got out of the car and blew them away with her shotgun.

That was yesterday. And the bloody images would not stop replaying in Zeke's head. Mary Lou's unrestrained savagery so intimidated Zeke that he was unable to make an attempt to flee, not even when she returned to the car to reload the shotgun from a box of shells she'd swiped from a Wal-Mart the day before. That had been his opportunity, his one big chance to put an end to this insanity. He was bigger than her. Stronger than her. He could have ripped the unloaded gun from her hands. Probably should have beaten her senseless with the weapon's butt end.

But he'd done no such thing. He just sat there, hands locked on the steering wheel, eyes staring straight ahead. Afraid to move. Afraid to even breathe. Then she had the gun loaded again and it was too late. She made him get out of the car and he'd done so immediately. Never in his life had he been so thoroughly cowed by another human being. He knew in that moment there was nothing he wouldn't do if she so instructed. At her command, he'd drop to his knees and lick the still-warm blood of the murdered innocents off the ground. He'd piss in their wounds, defecate on them, or perform any other humiliating act that crossed her fancy.

He had no doubt she would've made him do those things if she had thought of them. There had been ample proof of that in the days since she'd abducted him on that lonely stretch of Alabama highway. Like the time yesterday when she'd forced him to kiss and fondle the days-old corpse of a fat woman in the Wal-Mart bathroom. She took pictures of the morbid clinch with a Polaroid camera, laughing hysterically all the while. She later glued the snapshots to the dash of his car, and the sickening images had taunted him the rest of the way to Nashville.

Coming to Nashville was Mary Lou's idea, of course. She was a big country music fan and wanted to see all the sights. It didn't seem to matter to her that all her favorite country performers were probably dead. She wanted to see the Country Music Hall of Fame and maybe pillage some of the souvenir shops. She planned to enter the city tomorrow. He would accompany her, of course. He was duty-bound to do so as her "significant other", or so she'd told him. That was another thing. He wasn't just her prisoner anymore. Nope, as far as Mary Lou was concerned, he was her boyfriend—same as Billy had been until she'd blown his brains out.

She was completely out of her fucking mind.

Zeke strained against the lengths of black electrical cord she'd used to tie him to the headboard. He thought he detected a bit of give around his left wrist and was pretty sure he could get himself free if he had enough time to work at it. Mary Lou was gone for now. Out foraging or looking for other innocent people to slaughter for kicks. He gave his left wrist a hard twist. The cord loosened a bit more. The lower portion of his thumb was on the verge of being able to pass through the loop.

Then Mary Lou walked into the bedroom and all hope of escape fled. She leaned the shotgun against a wall and plopped down on the edge of the bed. "Trying to get away?"

Zeke sighed. "Sort of. I guess."

Mary Lou smirked. "I really oughta punish you for that. Give you a good thrashing. Put you in your fuckin' place again."

Zeke grimaced. He'd endured several "thrashings" at her hands already. They were not pleasant experiences. "Why don't you just kill me and be done with it?"

Mary Lou rolled her eyes. "'Cause then I'd get real fuckin' bored real fuckin' fast." She dragged the long nails of her right hand down his bare chest. "Anyway, I ain't gonna thrash ya today. Just don't feel like it."

Zeke felt an immense wave of gratitude wash over him, but he didn't want her to see how relieved he was. He looked away from her and said, "Whatever."

She gripped his penis. "Wanna fuck?"

Zeke grew hard in her hand.

Amazing.

He loathed this woman. She was a monster. She had no more regard for human life than she did for the life of a fly or mosquito. The memory of what the shotgun's blast did to that boy's face jabbed at his psyche like an icepick to the brain. Yet some helpless, primal part of his brain wanted what Mary Lou was offering. She climbed atop him and guided his cock into her already wet pussy. She rode him for a while, bucking and whooping as enthusiastically as a drunken secretary riding a mechanical bull on nickel beer night. After he shot his load up inside her, she climbed off him, jumped off the bed, and disappeared through a door adjacent to the bedroom. A sound of running water came from the bathroom. Zeke felt a fresh surge of revulsion—directed both at Mary Lou and at himself.

Because he'd enjoyed it.

So now he felt lower than dirt. He thought of the bodies of his sex partner's victims decaying on the ground outside and felt a tickle of bile at the back of his throat. An ache flared behind his eyes. So he closed them and tried to focus on anything other than the sex smell permeating the room. Like how he might get himself free of this nightmare his life had become. Since the night of his abduction, the death of civilization had become a secondary concern. He was at the mercy of a deranged person, and every moment that elapsed with his heart still beating seemed like a miracle.

She came out of the bathroom some twenty minutes or so later, still dripping wet from the shower. Her hair, which he was accustomed to seeing in a big, poofy style that had last been in vogue in the mid-1980s, was plastered to her scalp and hung halfway down her back. She moved to the foot of the bed, where she dried off—very slowly and methodically—with a fluffy white towel. She propped each leg on the bed as she dried them, giving him long looks at the glistening spot between them.

She winked. "Enjoying the show?"

Zeke forced himself to look at the ceiling. He tried to rid his head of the taunting images. He thought of disgusting things. Piles of shit and raw sewage. He recalled images of all the dead and mutilated people he'd seen in the last few days. So much death. So much misery. The word "tragedy" didn't seem adequate to describe it all. Catastrophe, he thought. Yes, that was closer. He imagined the pain suffered by the victims of those airborne monsters. Tears stung his eyes. He realized the sublimation tactic had worked when he saw Mary Lou standing again at the foot of the bed, her pretty face twisted by a frown.

"What the fuck is wrong with you?"

Tears spilled down Zeke's cheeks. His chest hitched, and a moment later he was sobbing uncontrollably. He was vaguely aware of Mary Lou yelling at him, ordering him to "stop acting like a fuckin' baby." But the stream of tears just wouldn't dry up. Then Mary Lou did a strange, unexpected thing. She curled up next to him on the bed and buried her face in the crook of his neck. She made shushing noises and stroked his hair. The notion of being comforted by the likes of Mary Lou struck him as obscene, but he was surprised to find something within him responding to her ministrations anyway. When his tears at last began to subside, he felt her mouth on his. He lay frozen for a moment, feeling again that reflexive flush of revulsion—but then he was kissing her back, drawing her tongue into his mouth and feeling a shudder of pleasure at its warmth.

It was the first time they'd kissed. She'd used him to get herself off a number of times, but never had there been any actual intimacy in the acts. A wave of heat suffused his body, made him ache with desire. Nothing other than that desire mattered now. Not the death of the world. Not Mary Lou's monstrous acts of murder. She was alive, and he was alive, and for now that was good enough. He gave himself over to her completely then. And she to him. It felt good to get lost in sensation, to forget everything but the pleasure of flesh. Maybe this was how they could keep that monumental sense of loss at bay—by literally fucking the pain away.

Mary Lou pushed away from him, smiled, and began to undo the lengths of black cord. When she was through, she tossed them to the floor. She sat next to him, smiling, waiting to see what he would do.

FROM THE VOID

Zeke rubbed at the sore spots on his wrists. He looked at Mary Lou, who regarded him expectantly.

This is it, he thought. *My big chance.*

He could get out of here. Or he could get to the shotgun, turn it on Mary Lou, and make her pay for her crimes. Instead, he put a hand at the back of her neck. Again, here was a chance. He could get both hands around that slender throat, push her to the bed, and choke the life out of her.

Part of him figured he *should* do it, after all she'd done.

But he didn't choke her to death either. He kissed her again instead, more fiercely even than before. When their lips parted, she made a low sound in her throat that was almost a growl. He took her then, parting her legs and driving his hardness deep inside her. In the midst of it, an image of the boy's face blowing apart flickered through his mind. Then it scattered, like ashes in a breeze.

Nothing else matters, he told himself.

Nothing but this.

Not anymore.

12

NASHVILLE, TN
September 29
12:39 p.m.

The image on the monitor went fuzzy again. Emma snarled and smacked the side of it with her palm. "Goddammit!"

Jake came into the bedroom and took a seat in the folding chair next to her. "Whoa, what's happening here?"

Emma sighed. "What's happening here is that Laura Brandner's stone-age computer is pissing me off. I'm about to chuck it out the window."

Jake looked haggard. His eyes were bloodshot, and his face had a gaunt, haunted cast. He hadn't slept much since that first night, when he'd awakened to the sound of an intruder in the apartment. He chased off whoever it was, the intruder zipping down the stairwell and out the building before Jake could get a good look at him. Not that a visual verification was really necessary. They both were sure it'd been Aaron.

Emma had slept through the whole thing, but when Jake told her about it the next day, her first impulse was to move to another location. They couldn't be safe with Aaron lurking about. She didn't want always to be looking over her shoulder, worried he might jump her at any moment. Plus, there was Abby to worry about.

But Jake convinced her to stay. He reasoned that a confrontation was inevitable. Aaron was a sick, obsessed fuck who would not give up until he had what he wanted. Moving would only slightly delay a showdown. Jake believed they should remain where psycho-boy could easily find them.

Sooner or later, he'd come after them again.

And Jake would be ready for him.

Emma's gaze went to the Glock pistol resting in Jake's lap. He'd taken it from Phil's safe at the Villager Pub. She frowned. "Do you really mean to shoot Aaron with that thing?"

Jake nodded. "I do."

Emma was again surprised to see grim determination evident in his eyes. "I never would have imagined you'd have that in you. To be able to kill a man, I mean."

Jake held her gaze a moment, then looked at the computer monitor. "I've changed. I can't be a pacifist in this new world." He looked at Emma. "It's depressing, I guess, especially in light of all we've lost. But surviving—and I know we mean to survive—means we have to adapt. It means we have to . . ."

"Become savages."

Jake shrugged. "Yeah. That's about the size of it."

"Well, it sucks."

Jake's smile then was small and sad. "I know. But I'm going to kill that man. I'm going to put this gun to his head and blow his fucking brains out. It's the only way. You can threaten him a million times, but he'll keep coming back. And if we fuck around and don't exterminate him like the fucking pest he is, one day he'll come back better armed than we are."

Emma sighed. "Unless we leave town."

"Right." Jake ran a hand through hair grown greasy over the last two days. "Which you said you'd never do."

Emma grunted. "Yeah. Well, maybe it's time I adapt to this fucked-up new paradigm, too. I mean, this town has been my home forever, but . . ."

Jake nodded but didn't say anything. There was a simple decision to be made. Leave, or make a conscious choice to have a man killed. And Emma knew it was her decision to make. Jake would abide by whatever choice she made. Emma supposed it was a tougher decision than it ought to be. The pragmatic and obvious choice was flight. But her heart was anchored to this town. She had been born here. Had grown up and lived here. Nashville was home. And, broken though it was, the city was all that was left to her of the world she'd known. So it made her furious to think she might have to leave it forever because of Aaron Harris.

"There's Abby to think of, too. We're her guardians by default. Doesn't matter that we didn't ask for the responsibility. It's just the way it is. We have to think of her safety first."

Jake nodded again—and again said nothing. He was waiting for Emma to steer herself toward the inevitable conclusion by talking it out. He knew what had to happen and so did she.

So she jumped ahead to it: "We have to leave. Today. As soon as we can."

Jake smiled. "I'm ready whenever you are." He looked at the computer monitor. "Any luck with that thing yet?"

Emma shook her head. "Laura's ISP is still up and running, amazingly. She's got cable internet, at least. Otherwise we'd have been fucked from the beginning, what with the phones being out. Turns out, though, that's been our only lucky break."

Jake arched an eyebrow. "Oh?"

Emma indicated the fuzzy monitor with a nod. "On top of everything else, this thing looks ready to die. Not that it matters. There's been next to nothing to see anyway. I've gone into chatrooms, posted messages all across the internet, mostly BBSs with a southern regional focus. The newest messages I've seen were posted the morning after those things attacked. A fair smattering of them, too. So there were other survivors, even some who identified themselves as being in Tennessee. That got my hopes up. There was this one sort of oddball guy right here in town. Called himself Captain Flash Wheeler. Posted a slew of messages claiming to have experienced some sort of religious epiphany. Claims he was a car mechanic before doomsday, but a vision told him he's the One True God."

Jake smirked. "Sounds like a nut. We're better off not hooking up with anyone like that."

Emma shrugged. "Maybe. He hasn't posted anything in over a day, either. I posted replies to other people who seemed to be nearby, suggested everyone still alive in the area hook up at a central location." The deep frustration she felt was evident in the way she slumped further in her chair and stared blankly at the monitor. "But no one's responded. Everyone still alive the day after is either dead now, on the move, or they've stopped paying attention to their computers."

Jake made a soft sound that was part laugh and part grunt. "I imagine surfing the internet is a pretty dull exercise without anyone out there to interact with, so I'm guessing that last scenario is the most likely one."

Emma pursed her lips. She looked at him a moment before speaking again, trying to decide whether he really believed that or was simply trying to make her feel better. "I don't know about that," she said at last. "I'm not saying I'm psychic, okay? Or anything like that. But sometimes I get really strong feelings about things, and when I get those feelings they're usually right. And it feels to me like there's no one out there in the world. Like the whole planet is one vast graveyard. All that's left is you, me, that sweet little girl, and that psycho asshole."

Now Jake really did laugh. "But that's not possible. There's other people out there. Somewhere. There has to be."

Emma was about to reply in a snide way when Abby came into the room. A curse died at the edge of her tongue when she glimpsed the child's face. Emma made herself smile, a broad grin that must have looked as phony as it felt. "Hey, sweetheart," she said, injecting a note of equally false cheeriness into her voice. "I thought you were napping."

Abby shrugged. She yawned and stretched her arms over her head, going up on her toes in a pose that made her look like a sleepy ballerina in pink pajamas. Then her arms flopped back to her sides and she came farther into the room. She craned her head and peered past Emma at the computer monitor. "That monitor's broken."

Emma smiled. "I know."

Abby looked at her. "It's old. Laura's good monitor stopped working. She bought this one at a pawn shop. A 'temporary fix'. That's what she said."

Emma sat up straighter in the chair and tried not to fidget. She was uncomfortable discussing the girl's aunt with her. Abby still talked about Laura in the present tense on occasion, and Emma supposed the girl still held out some faint hope the woman might yet turn up alive.

Abby came up beside her and leaned over the desk to touch the wireless mouse. She moved it across the mousepad and closed the internet application Emma had been using. The pointer moved across the screen and stopped at a folder labeled "Stories". Abby double-clicked the folder and a window displaying dozens of files opened.

Abby looked at Emma. "My Auntie was a writer. She wrote lots of stories. Some of them were even in magazines."

"Wow." Emma scanned the file names. Laura's titles hinted at stories with a literary or postmodernist bent. She smiled at Abby. "You must have been really proud of her."

Abby shrugged. "Yeah. But writing made her sad. She said she loved it, but that it was hard." She sniffled. "She said trying to be a writer was dumb. That she should have tried to be a doctor or lawyer instead. She said it would be the death of her one day." Abby swiped at her eyes, wiping away tears. "But she was wrong, wasn't she? Something else was the death of her."

Emma pulled the suddenly sobbing girl into her arms. She patted her back, stroked her hair, and made cooing, comforting noises. She looked over the top of the girl's head at Jake, who had averted his gaze. But his own eyes glistened with tears, too. He was trying hard to hold them back. And he was trying so hard to be strong for both of them. She felt the tug of another emotion, then, some welling of feeling within her. She was starting to love him, she guessed. Really love him. She didn't know how to feel about it, whether she should be happy or depressed. Because what was the point of falling in love anymore?

But she didn't have to think too long on that one. The answer was right here in her arms. This little girl. A precious life worth saving and nurturing. Unless things changed again in some strange and unanticipated way, the three of them likely had a good shot at long-term survival. Which meant she and Jake were obligated to become surrogate parents to Abby. There was a moral imperative here. The catastrophic events of the last several days had robbed them of each of their birth families. Therefore, the three of them had no choice but to become a new family, one forged in the fires of desperation, and from the need that dwelled within all humans to cling to one another, to find strength and solace and warmth in one another.

And, yes, love.

Jake looked at her now, saw the intent way she was studying him, and managed a nervous smile. He leaned forward in his chair and said, "Hey, Abby, what do you say you and me go do some more of those finger paintings?"

Abby sniffled and drew in a great, shuddering breath. She still had her face pressed against Emma's chest, but she seemed finished with this latest crying jag. "Okay," she said, the single word exhaled in a soft sigh. "But I paint better than you."

Jake chuckled. "Yeah, you're a budding Picasso, that's for sure."

Emma smiled and mouthed a "thank you" at Jake.

He winked and began to rise from his chair. Then he frowned and cocked his head in a way that made Emma think of a dog perking its ears. He stood the rest of the way up and began to move past Emma toward the window. Emma turned in her chair and watched him as he braced his hands on the sill and peered outside.

Emma's heart skipped a beat and she swallowed a hard lump in her throat. She had no good reason yet to be afraid, nothing tangible, but she'd seen and experienced so much awfulness recently that instant terror had become her default reaction to anything out of the ordinary.

"Jake?" she said, sounding more timid than she wanted in Abby's presence—but she couldn't help it. "What is it?"

He spoke without turning from the window: "Don't you hear that?"

Emma started to say "no", but then she did hear something—a distant rumble growing louder by the nanosecond, a sound felt as much as heard. It soon became a rising roar, and Jake turned from the window and bolted out of the room.

"Jake!"

Panic gripped Emma. She took Abby by the hand and together they ran after Jake. In the living room, they saw the apartment's front door standing open. Emma stopped in the center of the room and fixed Abby with the sternest expression she could manage. "Abby, I'm gonna go check on Jake. I want you to stay right here until we get back. Okay?"

Abby's young face reflected fear as well as a burgeoning defiance. "No! I want to come with you!"

Emma gripped the girl by the shoulder, squeezing hard enough to elicit a wince. "I mean it, Abby!" Her tone was too harsh. She knew it at once, but she couldn't help it. She had to make the girl stay here and then get after Jake. Damn him for running out like that! "Stay. That's an order."

She left then, figuring it best to get on with it and not give the girl a chance to pout or defy her again. She hurried down the single flight of stairs and dashed through the building's front door. Jake was standing in the center of the courtyard, his head turned skyward. She called out to him, but the roar was so loud now the sound of her voice couldn't penetrate it. She stood beside him and turned her head to the sky.

At first she saw nothing. Just that strangely washed-out sky they'd been seeing for over a day. Then Jake raised his hand and pointed to a seemingly empty patch of sky in the distance. Except—it wasn't empty. A wedge of something black came shooting over the horizon. A plane. Emma's heart raced and she had difficulty breathing. It was a fucking plane. And not just any plane. It was something of obvious military design. A Stealth bomber maybe. It came in low over the city, so low Emma feared at first it was about to crash. Her next thought was that the plane was piloted by some rogue Air Force survivor, a whacko who meant to bomb the city for the sheer fun of it. But it maintained a steady altitude as it blew overhead and shot toward the downtown area. No bombs or missiles fell. They watched its tail end disappear, and several moments elapsed before they realized they could hear again.

A sudden gasp burst from Emma's lungs. "Oh my God!" She turned a wide-eyed gaze on Jake. "What the fuck!?"

"I don't know." Jake shook his head. "Maybe . . . maybe there's some rudimentary form of government still out there. Maybe it's, uh . . . reconstituting itself. And this was some sort of recon mission." He shrugged. "Or some rogue pilot is out on a joyride. One possibility is as likely as the other, I guess."

He frowned. "Where's Abby?"

Emma gasped again. "Aw, shit." She smacked her forehead. "You had me so worried when you took off like that. I made her stay in the apartment."

Jake smiled reassuringly. "I'm sure she's fine."

Emma's brow creased. "Yeah. But let's go back."

They reentered the building and trudged back up the flight of stairs to the apartment, feeling tired now the adrenaline rush triggered by the plane's appearance had faded. Emma was first through the apartment's front door. She stared uncomprehendingly at the empty living room for a moment.

Jake came in behind her and moved into the middle of the living room, his head doing a slow swivel on his neck as he scanned the biggest room of the apartment for any sign of the little girl. "Where is she?"

Emma didn't reply right away. She was too busy trying not to panic. If she didn't keep a tight rein on her emotions, she'd start to hyperventilate, become a useless, gibbering mess. She needed to think clearly. But her brain was refusing to kick into gear.

"Abby! Where are you!?"

The sound of Jake's voice was the impetus she needed. She ran into the bedroom, saw at once the girl wasn't there, and threw open the door to the bathroom. Which also proved empty. Each empty room was like a taunt. Some force—God, or whatever—was providing her with a heart-squeezing object lesson, showing her what could happen when you didn't act responsibly.

Christ, she should never have left the little girl in the apartment. Should never have let her out of her fucking sight. The idea Abby might be dead occurred to her for the first time, hitting her with the force of a two-by-four to the head. She'd only been out in the courtyard with Jake for a minute. Maybe two. Such a miniscule stretch of time. But more than time enough for someone (Aaron?) to come up the back way and snatch the vulnerable girl. She might have screamed. More than once, maybe. But they wouldn't have heard her over the roar of the low-flying plane.

Jake came into the bedroom. "Is she in here?"

Emma saw it in his face. He hadn't found her in the kitchen. Or sitting on the stairs out back. "Oh my God." She covered her face with her hands. Shaking hands that pressed into her eyes to stem the flow of tears that wanted to erupt there. "Oh my God. Oh my God, Jake!"

Jake gripped her wrists and pulled her hands from her face. "Look at me!"

She looked at him, her eyes shining with desperation. "She's gone. Oh, she's gone, and it's all my fault."

He shook his head. "What do you mean?"

And now tears did sting her eyes. She wasn't strong enough to hold them back. But the tears shamed her. Were they for the missing little girl? Or were they a product of the massive guilt she felt for abandoning her? "I made her stay up here. She wanted to come with me. You shouldn't have run off like that. Y-you scared me. I thought Abby would only s-slow me d-down."

Jake's expression hardened. He bit his lower lip and looked away. She saw anger flash in his eyes, an emotion he'd never once directed at her. He turned and started to walk out of the room.

Emma hurried after him. "Wait! Where are you going?"

He didn't say anything, and Emma followed him out of the apartment. He stomped down the steps and kicked open the building's back door. It flew back and struck Emma in the shoulder on the backswing, sending a jolt of pain down her back. The pain barely registered. Everything was going to hell. It was amazing how fast everything a person held dear could be taken away. A thing she should've learned well enough already.

She chased Jake down Fairfax. "Jake! Goddammit! I'm sorry. I wasn't blaming you. Please stop. You're scaring me. We've got to find Abby. Please!"

Jake came to an abrupt halt in the street. He stood there with his back to Emma, his hands clenched at his sides. She watched his shoulders move up and down as he rapidly breathed in and out. He was trying to contain an outpouring of rage. Emma didn't know whether to take the struggle as a hopeful sign. She stopped ten feet from him, too afraid to touch him yet, or to get too close.

But she did manage to speak again. "I'm truly sorry. I fucked up. I got scared and did something really dumb. Please don't hate me. I-I love you, Jake."

His posture changed as the meaning of that last phrase registered. Some of the tension seemed to go out of him. He wasn't breathing so hard and no longer looked ready to explode. In a moment he turned and looked at her. "I love you too, Emma." The stern set of his features seemed to belie his words. But then his expression softened by the tiniest of increments. "I think I've loved you all along." He licked his lips and let out a huge sigh. "But that doesn't matter right now. We've got a little girl to find."

Emma moved closer to him, almost close enough to reach out and touch him—but she kept her arms at her sides. "Yes. Let's find her. But, why were you going this way?"

He pointed to something in the road. "That. I saw it as soon as I came out the door this time."

Emma wasn't sure she wanted to see what he was pointing at, but she made herself look anyway. She gasped and felt something brittle come close to breaking inside her. It was a pink Hello Kitty sandal. One of Abby's sandals. She looked at Jake through eyes full of tears. "It must have fallen off her foot when . . ."

She wasn't able to say it.

So Jake did: "When Aaron came running down this street with our little girl in his arms."

Emma sniffled. "Oh . . ."

Our little girl . . .

Neither had voiced it aloud, but they had already been thinking of her that way. It was a crazy way to feel. They'd known her just over two days. But they were learning that desperate circumstances had a way of accelerating the arc of a relationship. Emma loved Abby as intensely as she would a child from her womb. And now she was gone. Maybe forever. The thought drove back some of the swirling anguish trying to engulf her. Another, even stronger, emotion supplanted it. Anger. A burning, all-consuming rage, coupled with a sudden desire to commit murder.

She looked at Jake. "I'm going to kill him."

Jake blinked. Then he nodded. "Yeah."

The idea of taking another person's life would have repulsed Emma mere days ago. It wasn't the kind of notion civilized, enlightened people were supposed to entertain. Justice was a thing to be meted out by the law, to be determined in an orderly way by courts and juries. But civilization was no more, nor was there any semblance of a police force. Justice—or retribution—was now a thing to be determined on an individual basis by those few left standing.

In her mind, Emma had already judged Aaron Harris and found him guilty.

And the son of a bitch had to hang.

She nodded at the Glock. "We need another gun."

Jake looked up and down the street. "Yeah. But I don't think we've got time to go looking for one."

Emma wanted a weapon of her own. But Jake was right. They had to resume the search. Every second that elapsed with them standing here diminished Abby's already slim chances for survival. She started to say so, but her gaze was drawn then by a glint of something silver winking in the sunlight. At the curb outside a small house a half block down the street was an array of things some departing student had set out for the trash collectors (or local scavengers), including a ratty sofa, a television set, a microwave oven—and an aluminum baseball bat with a handle wrapped in fraying tape.

Emma almost smiled.

She walked past Jake and strode briskly toward the clump of collegiate detritus.

Jake hurried after her. "What are you doing?"

But Emma had already arrived at her destination. She answered Jake by drawing the bat from the overflowing trash can. She felt a kind of wild elation, the sort experienced by warriors about to enter battle. Sure, she didn't have a gun, but this was almost better. The bat had some real heft to it, but she felt it was short enough to wield pretty effectively. She imagined taking a swing at Aaron Harris's head and could almost hear the crack of his skull beneath the force of the blow.

Yeah.

She liked this bat.

She looked at Jake. "Let's get after that motherfucker and take our girl back."

Concern flickered in Jake's dark eyes. "Yeah. Let's do that." He touched Emma's arm, gave her a gentle squeeze. "But let's be careful, too."

Emma grunted. "Sure."

She brushed past him, returning to the fallen pink sandal. She scanned the surrounding area, trying to guess which way Aaron would have gone. And as she did she gripped the club's handle tighter.

~

Aaron Harris couldn't believe his luck. After two days of skulking about and waiting for the right opportunity to strike, he'd been unable to bear it any longer.

Enough fucking around, he'd thought. *I'm just gonna go get the bitch.*

So he'd gone to get her. But things didn't work out the way he'd envisioned. He didn't have Emma Singleton. Yet. But he did have another prize, one he suspected would soon bring the object of his most fervent desires into his possession.

It was funny how things worked out sometimes. You set your sights on one thing, completely devote all your energies toward accomplishing that goal, and something entirely unexpected comes along to alter your plans, and change them in some uniquely delicious way.

Aaron had never been a patient man. This brave new world he was so fortunate to inhabit was one in which he could do whatever he wanted whenever he wanted. He could walk into a store, any store, and walk out with anything he desired. Gold watches, diamonds, rubies, and other jewels. He could drive a car with a list price of a quarter-million dollars off the lot of a dealership or walk into a bank and walk out with piles of money.

He had done all of these things. The surface of a coffee table in the apartment where he'd taken up residence was covered with a fortune in glittering things. The irritating thing was how little pleasure he derived from them. By the standards of the old world, he was a rich man. But the old world had passed, and so this vast bounty was worth approximately nothing. The realization depressed him and served to refocus his attention on the one thing he wanted more than anything else.

Emma Singleton.

But even that had changed. He didn't want to kill her. At least not right away, and maybe not for a long time. He'd explored enough of the city over the last two days to know there was virtually no one else left alive.

So he'd hatched a new plan. A simple, two-phase scheme. Phase one would be the murder of that hippie asshole Emma was shacked up with. Then he'd beat the living shit out of Emma. Work her over and put her in her place once and for all. But he wouldn't kill her. Oh, no. Instead he'd keep her alive indefinitely, have her live out the rest of her miserable days as his slave.

The idea of Emma's subjugation so excited him he decided there was no point delaying the implementation of his scheme. So it was that he'd gone to the apartment he'd spied them coming out of on several occasions. He'd planned to burst in and do it, eschewing stealth in favor of stunning them with sudden, violent action. But fate intervened in a way he couldn't have anticipated. When the jet came roaring by, Aaron burst into the apartment and was stunned to see the little girl standing there all alone.

The little bitch creeped him out, the way she smiled at him and seemed so utterly unafraid of him. But Aaron grabbed her anyway, wrapping her up in his arms and retreating from the apartment. Outside he hurriedly ducked down an alley, crossed over to another street, ran another block, and ducked down yet another alley—and then finally arrived back at his commandeered apartment. He was pretty sure he was safe here for the time being. The area was densely packed with apartment buildings. Emma and her boyfriend would have no idea where he'd gone.

The girl—whose name he still didn't know—regarded him with eyes wide with fear. She made a sound that was muffled by the strip of duct tape covering her mouth. More duct tape, almost a whole roll of the stuff, bound her to a sturdy wooden chair. She squirmed in the chair, managing to make it rock sideways.

Aaron chuckled. "I wouldn't do that if I were you, little girl. You tip that chair over, I'll leave you right there on the floor. And that won't be any fun, will it?" He stood up and slowly crossed the room until he was standing right in front of her. "I know some other things that might be fun, though."

He pressed the flat of the hunting blade against one of her cheeks.

Sudden tears spilled from her eyes.

"Aw. Don't cry, little girl." He giggled now, that mad sound again. "Save your tears for later." He stroked her cheek with the flat of the knife. "For when I kill that tall friend of yours right in front of your eyes."

The girl's body began to shake harder.

Aaron's breath grew shallower as the idea taking shape in his mind grew more vivid. "And for when I make that cunt Emma beg for her worthless life."

He was so caught up in the murder fantasy he failed at first to notice the extraordinary thing happening. A strange sound took him out of the reverie. Then his eyes flicked downward and he gasped at the sight of the strip of duct tape peeling away from the girl's mouth, the sticky grey length moving apparently of its own accord, or as if it was being manipulated by an invisible hand.

Aaron stumbled backward. The knife slipped from a numb hand and clattered on the hardwood floor. He shook his head rapidly from side to side, instinct compelling him to deny the impossible thing he was seeing. "No . . . no . . . no . . ."

The piece of tape came completely away from the girl's mouth, revealing a smile that projected a raging malevolence, an expression that couldn't be the product of any mere girl's still-developing soul. Her eyes sparkled like dark jewels, twin points of focused hate and deadly intent. Her mouth opened and a deep and strange exhalation emerged, a throaty, hoarse sound, a sound hinting at a level of corruption so profound even the likes of Aaron Harris, rapist and murderer, could scarcely comprehend it. A terrible, creaking laughter followed, a big sound the girl's small body couldn't have produced. And yet here it came again, even louder this time, and the girl threw her head back and loosed a demonic bellow so huge it caused Aaron to clamp his hands over his ears and drop helplessly to his knees.

He saw the knife. It lay on the floor no more than three feet to his right. He knew he should grab it and attack the girl at once. Something monstrous had taken possession of her body. Something that would kill him in an instant if he allowed it to get loose. He tried to reach for the gleaming sliver of razor-sharp metal—and found that he couldn't move. He was frozen in place, the muscles and joints of his body locked as rigidly as the limbs of a statue. His gaze went again to the girl and he saw the sadistic amusement glittering in those cold eyes. She was controlling him. He didn't know how, but she was. She'd reached into his mind and switched off his ability to manipulate his body. He was certain she could stop his heart or still his breath with a thought.

He wanted to scream but could not.

The girl laughed yet again and tore free of her bonds in an astonishing display of superhuman strength. Then she came slowly across the room, her gaze locked with his as she continued to leer at him. There was a horrible glee in her expression, a dark joy that elicited a thin, reedy whine from Aaron's constricted throat. He prayed she would kill him fast.

She knelt to pick up the knife. She chuckled. Another sound utterly unlike the laughter of a girl. She traced the edge of the blade with the tip of a finger, then pricked the tip of the finger with the point of the blade. A tiny droplet of blood welled up, and the girl popped the finger into her mouth. She noisily slurped the blood up, then placed the tip of the knife against one of Aaron's eyeballs. He wanted nothing more than to flinch away from that cold touch, from that sharp, insinuating pinpoint hardness. But his eyeball didn't move. His eyelid didn't blink.

The girl laughed yet again.

And, in a voice like something out of a nightmare, said, "Some wishes don't come true, little worm. And some prayers are never granted."

She pushed the knife forward.

Very, very slowly.

13

ON THE ROAD TO NASHVILLE
October 1
2:00 p.m.

The green sign drew Warren's gaze away from the road. The sign showed a distance of 150 miles to Nashville. He pressed the BMW's gas pedal harder and the needle of the car's speedometer edged close to the 90 MPH mark.

Jasmine groaned and shifted in the front passenger seat.

Warren looked at her.

She was still asleep. He hoped she'd stay that way for a while yet. His somewhat reckless driving habits made her anxious and prone to shrill outbursts. But she'd nonetheless ceded the driving responsibilities to him, at least for the remainder of the journey to Nashville. He knew the way and was infinitely more familiar with this area of the country than she was, so it only made sense. Still, she'd been unable to resist chiding him for some of his more egregious acts of daredeviltry. She would gasp, and occasionally shout, warning him not to run into things he could see clearly with his own eyes.

Despite her occasional nervous outbursts, Warren liked Jasmine and enjoyed her company. She was smart. And funny sometimes. He

133

was especially glad to have her around in light of what had happened to Amanda. If he'd had to carry on alone in the wake of that horror, he wasn't sure he would've been up to it.

But carry on he had, through hundreds of miles and several states, enough to see there wasn't much left of this world. They stopped in several cities and smaller communities along the way. At no point had they encountered another living person. In one town they heard a dog barking somewhere in the distance, a forlorn, frightened sound. They called to the animal and spent hours searching for it, but it never turned up. The failure to find the dog depressed them and with great reluctance they resumed their journey south.

It wasn't just the absence of life they found disturbing. There was a fundamental change in the fabric of the world underway. The patches of impenetrable blackness were only one way in which this change was evident. The others were more subtle, but became increasingly apparent as the hours and days slipped by. The remaining world, those parts not eaten by the darkness, was withering. It was early fall in this part of the world, but it seemed to them that there should still have been abundant evidence of greenery in the countryside. But plant life was dead everywhere, turned brown in a shockingly short expanse of time.

Warren privately wondered how long it'd be before the rot infesting the world affected the atmosphere. He imagined a world slowly starved of oxygen and wondered what it would be like to suddenly discover he couldn't breathe anymore. The thought made him shudder, and he decided not to share it with Jasmine. She might think of it herself later—if she hadn't already—but for the time being he saw nothing good in giving her another reason to despair. God knew they had more than enough of those already.

Jasmine stirred again and this time her eyes fluttered open. She stretched, groaned again, and sat up straighter in her seat. "Where are we, kiddo?"

Warren suppressed a groan. "Stop calling me that."

A gently teasing grin touched the corners of her mouth. "What? Kiddo?" She said it in a tone of mock innocence. "That doesn't bother you, does it?"

Warren rolled his eyes. "You know it does. I've only told you that maybe six gazillion times these last couple days. Anyway, we're about 150 miles from home."

"From your home, you mean." Jasmine fixed him with a gaze that was very serious. "What do you expect to find there?" She sighed. "Look, I agreed to go along with this because, hell, it's not like we've got anywhere else to go. But I want you to be realistic. We've both seen what's become of the world. Your chances of finding anyone you knew still alive . . . well . . ."

She didn't have to finish the sentence. They both were well aware what those chances were. Warren was setting himself up for nothing but heartache. He knew it, but he had to go home anyway, had to see what had become of his family with his own eyes. Once that was out of the way, they could decide where to go next. Until then, getting home was his lone priority.

Warren shrugged. "We've been over this. I have to do it."

Jasmine was silent several moments. Warren tried not to fidget while she sat there contemplating things. He hated when women wanted to get deeply analytical about feelings and motivations. Inevitably you had to try to justify gut-level things that made no sense when talked about in a cool, rational way.

"What if I'd said no?"

Warren frowned. "Huh?"

Jasmine's tone was somber, her voice soft and subdued. "What if I'd told you I couldn't have anything to do with this? That we'd have to part ways back there in Maryland?"

Warren looked at her. "Would you have done that? Did you think about it?"

She sighed. "I did, yes."

"So why didn't you?"

She looked at him now. "Mainly because I thought of how desperately alone I felt in those moments after my husband died. I didn't want to feel that way again. And . . . I didn't want you to have to feel that way."

Warren didn't know what to say. He was torn between feeling hurt she'd seriously considered leaving him and being touched she felt concern for him on so elemental a level. His frown deepened. "I just don't get it. Why would you feel like you had to make a choice like that?"

She drew in a big breath, then immediately blew it back out. "Because I know what will happen if we stay together."

"What do you mean?"

"Sooner or later I'll want to kiss you. Or you'll want to kiss me. It's inevitable. We're human beings and we'll need that kind of comfort eventually, and we have no other alternatives. We'll kiss. And we'll make love. And I'm old enough to be your mother, for God's sake."

Her words all came out in a rush. Warren was stunned. He cleared his throat and kept his gaze locked on the road ahead. After several moments of uncomfortable silence, he sighed and said, "I know you've been through a lot. I've been through a lot, too. And I understand what you're saying. I really do. But . . . let's not get ahead of ourselves, okay? Let's focus on today and not freak out about what might happen in the future."

Jasmine didn't say anything for a moment. But she looked slightly less mortified when she at last turned her gaze on Warren again. "Okay. I'm sorry. I'm being stupid, I know. But those thoughts have been bouncing around in my head for days, and I had to let them out."

Warren nodded. "I know what you mean. Besides—" And now he infused his voice with a careful note of playfulness. "—for you to be my mother, you would've had to be, what, sixteen?"

Jasmine smirked. "Seventeen. Kiddo."

"Whatever. Pretty damned young, at any rate."

"It's been known to happen. At younger ages than that, even."

Warren laughed. "Yeah. To crack whores."

They drove on in silence for a minute. The interstate continued to unfurl ahead of them, winding away into the great wide nothing. It was amazing how empty the road was. Well . . . it'd *been* amazing for the first hundred miles or so. Now it was depressing. Sometimes they'd see cars stalled in the middle of the road, and once in a while they'd see gray, drooping corpses propped like crash-test dummies behind the steering wheels. There were fewer of the mangled wrecks in these rural areas. In fact, there were huge stretches untouched by any evidence of the previous week's calamity (save for the occasional black rip in the fabric of the world). Yet there was no sign of life on the highways of America. Just lots of metal coffins. Warren had felt compelled to inspect some of them early on. These cursory examinations revealed no obvious evidence of physical trauma.

Apparently, many millions of people had just up and died.

He thought again of the rot laying waste to the land around them and figured something from that other world—some invisible, odorless substance—had leaked into our world, something toxic to all life on earth. It was the obvious explanation for all this desolation, but it didn't explain why he and Jasmine were still drawing breath. He supposed a tiny percentage of organisms must be immune to the effects of whatever it was.

He wondered whether he should feel grateful for that. To be one of the lucky few allowed to keep on keepin' on. He sure didn't feel lucky. And there wasn't much he was grateful about these days.

In fact, there was just one thing.

He looked at Jasmine. And for the first time he allowed himself to fully ponder the implications of what she'd said. It made him remember some of his initial feelings about Jasmine as they stood in that Exxon parking lot, before Amanda died. He'd been struck by how pretty she was, especially for a woman her age (a thought that now struck him as ageist, oh irony).

So lost in thought was he that the sound of Jasmine's voice nearly made him jump: "Have you thought about what happens if we never find other survivors?"

"Huh?" Warren frowned. Despite everything, this wasn't a possibility he'd entertained. And now that Jasmine had voiced it, he found it profoundly disturbing. "But there must be other people. Not many, obviously, given what we've seen. But it makes no sense that we're all that's left of the human race."

Jasmine's gaze went to the empty countryside for a moment, then she looked at him in a pointed way. "Not necessarily. How many hundreds of miles have we come since we last saw another living human being? Two hundred? Three? More, maybe?" She shook her head. "And what if there are other survivors, but only a very small number scattered over the world? We might never see any of them."

Warren's frown deepened. "Are you trying to depress me? Is that it? Because if you are, you're doing a good job."

Jasmine made a sound of exasperation. "That's not what I'm trying to do at all. I just think we need to prepare ourselves for a pretty bleak future."

Warren laughed, a short, harsh burst of sound devoid of any trace of humor. "It's the end of the world as we fucking know it, and I don't feel even a little bit fine."

Jasmine sighed. "There's no need to be vulgar. I keep coming back to it because I truly believe we are unprepared for coping with this over the long term. You especially."

Warren's frown twisted, became a scowl. "Me? Are you serious?"

Jasmine's nod was emphatic, her gaze unwavering. "I am. What happens after Nashville? When you find that everyone you knew is dead, what then? I'm truly sorry to be so blunt, so heartless, but that's the reality you're facing and I'd be doing you a disservice were I to allow you to believe otherwise."

Warren knew he had no real cause to be angry. Jasmine was only telling him what he needed to hear. But knowing that didn't make hearing it any easier.

"Let's assume whatever's wiped out the rest of humanity doesn't kill us, too." She sounded solemn but steadfast, like a general on the verge of sending troops into the heart of enemy territory—to almost certain death. "Something else might yet come along to eradicate the rest of us. But say we get the opportunity to live out the rest of our natural lives. There are practical things to consider. The machinery of the world will run down sooner or later. Probably sooner, the way things are going."

She was talking now about another aspect of the creeping decay consuming the world, a part so disconcerting they rarely talked about it. The widespread death of plant and animal life could at least be attributed to something understandable, a poison or some other taint from that other world. But how to explain the way all things manmade appeared to be aging at an accelerated rate? Jasmine's BMW, barely more than a year old, had run as smoothly as it must have the day it came off the assembly line the first time Warren drove it. Now, only days later, its formerly finely tuned engine was making the kind of coughing and sputtering sounds he'd expect to hear from that of a poorly maintained old junker. The retractable roof was frayed at the edges and the car's powder blue paint was flaking away. They'd seen much evidence of the same phenomenon in all the blighted cities and townships they'd passed through.

It was all so odd. And inexplicable. Warren could think of no explanation for the phenomenon that made any rational sense. So he tried to think of potential explanations that didn't make rational sense, especially ones that challenged or inverted all his previously held concepts of reality. One theory disturbed him above all others— the possibility that nothing in this world was real. Not himself, not Jasmine, not the decaying world around them. Nothing. Instead everything, the world and all the people he'd ever known, were fleeting fragments of illusion, phantoms haunting the fever dream of some dying god. That would explain how the substance and shape of the world could have become so malleable. It was the kind of wacko idea stoners entertain when high on really good ganja—and then laugh about.

But Warren didn't feel like laughing this time. Screaming, maybe, but not laughing.

Jasmine continued: "What happens when one of us becomes seriously ill? What do we eat if all the canned and processed food of the world goes bad?" She waved at the countryside again. "Do you honestly believe anything will grow in that dead soil?" She looked out the window on her side. "I'll tell you this, Warren Hatcher. If it gets really bad—if we're starving to death, if I come down with some horrible illness—I'll take my life. And if I'm in such bad shape I can't even lift a pistol and put it to my head, I'll want you to do it for me."

Warren didn't say anything at first, but as he thought about it he realized his feelings on the subject very closely mirrored Jasmine's. "Okay. But only if you'll promise to do the same for me."

Jasmine kept her gaze trained on the countryside, but she said, "Okay."

Warren sighed. "I hope it doesn't come to that."

Jasmine didn't say anything. Warren realized she'd been thinking about this all along. She'd danced around the subject all day, trying to work up the nerve to say what she needed to say. He knew then she believed there was a dark end ahead for them, and there was nothing they could do about it. He tried to think of something he could say to ease her mind, at least for a little while, but he came up with nothing.

What he finally did say was, "Do you think there's a God?"

"I don't know." She looked at him. "What do you think?"

He shrugged. "I don't know, either. No one can really know a thing like that until they're dead, I guess, if then. I was raised to believe in a higher power. My parents weren't religious in the traditional sense. They didn't require me to adhere to some strict set of beliefs set down by long-dead men. They believed in a Creator, but not one you could identify as Christian, Muslim, Jewish, or whatever. It was just a fuzzy, non-specific belief in a benevolent force somewhere . . . out there." He indicated the sky above them by lifting his head. "There's no hellfire and brimstone in my past. I was always kind of grateful for that. Now . . . well, now it looks like the prophets of doom were right all along."

Jasmine's eyes narrowed to slits. "So you think this is God's judgment?"

Warren shook his head. "I didn't mean that." But the idea took root in his head, caused him to explore some theories he might not have considered otherwise. "But what if it is? I'm just thinking out loud here, so bear with me. This world around us, the road, the passing fields, the stalled cars . . . this is our reality now. But what if it's only an illusion? Or what if it's something else? What if it's hell?"

A glint of something that might have been fear sparked in Jasmine's eyes. "But that can't be. Can it? We're alive."

Warren arched an eyebrow. "Are we? Maybe we're dead and we don't know it yet. Maybe we've been dead since that first fucking day and everything since then has been an illusion. Think about it. It would explain all the weird shit. The blighted land. A new car that becomes a mobile wreck almost overnight. Think of all the fucked-up things you've seen this last week. Tell me how any of it makes sense. Unless, of course, we're in hell, or some purgatory. Maybe that's it. Maybe we're doomed to wander this highway forever, endlessly—"

"Stop!"

Jasmine's eyes were wide and gleaming now. She looked like a terrified animal, a small and helpless creature cornered by a larger predator.

"You're scaring me."

He sighed. "Sorry. I didn't mean to. I thought you wanted to talk about this."

Her expression softened as some of the tension eased out of her. "I did. Now I don't. If this is hell or purgatory, there's nothing we can do about it, no way we can escape it. I don't want to think about it anymore."

"Fair enough."

But now Warren couldn't stop thinking about it. He didn't believe they were in hell, or even purgatory, but he couldn't dismiss such notions as irrational or implausible. Not after all they'd seen and experienced. If there could be such things as alternate dimensions coexisting side by side—and the evidence of this was indisputable—then surely there could be such a thing as hell. Or dreaming gods. The only tangible evidence he had that he was still on a mortal plane was the beating of his heart. And he wasn't sure he could even trust the reality of that.

A loud BANG! jolted both of them. Warren stared through the windshield at the hood of the car. "Was that—"

The sound came again, louder now. Then again. Then the car jerked hard, making them both yelp. The car shuddered violently and began to slow down. Warren half-expected pieces of it to start falling off.

"Shit!"

He pounded the steering wheel with a fist and pressed the gas pedal to the floor, but it was no good. The car lost power and began to coast. In a few moments it came to a dead stop in the middle of the road. Warren sat there for a while with his hands clenched around the wheel, completely incapable to comprehend what had happened.

Then Jasmine sighed. "Car's dead."

Warren shook his head. "How can that be? How—"

But Jasmine was already opening the door on her side. There was a groan of metal rusted to an impossible degree. She stepped outside and left the door standing open. Warren felt a touch of exasperation, but he immediately realized it was pointless. Why ask how something so inexplicable could happen? There were no answers to be had. So he sighed and pushed a button to trigger the trunk latch. Then he got out of the BMW and stared over the roof at Jasmine. She had put her sunglasses on and was staring at the road ahead.

She said, "So I guess we're on foot now."

Warren moved to the rear of the car, opened the trunk, and hauled out their bags. "I guess so. I don't think we'll find another working vehicle, either." He laughed humorlessly. "The horseless carriage has been consigned to the ash heap of history."

Jasmine joined him at the car's trunk. She picked up a bag and slung it over her shoulder. "You know how I said I didn't want to talk about the weird stuff anymore?"

Warren nodded. "Uh-huh," he said in a careful tone.

Her chin angled downward, then lifted again. She was eyeing him up and down. "It's funny how selective the decay is. My car aged thirty years in under a week. Our clothes look a little careworn. But you and I, physically, seem unaffected."

Warren pursed his lips. "Hmm . . ."

He thought again of the slippery nature of dreams, and of a god in the throes of some awful dementia. And he suppressed a shudder.

Jasmine folded her arms beneath her breasts. "I wonder why."

Warren smiled wryly. "Well, look who's asking the hard questions again. Jeeze, I don't have a fucking clue why the rot isn't affecting us. I'm just glad it's not. Christ, I'd hate to have to deal with incontinence or senile dementia on top of all this insanity."

"Or any number of other common old-age maladies. Erectile dysfunction, for instance."

Warren groaned.

"I'm just teasing you."

"I know." Warren glanced briefly at Jasmine's feet. "How long can you go in those heels? I hope you're not planning a hundred-some-mile hike in them."

Jasmine shrugged. "I'm sure there'll be an opportunity at some point along the way to avail myself of more appropriate footwear." She smiled. "Okay, non-sequitur time, and I don't mean this to be maudlin, but I couldn't have picked a better companion to travel through this horrible time with. You're a good man."

Warren suppressed another groan. "That's sweet of you. But you're lucky you didn't know me before the world went kablooey. I was the quintessential fuck-up. A decent guy, maybe, but a pitiful mess. That's the unvarnished truth."

"Maybe. And maybe your problems in the past were far more superficial than you believed. You've been through a trial by fire and you've come through it admirably."

Warren didn't know what to say to that. He blushed and averted his gaze. Then he felt her fingers lift his chin. She made him look at her again. She was close enough he could feel her breath on his face. She kissed him.

He shuddered. And he let the bag he'd been holding fall from his fingers and land on the road. Then he pulled Jasmine Holtz into his arms and kissed her as fervently as he'd ever kissed a woman. She equaled his passion.

A little while later, they resumed their journey west on foot.

14

Zeke stepped out of the useless Ford Explorer with a grim expression.

Mary Lou screamed.

Again.

Zeke winced and closed his eyes, the shrill sound rattling his skull like the concussion of a grenade. The sting of her palm whipping across his face made his eyes snap open. He saw the boiling rage in her wide blue eyes and stepped backward. She advanced on him and he held up his hands, but she batted them away and seized a handful of his tattered shirt.

"Why won't any of 'em fuckin' work!?" Mary Lou's mouth sprayed spittle as she yelled at him, wetting his face with a fine mist of moisture. She shook him hard and screamed again. "Why, goddammit!?"

Zeke took hold of her wrists and eased them away from his shirt. He wiped saliva from his face with a shirt sleeve. Then he sighed and scanned the Ford dealership's parking lot. He saw rows and rows of trucks and cars, some of which were among the newest vehicles in the world. Next year's models. Mary Lou had been certain they would find a suitable replacement for Zeke's dead Lexus here. As certain as she'd been at the previous dealership. And the one before it. Lot after lot filled with new cars that looked ready for the junkyard.

He threw the Explorer's door shut and moved away from the car, turning his back on Mary Lou. He sensed her coming at him and tensed. The base of a fist pounded a spot between his shoulder blades and made him stumble forward a few steps.

"Don't you walk away from me, asshole!" Her voice grew even more shrill. Zeke wouldn't have thought it possible. She smacked the back of his head now. "Look at me when I'm talking to you!"

Zeke turned to face her. "Please stop doing that."

Her pretty features twisted, forming a deep scowl that almost made her look ugly. "Say what, motherfucker!? Since when do you get to tell me any fuckin' thing!?"

Zeke started to say something, a piece of truth that would only have inflamed her more. A thing he needed to say. Would have to say at some point. But he didn't feel like dealing with it right now. He hadn't technically been Mary Lou's prisoner since that long evening of sex and tears. He was essentially free to go any time he felt like it. But he didn't want to leave her. It was crazy. She remained as dangerous as she'd ever been, as completely nuts as she'd ever been, but he wanted to stay with her. So he was either desperately afraid of being alone or was as crazy as she was—he wasn't sure which yet.

He put a hand on her bare shoulder (she still had never put any clothes on). He gave the tensed muscle there a gentle squeeze and was pleased to feel it loosen up beneath his touch. "I'm not telling you what to do."

"Damn straight."

He nodded and continued to knead her shoulder. "I know. All I'm saying is you need to chill out a little bit."

Mary Lou knocked his hand off her shoulder. "Stop trying to calm me down. Okay, I'm freaking out. Can you blame me? What's wrong with all the cars? Why do they all look so shitty? Hell, why doesn't *anything* in the whole motherfuckin' world work anymore?"

Zeke wanted to know the answer to that himself. He didn't know what to tell Mary Lou, at least in part because there was no rational way to explain what was happening to the world. And he didn't feel comfortable speculating out loud about what might have been causing the rapid decay of most things man-made. He could only think of things based on theoretical possibilities so abstract he knew he could never make Mary Lou understand what he was trying to say. Vague concepts rooted in mysticism and the occult. Scientific principles so advanced they were as baffling to him as the otherworldly stuff. Things that would only be so much mumbo-jumbo to a girl like Mary Lou. Partly because it *was* so much mumbo-jumbo. Just a lot of clueless conjecture.

He cleared his throat. "I just don't know. I know you think I'm pretty smart. But—"

"You were on television." She said this as if it was equivalent to a degree from MIT or a membership in Mensa. "On the fuckin' news, man."

Zeke sighed. "Yeah. But I don't know as much about things as you think I do. I'm a pretty average guy in the brains department. When you see me on television, I sound like I really know what's what. But I'm just reading from a teleprompter most of the time." He shrugged. "Fact is, I don't know a whole lot more about the world in general than you do."

Mary Lou laughed and shook her head. "Well, ain't that a fuckin' gyp. I reckon I oughta trade you in for a rocket scientist fella."

Zeke smiled. He was happy to see that his self-deprecating speech had had the desired effect. In truth, he knew he was significantly smarter than Mary Lou. He was pretty sure her I.Q. didn't quite reach triple digits. Not that it mattered. It wasn't her brains he was attracted to. Hell, he knew he shouldn't find her desirable at all. As always when his mind drifted in this direction, he thought of the massacred family at Mountain High Apartments.

And—as always—he shoved the gruesome memories away.

"I'm afraid rocket scientists are in short supply these days."

Her lips curved into a mischievous grin. "So's every fuckin' thing, baby. There ain't no more doctors. No police. That I'm pretty happy about. No more plumbers. No more garbage men. No more pretty boy actors. No more hot rock stars." Her mouth opened and he saw a pink wedge of tongue flick against her bottom row of teeth. "Mmm, I think I'm gonna miss the rock stars most. Do you like Guns N' Roses?"

"Good to hear you've got your priorities straight. I think we're eventually going to miss the doctors and garbage men more than the rock stars. And anyway, wasn't Mr. Axl Rose a little before your time?"

Mary Lou shrugged. "He's a timeless fuckin' classic, man."

Zeke rolled his eyes. "If you say so."

He clasped hands with Mary Lou and said, "Let's walk out to the street. I want to get the lay of the land again."

"Okay."

Zeke picked up the lone bag they'd been toting around for the last couple days. They'd decided to travel as light as possible and the bag contained all their belongings. Some more clothes for Zeke, a flashlight that no longer worked, a Glock pistol, and a couple of books.

The only thing Mary Lou carried was her beloved shotgun. She walked with it propped over her shoulder. Zeke was pretty sure it wasn't even loaded anymore. Empty or not, the shotgun stayed with her at all times. It was a comfort thing, he realized. She was like some crazed redneck version of Linus from the Peanuts comic strip, with the big gun substituted for a blanket.

They reached the street and came to a stop. This road was called Broadway and it ran through the heart of the city. To their left the road led to the downtown area, the direction from which they'd come earlier in the day. There'd not been much to see there. A lot of dead people, a lot of dead creatures. And there'd been the expected evidence of the doomsday chaos.

In the other direction the road forked off. Broadway continued to the left and West End looked to be home to a thriving business district. Vanderbilt University was situated between these two main thoroughfares. Zeke had visited Vanderbilt once years ago as a guest lecturer and remembered the area reasonably well.

He nodded in the direction of Vanderbilt and Broadway. "Let's go that way."

"Why?"

Zeke shrugged. "No good reason, I guess. I know that area a little. I visited the school there a few years ago."

Mary Lou frowned. "School? What fuckin' school?"

"Vanderbilt."

Mary Lou cackled. "You mean them pussies who can't win a SEC football game to save their fuckin' lives? Them Ivy League motherfuckers?"

"Not quite Ivy League, but I get what you mean. Yeah, those fuckers."

Mary Lou shook her head and laughed again.

Zeke replayed the last thing he'd said in his mind and shook his head, too. Mary Lou was rubbing off on him. In a few more days he wouldn't be able to complete a sentence without saying "fuck" or "fuckin'" or "motherfucker".

As they started down the road, Zeke raised his head to look at a huge billboard that overlooked the fork in the road. The ad was the cover of some female country singer's newest album. She was pretty and looked remarkably like Zeke imagined Mary Lou would look with clothes on and her hair styled in a chic modern way. The billboard woman's face was frozen in a typical come-hither look.

But what got to Zeke was the name of the woman's new album: SALVATION ROAD.

He didn't know whether it was a good omen or an ironically bad one.

~

Captain Flash Wheeler emerged from his hiding place behind a blue metal desk in one of the Ford dealership's service bays and took up a position behind the Ford Explorer the departing intruders had tried in vain to start. He watched the naked woman and her boyfriend amble down Broadway. He recognized the man. He was that VNC guy, Zeke Johnson, the one who disappeared the day before the world died. A boob tube false prophet and idol, a man whose very existence had been a symptom of the sickness that had doomed the world. A blasphemer in the face of the One True God.

An entity also known (to himself) as Captain Flash Wheeler.

Flash had become aware of his divinity, and of his true identity, after surviving that long day of cleansing. Prior to that day, he had been employed by the car dealership as a mechanic. The name on his uniform was "Jeff". As in Jeffrey Wheeler. He had lived his life as the son of Bo and Julie Wheeler, as the third of five children, two of whom had died young after getting mixed up with some bad elements. He reckoned the rest of his mortal siblings were dead now, too.

He always felt a small tug of sadness when he thought about his earthly family. But the hurt never lasted too long, because he knew his true family was comprised of all the living things in the universe(s). He was their Creator, missing from this realm for millennia but returned now to shepherd home the survivors of the Great Cleansing. Thirty-some years ago his essence had embedded itself in the womb of Julie Wheeler, and in all the years since he'd remained blissfully unaware of what he really was.

Until the day of Awakening.

At the dawn of that day he'd been standing with a customer in the lot outside the service bay, the two of them discussing work to be done on the man's Taurus. His only clue that something momentous was about to happen was the sky's unusually dark hue. He'd thought a major storm front was moving in, which should have struck him as odd because the forecast the night before had called for sunny skies all day.

Then he heard that high screeching sound for the first time and looked up to see one of those huge winged demons dropping out of the sky. In those first moments, he'd been too shocked to run for cover, or to do anything other than stand there and meet his fate. The demon swooped over him, close enough that he could make out its face, which had features like a cross between a gargoyle and a bat. A very, very large bat. The wind from its huge, leathery wings blew him to the ground and he nearly lost consciousness as the back of his head struck the Taurus's rear bumper. When he was able to see clearly again, he sat up and watched the demon's teeth tear a fellow employee's throat apart.

He was possessed then by a foolish heroic notion. He got to his feet and stumbled a step or two toward the doomed man and his ghoulish attacker. Then strong hands gripped him from behind and pulled him into the service bay. Mac and Stu, two fellow mechanics, were his saviors. They were yelling things at him, words of panic and terror that were lost to him now. The three men and a handful of other dealership employees took cover in the dealership's offices. Eight of them survived that day. Mac and a secretary named Cindy Brewer left the next day to go looking for their families. The rest of his companions soon fell ill and died, victims of a mysterious and fast-acting malady that induced convulsions of intense agony for a period of hours before finally, mercifully robbing its victims of life.

By the time the last of them perished Flash had experienced the first of his revelations. It came to him in a dream on that second day, when Dean and Stu and Bobbi Jo had still been alive. In that dream a white-robed man with a long, flowing beard stood atop a great mountain and spoke to him in a booming voice. This man, it soon became clear, was an earlier incarnation of himself, speaking to him now through a kind of mental pre-recorded message. The dream image of his former incarnation told him the truth of how he had come to be reborn in the guise of so outwardly ordinary a man. He further revealed that Jeff's true name was Captain Flash Wheeler.

Which sounded like a strange name for a god—especially the One True God—but apparently it was true that God, meaning himself (or Himself, whatever), worked in very mysterious ways. But Jeff—Flash, that is—chose not to indulge in skepticism. Instead, he embraced his new identity with enthusiasm. He logged onto the internet via the departed secretary's computer and started spreading The Word about the second coming of the One True God via message boards and mass emails. But preaching the new gospel that way proved frustratingly ineffective. It was like screaming into a great, echoing void. Either there was no one left in the world, or, more likely, those left alive were a tad too busy struggling to survive to surf the web.

Then the computer stopped working. One day it had been running smoothly, the next it was dead. Flash found this annoying. Despite the lack of anyone online to interact with, the internet access had kept him occupied. When it was gone, he became too keenly aware of an encroaching emptiness. This feeling intensified as every piece of man-made equipment began to follow the computer into technological oblivion. The phones stopped working. Though he couldn't call anyone, he'd been in the habit of lifting the office phone off the cradle to hear the dial tone. Then the power went off, vanquishing both the heat and the artificial lights that made nights alone in the office marginally bearable. He considered driving away. Hell, he had his pick of cars, and a plentiful supply of gasoline. He could leave this place and search for a city with people and a functioning power grid. The people part of that equation was of utmost importance. What good was a God without people to follow Him?

But none of the cars worked. Turn the key in the ignition and all you got was a dead click. If you could even turn the key, that is, or get the keys into ignition slots crusted with rust. Flash couldn't figure it out. It was as if he'd gone to sleep one night and when he woke up it was a thousand years later.

He'd been on the verge of utter despair when he was visited again in his sleep by another vision. In this dream the white-robed man was standing not on a mountain like some prophet out of the Old Testament, but instead stood atop the huge billboard where Broadway branched off from West End. He looked funny up there, walking around in his robes atop the billboard and waving the huge old wooden staff around. Flash had giggled in his sleep at the image.

FROM THE VOID

The man stopped pacing and glowered down at Flash, who was somehow simultaneously asleep here on the office floor and was also standing in the street below the billboard. And when the man leveled that fierce glare at him, Flash knew the ancient deity had heard his laughter. He experienced a moment of searing terror, then reminded himself this was only a dream, or a vision, and that the man couldn't hurt him. He wasn't Freddy fucking Krueger, for fuck's sake. And besides, the man up there was an earlier version of Flash. Why should he fear himself?

"Because you are the One True God," the man's booming voice intoned, his eyes going wide and his hand curling tighter about the staff. "You have a destiny to fulfill. You must venture out into the world and meet your motherfucking destiny!"

Flash was almost jarred awake by the outburst. He'd read the Bible a time or two when he was younger and as best he could recall no one had ever used the word "motherfucking."

The white-robed man rolled his eyes. "I'm merely trying to communicate to you by utilizing a modern vernacular. Is that okay with you?"

"Uh . . ." Flash didn't give a damn about profanity issuing from the mouth of a possible biblical figure, but the knowledge that the guy could read his mind creeped him out. Earlier version of himself or not, that was just wrong. "I . . . suppose so."

Some of the anger left the man's face, but his gaze was no less fierce. "Listen to me very carefully, Captain Flash Wheeler." His voice had dipped to a lower register but remained just as compelling. "You already know what you are. You may not feel it yet. You likely wonder why it is you cannot perform miracles, heal the sick, and whatnot."

Flash was nodding along with every word. "Now that you mention it . . ."

"The reason for this is inextricably linked with your destiny. Your divinity lies dormant within you, a ripe seed hidden away in your soul, biding its time to flower in the light of revelation."

Flash frowned. "Rev . . . you mean like in the Book of Revelations? That would make sense, I guess, what with all this end of the world shit."

The white-robed man sighed. "No." Then his brow furrowed. "Well, maybe. But that's not important right now. I merely meant that your true nature, that of the One True God, will become manifest when you accomplish a special task. I'm talking about the very thing for which you were returned to this realm in this form."

"Uh-huh." Flash was nodding again, but not necessarily in agreement this time. "Could you be more specific, please?"

"No."

"Oh." Of all the possible answers Flash had considered, that had not been one of them. "Okay. I guess."

Then a flash of light encompassed all of existence for a moment. Flash jerked in his sleep and stepped backward in the street. When he could see again, the white-robed man was no longer atop the billboard. He was standing on the street now, maybe a dozen yards from where Flash stood. The man raised his staff and pointed it toward the Broadway side of the road split.

"Your destiny awaits you here, down Salvation Road."

"Er . . . actually, that road's Broadway."

The old man smiled, just barely, the corners of his mouth dimpling as a sound vaguely like a chuckle rumbled in his throat. It was the first time Flash had seen a less than serious expression on the man's face. Seeing it eased his fear a little.

"So it is." The man lowered his staff and regarded Flash more soberly. "But it is also Salvation Road. Know this, and know it well. You are a deity. You are you as I am me and we are all together. I'm paraphrasing, of course, but you get my drift."

"No." Of this at least Flash could be certain. "I don't."

"Have you never listened to the Beatles?"

"They were a little before my time, I guess."

The old man shrugged one shoulder. "Oh. Have you not been paying attention? I merely mean that we are parts of a greater whole, interlocking pieces of a larger truth. The body you inhabit is mortal flesh. It can be hurt. It can be killed. But that piece of you that is of the divine can never be extinguished and so you have no reason to fear what lies ahead."

Flash blinked rapidly. "Uh . . ."

"Don't try to process it all now, son. You have lived thirty-some years as a mortal. As a human being. And now the survival of what remains of your race is in your hands." The old man nodded in the direction of what he called Salvation Road. "A momentous thing will happen somewhere down there. A force that loves chaos and revels in bloody death lurks there. The darkness overtaking this world was unleashed by it. You, Flash, will shine a holy light into that darkness and turn it back."

FROM THE VOID

Flash wasn't sure about this. Being the One True God seemed a lot more fun before this Moses-looking motherfucker started in with the sacred duty crap. Part of him, the significant part that was still an ordinary guy, a mechanic and a fan of the WWE, wanted to wake the hell up and get the fuck out of Dodge. But another part of him was growing stronger by the moment, that bit of glowing consciousness that instinctively recognized the truth of what the scary man was telling him. There was something noble in that part of him, something brave and resolute, and it was eager to embrace this higher calling.

He sighed. "Fine. But how exactly am I supposed to do that?"

The man smiled again, but there was a deeper shade of sadness in the expression this time. "You will know when the time comes. Just as you will know when the time has come to begin your journey down Salvation Road."

"If you say so."

"I do." The man's image was becoming fuzzier as he talked. He was disappearing. Flash could see the outlines of buildings through his ephemeral form. And his voice took on an echoing quality. "One more thing. Two travelers will appear on the morrow. A man and a woman. You are not to approach them. Remain in hiding until they are gone, and do not follow them when they have left."

"Why not?"

But the old man was gone.

When Flash awoke on the office floor, he tried his best to convince himself it'd only been a dream and not a vision. He told himself the whole One True God thing had been a delusion from the beginning. He'd been through a lot, and he had simply cracked under the strain. In a still-functioning world, they'd be fitting him for a straight-jacket and sending him to the loony bin.

It sounded good. It sounded believable, even.

But he knew he was sane.

He felt in his gut that everything the man in his visions said was true, even the stuff he hadn't been able to understand. Especially that stuff, maybe. The realization alternately depressed and scared him, but what could he do?

And today the final, irrefutable bit of evidence had arrived to cast away all remaining scant traces of doubt.

The two travelers.

Flash watched them disappear down Broadway, sending a prayer in their direction as they moved down a dip in the road and out of his sight. Then with a heavy sigh he returned to the office to meditate and wait for guidance.

To wait for that moment or subtle signal that would tell him it was time.

Time to go meet destiny.

15

NASHVILLE, TN
October 2, 9:00 a.m.

They were arguing again. The same goddamned argument they'd been having for three days now. There'd been times when Emma had felt her anger rise up to a degree that frightened her. In those moments she wanted nothing more to drive a fist into the middle of Jake Dunham's face. There had been a time or two when she might actually have done it, but he was so tall that attempting it would have been a comical exercise in futility. Ah, but there was the aluminum baseball bat in her hands, her blunt instrument of choice. She could sure shut him up with one swing of this fucking bat.

Emma replayed that last thought in her mind and felt a strong surge of self-loathing. What had become of her? She couldn't allow this anger to consume her.

Still . . . the emotion stubbornly refused to recede. Nor did the desperation fueling it. She chewed hard on her lip a moment and refused to look Jake in the eye. They were on an external second-floor landing of an apartment building in Hillsboro Village. Her gaze swept over the parking lot, over the array of useless cars and motorcycles, and over the roofs of the densely packed neighboring apartment buildings. Over the course of the last few days they'd methodically searched every unit in many of those buildings. The ones they hadn't gotten to yet, they soon would, because so far they'd found no trace of Abby or her abductor—and Emma would not abandon this search so long as she was drawing breath.

She sighed and reluctantly allowed her gaze to drift back to Jake. She looked into his sharply gleaming eyes. She saw anger there, too. But not just that. There was concern there. Concern not just for the missing girl, but for Emma. And more than a little bit of fear. He was worried she was on the verge of cracking. Well, he was right. What he failed to grasp was that she didn't care. Not one little fucking bit.

"Look, you know I'm right." The anger was still there, was just the merest breath away from exploding outward, but Emma managed to at least *sound* calm and level-headed. "Every second we waste is another second Abby is with that man. If she's even still alive." Here her voice wavered slightly, but she recovered quickly and pressed on. "This whole process is too goddamned slow. It'll go a hell of a lot faster if we split up and search two apartments at a time."

And already Jake was shaking his head as vigorously as he had every time she voiced this opinion. And again Emma felt that insane surge of anger. This time she was perilously close to slipping over the edge. She didn't want that to happen. Oh, God, she didn't. And Jake, damn him, didn't seem to realize how precarious her grip on sanity was.

"Nuh-uh," he said, still shaking his head. "We just can't do that. You know how dangerous he is. Hell, we don't even know if he's in any of these apartments. I don't know why you're so convinced he is."

A fever began to burn behind Emma's eyes, and a dollop of perspiration appeared and rolled away from her left temple. Couldn't he see she simply couldn't take this any longer? This bullheadedness of his made her want to scream. Instead she said, "I've told you. It's very simple. He didn't have a big head start on us. He simply *had* to have taken refuge nearby."

Jake sighed. "You say that like it's fact, but it's not. He could be far away from here. But, God forbid, if he is here, and you happen to barge into his hiding place alone."

Breath hissed through Emma's tightly clenched teeth. "I. Can. Handle. Myself." Each word was a terse burst of menace and impatience stretched too far. Wild-eyed, she brandished the baseball bat like a serial killer stepping to the plate. She was pleased to see Jake take an involuntary step backward. Maybe it meant she was finally getting through his thick fucking skull.

And maybe it only meant he was becoming afraid of her.

Emma waited for the expected surge of self-loathing to come again. This time, however, it did not. Later, she would likely be repulsed when she replayed this whole incident in her mind, but right now she didn't care. Right now Jake Dunham needed a dramatic shock to his system, something to shake him out of this obnoxious role of the protective, chivalrous male.

"Get this straight, Jake. This argument is over." She waved the bat again and Jake took yet another step backward. "We've done it your way for days, and if we keep doing it your way, we'll never find Abby. So now we're gonna do it my way. You shut your fucking mouth for a while and do what I tell you." She nodded at the door behind Jake. "You look there—" Her head jerked in the direction of the adjacent apartment. "And I'll look in there. Now."

Jake's expression had changed, hurt replacing concern. Seeing it made Emma's heart ache, but she couldn't back down now. Hurt feelings could be sorted out later, after they found Abby. And if not—if they never found Abby, and if the hurt ran too deep—then so be it.

She turned away from Jake, planted one foot and drove the other hard against the apartment's closed door. The rotting wood splintered. The decay of all things manmade was the one thing that had worked in their favor thus far. Gaining access to locked rooms and buildings was never difficult. One more kick and the door flew open, the locking mechanism remaining in place as it separated from the rest of the wood. Refusing to even acknowledge Jake's hurt feelings with a parting glance, Emma rushed immediately into the apartment.

It was dark inside. The power had been off for days, so she was accustomed to entering rooms cloaked in shadow. For safety's sake, they'd confined their searches to daylight hours. And right now the sun was high in the sky and darkness was many long hours away. Still, there was something about this darkness that sent a shiver through her. It was a deeper darkness. And she knew with sudden certainty that she'd happened upon a Bad Place. The source of her anxiety wasn't just the deeper shade of black overlaying everything. This darkness felt . . . sticky. Like something that could draw her in and swallow her.

A line of poetry floated into her consciousness—strangely, she heard it as the whisper of a little girl: "Will you step into my parlor?" said the Spider to the Fly.

She shuddered.

She suddenly wanted nothing more than to flee this place. To grab Jake and get far, far away. Or leave his sorry, obstinate ass behind if he decided to play Mr. Stubborn again. In that moment—fleeting though it was—she wavered on the brink of abandoning the search for Abby and placing her own safety above everything else.

Then the moment was gone.

She drew in a deep breath, counted slowly to ten, and listened to the heavy THUMP-THUMP-THUMP of her heart. She was still afraid. Hell, yes. But she wasn't going to surrender to fear. She tightened her grip on the bat and lifted it a little higher, anticipating an imminent battle with . . . something.

She still couldn't precisely identify what was wrong here. There was no visual evidence of any reality rips. The place looked as whole as it had been prior to doomsday (albeit a good deal more decrepit). The wrongness was based on nothing more than feeling. Something alien was here, some dark essence not visible to human eyes, and she felt it more strongly with each step she took deeper into the apartment.

She swallowed hard as a film of sweat formed on her forehead. A bead of moisture gathered at the spot between her eyebrows, then began to roll down her face. A salty taste filled her mouth. By the time she realized her legs were shaking she was already several feet into the living room.

A coffee table was covered with mounds of glittering things. Diamonds and rubies. Gold watches and rings. Pieces of shimmering Waterford crystal. These jewels seemed unaffected by the rot laying waste to everything else, and so only amplified the shabbiness of this crumbling abode. She let the glitter hypnotize her for an indefinable period of moments. Then she bit her lip hard, piercing soft flesh and drawing a drop of blood into her mouth. She gritted her teeth and tried to bring back the tight focus of her rage. She had to be very careful here. There was something very like dark magic at work in this tainted place. She felt as if she'd nearly succumbed to a spell, a supernatural trap meant to stupefy her long enough to leave her vulnerable.

The little girl's lilting voice came again: *Will you walk into my parlor?*

Emma blew air through her nostrils. "Shut. Up."

157

FROM THE VOID

She moved to the center of the living room and turned slowly around, keeping the bat cocked at her shoulder. She saw an entertainment center filled with an array of electronic equipment that might have impressed her a week ago. Now it was a pile of useless junk. She saw a sofa and a recliner. The leather upholstery looked cracked and faded. More junkyard debris. She saw a bookshelf and realized one of the underlying smells she'd detected upon entering was mildew combined with the odor of rotting paper.

A nervous breath shuddered out of her as she completed her survey of the living room. There was nothing alive here. But the piles of useless jewels intrigued her. She had no doubt it was all genuine stuff. God knew how many thousands of dollars it had been worth a week ago. She doubted the apartment's original tenant had left this strange and empty treasure here. Not unless he or she had been a jewel thief. But she doubted that. Something about all this soulless glitter made her think of Aaron.

Prior to snatching Abby he'd had days during which he might have been engaged in any number of oddball activities. A man as superficial as Aaron Harris wouldn't be able to resist the opportunity to avail himself of a fortune that was there for the taking.

This had been his hiding place. These jewels his spoils of the apocalypse. The certainty of it struck Emma hard. Her breath exploded out of her, as if she'd been struck in the gut with a medicine ball. A helpless whimper issued through her lips. A terror beyond even what she'd felt upon entering this awful place consumed her. Because if Aaron had been here, that meant—

"Abby was here," she said in a voice as brittle as an old man's hip.

Her gaze snapped to the left. She took in the tiny dining room—with its table piled high with packets of rotting cash—and the small adjacent kitchen area, and saw at once no one was there. Then her eyes flicked right, to the dark hallway beyond the living room, and she experienced a moment of precognition so intense it nearly robbed her of all strength. She braced the end of the bat against the floor to keep from falling to her knees.

Then, when she was certain she could proceed without tumbling face-first over the glittering coffee table, she raised the bat again and began to move toward the hallway.

And the darkness there really was deeper. She felt the air growing thicker around her as she neared it. It occurred to her it might be a really good idea to call out to Jake now. To hell with their petty war of wills. She did *not* want to face this alone. She opened her mouth, but no sound came forth. Her jaw trembled as the words she hoped to summon fizzled and died before reaching her tongue.

She simply could not speak here. Not now. She was close to the heart of some dark secret. Something that radiated a malign sickness of the soul. She didn't wish to alert it to her presence. Even her breathing—and even the beating of her heart—seemed too loud. A more rational part of her mind spoke up, reminding her that if anything was here (whether it was Aaron or some unfathomable supernatural entity), it had likely been aware of her intrusion into its lair from the moment she'd kicked the front door open.

The thought stopped her in her tracks.

She came as close to surrendering to cowardice as she had at any point since entering the apartment. But she just stood there, quietly shaking, allowing several seconds to pass while her resolve reasserted itself. She moved into the hallway and felt an unnatural cold envelop her, a deep chill that raised goosebumps and penetrated her flesh to the bones.

The darkness swallowed her.

Yes, that was precisely how it felt. Because now she could see nothing. There was only black. Her heart lurched and panic burst in her brain like a struck match. She whirled about and prayed she'd see a dimly visible living room. But there was only more blackness. It was as if she'd been sucked into some horrible, lightless void, a realm entirely removed from her own world. The spark of panic grew into a fire and she began to hyperventilate.

Christ! How could she have been so dumb? Her desperate need to recover Abby had obliterated her common sense, as well as her ability to reason objectively. *Of course* the hallway had seemed unnaturally black. It wasn't there anymore. She'd walked straight into one of the black openings through which those hideous creatures had come surging into her world. The invaders were all dead, but many more of their winged and screeching red-eyed brethren would be lurking here, waiting for idiotic humans to wander into their realm. She might well have surrendered utterly to panic and terror then . . .

But then she heard something.

A sound very like one that had escaped her own lips moments earlier. A human sound. A pathetic, mewling sound.

A whimper.

She forgot her own fear for a moment and focused on the sound.

FROM THE VOID

The sound came again. And again. She swallowed thickly and willed herself to focus only on concrete reality, rather than on the absence of visual proof of her location. She tested the ground beneath her feet, rocking her Doc Martens slowly up and down. There was a yielding softness there, with hardness beneath it. She laughed in the echoing darkness.

Carpet.

She let out a big breath. Then she reached out with the bat and felt it connect with something solid to her left. She moved the bat in the opposite direction and detected another solid construct to her right.

Hallway walls.

She laughed again.

And how strange that sound was here in this sticky darkness, with this chill sliding over her flesh like a madman's cold caress. Yet she couldn't help it. The relief she felt at still being in her own world—even as tainted as it had become—was overwhelming. She laughed some more, stopping only when she heard the whimper yet again.

She tried to discern whether it was a sound made by an adult or a child. Because if that was Abby making that sound, she would have to force herself to push deeper into this awful, perfect blackness. If it was Aaron, he could rot here as far as she was concerned.

Again the sound came.

It was weak. A frail, brittle thing dancing on the fine edge of death. It was the sound of someone who wanted to cry, but hadn't the strength. The sound was so pitiful it stirred sympathy within her. Even though she was certain it was not Abby making that sound. She was certain she detected a faint masculinity in that trembling timbre. Which meant that it could only be Aaron. Some of the darkness that had been filling her heart for days began to recede. Her hate for the man didn't die. Regardless of how much he was suffering now, he was a monster. But her basic humanity began to reassert itself, because this was the sound of someone who had endured unspeakable torture. She had no firsthand experience with such things, but she felt the truth of it as clearly as she'd ever felt anything.

She cleared her throat, swallowed hard, and managed a single word: "Aaron?"

The whimper again, louder than before, followed by a rasping moan. Then a sound that might have been a single, cracked word. But that dim voice was too distant to be intelligible.

Keeping the bat poised in front of her, she began to move forward again. "Keep talking. Or moaning. Whatever sound you can make. I'm coming."

He managed another brief moan, a sound that turned into a weak sob.

I'm coming, she thought. *I am, really. But not to help you, you miserable bastard. I'm coming to find Abby. If she's dead in there, you haven't even begun to suffer. And if she's gone, I'm putting you out of your misery, you son of a bitch.*

One step forward became two. Then three and four. Then ten. And still there was only blackness. But then the moaning became more distinct. There was a flash of light to her left and she took an involuntary step sideways, raising one hand to shield her eyes against the glare. She blinked hard and carefully peered beneath her hand.

What she saw was a doorway that had swung suddenly open. Beyond the doorway was what had formerly been someone's office. There was a desk with a computer. And a folding, cafeteria-style table against the far wall, upon which sat a fax machine and copier. Huddled in a ball on the floor beneath the table was Aaron Harris.

That thirst for vengeance, there all along but lately consigned to the background as she dealt with more pressing concerns, became paramount again. This consuming rage pushed her forward and through the doorway before she was even conscious of being in motion. She stopped abruptly inside the doorway, the cold hand of fear seizing her heart again. She could see the whole room now. Abby wasn't here. But there was a chair in the middle of the room that had strands of shredded duct tape clinging to it. There were dark stains on the chair and the floor beneath it.

He tortured her there, a sinister voice seemed to whisper in her ear. *That's her blood. And when he was through making her suffer, he killed her.*

"Shut up," she said, hoping that leering, reptilian corner of her subconscious would fall quiet once and for all.

She looked at Aaron, curled there in a fetal ball, hands over his face, a low moan issuing through fingers that looked white as bone. She tested her grip on the bat, swinging it in a practiced way, like a baseball player warming up in the on-deck circle. In her mind she saw the fat end of the bat connecting with his skull. The image was so vivid she could almost hear the CLACK! of metal striking bone. She was at once repulsed by and sickly satisfied with the grisly visualization. She imagined raising the bat again, bringing it down and reveling in the sound of this monster's skull shattering. A warm, almost sexual

161

tingle ignited somewhere inside her and spread like wildfire through her body.

What's happening to me? she wondered.

Had she actually become so debased in the course of just a week that she might actually get off via the act of killing another human being? That couldn't be. Only very sick people could derive that level of pleasure from murder. This was more evidence something was fundamentally wrong in this place. Something evil and insidious had seeped into her and was poisoning her spirit.

She felt the undeniable truth of this, but it didn't change anything.

That sick warmth was still there—was in fact intensifying.

And it was not to be denied.

She imagined the bat coming down again and again, reducing the monster's head to a pulpy crimson mess. She couldn't see her face of course, but had there been a mirror in the room, the sight of her wide-eyed, smiling visage would have horrified her. The desire to kill became such that her reasons for committing the act hardly mattered. She was only dimly aware of droplets of saliva leaking from the corners of her mouth as she moved deeper into the room, raising the bat as she advanced on her helpless quarry. The thing that stopped her was an upward glance as she neared the table.

Her gaze locked on the light fixture and the blazing electric bulb on the other side of an opaque square. She stared at the light a long time, her fuzzy mind laboriously trying to discern what was wrong with this sight. And when it came to her, the fog swirling in her mind dispersed at once.

She frowned and gave her head a hard shake. "What . . . the . . . fuck?"

How could the power be on in here? Everywhere else in the city, things that ran on electricity were as dead as the dinosaurs. But, somehow, in this one room in this horrorshow apartment, current still coursed through hidden wires. It made no sense. In order for current to flow, a power grid would still have to be functioning somewhere. And she'd seen enough in the world outside this place to be pretty sure that wasn't the case. So what she was seeing wasn't possible.

Unless . . . well, unless something other than the machinery of man had restored the power to this grim corner of the world. Some force that wanted her to see something. For the first time since entering the room, she wanted something other than vengeance.

She wanted to flee.

But she could not. She had come all this way. Turning back now would render all she had endured a waste. So her gaze went to Aaron. Her quarry. Her prey. And he did look like a cornered animal, a wounded, whimpering beast with his leg caught in the steel teeth of a trap. Though she wasn't aware of it, the corners of her lips rose upward and she made a low sound of pleasure.

When she reached the table, she swept the fax machine and copier to the floor, where they landed amid a sound of shattering plastic. Then, with a sound halfway between a grunt and a rising roar, she gripped the edge of the table with one hand and flipped it over. Aaron's legs flailed weakly as he pushed himself up against the wall, seeking shelter no longer available, and covered his face with his hands.

Smiling broadly, Emma gripped the bat with both hands again and raised it over her head. "Look at me."

But the broken man's hands did not come away from his face. He wailed and shook his head. Emma snarled and drove the tip of a heel hard into his stomach, causing him to wail again and raise his knees to his chest. Emma screamed and kicked repeatedly at his legs, driving them back and exposing his stomach again. This was followed by a series of brutal kicks to his abdomen. Still, maddeningly, the condemned man's hands remained over his face.

Emma screamed again. "I WANT YOU LOOKING AT ME WHEN I KILL YOU, MOTHERFUCKER! I WANT YOU TO SEE MY GODDAMNED FACE WHEN YOU DIE!"

Despite enduring what must have been overwhelming agony, he refused to acquiesce to her wishes. And Emma's patience, what tiny shred of it still existed, that is, evaporated. She kicked hard at his hands, mashing and snapping the bones in his fingers with the heel of her boot.

So that at last his hands came away from his face.

The bat fell out of Emma's hand. Her mouth opened wide and she forgot to breathe for a long moment while her reeling mind attempted to process this fresh horror. A whimper died in her throat and a constricted rush of breath came rolling out of her open mouth instead.

"No," she managed to say at last. What she was seeing was not only horrible but inexplicable. She didn't speak out of pity for Aaron. She still had none. That one word was born of her mind's inability to accept this hideous and bizarre reality.

163

It came again. "No."

His eyes were gone. Something hot, some burning tool, had been applied to the empty sockets. Where once there had been eyes there now were only twin patches of cauterized flesh. The head twitched and rolled upward, instinct causing him to search for something he couldn't see. How strange his face looked without eyes. With empty eye sockets. Like a mask, a bland, featureless thing one might buy at a drugstore for Halloween.

Emma's face twisted into a grimace and her stomach did a slow roll. She was grateful she hadn't eaten yet today. As it was, her gag reflex caused her throat to spasm dryly. She heard a sound behind her, the creak of a floorboard, and jumped, a scream bursting from her lungs. Sure she was about to face the person or thing responsible for Aaron's horrific condition, she scooped up the bat and whirled to face the intruder.

And tears sprang to her eyes when she saw it was only Jake. "Oh, Jake . . ."

The blanched pallor of his cheekbones told her the trip through the hallway had been no less harrowing for him. Her eyes beseeched him with a silent desperation that penetrated any lingering hurt he may have been feeling from her earlier treatment of him.

He moved farther into the room and peered past her at Aaron.

An expression of disgust creased his features. "Oh my God. What happened to him?"

Emma tried to say something, but the words emerged as an unintelligible croak. She cleared her throat and drew in a calming breath. "I don't know. I . . . I was about to . . . ." Tears filled her eyes again and she wiped them away with growing impatience. "I was about to kill him. He had his hands over his eyes. I wanted him to see me. So I kicked him. And . . . and . . ."

Jake came to her then. He laid a hand on one softly shaking shoulder. "It's okay." He sighed. "Have you had a chance to ask him about Abby?"

Emma shook her head and sniffled. "No . . . I . . . I just . . ."

He made a shushing sound. "All right. Okay." He pulled her close and kissed the top of her head. The simple affectionate gesture was enough to dispel the last traces of the dark urges that had infected her. She felt suddenly human again. She recalled the arousal (there was no other word for it) she'd felt moments ago and a sudden sob rolled out of her. Followed by another. And another.

Jake pulled her into his arms and she buried her face in his chest. He stroked her hair and made more shushing noises while she cried it out. After several moments of this, she forced herself to snap out of it. This was neither the time nor the place for a breakdown. She broke the embrace and tilted her head up to look Jake in the eye.

Her voice was small and frightened. "There's something wrong here."

"No kidding."

She shook her head. "No, I mean *really* wrong. Really, really fucking wrong. There's something . . . not natural at work here. Some kind of dark magic. I feel like Alice after stepping through the looking glass. Or whatever the Satanic equivalent of such a thing would be."

Jake frowned. "Come on. Be serious. You don't think . . . what, the devil, or Satan, whatever is responsible for this."

Emma shook her head again. "No. Not exactly. But something just as bad." Her voice teetered for a moment on the brink of breaking again. She swallowed hard and pressed on. "Something from that other world, maybe. Something worse than those demon things. You came through that hallway. I know you felt that wrongness." Her gaze flicked upward a moment before settling again on Jake's skeptical expression. "And look at that light. We have to get out of here."

Jake sighed. "Yeah. But let's have a word with Mr. Child-snatcher first."

He clasped hands with Emma and they moved closer to the trembling figure still huddled against the wall.

"Aaron, I want you to listen to me." Jake's voice rang out with an authority Emma hadn't expected, but she was glad to hear it. It helped her get in touch with her own inner strength again. "I can see that something bad happened to you. You've suffered. Maybe you feel like dying, or like you've got nothing left to lose anymore. But I'm here to tell you that's not the case. You're still alive, buddy. And that means you can still hurt some more. Whoever did this to you may have taken your eyes, but I know your mind's still intact in there. Unless you want me to go to work on some other sensitive areas of your body, you'll tell me some things I want to know." He paused a moment to let the words sink in. "You hear me, Aaron? I'd like an answer right now."

A strange, dark thrill slithered through Emma as she listened to these words. They were the same words—or close enough—she'd wanted to say to Aaron herself before the killing fever gripped her.

Thinking that scared her. Made her think the soul sickness was getting a grip on her again. And maybe on Jake, too.

Aaron rolled onto his side and coughed hard. A wad of pink-and-yellow phlegm flew from his mouth and stained the carpeted floor. Then he sighed. And said, "I hear you."

Jake nodded, a gesture that had the startling effect of nearly causing Emma to laugh. Why nod for a man who can't see? A corner of her mouth twitched, nearly lifted in a smile. She bit down on her lip and tried to remain focused long enough for Jake to conduct this interrogation.

Jake said, "Who did this to you? Where's Abby?"

And now there was laughter in the room.

But it issued from a surprising source—the disfigured man on the floor.

Jake's expression sharpened and he took an abrupt step closer to Aaron's prone form. "Nothing's funny here, asshole. Stop laughing, or start hurting. Give us some answers. NOW!"

Aaron seemed to sense the very real threat in Jake's voice because the laughter dried up and gave way to another moan. "I'm sorry. Please . . . it's just that there's something you don't know . . . something you won't believe . . ."

Jake grunted. "Try us."

And now Aaron turned his head toward them. If he still had eyes, his gaze would be locked with Jake's. Seeing this creeped Emma out.

Aaron said, "Abby did this."

There was a long moment of stunned silence.

Jake was seething. "You're fucking with us. We're about done with your shit."

A sound that might have been a giggle trilled out of Aaron's mouth. "Do what you want. Sooner or later I'll be dead, and that's all I want now. But I'm telling you the truth. Abby did this. She's not human."

Jake and Emma exchanged perplexed glances. Emma's immediate instinct was to say this was all a lie. That this was just a madman taunting them with sick untruths in his last moments. But something analytical within her was at work, examining everything she'd known of Kelly and Laura prior to doomsday, lingering for a long time on how she'd never—not once—seen Abby with the women. And on how they'd never once so much as mentioned the little girl.

She could see Jake was thinking the same thing.

But this was crazy.

Right?

There were all kinds of legitimate reasons why neither of them had previously been aware of the girl's existence.

And yet . . .

Emma slipped her hand from Jake's and knelt next to Aaron. "Aaron, this is Emma. What do you mean when you say Abby isn't human?"

"I mean she's not human. There's a real little girl there, but it's just a shell. A host. There's something evil living inside it. Some monster." Aaron swallowed hard, coughed again. "I brought her here. Taped her to that chair. But she broke free. She reached into my mind. She paralyzed me. And she used my knife on me."

Emma still wasn't sure she believed any of this. Believing it would shatter a number of very important illusions she'd constructed for herself in the last several days. But she didn't scoff at what Aaron was saying. She could hear the belief in his voice.

"Where is Abby now?"

Aaron opened his mouth to answer—

—and a lilting, bell-clear feminine voice spoke behind them: "Why, I'm right here." A giggle. "Said the spider to the fly."

Emma surged to her feet and wheeled around. And there was Abby, standing in the doorway. Emma felt none of the relief she'd expected to feel in the moment of reunion. Because when she looked into that insane, blazing gaze, she knew what Aaron had been saying was the truth. Every last bitter word of it.

Aaron wailed and rolled up against the wall again.

Abby laughed. "Pathetic, don't you think? He was fun to play with for a while. Just as it was fun manipulating the emotions of two simpletons."

Emma's eyes welled with helpless tears. Part of her knew it was stupid to lament the loss of something that had never been real—especially in light of the danger they were facing—but she did so anyway. How could she have been so blind? How could she have been so foolish?

Abby threw her head back and laughed heartily. It was a big, expansive sound, bigger than anything a little girl's lungs should have been able to produce. Then, grinning broadly, she locked gazes with Emma. "How? I'll tell you how. Because you are a primitive, stupid thing. Like the rest of your race. I let that man take me because I thought it might make things more interesting for me. And it has. Oh, it has."

Emma's hand sought Jake's, found it, and pulled him close. She savored this bit of simple human intimacy, knowing she might never experience it again. She tried to keep the quaver out of her voice when she said, "What are you going to do to us?"

Abby sucked moisture from the corners of her mouth and rolled her shoulders in an exaggerated shrug. "Well, let's see. Hmm, you know, I think I'm going to let you go."

She laughed.

Just taunting us, Emma thought bitterly.

But Abby gave her head an emphatic shake. "It's true. I'm letting you go." She laughed again. "Are you listening? I'm letting *you* go." Heavily emphasizing the word "you" this time. "Your boyfriend, though . . ."

Before Emma had time to consider the implications of this, Abby's head snapped forward and her nostrils flared. Her mouth opened wide and something black emerged. An indistinct black mist. It coalesced in the air, became a dark bolt, and shot toward Jake. The bolt punched through the middle of his face and exited through the back of his head before he could so much as flinch.

The body toppled to the floor and Emma screamed.

And screamed.

"Enough."

The next scream died in her throat at the sound of Abby's voice. "There aren't many of you humans left to play with. So I'm leaving you alive for another day. But make no mistake, sweet Emma. I'll be back for you."

Abby turned and walked out of the room, whistling a cheerful tune as she went. By the time the sound receded the unnatural blackness gripping the hallway was gone. And the light in the ceiling fixture snapped out.

Emma stood in the natural gloom of the room, alone now except for Aaron. Her mind went blank, a defensive move on her psyche's part.

She dropped to her knees. And a moment later toppled over.

Unconscious.

16

One of the special joys of Warren's younger days had been the too-infrequent occasions when his dad, Earl Hatcher, would take him to the local minor league baseball team's home games. Earl was a truck driver and so wasn't home enough to make it a regular thing, but every summer the father and son would go to three or four games at Greer Stadium in Nashville. Greer was a typical minor league ballpark, small and utterly lacking the pizzazz and glamour of a major-league park. This distinction was not so evident to the average little kid, however, and to Warren a visit to Greer was every bit as momentous an occasion as a pilgrimage to the House That Ruth Built was for a Yankees fanatic.

He and his dad always sat in the outfield bleachers beyond the right-field wall. What his dad called the "cheap seats." His dad's idea of a joke. At Greer, all the seats were "cheap seats." Earl Hatcher was not a social man (a trait inherited by his son) and he preferred this sparsely populated section of the stadium to the more densely packed bleachers along the first and third base lines. Some nights they had the entire section to themselves. Earl was a big baseball fan and he often became so immersed in the games he appeared to forget his son was there with him.

But Warren didn't mind. Just being at the ballpark in the company of his dad was enough to keep him happy. He would fall into fantasy at times, sometimes so deeply he lost track of what was happening in the game for more than an inning at a time. A favorite fantasy involved having the ballpark all to himself, utterly devoid of other fans, players, and concessions workers. He imagined being able to walk unfettered across the bright green outfield grass, saw himself running around the bases and sliding into home plate head-first like Pete Rose. The fantasy was tantalizing, and more than a little frustrating, mostly because he knew he'd never have the opportunity to do those things. Not like those lucky kids who—through some complicated process he couldn't fathom—got invited onto the field to participate in some special pregame ceremony or activity. It was firmly in the realm of the Not Possible.

Walking straight down the middle of this stretch of interstate reminded Warren strongly of those feelings. Until recently, doing this would get you flattened by an oncoming semi within seconds. But now the semis were rusting hulks. Artifacts of a prematurely ancient culture. The asphalt beneath his feet was cracked and faded. He felt like a time-traveling archaeologist traipsing through the ruins of a civilization fallen to dust long ago. But he also felt a bit like a little boy walking across the green grass of a ballpark's outfield. No longer fantasizing about a waltz through the realm of the Not Possible, but lost in the terrifying land of Things That Should Not Be.

He glanced to his right at Jasmine. Her expression was unreadable, but he thought he detected a glint of faraway things in her unfocused gaze. It was the way she always looked lately. Making love hadn't brought them closer emotionally. If anything, it'd had the opposite effect. She seemed cooler to him, less responsive to his efforts to engage her. Today, for instance, they'd exchanged hardly more than a half dozen sentences since this morning.

Ah, but she still came to him in the night. With a desperate desire burning in her eyes, pulling off his clothes, and fucking him with a fervor that always excited him in the moment—but always left him puzzled in the awkward ensuing silence. He'd tried talking to her about it that first night, but not since then. She'd listened to his earnest entreaties in stony silence that time, then had quietly dressed and walked away, leaving him to sleep alone. He hardly slept at all, and what little sleep he did get was fitful and plagued by dreams about red-eyed zombies and demons. When the sun came up the next morning, he was surprised to see her standing near him, her bag slung over her shoulder, apparently ready to resume their journey together. He'd half-suspected he'd never see her again. And though he'd been overjoyed to see she was still with him, he'd forced himself not to express this feeling, lest she leave him again.

He knew he had to cut her some slack. She clearly remained uncomfortable about being intimate with someone so young. Also, she was still grieving over the loss of her husband, the love of her life. Probably she imagined she'd betrayed his memory in some way by sleeping with another man so soon after his death. Those things alone likely would have been enough to make her moody and distant. Add the end of the world into the mix and . . . well, he had to count himself lucky to have her around at all. And as long as she was still around, there was hope. She might yet resolve the angst consuming her and then they could be closer.

She became conscious of his gaze. He could tell by the way she closed her eyes and breathed a slow sigh. As if being looked at was a burden. Her eyes fluttered open and she looked at him, her expression wary. "What?"

Warren's heart jittered. "Um . . . nothing."

"Okay."

Warren opened his mouth to say something else, to tell her to cease this quiet hostility once and for all. He wanted her to admit they needed each other. But he said no such thing. He closed his mouth and let his gaze go back to the road ahead.

The Nashville skyline loomed off to the right, beyond a line of dead trees shrouding the 440 parkway. He felt a rising tide of melancholy as he glimpsed the familiar outlines of buildings he hadn't seen for more than four years. There was the AT&T building, the so-called "Bat Building" because of the blue glass of the windows and the spires on either side that made it resemble Batman's cowl. But it was no longer the gleaming monument to commerce it had formerly been. The blue glass had turned a dingy brown and the spires were black. It looked like a vision out of some medieval fantasy, an edifice suffused with dark magic and evil. He felt for a moment like Frodo nearing the end of his quest, about to enter Mordor. The notion was silly, but it sent a shudder rippling through him.

He was gripped by a sense of foreboding so strong it nearly

stopped him in his tracks. He slowed and nearly stumbled as Jasmine moved ahead of him. The gap between them lengthened quickly and Warren knew he should call out to her, tell her to wait up. But he said nothing and she got farther and farther away, her back squarely to him, seemingly oblivious or uncaring, or both. He came to a dead stop and she was more than fifty feet away. A voice at the back of his brain, a thing that sounded defeated and lost, told him to let her keep going—that the sooner they ended this exercise in misery the better.

But that intense feeling of dread kept penetrating deeper and he became sure of one thing—whatever awaited him in this city, he didn't want to face it alone. So, at last, he cleared his throat and called out to her, "JASMINE!"

She kept going for another few feet, so he called to her again: "JASMINE!"

She took another step forward. Then another. And another. But she was slowing. Warren knew she'd heard him. And he knew something else, sensed it as clearly as he'd ever discerned anything. On some level she'd known he'd faltered. She'd known she was leaving him behind. And she would have kept right on going had he not called out to her. Part of her clearly wished he'd kept his mouth shut.

She had come to a stop now, but her back was still to him. Warren was torn between a strong urge to go to her at once and a new impulse to just stand here until she tired of waiting for him and continued on without him. The latter notion was born of hurt feelings. But the fear he felt at being alone in this broken city outweighed—for now—that hurt.

Warren put one foot in front of the other and began walking. But Jasmine was so far away—had gone nearly a hundred feet before stopping—and suddenly walking wasn't good enough. He jogged the rest of the way and stood panting next to her for a moment. He looked at her, but she stared straight ahead. His gaze remained on her for several moments as he tried to think of a way to verbalize the paralyzing fear that had overtaken him. She removed the dark sunglasses hooked over the collar of her dress and slid them on. Only then did she look at Warren. Looking at those twin black ovals elicited another pang of hurt. He saw the sunglasses for what they were to her—a deliberate buffer between her feelings and his.

He knew then he couldn't tell her what he'd felt. Either she wouldn't want to know, or she'd dismiss it with a put-upon sigh and start walking again. So he said, "Sorry. I'm just tired."

She watched him from the other side of the dark lenses for a long moment. He grew intensely uncomfortable and had to fight the urge to fidget. Then she sighed and said, "That's going to happen when you walk all day every day for four days straight."

Warren groaned. "*That's* what you're being so pissy about?"

She whipped off the sunglasses and directed a high-intensity glare at him that made him wish she'd go back to being aloof and uncaring. "Why, yes, that's it exactly. You are such a perceptive little boy. I agreed to accompany you on this grand fool's errand, granted, but I might have given the matter a second thought had I known it'd turn into a goddamned Bataan death march. What on earth made you think I wouldn't mind marching nonstop from the crack of dawn until sunset, day after godforsaken day?" And now a spark of startling cruelty ignited in her clear blue eyes. "Why the hurry? There's no one alive here. Whatever was left of your family dried up and blew away days ago."

Warren nodded and directed his gaze at his shoetops. He didn't want to look into Jasmine's blazing blue eyes, didn't want to see the fury and resentment that had been eating away at her. Not simply because the intensity of it hurt him, but also because he feared gazing upon that anger too long might ignite a smoldering anger of his own. He laughed humorlessly.

She moved another step closer. "What's so funny, Warren?"

He said nothing. Just laughed again.

She slapped him. "Stop that."

Warren put a hand to his stinging jaw and rubbed it slowly, watching Jasmine now through thin-slit eyes. There hadn't been much real force behind the blow, but a primal part of him ached to respond in kind. The impulse was gone in an instant, leaving in its wake a wash of shame.

Her expression changed subtly, as if she'd read his thoughts. There was a wariness in her gaze now. "Do you want to hit me, child?"

Warren blinked hard. "No. I don't want to." Which wasn't a lie. The fleeting fantasy notwithstanding, he couldn't seriously imagine doing such a thing. "And even if I did, how would that be any different from what you did?"

"I don't suppose it would be any different." She laughed, but there wasn't the slightest hint of a smile on her face. "But you better not expect me to apologize for that. You had it coming."

Warren arched an eyebrow. "Did I?"

She nodded. "You bet your ass."

"Why?"

She heaved a sigh and slid the sunglasses back on. "I'm done with this conversation."

Several moments of uncomfortable silence ensued, during which Warren tried to decide whether to tell Jasmine she was free to leave him and should go her own way. Whatever sense of respect they'd had for each other had deteriorated to the point of near nonexistence. If they'd been a couple facing a similar emotional crossroads prior to doomsday, the solution would have been obvious. Life, he would have told himself in that situation, was too short to waste in the company of someone who simply doesn't respect you.

But in this new reality you couldn't blithely blow someone off, even if they were being unreasonable to an egregious degree. Not unless you wished to face the almost too bleak to consider prospect of living out the rest of your life completely alone. And not simply "alone" in the sense of not having a bed companion, but as in completely shut off from all human contact.

Forever.

A prospect Warren found so depressing he couldn't bring himself to tell Jasmine to fuck off. What he said instead was, "Fine. But as long as we're sticking together, I wish you'd do me one little favor."

"And what would that be, little boy?"

His gaze turned stony. "I'd like for you to stop calling me 'little boy'. Or 'child'. I know that on some very basic level our age difference disturbs you. But you should fucking get over it. If I'm old enough for you to fuck every night, I'm old enough to be treated like an equal."

He brushed past her then and resumed walking at a much brisker pace than before. His heart was racing and he could barely breathe for a moment. He was afraid that last jab had been too harsh. He kept his gaze straight ahead, fearing that if he glanced back, he'd see Jasmine walking off in the other direction. He hoped like hell that wasn't happening. Despite everything, he wanted her to stay with him.

But he was glad he'd said what he said.

Ahead of him loomed another big loop in the road. His gaze went to a faded road sign that'd once been bright green. Somewhere beyond that loop was an exit, a path off this bleak highway that would lead him straight into the heart of a dead city. He began to think about what he might find there and a deeper darkness began to tinge his thoughts, obscuring, for a while, his conflicted feelings for Jasmine.

~

Jasmine stood there watching Warren stride purposefully down the road. Part of her wanted to see him disappear forever once he moved beyond that coming bend in the road. A feeling fueled in large part by the angst she felt over the intimate turn their relationship had taken. She felt guilty of both betraying her husband's memory and of robbing the cradle. Warren's instincts in that regard were dead-on accurate.

But in the end it hardly seemed to matter. Everything kept boiling down to a simple, inescapable fact—she didn't want to be alone. And Warren, despite being very young and therefore naive, was all she had. She had no other friends left, no other men from whom she might choose a more appropriate (i.e., older) suitor.

She watched Warren's back grow smaller in the distance.

And smaller still.

Then she sighed.

She started walking—slowly at first, but faster and faster with each step. A quiet desperation hurried her pace, a primal impulse from the murkier depths of her subconscious. He was moving faster than she was, almost faster than she could manage without actually running. A vague sense of desperation sharpened, became almost all-consuming. She almost had to laugh when she realized abruptly what was spurring her forward.

Some part of her knew her previous wish to see Warren gone had never had much substance. It'd been a product of her ego and battered psyche. When she'd been faced with the very real possibility of having to do without him, all that had been swept away like so much flotsam in the wake of a tidal wave.

And he was still too far away.

Still moving too fast, like a man hurrying to the site of some emergency. She felt a surge of genuine concern for him then. The young man was determined to find out what had happened to his loved ones. All the evidence indicated he was heading straight to the bottom of a deep well of grief. She thought of what she'd said to him earlier about his family and felt shame.

"Damn it, Jasmine," she muttered. "Sometimes you really are an unfeeling bitch."

She began to run then, jettisoning those last shreds of ragged ego.

"Warren!" she called out to him. "Please wait for me!"

So she was begging now. She almost laughed. You couldn't get less aloof than this. A ghost of the old feelings came back when she saw him stop and turn to face her. Just a brief, flickering spark of ego that was gone in less than the space of a heartbeat.

She kept running.

And she saw Warren smile.

A great relief swept over her. A smile of her own stretched across her face, her first purely genuine smile in days. Everything was going to be okay now. She and Warren would talk everything out when they made camp tonight, honestly and openly address all their feelings and concerns. Then they'd be able to put all this angsty crap behind them and move on, maybe figure out how to make a decent (or at least bearable) life for themselves in this inhospitable new world.

Then there was a flash and the whole world went white.

Jasmine could still feel the road—the cracked and faded asphalt, with its dangerous, pocked surface—beneath her pounding feet. But she couldn't see a thing. Not Warren. Not the road. Nothing. Just this blinding white light. Then her foot dipped into a hole in the asphalt and she pitched forward. She struggled for a moment to regain her balance, but it was no use—she was going down too fast, and the bag slung over her shoulder was suddenly like a big hand driving her to the ground.

Her knees struck asphalt and she felt a jagged hardness shred her skin and draw forth a rush of warm blood. She screamed and fell flat against the road's surface. Then, screaming again, she rolled onto her back and stared up at that forever expanse of nothing.

"WARREN!" she screamed. "WHAT'S HAPPENING!?"

A silent moment elapsed while she waited to hear him respond. But he didn't say anything. Either he didn't hear her—which didn't seem possible—or he was ignoring her. She doubted the latter. If she'd learned anything about Warren in their brief time together, it was that the boy hadn't the merest spark of cruelty in his soul. He thought he was so dark. A brooding poet type. But he was so innocent, really. And so basically good, so decent. He wouldn't leave her to writhe here in agony.

Speaking of "here" . . . where was that, exactly? What on earth was happening? Whatever it was, it wasn't natural. Some unfathomable supernatural phenomenon was at work. Realizing this should have deepened the sense of terror engulfing her, but, curiously, it actually served to calm her some. It explained why Warren hadn't come immediately to her aid. For some reason, he couldn't. It was as if some ethereal cocoon had closed around her, separating her from the rest of the world while inexplicably leaving her connected to it in a tactile sense.

Then a face appeared above her. A pretty, almost angelic face, floating there in the midst of all that white. She began to perceive the outline of a small body. The image gradually clarified, and she began to perceive the shape of the world beyond it. It was her world. Earth. Barren, defeated Earth. She glimpsed a man-sized shape in the distance and knew it was Warren, though she still couldn't see him clearly. Everything was still shrouded in bright white.

The face was that of a smiling little girl. Nine years old, maybe ten. She wore her long brown hair in braided pigtails. Jasmine knew she should feel joy at seeing another human being, but she did not. There was something wrong with this girl. Her eyes were twin dark points of gleaming malevolence.

The girl laughed. "Hello."

Jasmine clenched her teeth and managed to speak through the pain. "Wh-who . . . are you?"

The girl laughed. "I am your lord and master."

Jasmine frowned. What an odd thing to say. She didn't know how to reply, so she said, "Where's Warren? What have you done to him?"

The girl's almond eyes flicked in his direction. Then she looked at Jasmine again and smiled more broadly than before. "Oh, him." She adopted a tone of mock consolation. "Well, you'll have to do without him from now on. He's mine now."

The scream that leaped from Jasmine's throat then was of such intensity it shocked her. She screamed again and said, "NO!"

The girl laughed yet again. "Afraid so, bitch." She glanced at Warren again, and now her grin morphed, became a sly smirk. "Hmm, I'd originally thought he'd just be my new plaything, but a look into his mind has proven most interesting. I think I have another use for him."

The white brilliance flared again, blotting out all of reality for an indeterminate time. Jasmine lost consciousness at some point, even experienced fleeting, dark-tinged dreams. Then she came back to herself, blinking slowly as she realized the awful shroud of white was gone.

That wasn't the only thing that was gone.

"Warren!"

She got to her feet and turned in a slow circle, searching for any sign of her young companion, but there was nothing. It was as though he'd disappeared into thin air. She supposed it was possible he'd really left her behind while she was in the clutches of . . . whatever that thing really was (she was certain it'd only been masquerading as a young girl). But she didn't really believe that. The stretch of road ahead was too long and wide open—he simply couldn't have gotten far enough to have disappeared from sight during the brief time she was incapacitated.

You don't know that, whispered a voice from the darker recesses of her psyche. Think about what happened. *Was it really mere minutes that elapsed while you were in that white void—or was it hours?*

Jasmine's instinct was to dismiss the notion as absurd, but, to her dismay, she found she was unable to do that.

An echo of low, black laughter came to her like the sound of waves lapping at a distant shore. She whirled about, scanning the road for any indication of the source of the laughter. She caught a glimpse of something at the far side of the road, a small shape sprawled on the ground next to a fallen motorcycle. A tuft of brown hair moved slightly in the gentle breeze.

A fresh knot of fear twisted its way through her guts as she began to move carefully toward the other side of the road. She couldn't be seeing what she thought she was seeing. This person was dead. Long dead, from the looks of it. But the clothes and hair were the same. Same braided brown pigtails. The same pajamas. By the time Jasmine arrived at the motorcycle, it had become next to impossible to believe she was seeing anything other than the body of her tormentor.

The body lay curled against the skeletal remains of the motorcycle's deceased driver. A grinning, fleshless skull was pressed into the hollow of the girl's throat. As unsettling as the grisly tableau was, Jasmine nonetheless felt compelled to investigate it more closely. She knelt next to the very still body and reached out to it with a trembling hand. Her fingers skittered over the cool, smooth flesh of the dead girl's cheek, then dipped lower, sliding between flesh and rotting bone. Her fingers pressed into the flesh, seeking a pulse, but of course there was none.

Jasmine's mind swirled with a confusion of thoughts and emotions, a dark, flashing kaleidoscope of jangled, half-formed ideas and suspicions. Finding the girl's corpse did nothing to allay either her fear or the concern she felt for Warren's safety. That dark, malign intelligence she'd sensed upon looking into the girl's eyes was still out there somewhere. She imagined something malleable and without solid form, a life force alien to this world, a parasitic consciousness able to enter and take over the minds and bodies of human hosts.

A theory the child's death seemed to verify. If she was right, it could mean only one thing—that creature, whatever it was, had moved on to a new host.

Warren . . .

Tears stung her eyes and she felt a sob beginning to work its way up her diaphragm. She didn't attempt to suppress it. This seemed as good a time as any for a total mental meltdown. Everything had gone to hell.

One of the dead biker's skeletal hands came to life and clamped tightly around her wrist. Jasmine screamed and tried to pull away. Even as she struggled, her mind reeled, refusing at first to accept this new level of insanity. She could accept the concept of disembodied, parasitic life forms from another world, but animated skeletons were another whacked-as-hell matter altogether.

The skeletal hand held her fast, failing to yield to her furious flailing. Which was crazy. The brittle old bones should have snapped easily, but they seemed as solid and durable as titanium. When the skull's jawbone began to move, Jasmine thought she might truly lose whatever little left of her sanity.

Dry, musty laughter emerged from that dead mouth. The lack of vocal cords appeared not to be an issue for Mr. Bones.

Jasmine screamed.

Yanked against the skeletal hand with all her might . . .

. . . and fell backward onto her ass.

She scooted rapidly away from the skeleton and dead child, stopping only when she'd put a good twenty feet between herself and the ghoulish scene. Then, panting rapidly like a dog in dire need of a drink from its bowl, she sat there staring at the motionless skeleton for several long moments. She half-expected it to get up and come shambling toward her. When her pulse had dropped back to a normal range, she got shakily to her feet and began heading down the road.

Toward the city.

And whatever awaited her there.

17

OCTOBER 6
Noon

Mary Lou's face was a study in tight-lipped concentration as she worked the can opener's little crank and steered it along the edge of the lid of canned veggies. Though the opener had still been "new" in the package when she'd swiped it from the kitchen utensils section of the grocery store, it functioned like some decades-old rickety relic. She managed to separate lid from can at last and flipped the tiny silver disc in disgust. "Swear to motherfucking god, Zeke, we ever run across any other living, breathing people, we're gutting the fuckers and roasting them over a fuckin' fire."

Zeke looked up from his own hearty meal of Spam. "Um . . ."

He didn't know what to say. Mary Lou had changed some for the better since those first harrowing days he'd spent in her company. Had mellowed out significantly. Still, this was the same woman who, at gunpoint, had forced him to mock-copulate with corpses. She was the same murdering lunatic who'd gunned down a family of three for no good reason. So he couldn't dismiss out of hand the possibility she was dead serious about engaging in cannibalism.

She sneered and shook her head, bugging out her eyes in an

180

exaggerated way. "What do you mean, 'Um . . .'?" She repeated his inarticulate utterance with mocking disdain, making it sound like something said by a drooling, lobotomized idiot.

They sat facing each other atop two checkout registers in a Harris Teeter grocery store on 21st Ave. Most of the food in the place had gone bad long before their arrival, but the canned goods were still in fine shape. They'd gone through dozens of cans of vegetables, soup, and ravioli in the last few days. Their preference was anything ready-to-eat, but they'd cooked some things over a fire in a makeshift pit in the parking lot.

Zeke cleared his throat. "Um . . ." He mentally smacked himself. "Well, you're not serious, right?"

Mary Lou grunted between swallows. "Fuck yeah, I'm serious. You think I'm gonna eat nothing but this shit the rest of my life?" She held up the can of veggies, sneered at it, and tossed it over her shoulder. "Fuck that, man. I need meat. Something to fill my belly. I've had I don't know how many goddamned cans of processed crap-ola since the other day, and I still feel like I'm fuckin' starving."

Zeke hated to admit it, but Mary Lou's rant had struck a nerve. He had a sudden, powerful craving for New York strip, a gnawing hunger a million cans of Spam couldn't begin to allay. He wished fervently there was some sort of animal life about, anything he could trap and kill. A dog or cat, or even a goddamned squirrel. But there was nothing alive out there. This new world was one without parallel in the planet's history. This wasn't a new Stone Age. There was no prey to hunt with a spear.

Mary Lou chuckled. "Yeah, you feel it, too. I can see it in your fuckin' eyes. You need a good chunk of long pork." Another chuckle. "I wonder what part of the human anatomy tastes best. Hmm, I reckon it depends on whether you're chowin' down on a dude or a chick. How's a portion of fried tit sound to ya, Zekey-baby?"

Zeke groaned. "Mary Lou . . ."

"Myself, I could go for six inches of roasted tube snake and a side of fried balls." She grinned broadly. "And maybe a bit of brain soup."

Zeke swallowed his rising gorge with great difficulty. "Let's talk about something else, okay?"

Mary Lou cackled. "I bet one of these cans of veggie soup would go real good with some fried eyeballs."

She was messing with him now, treating the issue of cannibalism like a joke. But it wasn't funny. Sick humor aside, she'd made it clear she was dead serious. Though it seemed less likely with every passing day, it was still possible there might be other survivors out there. It was even remotely possible they might encounter one or more of them somewhere along the way. And when (or if) this happened, Mary Lou had every intention of killing them. Then cooking them. And eating them.

And what will I do? he wondered. *Stand there while it happens, watching from the sidelines like the ineffectual coward I am?*

The memory of the apartment complex slaughter continued to haunt his dreams. He still felt great shame at having done nothing to prevent the senseless loss of life. Any attempt at intervention on his part would likely have resulted in the loss of his own life, but knowing that failed to make the memory sting any less.

The humor seeped out of Mary Lou's expression and she stared silently at him for a time, examining him in the dispassionate manner of a pure sociopath. He'd seen her look at him like this a few times before, and it always unnerved him. Sometimes he dreamed about her coming to him in his sleep, not to rouse him for fucking, but to slit his throat or bash him over the head. He knew this wasn't mere dreamtime paranoia, that it was very much in the realm of possibility.

So why don't I leave?

A question easier asked than answered. He could do it easily. All he had to do was wait until she was asleep, then get up, grab his traveling bag, and walk away. He could be miles down the road before she realized he was gone.

Mary Lou squinted. "The fuck're you thinking about?"

Zeke shook his head. "Wha . . . ?"

Mary Lou smirked. "Don't gimme that innocent shit. You were thinkin' on somethin' pretty deep there. You best not be doing any scheming, boy. You try anything you oughta not try, and ol' Mary Lou's apt to go off on your ass."

Zeke said nothing for a moment while he worked to decipher the threat. It almost seemed as if she'd been reading his mind. Either that, or she was one of the most intuitive people he'd ever met. He decided to divert her attention by changing the subject. "Did you feel anything when you gunned that family down?"

Mary Lou stared at him a moment, her expression contemplative. She was seriously thinking about his question. Zeke was surprised. Then a hint of a smile played at the corners of her mouth. "Okay, Mr. Fancy Pants. Mr. Shrink. Mr. I-was-on-TV-so-I-know-everything. I'll tell you what I was thinking about."

Zeke swallowed a lump in his throat. "Okay."

Mary Lou's face seemed to crumple. Her brow furrowed, the corners of her mouth turned down, and her jaw trembled. She seemed more vulnerable than Zeke had ever seen her. Hell, she seemed on the verge of expressing genuine human emotion, a development Zeke found at once welcome and disturbing.

Then she said, "I was thinking about my troubled childhood. I grew up in a mobile home in Huntsville, Alabama. And not one of them doublewides, neither. A real tiny one. I lived there with my mommy, my daddy, my cousin Tammy, my brother Stu, my other brother Emery, my little sister Nadine, and our crippled granny." She shook her head. "You ever tried living in a itty bitty trailer with seven nasty-ass motherfuckers?"

Zeke shook his head. "No."

Mary Lou's eyes misted over. A single tear spilled from the corner of one eye and rolled slowly down her cheek. She wiped it away and sniffled. "Sayin' it was cramped up in there is a goddamn fuckin', whatchacallit, a understatement, that's what. Anyways, over time I got to hate people. I mean, just flat-out fuckin' *hate* the human fuckin' race, man. Everything about fucking people. The fucking odor of their flabby bodies. Their farts. Their bad breath. The noises they make in their sleep. And lemme tell ya, eight people crowded into one goddamn trailer at night make one hellacious motherfucking noise."

Zeke felt himself growing numb as he listened to her story. He believed what she was saying, but it was so hard to picture, and so far removed from anything in his own experience. So all he could say was, "Uh-huh. Go on."

She smirked. "Oh, I'm just gettin' to the good part." She heaved a sigh, and another tear squirted from the corner of her eye. "The worst thing was when somebody would be fuckin' somebody else in the trailer. They'd go in the back room, draw the curtain, but you could hear all the action. And the fuckin' trailer would rock. It was bad enough when Tammy and Emery would go at it, but when Mommy and Daddy got to makin' the beast with two backs, it was more than I could stand. 'Specially when I got to be of a certain age. One summer when I was fourteen I hooked up with Skeet Carson, an ex-con who lived in our trailer park. We were getting all hot and heavy, and he started getting all deep and shit. Asked me what I wanted most outta life. So I told him."

Mary Lou descended into sobs then, and Zeke debated whether he should go to her, take her into his arms. Ordinarily it was the obvious thing to do when a woman was baring her soul to you this way. But nothing was obvious to Zeke in this situation. He was genuinely curious to know what trauma lay at the heart of Mary Lou's insanity, and he wasn't at all certain she wouldn't clam up—or worse, fly into a psychotic rage—if he were to go to her.

But the sobs were soon displaced by odd, humorless laughter. "I told that crazy sumbitch the one thing I wanted more than anything else was to see my worthless family dead. Every single goddamned one of them. I told him I didn't think I'd really be happy until I was free of them."

Zeke gaped. Something heavy seemed to slide down his gullet and settle in the pit of his stomach. "Oh, no."

Mary Lou nodded. "That evening I fell asleep at Skeet's place after having some of his whiskey. Didn't drink that much, but I was out like a light. He doped it. While I was out, he took his shotgun and paid a visit to my family's trailer. He blew 'em all away. You should've seen the inside of that place the next day, man. Looked like something out of a Halloween haunted house, the kind fixed up with fake props and shit. Big splashes of blood all over the walls. Pools of dried-up blood on the carpet. Later, after the police were done checking everything out, I found some teeth Skeet's shotgun blowed outta somebody's head. They were on top of the fridge."

Zeke said, "Oh my God."

Mary Lou grunted. "Yeah."

Zeke shook his head. "So . . . whatever happened to Skeet?"

She rolled her eyes. "Cops took him down a couple days later. He'd made it up to Kentucky, where he was holed up with kin. He confessed, and was sentenced to seven consecutive life sentences."

Zeke frowned. "Really? In Alabama? That sounds like a slam dunk death penalty case to me."

Mary Lou shrugged. "Yeah. Probably woulda been. But I testified on his behalf. You know, as a character witness. Made it sound like my whole family had been taking turns sexually abusing me, and that Skeet did what he did to protect me."

Zeke gaped at her. "You're kidding. Why would you do that?"

Mary Lou smiled. "Because it was the most romantic thing anybody ever did for me. Still is, I reckon."

Zeke shook his head again as his voice emerged in an amazed

whisper. "Holy shit." Zeke ran a hand through his greasy hair. "But . . . how's this explain why you killed those people?"

Mary Lou's head tilted forward and her eyes widened. "Don't you get it? I don't like other people around me. I told you before, back when I took you prisoner, but you didn't get it then, either. I told you I was *glad* the world was ending and that everybody was dying." She slid off the counter and began to approach him. Zeke tensed, not sure whether he should welcome her with open arms or make a run for it now. She laid her hands on his knees and leaned forward, pressing her bare nipples against the slowly decaying fabric of his shirt. "I only need you, baby. Anybody else is in the way, far as I'm concerned."

Her tongue darted out and flicked against his lower lip. A shudder went through Zeke's body and he had to fight a sudden urge to pull her into his arms. He drew in a steadying breath. "And what about Earl? Was he your one and only before I came along? What happens to me if someone better comes along? Do I get my brains blown out, too?"

"No, silly." Mary Lou caught his lower lip between her teeth, chewed lightly on the bit of flesh for a moment, then let it go. A thin strand of saliva connected them for a moment, but she severed it with another flick of her tongue. "The gun doesn't work anymore, remember? I'd have to slit your throat."

Zeke trembled as she planted a series of feathery kisses all over his throat while her hand went to his crotch and massaged the suddenly swelling bulge there. Though he was on the verge of surrendering to her, he managed to say, "That's not very comforting."

Her mouth roamed higher and she nipped at his earlobe. "It ain't meant to be, baby." She began to pull his zipper down. "I've got to keep you on your toes." She chuckled throatily. "Got to maintain that dangerous edge that turns you on so much."

Zeke gasped as her hand found the swollen shaft of his cock and began to stroke it roughly, squeezing and twisting it while she continued to nip at his ear. He was very close to not being able to think about anything other than what she was doing to him. And maybe that was the point.

He sighed—then gripped her by the wrists and reluctantly forced her to stop doing those oh-so-pleasurable things to his body. "I'm going to tell you what I really think, Mary Lou. If that's even your real name. I think if anything you've told me about your life is true, it's filtered through so much bullshit as to be nearly unrecognizable. I think you're playing a role. Maybe you really are redneck through-and-through, but you're a lot smarter than you like to let on."

Mary Lou's grin was sly and mischievous. "Is that so?"

Zeke nodded. "Yeah."

Mary Lou sighed and rolled her eyes. "Whatever, man. You wanna fuck or not?"

Zeke held her gaze a moment, then shook his head again. "You're mentally ill."

Mary Lou laughed. "No shit. You're really swift on the uptake." She wrenched a hand free of his grip and grabbed his cock again. "It's the end of the world, sugarpie. So what's it really matter?"

Zeke stared at her for a long moment. He sighed. "I give up."

She leaned closer and her hot breath tickled his face. "It's about fucking time."

Then she slithered down the length of his body and took him into her mouth.

Zeke gasped and gripped the edge of the counter while Mary Lou's skilled tongue temporarily made him forget all his concerns. He closed his eyes and focused on the amazing physical sensations. He only opened them again when he felt himself rushing toward a climax.

And then he nearly screamed. A man standing just inside the entrance to the store. A lean, good-looking guy of average height with his arms crossed over a frayed Ramones T-shirt. He was a young man, maybe twenty-five, with dark hair and a piercing gaze. He was smirking at them, the way a friend would upon accidentally interrupting a roommate's encounter with a girlfriend. Zeke was so startled by his appearance that he abruptly ejaculated into Mary Lou's mouth.

She held fast to him, bearing down on him harder than before, coaxing out every last drop of jism. Then her mouth came away from his cock and she looked up at him with a smile. "Mmm . . . did you like that? Or was your tortured conscience bothering you the whole time?"

Zeke cleared his throat. "Um . . . we have company."

The smile faded from Mary Lou's mouth, replaced by an expression every bit as cold and lethal as the one she'd worn while gunning down the family of three. She wiped her mouth, stood up, and turned to face the intruder.

She folded her arms over her breasts and said, "Who the fuck are you and what the fuck do you want?"

The young man laughed and shrugged. "Sorry to barge in like this, but I heard voices." He shook his head. "I might have loitered outside a while had I known what an intimate scene I'd be interrupting." He laughed again. "But heck, I hadn't heard another human voice in going on a week. The silence was starting to drive me crazy, know what I mean?"

Zeke hopped off the counter, zipped his pants up, and moved into position next to Mary Lou. What the man was saying seemed reasonable enough, but something about him was disturbing. There was something off about him. Something darkly feral in those intense eyes. And there was the matter of the way he'd stood there smirking and watching Mary Lou give him a blowjob. Zeke was sure he detected a hint of something predatory in those eyes, an impression strengthened by the stranger's cocksure stance and smug expression.

Zeke laid a hand on Mary Lou's shoulder. "Take it easy," he told her in a whisper. He could feel the tension building within her. He remembered her talk about cannibalism and thought of a tigress preparing to pounce upon prey.

The young man held his hands out in a conciliatory gesture and said, "Hey, there's no need to be uptight. I don't mean any harm." He smiled. "I guess maybe it hasn't been too bad for you guys. You've had each other to hold on to. But me . . . ?" He shrugged and moved an ambling step or two closer to them. "I've been alone since day one. Surely you can imagine how desperate I must be for human company."

Mary Lou shrugged off Zeke's hand, moved quickly to the counter where she'd been sitting before, and picked up the big hunting knife that had replaced the useless shotgun as her weapon of choice. She stepped around the counter and waved the gleaming piece of metal at the intruder. "You got two choices, motherfucker. You can turn around and leave this place. And this is *our* place, bitch. We ain't sharing it. Or you can stay and be dinner."

The young man's eyes bugged out and he put a hand to his chest. "Whoa. Oh, I'm so scared. Please don't hurt me, little girl."

Zeke groaned. "Oh, shit."

Mary Lou snarled and leaped forward, raising the knife high over her head. The intruder never stopped smiling, but Zeke saw something flare in those eyes, a hint of alien redness that sent a chill through him. He wanted to call out to Mary Lou, to warn her back, but it was too late. Her hand came down in a vicious arc as she neared the man, and for a moment Zeke had hope she might successfully rip his throat open.

But the man's arm snapped in her direction so quickly it was a blur. Zeke thought of a frog snagging a fly with its tongue. The man's hand seized her wrist and shook the knife loose. He gripped her by the bicep with his other hand and began to bend her arm backward. There was a sound of snapping bone and cartilage, followed by a shriek from Mary Lou.

Zeke screamed and attempted to rush to her aid.

But the man's gaze swiveled in his direction. Zeke felt . . . something . . . enter his mind. He couldn't comprehend what was happening to him, or how it had happened, but he knew the stranger was projecting some kind of energy into his brain. Something like liquid light that moved like lightning through all the nooks and crannies of his psyche and stopped Zeke in his tracks.

He stood there helplessly while the man tore Mary Lou's arm completely off her body. Blood jetted from the stump at her shoulder. Mary Lou had a stunned look on her face, like she couldn't believe what was happening to her. Zeke couldn't believe it either, but he couldn't deny the truth of his eyes. Then the man—who clearly was something much more than a mere man—gripped Mary Lou by the neck and twisted her head off.

Zeke would have cried then had he been able to, but his tear ducts were as frozen as the rest of his body. A wave of grief washed over him as Mary Lou's headless body stumbled backward several feet before toppling to the floor. The sense of deep loss surprised him. He realized he'd come to truly care about the crazy redneck woman, despite what he'd seen her do.

Holding it by a gore-smeared length of yellow hair, her killer swung her severed head in a swooping motion, like a softball pitcher gearing up to deliver a pitch. Then he let the head go and it went sailing over Zeke.

The man cackled. Then he looked at Zeke and his expression sobered somewhat. He walked over to where Zeke was standing and stood before him with his arms crossed again. "Now . . . Zeke . . . I don't think I'm quite ready to kill you yet. There's someone I want you to meet. First, though, I think we'll need to manipulate your memory a bit."

More cackling. "Quite a bit, actually. Wow, I made a mess of that bitch, didn't I?"

Zeke seethed inwardly. He ached to brutalize the smiling young man with his fists.

The man made a tsk-tsk noise and shook his head. "Now, you watch that temper of yours, okay? It could get you into trouble." The man's smile faded as he peered more intently into Zeke's eyes. "Ah, but you've always been a tad on the impulsive side, haven't you? Well, we'll have to fix that."

Zeke found he was suddenly able to speak. "Who are you?"

The man shrugged. "Who I really am doesn't matter. Yet." He smiled. "But for now you can call me Warren. Warren Hatcher."

Zeke's breath hissed between tightly gritted teeth. "I'm going . . . to kill you . . . Warren."

"Oh, I don't think so."

And "Warren" splayed the fingers of a hand against the side of Zeke's face. "Time to forget."

Zeke's rage level surged still higher, then began to fade.

Mary Lou, he thought. *I'm sorry, Mary Lou.*

Another moment passed. He grew calmer.

He wondered who Mary Lou was.

And then, just like that, he didn't know the name anymore.

18

Emma sensed the stranger's presence before seeing her. She glanced to the east, where Broadway met 21st Avenue, and glimpsed a dim figure moving in her direction. A woman, she was pretty sure. That, or a man with a very feminine hip swivel and a wardrobe preference indicating an interest in women's clothing. She watched the figure draw closer a moment longer and grew certain the stranger was a woman.

Emma considered her options. She could stay where she was—in a chair at a table outside Provence, the cafe that had once employed Laura Brandner—or she could bolt. A quick dash through the cafe and out the back entrance would work best.

Emma stayed where she was. She lit a cigarette with a match and drew in a lungful of smoke. Four days had passed since Jake's death. She felt empty inside right now. But other times she was full of rage and sorrow. She alternated between these extremes like an unmedicated manic depressive—which, she figured, was sort of what she was. Not that it mattered. There were no more psychiatrists left in the world. No more little pills to pop to make her problems go away.

Well, maybe the pills still existed. But she felt not the slightest impulse to break into a pharmacy and start testing a bunch of psychotropic meds on her already too-fragile psyche.

She winced at a sudden flash of memory . . .

. . . .*she comes to after passing out, consciousness creeping back like an unwelcome stranger tapping on her bedroom window at night. She doesn't want to be here. Doesn't want to face the hard things she knows await her in the waking world. But she wakes anyway, in a room shrouded in shadow. The same room where (go ahead, say it) . . . where Jake was killed by some kind of monster in a little girl costume.*

There's a physical presence above her, ON her, something heavy crushing the breath out of her lungs. Then she feels breath hot on her face, feels hands clutching at her breasts, straining to rip open her shirt.

She screams, a piercing sound in the darkness.

He giggles.

It's Aaron, the awareness hitting her like a brick to the jaw.

"You thought you were through with me, didn't you, you dirty little bitch?" Another giggle. Then another. A whole series of them. He sounds insane. "Thought you'd put old Aaron in his place once and for all. Well, you were WRONG, whore!"

A fist crashes against her jaw, making the back of her head bounce off the floor. She cries out and wavers on the brink of another descent into unconsciousness. But something within her—some last dying flicker of survival instinct—rallies and she snaps back. The world—with all its awful realities—comes into clear focus again. She hears the tearing fabric and screams again.

Aaron giggles. "Ooooh, I LOVE that sound! You always got me hot. Just the thought of you—just the sight of you—got me all bothered. Still does, bitch." She feels the proof of his words in the hardness pressing against her thigh. "I should've figured out long ago I'd have to take you by force." Giggle. "Well, you know what they say, whore . . . better late than never."

Emma feels her shirt come away from her body in tatters. Then Aaron's rough hands are on her bare breasts, squeezing and twisting, and Emma screams yet again. And Aaron says, "Oh, yeah . . . keep doin' that." The sound that emerges from his throat then is a throaty chuckle. "That little bitch took my eyes, but guess what." He leans closer to her and flecks of spittle strike her face as he speaks in a hoarse whisper: "Everything else still works. I can still do everything I ever wanted to you."

He shifts his weight then and Emma hears the snickering sound of a zipper being pulled down. The crushing weight has lessened. Her eyes have adjusted to the darkness by now and she watches Aaron shift his body again, this time to facilitate the removal of his slacks. She sees the upthrust outline of his pecker in the darkness and makes a decision.

Her hand darts forward and seizes him by the balls. The next scream that fills the room is made by Aaron Harris. He tries to thrash away from her, but Emma holds fast to his scrotum, scooting across the room with him, increasing the pressure with both hands now. A fist comes hurtling toward her, but she evades it easily and bears down harder than ever. She finally releases him after she feels something give beneath her crushing fingers. She gets to her feet and staggers out of the room, leaving her blind attacker thrashing madly on the floor . . .

Emma blinked and looked again toward Broadway.

The woman was a block closer now. Emma could discern a little more about her. She was a trim woman of slightly better than average height. And she was older than Emma. Maybe forty or so. Though it was hard to be sure from this distance, she seemed quite attractive.

Great. Emma snorted. *At least I won't be too repulsed if I'm forced to spend the rest of my life with only another woman around as a potential sex partner.*

It was a passing thought, was nothing like a real possibility she was considering. But as she thought about it a bit more she realized there might come a time when her little joke would no longer seem quite so funny. She flicked the cigarette away and watched it smolder in the open mouth of a corpse.

Emma turned up the collar of a sweater she'd taken from the window display of a 21st Ave. boutique and shivered. It was getting colder lately. She'd have to look into acquiring a hardier wardrobe sometime before winter. The thought triggered a small grunt of laughter. Maybe she and this woman could walk across town to the Hecht's department store. They could pretend to be two fabulous pre-apocalypse babes on an unlimited shopping spree. Oh, what fun.

She closed her eyes, slumped down in the chair, and let herself slip into a light sleep. She entered a dreaming state within seconds. She was at a New Year's Eve ballroom dance with Warren Hatcher. Warren looked more handsome than she'd ever seen him in real life, clean-cut and wearing a dazzling tux that fit him perfectly. And she was wearing an elegant white gown that reached her ankles. They danced together, swirling across the gleaming floor in perfect synch. She was only peripherally aware of the other dancing couples at first. Until she bumped into someone and Emma turned to offer her apologies. Then she saw all the other dancers were ambulatory corpses. Skeletons with an overlay of gray, papery flesh.

Emma jerked awake at the same moment a shadow fell over the table. Fear filled her body like ice as she gripped the arms of the chair and looked up expecting to see the Abby-thing. But it was only the woman she'd seen walking down the street before. She let out a big breath and managed a trembling smile.

"Hello." She swallowed hard and sat up straighter in the chair. "I, uh . . . I'm glad to see you." Emma wasn't one-hundred percent convinced she believed that, but what the hell. "I haven't seen anybody for days."

The woman's slack expression didn't change. "I'm looking for somebody."

"Uh-huh." Emma managed not to roll her eyes. She also managed not to immediately express the opinion that whoever the old broad was looking for was probably dead, dead, DEAD. But just barely. "Does this person live around here?"

"He used to." The woman's flat inflection matched the look on her face. "We both came from up north. But he used to have family here and wanted to check on them. He knew they had to be dead, but he wanted to see for himself. We walked for days and days. Then . . . we got separated."

"Uh-huh." Emma nodded. She was aware of an urge to slap the woman. Part of it was to make her stop sounding like a goddamned emotionless robot. A bigger part of it, she realized, stemmed from a general irrational anger. She ached to lash out at something . . . anything. For a brief, flashing second, she figured this woman's face would make an excellent choice of punching bag. Then the feeling was gone and she felt her own numbness slowly return. "When was this?"

She sounded disinterested, like someone who couldn't give a fuck one way or the other what happened to this lady's boyfriend, lover, husband . . . whatever.

Which—for the moment, at least—was true.

The woman sat in the seat opposite Emma and let her bag drop to the sidewalk. She folded her hands in her lap and stared intently across the table. "Yesterday afternoon. About this time, actually."

Emma's brow furrowed. "How did you get separated?" She laughed, a harsh sound bordering on derisive. "It's not like there's teeming masses of people to get lost in." She smirked, a bit of the previous surge of anger manifesting now in a petty jab of cruelty. "Maybe he separated himself from you on purpose."

The woman's eyes widened a bit, evincing a secret hurt. Seeing this gave Emma a sense of cold satisfaction.

Got to you, bitch, she thought. *Finally.*

And then, *Jesus, what's wrong with me? What am I turning into?*

The woman's voice was terse: "It. Wasn't. On. Purpose."

Emma held her gaze a moment, intensity meeting intensity. Then she sighed and looked away. "Okay. I'm sorry for being such a bitch. I lost my own man a few days ago." She laughed again. "I'm bitter and all fucked up."

"I understand." The woman started to stand. "I suppose I'll be moving along now."

Emma frowned. "Don't do that. Not yet." She nodded at the chair. "Sit down. Please."

The woman regarded her in an appraising way a moment longer, chewing her lower lip as she studied her. Emma was sure she detected a hint of general distaste, but she decided she'd give the woman the benefit of the doubt. For now.

Then she smiled coldly and extended a limp hand. "I'm Jasmine Holtz."

Emma shook the woman's hand, but released it quickly, uncomfortable with even this mild intimacy after so long a period of utter aloneness. "Pleased to meet you, Jasmine. I'm Emma."

Jasmine smiled again—a bit more warmly this time—and sat back down. She stared at Emma for a minute before saying, "So . . . what happened to your man?"

Emma averted her gaze again, directing it now at the smashed storefront across the street. "Well . . ." She sighed. "Jesus, it's hard to explain. And so fucking strange." Her gaze settled on Jasmine again. "You'd never in a million years believe me."

Jasmine's smile faltered. "Oh, there's not much I'd have trouble believing anymore."

Jasmine's words echoed inside Emma's head for several moments. Though innocuous on a surface level, the statement conveyed a greater internal weight. *She's right*, Emma thought. *Nothing seems far-fetched anymore. Demonic baby clowns could come shooting out of my ass right now and I'd probably take it in stride. Well, aside from the severe rectal pain, that is.*

She laughed then, tossing her head back and letting gales of mad mirth roll out of her. Then, just as abruptly, the laughter transformed into gut-wrenching sobs and hot tears obscured her vision. This went on for several minutes. Part of her half-expected—and even wanted—Jasmine to console her in the instinctual ways people often do in the presence of a person in distress. A hug combined with empty-but-heartfelt reassurances would have been nice. A hand patting her shoulder would have sufficed. But by the time Emma regained some measure of self-control, Jasmine hadn't moved an inch. She just sat in that chair watching her with her hands still folded primly in her lap.

God . . . she's so fucking cold.

Emma supposed she shouldn't judge the woman. No telling what she'd been through in the days since the old world ended. Anyone still alive at this point had endured far more than their fair share of traumas.

Jasmine smiled, a half-hearted expression that didn't reach her eyes. "I'd offer you a tissue if things were still the way they ought to be."

Emma chuckled and wiped the remaining dabs of moisture from her eyes with the backs of her hands. "That's the right way to put it, isn't it? 'The way they ought to be.'" She sighed. "God, but I miss the world we knew. So, okay, it wasn't perfect. There were wars and famine. Political scandals and rampant crime in the big cities. Child abuse, rape, and murder. But at least it was a world full of people. Not like this . . ." She indicated both the street and the world beyond with a sweep of her hand. "This wasteland. The old world, despite its faults, was a vital place. And there were a lot of good people striving to make it a better place."

Jasmine said, "Well, they're all dead now."

Emma looked at her. "I'm not saying this to offend you or anything, but you seem awfully blasé about the whole thing. As if the death of civilization and the end of the fucking world means nothing to you."

Jasmine shrugged. "Of course it means something to me. But it happened, and there's nothing I can do about it. When this process was just beginning, I lost my husband Gary to a heart attack. We watched the president die on live television and Gary was dead a few minutes after that. There was nothing I could do about that either. I let myself get attached to my young friend from New Jersey. Now he's gone, too. So I've decided I'll be better off if I work at feeling nothing at all."

Emma frowned. Something in Jasmine's speech resonated in a

way she couldn't identify at first. She replayed the woman's words in her head, examining them for some clue. Then it came to her. Her "young friend", a man, was from New Jersey. But he apparently had had family here in Nashville.

No, it can't be.

The last Emma had heard, Warren Hatcher, the man she'd loved so intensely years ago, was living in New Jersey. And was supposedly attending Rutgers University. According to Dan Brooks, Warren's best friend in high school, he'd picked New Jersey at random on a map. Had just closed his eyes and stabbed an index finger at an atlas. At the time Emma had figured Dan was exaggerating. Thinking about it now though, she knew it was the kind of impulsive thing Warren might have done. He'd stated a desire to get far away from her after their painful split, and so he had.

Emma didn't often allow herself to dwell too long on thoughts of Warren and their doomed relationship. The memories were too painful. They'd met in the summer after high school graduation. Both had big plans for those first steps into the adult world. Warren wanted to become a great writer. A Hemingway or Faulkner. He was planning to attend college as an English major. And Emma wanted to be a professional singer. They bonded initially over their mutual creative ambitions, but the love that bloomed that summer soon overwhelmed everything else, including their plans for school and the future. They spent all their time together. Doing romantic things. Crazy things. Warren drank a lot, but Emma didn't care. She kept up with Warren that summer. The drunkenness made sense to her then. After all, so many great artists of the past had spent their days pickling their brains and livers with alcohol. Why should they be any different?

The summer slipped away and the time approached when they'd have to register for classes at their respective colleges, which were two hundred miles apart. A gloom descended as they began to face the reality of separating for the fall. Then Warren did what she would later come to see as a typical self-destructive act. He showed up at her parents' house in an old junker car. A lime-green Chevelle. Warren had spent the bulk of his summer savings on it. He took her for a ride in the country, during which he asked her to ditch school and journey across the country with him in the Chevelle.

Emma had a short-lived panic attack when she realized Warren wasn't joking. She knew instantly what a bad idea accepting the invitation would be. Her first-semester tuition had already been paid. And her parents were so proud she was going to college, even if they had reservations about her choice of major. If she ran away with her boyfriend, their hard-earned money would go to waste. They could get a portion back, maybe, but not all of it. Also, she and Warren were very young. They had their whole lives ahead of them. Maybe they were meant to be together, and maybe they weren't. If they threw away the opportunities available to them now, maybe they wouldn't be there again should they come to their senses later.

But they were in love. And so Emma went with Warren. They spent three months driving around the American South, picking up work where they could and living virtually hand-to-mouth. They learned a painful truth in that time. That no amount of romantic fantasy was enough to keep you going when you were living on the brink of starvation and had only a handful of pennies to your name. About the time she should have been wrapping up her first semester at college, Emma surrendered to the inevitable and asked Warren to take her home.

There'd been every bit as much hell to pay as she'd expected upon her return. Her parents forbade her from seeing Warren as a condition of being able to stay at their house. She bristled at being treated like a child. She was eighteen. Young, yes, but legally an adult. She could do what she wanted. So she kept seeing Warren in secret. Eventually she started school while Warren spent his days crashing at Dan's apartment and drinking. This went on for almost a year, Warren floundering while Emma slowly warmed to the challenges of college life. Then came the first in a series of ultimatums. Warren either had to get his act together or she'd leave him. Each time Warren made a promise to either look for a better job than his convenience store gig or go back to school. Preferably school, as far as Emma was concerned. And every time Warren failed to live up to his word.

So, finally, she left him. And Warren skipped town without so much as a goodbye phone call. If Emma had harbored any illusions of going blithely on with her life without Warren, they were shattered when word reached her that he was gone. In many ways she'd never quite recovered from the blow. She dropped out of school and started tending bar at the Villager, where she'd been until doomsday.

The man responsible for breaking her heart couldn't possibly be back in Nashville. The odds against that had to be astronomical. She figured this was nothing but coincidence. Still . . . she had to ask the question. "Jasmine, your 'young friend', what was his name?"

Jasmine smiled again, but this time her eyes did sparkle with some unidentifiable emotion. It might have been love. It might have been sadness. Probably it was a mixture of both. "His name is Warren."

Emma's thunderstruck expression made Jasmine's smile fade and morph into a frown. "The look on your face reminds me of my brother-in-law Frank when his only son announced he was gay at a family reunion." She pursed her lips and narrowed her eyes as she watched Emma struggle to form words. "The young man's last name is Hatcher."

Emma gasped.

A deep weariness seemed to draw Jasmine's features downward, making her look the way Emma imagined she would ten years hence (assuming she, or anyone else, was still alive in ten years, of course). The woman lazily went through the motions of lighting a cigarette. She turned her head up and blew smoke at the washed-out sky. She looked at Emma again and sighed. "I take it the name has some significance for you."

Emma could only nod. She was still reeling from the dual revelation. Warren Hatcher, her truest love, somehow had survived not only doomsday but the nameless infection that wiped out most of what remained of the already decimated human race. And he had come back to Nashville. She supposed there could theoretically be another young Warren Hatcher with the same connections, some cruel doppelganger delivered by malevolent fate, but she didn't believe that for one second.

Her Warren was back.

And just like that all the troubles they'd endured in their time together as a couple seemed so petty, like so much nothing. She knew if Warren were to appear before her now, she would throw herself into his arms and hold fast to him forever, the painful past and all its angst forgotten for good. But as soon as this bit of knowledge crystallized in her mind she became aware of the less-than-friendly way Jasmine was now regarding her. She was puzzled for only a moment, but then it all came clear.

I let myself get attached to my young friend from New Jersey . . .

Of course. Jasmine's words took on a deeper significance now. "Attached" was an obvious euphemism. She was in love with Warren. Or, at the very least, she'd been fucking him. The knowledge darkened her thoughts and feelings and set her blood to boiling. On one level, she knew this incipient rage was ridiculous. She'd forfeited whatever claim she held over Warren years ago. On a more primal and much more irrational level, she didn't give a fuck.

Warren Hatcher belonged to Emma Singleton. Not this hag. This cold bitch with the dead eyes. Emma felt a sudden urge to leap across the table and claw those eyes out, but she managed to restrain herself.

Jasmine peered closely at her, seeming to sense the hostility raging beneath the surface. Then she took another puff from her cigarette and smiled wryly. "It makes sense, I suppose. We're pawns on a cosmic chessboard, aren't we? We're being manipulated by invisible hands, drawn toward some inevitable fate. You were his girlfriend, I take it. His high school sweetheart, perhaps." She chuckled. "Clearly you and Warren are meant to be together again."

But the smirk touching one corner of her mouth made the sarcasm in her words plain. And Emma knew the bitch wouldn't surrender her hot young stud without a fight. Knowing this made her anger burn brighter a moment longer—until the absurdity of this little dance struck her, eliciting a humorless laugh of her own.

"I doubt that. After all, Warren's not here. For all we know, neither of us will ever see him again." Emma felt grimly satisfied at the way Jasmine's eyes flared at that suggestion. "By the way, I wasn't just a girlfriend. I was the love of Warren Hatcher's life. And vice versa."

Jasmine's smirk returned. "It's funny, though. I don't recall him mentioning you." Another puff from her cigarette. "I suspect he's simply moved on emotionally while you have not."

Emma laughed. "We're very close to blows, you and I."

Jasmine flicked the cigarette away. "Oh, please. You're welcome to him, if you like. You should know something, though. Warren's not exactly . . . himself anymore."

Emma frowned. "What's that supposed to mean?"

Jasmine opened her mouth intending to elaborate (or so Emma supposed), but her mouth froze in an open O for a long moment and her eyes went wide, staring at something beyond where Emma was sitting. "Oh my God."

Emma's frown deepened as she turned slowly around to see what Jasmine was gawking at.

She nearly fell out of her chair.

Warren was standing on the sidewalk a dozen feet away. Lurking behind him was a distantly familiar-looking man. The stranger's expression was befuddled. He seemed confused and haunted by something at the same time. But Emma had no room in her brain now for analyzing him. Warren was *here*. A tide of powerful emotions threatened to carry her away and she was only dimly aware of tears spilling hotly down her cheeks.

Warren smiled. God, he was as handsome as ever. More so, maybe. He seemed suffused with some inner, almost otherworldly glow. He looked almost godlike to her, standing there backlit by the diffused sunlight. "Emma. It's good to see you again."

Emma leapt from her chair and into his arms, as she'd imagined she would moments ago. Her love had been returned to her. It was a miracle. At last she had something to hold on to—and live for—again.

Then Jasmine said, "It's not—"

The older woman made a sound like something had suddenly become caught in her throat. But Emma paid her no mind. Nothing else mattered anymore. Nothing except that she was back in Warren's loving embrace—where she belonged.

Warren laughed softly and patted her back. "Aren't you forgetting something, Jasmine? Your manners, perhaps. Yes, I thought so."

He laughed again.

Something in that sound triggered a faint alarm at the back of Emma's brain, but she ignored it. She kissed Warren on the mouth, then pulled back a bit and beamed at him with tears still streaming down her face. "I thought this day would never come."

Warren's arms encircled her waist, the fingers of his hands interlacing at the small of her back. His eyes sparkled as he said, "I always knew it would."

A sudden thought pierced Emma's joy. She tensed in Warren's arms as she said, "Why didn't I see or hear you coming down the street?"

Warren's breath was soft against her ear as he said, "Shhhh. You forget about that."

And she did.

~

"It's almost time for you to start walking down that road, Flash."

Flash looked straight ahead, avoiding the old man's gaze. "You've been lying to me."

Flash was sitting behind the useless wheel of a Ford truck. He'd shifted his base of operations—meaning his body and several warm six-packs of beer—to the cab of the rusted hulk a day ago. He liked to sit here and stare through the glass. With enough beer flowing through his veins, he could almost believe he was home again, sitting in his recliner and staring at his widescreen television. But when he was closer to sober—like now—the windshield was less like a television screen and more like a window, one with a view of the Gates of Hell.

Because that was how he'd come to think of Salvation Road.

The entrance to a place of damnation.

"Salvation Road isn't the way to hell, Flash," said the man sitting in the seat next to him. "How many times do I have to tell you this? It's—"

"Yeah, yeah," Flash cut him off. He'd had a lot of time to mull over the outlandish things the man had told him, and his patience was nearly at an end. "That's where my destiny lies. Salvation Road is where good will finally triumph and evil will be vanquished forever and ever. Blah blah blah, yadda yadda yadda."

The old man sighed. "It's true."

Flash looked at him. And this time when the old man turned his piercing gaze on him, he didn't look away. That sense of cosmic awe he'd experienced before in the man's presence was absent, was probably gone forever. Because he now knew the mysterious codger wasn't some biblical apparition. Nor was he, as previously claimed, a former incarnation of Jeff Wheeler able to appear to him only in visions. That'd been so much hocus pocus and trickery. He was a real flesh-and-blood man, and he was right here with him in the truck now. For real.

Yet, for all his deceit, he was something more than an ordinary man. He possessed the ability to reach into Flash's mind and make him see things that weren't there, make him feel things he knew he shouldn't feel. Knowing this scared Flash some, but not as much as one might think. Despite the manipulation and trickery, he sensed nothing malevolent in the old man. Quite the opposite, in fact. Flash believed the man meant to set him on an important journey. There was a noble purpose at the root of all this, he was sure of it.

A conviction that made him no less cranky about the lies. "Maybe it's true. But that'd make that one of the few true things you've told me." He grunted. "Hell, maybe the only one."

The old man didn't say anything. He averted his gaze from Flash and stared out the windshield. He let his head settle against the headrest as he closed his eyes.

Flash grunted again. "I'll take your silence as a confession of your sins."

The man's eyes fluttered open. He looked at Flash through red-rimmed irises. "Okay, Flash. Or Jeff. Whatever you'd prefer to be called. It's true. I've filled your head with grand lies. If you feel used and misled, I regret that, but I am not truly sorry. You *do* have a pivotal role to play in a great drama, a genuine showdown between what your race would think of as good and evil. It's not so simple, so black and white, as that, but it's the best way I have of putting it for you."

Flash shook his head. "Why didn't you tell me this from the beginning? Why all the special effects? Why make me think I was some kind of second coming?"

The old man smiled. "Now you tell me something true. Didn't you feel more motivated to do this important thing when you believed it was the fulfillment of some ancient religious prophecy?"

Flash finished off a beer and chucked the can out the open window on his side. "I guess I did." He looked at his companion and nearly chuckled. They must be quite a sight, the two of them. Sitting here in this truck, drinking beer. Like a couple of rednecks out for a joyride through the post-apocalyptic wastelands. Like *Hee Haw* gone to hell. "Who are you, really? Hell, *what* are you?"

The old man stared at him for a long moment, some of that old intensity returning to his gaze now. Then he said, "Before I try to explain that to you, tell me one thing. Will you do this thing for me?"

Flash sighed and didn't immediately reply.

The old man pressed on: "I have to know. Because if the answer is no . . . frankly, I'll have to force you to do it. And I can. Have no doubt of that. But I'd prefer you go of your own free will." A pause. "So . . . will you?"

Flash laughed bitterly. "Either way, it's not really my will, is it?"

"I suppose not."

"You suppose not." Flash rolled his eyes and popped the tab on another beer. "Why me? Why not anyone else still around the day you came to me?"

The old man stretched, groaned, and sat up straighter in his seat. "Goddamn, but this body is so feeble, so nearly useless." He made a clucking sound. "Ah, well. Nothing to be done for it now. Flash, I chose you for this role for the simplest of reasons. You were there. I arrived through a crack in the fabric of your reality moments before the unleashing of the Shoth, those flying beasts. I knew what was about to happen. And that there was nothing I could do to stop it.

Your world was already doomed. But I also knew there was a slim chance I might later be able to avert the total extinction of your race. To do that, I would have to bide my time. And I would have to hide. I hijacked the body of the man you came out to meet that day. That body is my host. Here, I'll let you see him as he really he is."

The air around the old man seemed to shimmer and suddenly the flowing white robes and long white hair were gone. Physically, he still appeared the same. But now he wore glasses with thick frames and lenses and a business suit that looked like it had last been in style around about 1978. The man smiled at him. "This is the 'strange' man your coworker told you about that morning. Mr. Gabe Hassler. A 'talent agent', or so he billed himself. Mainly he just bilked money from the legions of dreamers who came to this city in hopes of becoming famous singers. Though I'm in control of his body and mind, he's still sort of here. It's a unique symbiosis. When I make references to things in your culture, that's Gabe shining through."

Flash scowled at the image. "I think I prefer the illusion."

"Very well then."

The air around the old man shimmered again and the white robes and flowing hair returned.

Flash's brow furrowed as he thought a moment. "So . . . you came from the same place as those . . . Sloths?"

"Shoth." The man nodded. "And, yes, I did."

"And you say you came here to save the human race from extinction?"

Another nod. "Yes."

Flash, thinking hard, pursed his lips and drummed his thumbs against the cracked steering wheel. "But those flying things . . . they're all dead. Are you telling me there's some other threat, something else that's come here from your world?"

"I am indeed."

Flash frowned. "Whatever it is, it couldn't possibly be worse than those things."

The old man's features took on a much more solemn cast. "Oh, but it is. Much worse by far." He sighed. "This thing, this *force*, is like me in many ways. We have the same origin. If you were to see either of us in our true forms, your limited senses would perceive a free-floating energy cloud. Something constantly shifting, amorphous and malleable. Like me, this other being is able to infiltrate the minds of other creatures. Like me, it is able to inhabit the bodies of other creatures. As I am doing now with Mr. Hassler. As it is doing now with . . ." He indicated the stretch of Broadway beyond the Salvation Road billboard. ". . . someone . . . out there."

Flash glanced in that direction and shuddered.

The old man continued, "Unlike me, this other being is interested primarily in spreading death and destruction, and in subjugating and humiliating those it chooses to keep alive. I was its adversary long ago. A great war was waged between the forces of light and darkness, a conflict that devastated the world we come from nearly as thoroughly as this one has been devastated. For a time longer than several of your centuries, the opposing armies stood at a virtual stalemate. Then, perhaps because I'd grown complacent, the tide began to slowly turn in favor of darkness. And darkness eventually prevailed. I went into hiding, making myself effectively invisible to my enemies. But I monitored the activities of my adversary. I knew I would not be able to prevent it from spreading its dark influence to other realms, but I believed if I were very watchful and very careful, a chance might arise, an opportunity to extinguish the darkness forever."

Flash blew air through clenched teeth. He looked at the billboard overlooking Broadway. SALVATION ROAD, it read, AVAILABLE OCT. 7. The significance of the date hit Flash and elicited a humorless laugh. "Let me guess, you want me to walk down 'Salvation Road' tomorrow?"

The old man nodded. "I do."

Flash nodded at the billboard. "The date there. That's tomorrow." His grin was a strained thing, almost a death's head rictus. "That's more of your trickery, isn't it? What date is your illusion covering?"

The old man glanced at the billboard briefly. "That's no illusion."

Flash frowned. "Huh."

"It's pure coincidence."

Flash grunted noncommittally. He wasn't sure he believed in such a thing as "coincidence" anymore. While he was glad to know the truth behind the manipulative creature's illusions, he had a feeling there was an even grander, and much more unfathomable, scheme of things. Maybe the date on the billboard was coincidence, but Flash wondered if maybe—just maybe—it might be a bit of the *real* One True God's handiwork, a subtle sign, a personal message from the Almighty to Jeff "Flash" Wheeler. He thought it was more than a little bit possible, and it was this possibility more than anything else that at last brought him some measure of peace.

"One more thing I want to know before we get down to business . . ."

The old man let out an abrupt fart. His nose crinkled and his cheeks turned pink from embarrassment. "Sorry about that. It'll be a pleasure to abandon this foul shell after tomorrow." He smiled meekly. "What is it you wish to know, Flash?"

"Why 'Flash'? Where'd that come from?"

The old man smiled. "You really don't remember?"

Flash frowned and shook his head. "No."

The old man drank some beer and chuckled. In that moment, he reminded Flash strongly of his Uncle Ben. "When you were very young, little more than a toddler really, your Uncle Ben used to babysit you."

The reference to his uncle gave Flash a start. "Uh . . ."

The old man chuckled. "Come now, surely you realize it's by design that I resemble the man. Anyway, your uncle used to read comic books to you. *The Flash* and *Captain America* were two particular favorites. He took to calling you 'Captain Flash'."

A sudden tear spilled down Flash's cheek. "My uncle . . . he died when I was in first grade."

"I know."

Flash looked at him. "And you got all this by looking into my mind?"

"I did."

Flash wiped the tear away and smiled. "I guess that ought to piss me off, but it doesn't somehow. Yeah. I remember now. Ben was a good man." He shook his head. "And I reckon I'd rather face some ancient evil as Captain Flash than as Jeff the Mechanic."

The old man nodded. "So be it."

"So . . . how are we taking this son of a bitch down?"

The old man grinned. "I thought you'd never ask."

19

Emma cried out as Warren thrust roughly into her again and again, causing the headboard to slam repeatedly against the bedroom wall. He loomed high over her, with his back arched and his palms braced against the headboard, snarling, his face contorting like a madman in the grip of delirium. It was strange. Warren had never been quite so . . . animalistic when they were together before. The out-of-character lovemaking style might have disturbed her, but the pleasure she was experiencing was so intense she had little room in her mind for anything other than physical sensation.

They were back in the apartment she'd previously hid out in with Jake and Abby, fucking on the bed once shared by Kelly and Laura. The room was dark, but the door was partially open, and flickering candlelight was visible from the living room. Jasmine and Zeke were out there. Emma experienced flashing moments of embarrassment, knowing they were practically witnesses to her coupling with Warren. In more normal times, she would have been mortified by the situation, would in fact never have allowed it to happen.

But there was nothing normal about the way things were now.

For one thing, Warren was . . . different. Oh, outwardly he seemed the same. And his voice remained the smoky, sexy drawl she remembered from years ago. But now he radiated a swaggering confidence and charisma he hadn't possessed before. It turned her on. She clawed his body, raking grooves in his flesh along his sides and down his back. She felt higher than she'd ever felt before, intoxicated on the sizzling adrenaline rush of pure lust. She wished this magnificent experience would never end. Never mind that her body ached all over from being pushed beyond the normal limits of physical endurance. The pain was a small price to pay for these dazzling sunbursts of ecstasy, powerful waves of sensation that rolled out and came surging back in, over and over, stronger and longer-lasting each time. Occasionally Warren would withdraw and flip her over, enter her from behind, poking alternately at her ass and pussy. He seemed determined to have her every way a man could possibly have a woman. Emma might have chalked this thirst for variety up to a long period of sexual deprivation—except there was none of the tentativeness she would have expected in a man who'd gone a long time without.

Warren pulled out and flipped her over yet again. Again, his strength astonished her. He was tossing her around like something with little more substance that a ragdoll. Her breath exploded out of her lungs and her face was pushed deep into the pillow as he slammed into her again.

Her ecstatic scream was so loud it masked his burst of mad laughter.

It seizes the Emma-thing by the hair and jerks her head back as it begins to pump harder and faster into her. It loves the screams it is able to elicit from her with this new body. The act itself is pleasurable, but what it likes best about the human sexual act is the way its innate savagery so easily strips away all pretense of civility or refinement. It has reduced Emma-thing to the level of an animal in the wild, a mindless thing, a prisoner of the senses.

But already it grows weary of the creature. It has broken her completely and feels there is little fun left to be had by punishing her this way. It thinks of the others in the outer room. In its mind, it can see them sitting silently on the sofa, shifting nervously now and then as they listen to the shrill music of two animals fornicating with abandon. It laughs, imagining all sorts of delightful games it might play with them. As well as numerous creative methods of torture and humiliation.

First, though, it must finish this stage of Emma-thing's punishment. It grasps her by the neck with both hands and smiles at the delicious sight of her bulging eyes. It can taste her thoughts, and reflected in those eyes is the knowledge that she might die at the hands of the man she loves more than anything else. It sees she is not completely opposed to this possibility. Just one more indication of how completely in its thrall she is. It could theoretically keep doing this thing to her indefinitely, so complete is its ability to regulate the host's body. But now it chooses to relax the tight control it has exerted and suddenly the host's body is speeding toward orgasm, pounding Emma-thing so hard the bed groans from the strain. At the moment of orgasm, there's a sound of splintering wood as the bed frame gives way and the mattress and box spring collapse to the floor.

It pulls away from the woman, leaving her panting and close to unconsciousness. It dresses itself in the host's clothes and stands staring down at her for a moment. She looks like a limp, broken thing, the discarded victim of a wild predator.

It smiles again. The expression feels less offensive now. The result, perhaps, of too much time spent in human shells. Soon, though, the last of these execrable creatures will be dead and it will again be able to assume its natural form.

But first . . .

Jasmine's breath caught in her throat as she watched Warren walk into the room. Though the sounds of sex had ceased several minutes earlier, she was surprised to see him. A storm of conflicting emotions buffeted her soul. She felt equal parts rage, jealousy, and fear. The jealousy was to be expected. Just two nights ago she had been the one on the receiving end of Warren's attentions. And now tonight she had to sit in this room and listen while he put it to some other bitch. It was a brazen, heartless, inconsiderate thing, and this—at least in part—was what led to the anger.

But then there was the fear.

She was afraid of Warren. Partly because he was behaving in ways utterly unlike what she remembered from before they'd arrived in Nashville. But mostly because there was something just . . . wrong . . . about him. She couldn't quite pinpoint what it was, but when she looked into his eyes she couldn't hold his gaze for long. The intensity she saw there made her want to find something to hide behind, anywhere where she'd be shielded from that crazed, feral gleam. Her fear was also fueled by the fuzziness of her short-term memory. She remembered walking with Warren for days, all those miles of desolate interstate, every grim bit of it until they were almost in Nashville.

Then—

Nothing. Until, that is, Warren and Zeke, the cable news guy, had shown up at that sidewalk table. She had no idea how she'd come to be at that table. Or why she'd been sitting there with that bitch

Emma. The missing portion of her memory troubled her, so much so she'd refrained from mentioning it to the others. She had a vague sense she had become separated from Warren at some point prior to this meeting, but she remembered nothing specific about that. She ached to question him about it, but some instinct stilled her tongue. She didn't know why, but she sensed broaching the subject would be a bad idea.

She kept her gaze trained on the coffee table as Warren took a seat in a recliner opposite the sofa. She didn't realize how terrified she was until she looked at her lap and saw her tightly clenched hands shaking.

"Look at me, Jasmine."

She didn't want to look at him. But the words conveyed a command, not a request. And she knew she could only obey. Shivering like a person trapped outside in the middle of a blizzard, she raised her gaze and tried not to whimper at the sight of Warren's grinning face.

That's not him, she thought. *I don't know who, or WHAT, it is. But it's NOT him. It's just something masquerading as Warren.*

Warren laughed. "My, but you're a resilient creature. I wiped that part of your memory, but on some level you still know the truth."

Now Jasmine did whimper. Because the charade was over. The thing wearing the Warren mask was speaking solely as itself now.

It laughed again. "I could finish the job, you know. Reach into your mind and do a deeper cleansing of your memory. And I could do so much more. Do you know that with just a thought I could pop a vessel in your brain and make you have a stroke? Maybe that's what I'll do when I'm done playing with you. Just use you up the way I used up the other female, then leave you helpless and drooling on the floor." More debased laughter. "That would be more satisfying than killing you outright. I quite like the idea of leaving you to stew in your own shit and piss, gawping there on the floor like a landed fish."

Jasmine sniffled. "Please . . ."

"I love that word." There was an obscenely rapturous look on its face. "It conveys so much, doesn't it? Desperation. Surrender. Utter helplessness. It's one of my greater pleasures, making lesser beings beg and mewl."

Jasmine wanted to say it again, in fact. She had never been so frightened in her life, not even in those first moments after Gary died. But she bit her lower lip, turning the word back before it could roll past the edge of her tongue. She was determined not to give this foul thing the satisfaction of hearing her beg. At least for this moment. At least until it forced her to break down. It was a small thing. But it mattered, goddammit. She would not willingly surrender the last frail shred of her dignity.

The look of rapture on its face gave way to a glower. "Say it again. Now."

Jasmine bit down harder on her lip. She felt flesh part beneath her rending teeth and the salty sting of blood on her tongue. This was her last stand. The last remaining iota of defiance she could muster. Then she felt a presence in her head, a warm tickle, and in a flash she saw herself sprawled on the floor, her mind ripped apart and her body rendered useless.

So she blurted it out: "Please!"

It cocked its head, made Warren's handsome face grin. "Please what?"

Jasmine released a big breath, then drew in a deep lungful of air. Her fingernails etched bloody grooves in her palms as she struggled not to hyperventilate. She swallowed hard and said, "Please don't hurt me."

The thing made Warren's face screw up like a man pondering one of the universe's most impenetrable mysteries. Then it smiled again. "Okay."

Jasmine felt the warm tickle recede from her head.

She breathed a relieved sigh and sniffled again, hot tears racing down her face as she tried not to think about the possibility she was nearing the end of her life. That a descent into eternal darkness might only be moments away.

"You don't want to die do you?"

She shuddered and shook her head. "No." Her voice was barely audible. "I don't."

"Then come over here and sit at my feet."

Jasmine experienced a flash of panic. She considered a run for the apartment's front door, but dismissed the idea at once. She wouldn't get two feet before the thing stopped her with nothing more than a thought. So she stood and moved haltingly toward the grinning thing in the recliner. It bade her forward with its gleaming eyes, and soon Jasmine was kneeling in front of it.

It said, "Lay your head in my lap."

And she did, feeling broken, utterly robbed of any will of her own, like a whipped dog desperately attempting to curry the favor of its abusive master.

Then it was stroking her hair and saying, "That's a good girl. You've learned your place." It chuckled. "Now let's see about Zekey-boy, eh?"

Emma managed to recover some measure of her wits while Warren entertained himself with the debasement of Jasmine and Zeke. She came back to herself slowly at first, like a heroin junkie coming down from a rush. Voices floated in from the living room, but at first the words were meaningless noise. She detected cruelty in the male voice, and fear in the female's. She focused on those base feelings until her head felt marginally clearer, then the words started to register.

She sat up and moved to the edge of the bed, listening in growing horror as Warren played some sadistic mind game with the woman named Jasmine. She thought at first they were acting out a kinky master-slave scenario, maybe some routine they'd worked out during their days spent walking across the country together. This thought sent a flash of jealousy through her and she came close to dashing out to the living room to kick the bitch's ass. But she sat there and listened some more, and the jealousy faded. What she was hearing was no game, she was sure of it.

There was something desperately wrong with Warren. This cruel man was nothing like the Warren she remembered. That Warren, though flawed, had been a man worthy of love and devotion. At least until he became almost terminally self-destructive. But this person that looked and sounded like Warren was a stranger. It was as if some malevolent being had hijacked Warren's body.

Emma's eyes went wide at the thought.

She flashed back to the confrontation at Aaron's hiding place, saw that little girl walk out of a black supernatural soup into that too-brightly lit room. The girl's eyes had possessed the same strange, leering gleam she'd seen in Warren's eyes. A possibility so awful it nearly made her cry out bloomed in Emma's mind like a black flower. The girl was a vessel, a flesh and blood prisoner of some darker consciousness. If the thing that had possessed Abby could leap to another body . . .

Emma rose slowly from the bed and moved in careful steps to the door. She kept her mouth closed, suddenly certain it was crucial she not make a sound. She reached the door and stood behind it, listening as Warren (*not him, only looks like him* . . .) ordered Zeke to do

211

something that made her stomach churn.

She didn't want to see what was happening. Could hardly bear the thought of it. But she had no choice. She needed visual confirmation, a final bit of condemning evidence, before she could write Warren off forever.

She took a careful breath and shuffled one foot to the left, then peered around the edge of the door.

At first her mind couldn't process what she was seeing.

It was too insane to be real.

Zeke Johnson was sitting on the floor next to the coffee table. His cheeks looked bloated and were speckled with gore. His right hand was pressed through his open mouth and his jaw was moving in a mechanical way as he worked at chewing off his fingers.

Emma's stomach clenched and she felt nausea rise in her throat. She felt the strength seep out of her legs as she gripped the edge of the door in an effort to keep from falling, but she only succeeded in pulling the door the rest of the way open—and thereby exposing herself to the monster inhabiting Warren's body.

It looked at her, grinning as if it'd been aware of her scrutiny all along. She realized with a dawning sickness it probably had been. Jasmine looked up from the thing's lap and showed her a sick, demented smile. Blood dribbled from the corners of the woman's mouth. The creature had done something to her brain, had either short-circuited it or rewired it in some fucked-up way. Either that, or she'd simply snapped from bearing witness to so much horror. The expression on the woman's face made her look more like a rabid animal than a human being.

The thing that looked like Warren giggled, reminding her so much of Aaron Harris her skin crawled. "Look everybody. Emma's come out to play. I had a good time with that nimble little body of hers. What say we see what else we can do with it, eh?"

Emma shook her head. "Nuh-nuh . . . no."

Another giggle from the Warren-thing. "No? Oh, I don't think so."

But Emma's terror and physical shakiness overwhelmed her before the creature could issue a command.

She let go of the door and fell unconscious to the floor.

20

OCTOBER 7
High Noon

"It's time."

Flash heard the voice in his head in those last blissful moments of sleep. He'd been dreaming of a better, happier life in a lush and green paradise somewhere far from this blighted world. A place where the sun always shone and the sky was always the same achingly brilliant hue of blue. And the most common sounds were laughter and birdsong. There'd been a smile on his face while he dreamed of this place, but the expression faltered at the sound of those two words. In the final seconds of the dream the bright blue sky suddenly darkened and a cold wind came sweeping across the verdant land.

Then his eyes snapped open. The first thing he saw was the damnable billboard. And the washed-out, faded blue of the sky overhead. He was still in the truck, but the old man was gone now. Flash knew he'd never see him again.

"I'm on my own from here on out," he said, addressing the comment to the peeling image of the female country singer. "With only you to watch over me. And somehow I don't think you're gonna be any help."

Flash sighed. "Ain't nothin' for it, I guess."

He pushed open the truck's creaking driver's side door and stepped outside. He moved to the front of the truck, where he groaned and stretched, working out the kinks in his body. Sleeping in the truck meant surrendering a significant degree of physical comfort, but that he could deal with. He'd found a strange measure of peace during his time in the truck and wished like hell he could drive it down Salvation Road. He'd feel so much more secure and confident behind the wheel of a vehicle like the F-150. But this was like wishing away the last few weeks or something else equally impossible, so he put it out of his mind.

Flash could almost hear the old man's voice again: *So get on with it, then.*

So he started walking. A tremor of excitement swept through him as he crossed the dealership's parking lot in the space of a few seconds and started down the road. He felt fear, too. A lot of it. He dreaded the confrontation with the dark thing. But he was going to meet his destiny. Which wasn't quite the destiny he'd envisioned initially. He wasn't going forth as a warrior. Not exactly. He was more of a vessel. A messenger of salvation. A means to a noble end.

Emphasis on "end".

The old man had made it clear Flash was in the last hours of his mortal life. He had to know and accept this before carrying out his mission. And though he was afraid (terrified, even), accept it he did. At least in part because he had an inkling the glimpse of paradise from his dream was something more than a wishful fantasy. He wouldn't have been able to precisely say why he felt this way, but he did. Felt it down to his bones. He'd been granted a peek at the better place that awaited him beyond life in this broken world.

With each step he took down Broadway, he grew more anxious to make the transition to that place. It would be such a relief to be delivered from this land of nightmares.

First things first, he told himself. *You've got a job to do.*

As he passed beneath the billboard and took his first steps down Salvation Road, it was exactly ten minutes past noon.

~

"Do you know what I am yet?"

Emma looked up from her kneeling position on the apartment floor. Warren's smirking face loomed over her. No, not Warren. She willed herself to think of the thing standing before her only as an *it*.

An unfathomable monster in a pretty mask. The creature's lips and chin were smeared with blood. She looked into its eyes and tried to discern even the faintest flicker of her lost love's essence there. But she saw only that infernal malevolent glee, a gleaming enthusiasm for slaughter and degradation.

She coughed. "You're the devil."

It threw its head back and laughed. Then, still grinning broadly, it looked at Emma again. "How quaint. I'm aware of your devil concept, of course. Do you know that when I touch the minds of you humans I absorb every bit of knowledge gleaned throughout the course of your pitiful lives?" It laughed again. "I know everything about you, for instance. Your most private thoughts. Your most shameful fantasies. The things you can't bring yourself to tell even those closest to you. And I have to tell you, I don't think even Warren, masochist that he is, would go for some of those things. You're a sick little bitch, you know that?"

Emma said nothing. She was beyond feeling mortified now. Since coming to after her fainting spell, she'd been made to endure levels of humiliation she would never have dreamed possible. And had been made to do things so revolting she was now beyond being shocked.

The Warren-thing's nostrils flared. "Oh, I wouldn't say that. The worst is yet to come for you. You have my most sincere promise on that count."

Emma's gaze went back to the floor. She shuddered, feeling the thing's hot gaze roam over her body. She was naked, but her torso was soaked with gore. Most of this derived from the things she'd been made to do to Zeke Johnson with the kitchen knife. Some of it was from cuts to her own flesh. The coagulated blood felt sticky on her skin, and she ached to wash it off. Every time she shifted her body, dry brown flakes of it fluttered to the crimson-stained carpet.

The creature put two fingers under her chin and forced her to look at him again. Those nostrils flared again. It was becoming excited. Emma knew what was coming next. She somehow managed not to whimper.

"Know this—I'm worse than any imaginary devil."

Emma did know it.

Then the thing was pushing her backward and forcing her legs apart. Her body, manipulated by the drooling creature, shivered with excitement.

She screamed.

~

Jasmine screamed, too.

Her eyes snapped open and her body lurched on the floor as she emerged from a nightmare of screaming demons and unspeakable atrocities. Short-lived relief flashed through her like a jolt of electricity, then true awareness returned and she realized with despair she was only trading one nightmare for another. And this one, the waking nightmare, was infinitely worse than the one she'd left behind. Because it was real. Regardless of how desperately her mind tried to rebel against it.

Warren was on top of the girl again, his butt pistoning up and down in fast but precise strokes, like a machine in a factory. The girl screamed and screamed. The sound was agony laced with pleasure. Jasmine was sickened to find herself dimly aroused. This was the creature's influence at work, she suspected. The taint of its intrusion into her mind. A twisted, infected part of her wanted what Emma was getting.

But another, increasingly strong impulse was making itself known. A desire to get up off the floor and get the hell out of here while that vile thing was occupied with the other woman. The idea frightened her as much as it tempted her. Because if that thing caught her in the act of trying to flee, it would stop her. And it would surely punish her in some exquisitely awful way.

Perhaps instinctively seeking some vivid evidence of the worst that could happen, Jasmine glanced at Zeke Johnson. The former newsman was alive and conscious, but he'd been made to endure hours of seemingly endless tortures. He sat shivering on the couch, his nude body swathed in gore, his eyes glassy and staring. The memory of his shrill, almost girlish screams was so clear in Jasmine's memory it was as if she was hearing them all over again. He was just a shell now, an irreparably ruined thing. She looked at the cauterized stumps where the fingers of his right hand had been and recalled that awful stench of burning flesh. The thing made Emma do most of the dirty work where Zeke was concerned.

But Jasmine hadn't been left out of the festivities. She'd wielded a knife of her own on Emma, inflicting dozens of non-lethal cuts on the younger woman's torso. At its direction, but not necessarily under force. Not by the strictest definition of "force", at least. Something inside her had snapped in the midst of that orgy of blood and madness, some crucial bit of her sanity had temporarily fled her. She'd felt debauched, like a willing participant in some satanic ritual. She did what he ordered without hesitation, eagerly, reveling in it, as if she believed the only way to survive this time of madness was to embrace it.

But then there'd been a long period of unconsciousness. Now that she was awake again she felt like a mental patient jolted out of a delirium, temporarily transported back to the land of (relative) sanity via the miracle of psychotropic medication. She experienced a surge of horror at the memory of the things she'd done, and especially at the way she'd felt while doing them.

Her gaze flicked back to Warren and Emma.

The machine was still pounding away.

Get out, a voice seemed to whisper in her ear. This felt strangely like more than an internal voice, almost like some disembodied consciousness giving her direction. *Get up and take a walk down Salvation Road.*

She frowned.

Salvation Road?

What the hell is that supposed to mean?

But the voice didn't come again. That was okay, though. It'd given her the last extra bit of motivation she needed to overcome her terror of retribution. She braced her hands on the carpet and pushed herself slowly up, keeping a wary eye on the rutting couple all the while. First she got to her knees, then, very carefully, to her feet. She kept her mouth closed the whole time, not wanting the thing to hear her breathing.

She was five feet away from the open front door of the apartment. She wasn't sure she would even be attempting this had the door been closed. She sent a silent prayer of thanks to the God she'd no doubt offended countless times over the last several hours and began edging toward the door. She shot a quick glance in Zeke's direction, worried he might give her away in the last moment, but he still seemed catatonic.

Jasmine moved backward through the opening, the bare soles of her feet bumping against the threshold. Though she managed not to stumble, she for the first time considered the potential difficulties of attempting a rapid getaway barefoot. It would be an impediment for sure, but not one she could allow herself to dwell on now. She was in the hallway outside the apartment, and all at once freedom no longer seemed like a remote fantasy. It was a treasure there for the taking.

FROM THE VOID

All she had to do was reach out and grab it. So, trying her best to step lightly, she moved quickly down the dusty wooden landing and reached the staircase in a matter of moments.

Her heart raced as she descended the steps to the first floor, first with care and precision, then with increasing abandon. She glanced backward as she reached the first floor and saw no sign of pursuit. She heard more of Emma's squeals and screams and knew she still had an opportunity to get one hell of a head start. But it wouldn't do to linger even a moment longer.

So she pulled open the building's creaking front door and dashed outside. The diffused sunlight fell warmly on her skin as she streaked across the courtyard and through the debris-covered front yard to the street beyond.

She turned left on 21st and kept on running. If she had to—and if her body could bear it—she figured she might keep running until she was out of the city.

~

As Flash moved at an unhurried pace down Broadway toward 21st, he allowed himself to be distracted for a time from the approaching rendezvous with the dark one. Nostalgia for the world he'd known washed over him as he surveyed the array of familiar haunts and landmarks. Coming up on his right was Noshville, the New York-style deli that had been one of his favorite places to have lunch. The once immaculately white facade was now tinged a deep brown and the windows were shaded with what looked to be an indelible layer of sludge and/or dust. A little farther along, up on the left, was the Great Escape, which, true to its name, had been a great place to hunt for rare old records and comic books. Its windows were smashed out and Flash had an amusing image of crazed comics geeks looting the place the day after the demon attack, carrying out armloads of Mylar-sealed treasures. Of course, those same geeks would all have been dead a day or two later, victims of the creeping, invisible infection from that other world. The realization was a sobering slap in the face, and Flash was no longer amused.

Prior to beginning his fateful walk down "Salvation Road," Flash hadn't quite grasped the extent of the mystery malady that had struck down most of his fellow humans. What he'd known had been strictly limited to what the old man had been able to tell him. Things that meshed with his memories of his dying coworkers. That had been bad enough. What the old man told him was worse by far. When

Flash had at last understood that nearly everyone else on earth was dead, he'd experienced a deeply cosmic, utterly unquantifiable horror. In some ways it'd been too big a thing to truly absorb, at least on that abstract level.

But now he was seeing it for himself and there was no longer anything at all abstract about it. He saw bodies and parts of bodies everywhere. But they didn't look the way he imagined bodies dead less than two weeks should look. The state of decay in most cases was so advanced the victims appeared mummified. He tried to imagine what it must have been like for these poor bastards. First realizing you were sick and getting sicker. Then knowing there was nothing you could do about it. That there was no one around to help you, and that it would only get steadily worse, until an agonizing death came and draped a thick, black blanket over the horrors surrounding you.

Tears welled in Flash's eyes, and he wiped them away as he moved along the curve in the road where Broadway gave way to 21st Ave. Behind the grief and tears, though, was a boiling rage. If what the old man had told him could be trusted—and Flash believed it could be—the dark thing he was about to meet had deliberately set in motion the process that shredded the veil of "reality" separating the two co-existing worlds. It likely hadn't known the two worlds were so thoroughly incompatible, as its original intentions had probably included a prolonged campaign of terror and subjugation. Decades, or even centuries, of a bloody reign. The dark thing had grown bored with its own world—or so the old man hypothesized—where there'd been precious few living creatures (other than the Shoth) left to kill. So though the tragedy that was the decimation of the human race was immense, Flash decided he was at least glad the goddamned thing had been deprived of its most coveted prize, a new world full of things to hurt and terrorize. Looking at it in that light, the creeping rot could be seen as a kind of mercy, albeit an unintentional one.

But knowing that did nothing to temper the fury brewing within him. A grim smile twitched at the corners of his mouth as he imagined the coming moment of confrontation. Especially that wonderful instant when the dark thing would realize what was about to happen—a thing it would have absolutely no defense against.

~

The thing ejaculated into Emma, pounding her against the floor as hard as it possibly could. Emma cried out again, purely from pain this time. She was certain the creature meant to snap her spine before it was done. But then it abruptly withdrew from her and she was still intact, albeit bruised and battered. Some of the knife-wounds to her torso were bleeding again, but she didn't care. At least the vile thing was off (and out) of her again.

Her head rolled numbly to the left and she saw the kitchen knife she'd used to torment Zeke lying discarded on the floor. She considered grabbing it and drawing it quickly across her jugular vein, but she didn't have the strength. Right now even breathing hurt. She closed her eyes and hoped she'd at least be allowed to sleep a while. It was the only means of escape currently available to her. She wondered vaguely how much more punishment her body could take. Surely not much more. She harbored a dark hope the abuse would soon reach such an extreme level her heart would simply give out. She didn't really want to die, not down to the deepest core of her being, but death seemed the only permanent way out of the hell her life had become.

She was drifting down toward unconsciousness when she was jolted wide awake by a yell so piercing it made her chest constrict with terror, and for a moment she was sure her wish for death was being granted. Then there was another yell, louder than before, and her heart kept on beating.

Somehow she found the strength to prop herself up on her elbows. The anger exploding out of the creature filled the room like the heat flash from a bomb blast and sent a burst of adrenaline coursing through her body. The thing stood in the middle of the room, spinning around in a fast circle, its eyes wide and searching. At first Emma couldn't fathom the source of its rage—then it hit her.

And she smiled.

Jasmine . . .

Though she hadn't liked the woman, a thrill close to elation made her grin as she realized Jasmine was gone. Somehow, while the thing had been busy raping Emma, the other woman had managed to emerge from the state of near-catatonia she'd been in for hours and slip out of the apartment. All without making a sound. And it was plain that the creature hadn't had the slightest inkling of what was happening. Which sort of blew its pretense of omniscience all to shreds, didn't it?

Emma realized there was a grin stretched wide across her face and made it go away before the creature could focus on her. She was happy verging on ecstatic at this turn of events, but this joy was tempered by the knowledge she would likely soon endure the brunt of the thing's rage. She didn't look forward to that, but she remained thrilled that it had finally been thwarted, and she silently urged Jasmine on.

Get out of town, you fucking bitch, she thought. *Run like the goddamned wind!*

The creature was still stumbling about the room, its eyes still wide and uncomprehending. Emma saw what was about to happen a moment before it did. One of its feet landed on the discarded knife. It screamed and then was flailing backward, falling hard to the floor. Emma laughed. She couldn't help it. Let the fucker do as it wished to her. This was too wonderful a turn of events not to express her delight.

The thing groaned and managed to struggle into a sitting position. It looked woozy, its eyes red and glossy. Its gaze was unfocused for several moments—until another trill of helpless laughter from Emma caused its head to swivel in her direction. The expression it showed her exuded befuddlement. Seeing it caused her to laugh yet again.

It shook its head in amazement. "How could she be gone?"

Emma smiled. "I guess you're not quite so all-powerful after all, huh?"

Now it glowered at her, its nostrils flaring again. "You must not mock me."

Emma laughed harder than ever. Great, heaving belly laughs. So immense was her amusement that she was unable to speak for a time, even as the creature screamed and raged at her, demanding her submission. It wasn't because her fear had deserted her. Quite the contrary. It was greater than ever. But the part of her that feared this thing was overpowered by a kind of mad fatalism. She was going to die. No matter what. She was going to suffer. A lot. No matter what. So she might as well laugh in the fucker's face while she could.

But the laughter abruptly ceased when it surged upright, seized her by the neck, and lifted her off her feet. Its face was inches from her own as it screamed at her: "I AM THE DESTROYER OF WORLDS AND LORD OF THE WASTELANDS! YOU WILL NOT MOCK ME!"

A choked gargle issued from Emma's constricted throat, a sound that could have been mistaken for a desperate plea for mercy—if not for the quivering grin still stretched across her sweat-shiny face. The thing screamed again, lifted her higher, flexed its arms, and threw her

221

across the room. Emma was airborne for only an instant, but in that time she felt almost giddy, like a kid again, strapped into the wickedest roller coaster at Six Flags. Then she hit the wall, hard, and tumbled to the sofa below, knocking Zeke sideways as she bounced off the edge of the sofa and rolled to the floor. Her whole body sizzled with pain as her open mouth tasted dirty carpet. She sensed the thing coming at her, charging hard, and tensed, certain it was about to fling her across the room again.

Instead, it upended the coffee table and tossed it aside. Then, gripping a handful of her hair, it hauled her upright and forced her into a kneeling position. With its other hand, it gripped its genitalia and pushed it toward her mouth. "You will submit to me. You will pleasure me. You will worship me."

And Emma laughed again. She raised her gaze to look right into the thing's blazing eyes. "You're so pathetic."

A momentary flicker of confusion shone in its eyes. Its mouth twitched. "You've lost your mind, haven't you? You're ..." It frowned, seeming to strain for a word. "... you're *hysterical*. I've broken you utterly."

Some of the giddiness drained out of Emma then, but she remained resolute. "Keep telling yourself that. It really is funny, though. For a self-styled 'destroyer of worlds', you're not very impressive."

Its eyes went wide at that statement. "Empty words. This is nothing more than bravado. You know you are doomed, so—"

"I'm telling the truth as I see it," she cut him off. "You've got all these powers and unearthly abilities and look at the shabby use you've put them to. Yeah, you're plenty scary, but from what I've seen, you're little more than a garden-variety pervert. You want to force yourself on me one more time?" She laughed disdainfully. "Go ahead. It means nothing. And what'll you do when you've used me up? There's no one left to terrorize. This world is dead."

It nodded. "And I killed it."

Emma shrugged. "Did you? My, but that's interesting. You come here on some kind of inter-dimensional crusade or jihad, or what-thefuckever, kill damn near everybody on the planet, and other than rape you can't think of anything to do with the last bitch standing. So ultimately everything you've done is meaningless."

It tightened its grip on her hair, eliciting a wince of pain. "I'm done listening to you, cunt. You are nothing. You are beneath me. And I don't have to justify myself to you."

Emma started to retort, but it twisted her hair tighter still. "I said I'm *done listening to you.*" For a moment its face contorted with rage, then it grinned so broadly the taut skin of its cheeks resembled half-moon-shaped peach wedges sliced with razor-precision. "But I'm not through debasing you. You imagine you can shame me into doing other than what I wish to do? Laughable." It chuckled. "But to prove to you I'm not quite out of tricks, I think it's time you were reacquainted with a mutual friend of ours."

Another pained wince turned into a frown, and Emma said, "What are you—"

"He's talking about me, sweetheart."

Emma's mouth dropped open at the sound of that hated voice. She shook her head as a combination of horror and disbelief settled in her stomach like a lead weight. "No."

"Oh, yes."

The creature relinquished its hold on her hair and stepped away, allowing her to see Aaron emerge from the kitchen area. He grinned as he walked slowly toward her. The way the skin crinkled around the folds of flesh where his eyes used to be made her stomach flip. He started shedding his clothes as he neared her, undoing the buttons of his shirt slowly, as if performing a striptease. His shirt fell away from his torso and dropped to the floor. Then he undid the button of his khaki trousers and slid the zipper down. He barely broke stride as he stepped out of the pants and kept coming toward her. She had a weird feeling of being ogled, as if he could see her even without his eyes.

"Oh, he can see you. As clearly as you can see him." The creature laughed. "I've enhanced the perceptive abilities of his brain in preparation for this special moment. He no longer needs eyes."

Emma shook her head again. "That's crazy. That can't be."

Aaron licked his lips. "But it is."

Emma felt bile in her throat as she watched Aaron's organ grow hard as he came closer to her. A whimper emerged through clenched teeth. The mad laughter of moments ago seemed as far away as the happiness she'd once known with Warren Hatcher. "Please . . . please don't do this."

Aaron laughed. "Don't be ridiculous. Mind you, I don't mind hearing you beg. It's music to my fucking ears, matter of fact. But it's pointless. You're about to get what's been coming to you for a long time and there's nothing you can do to stop it."

Then he was standing right in front of her, his stiff cock pointing at the top of her head like a divining rod.

Emma closed her eyes.

Aaron slapped her. "Look at me!" He laughed again. "Hah! Remember when you said that to *me*, bitch?"

Emma's eyes fluttered open and she looked up at Aaron through a veil of tears. "You don't have to do this. There's got to be some spark of humanity left somewhere inside you. This thing killed the rest of our kind. It destroyed our world. Doesn't that mean anything to you?"

Aaron nodded. He licked his lips again. "It does. It means I owe this motherfucker a debt of eternal gratitude. Our race needed wiping out, in my opinion. And, hell, he did me the favor of leaving you alive. You're all I need of the human race." He made a low moan of pleasure. "And you'll be happy to know I don't plan to kill you. You're gonna live out the rest of your natural life as my slave. Starting now."

Emma shook her head again. "No." But there was little conviction left in her voice now.

The creature said, "Take her now."

And so Aaron did as his new master bade.

~

Flash was pretty far along Salvation Road now. So far there was no evidence of unusual activity anywhere. There was no activity of any sort, unusual or otherwise. This was a dead place. He was now passing through what had been the trendy Hillsboro Village stretch of 21st Avenue. To his left and right were an array of once-posh cafes and boutiques.

Here and there were the jagged black slashes in the fabric of reality, but he wasn't afraid of them now; they looked as dead as the world around them. As he continued on down the road and surveyed his surroundings, he found it hard to believe anything momentous could occur here.

Yet he believed everything the old man had told him. Somewhere along Salvation Road lurked a creature which, if it wasn't the ultimate evil in all of the multiple planes of existence, it was pretty close.

And, Flash mused with a wry, tired grin, *it's my job to defeat it. It's a crazy old world, ain't it?*

Flash was thinking about the odd scheme outlined by the old man last night when he moved around the hulk of a rusting box truck and saw a beautiful woman appear in the distance. He couldn't quite make out her face yet, but he could tell she was beautiful by the outline of her slim yet shapely body and by the way she moved, somehow graceful even in the obvious throes of panic. She moved like a gazelle streaking across an African plain.

She hadn't seen him yet. And Flash didn't want to spook her, so he moved back behind the box truck and peered around a flap of rusted metal to observe her approach. He stood stock-still, listening for her approach. For maybe thirty seconds, there was only more of that same silence and dead stillness. Then he heard the first sound of bare flesh slapping against pavement, followed by the huff of labored breathing. Flash waited a little longer, standing still until he was sure the woman was no more than twenty feet or so away.

Then he stepped back outside and into her path. She came hurtling at him, too fast to see the new obstacle in her way, and Flash braced himself for impact. She ran straight into his open arms, shrieked, and they both went tumbling to the ground. Flash landed painfully on his back, absorbing the worst of the impact. The woman's wide, bugged-out eyes stared crazily at him, then she tried to pull away.

And Flash said, "I'm not here to hurt you, Jasmine."

The use of her name made the woman freeze. She gaped at him, her mouth hanging open, making her look like an awestruck child watching a Fourth of July fireworks display.

Flash sighed and sat up, wincing at the way his back suddenly ached. "I'm here to help."

Jasmine shook her head. "How did you know my name?"

"I didn't until just now. It's weird. The old man told me I'd know your name, that it'd come to me, and goddamned if he wasn't right."

Jasmine kept on shaking her head. "You sound crazy."

Flash smiled. "I know. It can't be helped, really. But I'm not crazy. And I meant what I said. I'm here to help. Somewhere along this road is a place, probably an apartment, where a very bad entity, a kind of demon or dark god from another world, is doing a very bad thing. I'm supposed to defeat it. And I have a notion you know where this thing is."

Jasmine shook her head yet again. "Maybe I do. But you can't make me go back there."

Flash's expression became more solemn. "I don't intend to. I just need you to point the way. I'll take care of the rest myself."

Jasmine laughed harshly, a humorless, despairing sound. "You really are crazy. Nothing can beat that thing. I shouldn't tell you where to go. It'd be suicide."

Flash gripped her wrist hard, making her share his sense of urgency. "Tell me."

Jasmine tried to twist free of his grip, but he held fast to her. So she surrendered, but her eyes were aglow with a defiant intensity. "Fine. I'll send you to your death. You can't say I didn't warn you."

"Tell me," Flash said again.

So she told him where to find the dark thing.

~

Aaron came almost instantly. When he was through bucking against her, he pulled out of her and stood up, throwing his fists exultantly into the air. He let out a child-like yell and jumped up and down. Unable to bear the sight of the vile man's triumph, Emma rolled onto her side and sobbed silently into the hanging sofa skirt. It was so monumentally unfair and wrong. She'd fought so hard to fend the sick bastard off in their previous encounters, had thought him vanquished forever after leaving him alone and sightless in that apartment. But now, through some miracle of dark magic, he was having the last laugh. Quite literally, so it seemed. She should've bashed his brains out when she'd had the chance, she reflected bitterly.

Emma remained on her side, her face hidden, until the creature said, "Look at us, Emma."

A command. Her instinct was to resist, but she felt the first pinprick spot of warmth touch her brain and decided resistance was futile. She rolled onto her back and stared up in mute horror at the two naked monsters. The tableau was at once absurd and utterly terrifying, like some drug-induced hallucinogenic vision. A leering, waking, psychedelic nightmare.

Aaron grinned and said, "I wish I had a camera. She looks so hot all beaten up, sweaty, and broken like that."

The creature said, "I tire of you."

Aaron was still grinning when he said, "What?"

His eyeless gaze was still riveted to Emma's chest. He never saw the creature reaching for his back. But he flinched when he felt fingers press against his spine. Then his mouth popped open and his limbs jerked spasmodically. He shook his head back and forth and appeared to be trying to scream. The creature turned Aaron's body sideways so Emma could see what was happening to him. Her lips curled in disgust at the sight of the creature's hand pushing through the flesh of Aaron's back, sliding in as easily as a hand pressing through cookie dough.

It smiled at her and spoke in an incongruously conversational tone. "See the way he's twitching? I have my hand wrapped around his spine. In a moment I'll tear it out of his body and leave him senseless and dying on the floor."

Emma sat up. She pulled her knees up to her chest and wrapped her arms around them. She let out a big breath and said, "Okay."

The thing's smile widened. "That's it? Just 'okay'? Where's your humanity? Surely you must have some small spark of it somewhere way down at the bottom of your broken soul. Right?"

Emma's mouth was a tight, grim line. "No. I don't think I do."

The thing winked. "Good."

Then it finished the job on Aaron, doing exactly as it had promised. Emma watched stone-faced as the grisly mess that was all that was left of Aaron dropped to the floor. The creature, grinning, held the extricated spine in its hand like some kind of bloody trophy.

"Am I your hero now?" it asked in a smooth, quietly insinuating voice. "Am I your knight in bloody armor? After all, I just vanquished your most hated enemy."

Emma's face remained expressionless as she said, "No. You haven't."

The creature's face exhibited mock offense. It slapped its free hand against its chest. "No!" Then it shook its head and frowned. "You've cut me to the quick."

"I'd like to cut you," she said, her voice flat, uninflected. "I'd cut your heart right out."

The thing's expression took on a quizzical cast. "Would you really? Because surely you know that in doing so you'd be killing your long-lost love as well." It laughed at the obvious flicker of doubt that crossed her face. "Oh, it's true. He's still very much in here with me. And I could return him to you if I wished."

"Shut up." Emma's face hardened again. "You're lying. You're just taunting me."

The creature shook its head. "I am not."

It knelt to pick up the discarded kitchen knife.

Emma flinched and braced her palms on the carpet, preparing to scoot backward.

"Relax." The thing's voice remained low, calm, almost soothing. "I'm not going to hurt you. Not this time. In fact, I am giving you the opportunity you've desired."

It flipped the knife around, holding it by the blade, proffering it to her.

"Take it."

Emma bit her lip. Her gaze flicked from the knife to Warren's face and back again. She hesitated only a moment longer before snatching the knife from its hand. Gripping it tightly in her fist, she surged to her feet, snarled, and raised the blade high over her head. The creature stood there smiling, with its chest thrust forward in invitation.

Emma cursed herself for hesitating, but she couldn't help it. She had to know something before slamming the blade into Warren's body. "Why are you doing this? Why would you do all you've done then let me kill you so easily?" She trembled and helpless tears leaked from her eyes. "You're fucking with my head again, aren't you?"

The thing's expression was very solemn. It exuded a degree of sincerity so convincing Emma almost bought it. The eyes lacked that maniacal fire she'd become used to and now had a soulful look that reminded her painfully of Warren. "You nailed it earlier. Except for you, there's nothing left in this world. Without lands to conquer and living things to subjugate, my existence is an empty, joyless thing. I'm asking you to kill me as an act of mercy. If not for me, then for Warren."

Emma's hand was still high over her head, but it was shaking badly. "Why won't you kill yourself, then?" She sniffled as more tears coursed down her face. "Leave Warren's body and . . . and . . ."

It smiled again, almost warmly. "Ah, there's the rub. I can only be killed in a corporeal form. Therefore, if you wish me dead, you must also kill your lover. Remember, I'm responsible for the deaths of billions. Surely you can make this sacrifice to avenge all those lost souls."

Until that moment Emma had believed her heart to be a dead thing, a cold lump devoid of human feeling, but now she knew she'd been wrong. It was as alive as it'd ever been, just weary and battered. And now she could feel that still-pulsing vitality too painfully as she considered Warren Hatcher and the way the love they'd once shared had shaped their lives. She loved him still, and could never love another so intensely. Though much pain had stemmed from their relationship, she believed a life in which they'd never crossed paths would've been a lesser life, a duller, colorless existence. She knew Warren would say the same. Accepting this was easy. What wasn't easy was the way thinking about it made her not-dead-after-all heart feel like it was breaking all over again—and for the last time.

Her eyes narrowed to glistening slits as her voice emerged in a terse whisper: "Yes. I can make this sacrifice."

The creature smiled again. It thrust its chest forward further still, spread its arms in a Christ-like crucifixion pose, and closed its eyes. "I await your vengeance and mercy."

Emma's body tensed as she psyched herself up to do what she had to do. Then she let out a breath, stepped forward, and began to bring the knife down.

"STOP!"

Emma's arm continued its downward arc, but the abrupt intrusion of the stentorian voice—coupled with a change-of-plans command issued by her brain in the last possible nanosecond—sent the knife veering of course. The blade sliced a crimson line down the length of a thigh before it went flying out of Emma's hand.

The creature cried out in pain as its eyes snapped open. Emma staggered backward as the thing whirled to face the intruder. Her legs met the edge of the sofa and she fell backward, sending a cloud of dust into the air as her rear end landed hard on a cushion. She made no effort to get up. She sensed that whatever was about to happen next was out of her hands, and she felt strangely like a movie theater patron sitting in her seat and waiting for the lights to go down and the show to begin. Zeke sat up and turned slightly in her direction, blinking slowly at her, some dim hint of awareness finally dawning in his bleary eyes. Then his gaze went to the apartment's front door.

A man neither of them had ever seen before stood inside the front door. He was an affable-looking and slightly heavyset man in his mid-to-late thirties. He was wearing what Emma assumed was a mechanic's uniform. A patch sewn on a front breast pocket showed his name to be Jeff. He was a shade over six feet tall, and his electric blue eyes were his most distinctive feature. They were piercing, movie idol eyes. And right now they were riveted on the Warren-thing.

The creature seemed temporarily disconcerted by the man's sudden appearance. Emma had a feeling it wasn't used to situations in which it didn't perfectly control every aspect of what was happening. But it recovered quickly, snarling, curling its hands into fists as it bore down on the mechanic. Emma cringed, knowing in a moment she'd see the mechanic, Jeff, be torn apart.

But the creature never got within six feet of the man, who never flinched, never retreated even an inch.

"That's far enough."

The thing stopped dead and let out a startled whuff of breath, as though he'd walked straight into an invisible wall. Its face contorted wildly, the facial muscles seeming to want to twitch in several different directions at once. A vein stood out in stark relief on its temple and its eyes filled with red. Emma was sure it would've stroked out if its rage level had increased even the slightest increment in the next moment. Instead, its rage gave way to confusion, and perhaps even the first hint of fear.

It inhaled and exhaled deeply several times, calming itself. Then it said, "Who are you?"

The man smiled. The expression made him look handsomer, seemed to enhance the sparkle of his sky-blue eyes. "I am Captain Flash Wheeler. And I've come to put a stop to your shit. Right fucking now, asshole."

The creature laughed. "I see. And how do you propose to do this? You are only a man, and no mere man can hope to vanquish me."

The man—Jeff, Flash . . . whatever—was still smiling. Emma stared at him in amazement. There wasn't the least indication of fear in either his posture or expression. She didn't want to allow herself to hope. She could imagine nothing crueler than the extinguishing of a revitalized sense of hope. But the feeling was there anyway. Some instinct told her this man, Flash, might really be able to do what he promised. But that was crazy. The logical thing to conclude about his lack of fear was an attendant lack of knowledge. He couldn't possibly know what kind of unfathomable evil was residing in Warren's body. He saw a man, not an ancient, amorphous monster.

But Flash's reply provided a deeper level of astonishment: "It's true. I'm a man. One of the last living members of the species you've nearly exterminated. But I am also more than a man. Dwelling within me now is the essence of your oldest surviving adversary, an entity you believed dead long ago. I am his vessel. Through me his vengeance will be unleashed. Your reign of darkness has come to an end."

The creature's face blanched. "No." It shook its head vigorously. "It can't be." It ventured another laugh, but this time the sound was hollow, humorless, its fear bleeding through in the form of a slight quaver. "I don't believe it. You're a pretender. You caught me off-guard, stopping me with a bit of flimsy magic. But now that I know the truth, I'll break your puny spell, step through this wall as easily as I'd move through a layer of mist."

Flash didn't say anything. He kept smiling.

The creature tried again to move toward him—and again met resistance. It flailed against the invisible wall for a moment, then stumbled backward, an expression of uncomprehending fear and confusion dawning on its face.

"This is impossible."

Flash slowly shook his head. "No. For time beyond calculation, you've terrorized and murdered those weaker than you. You've wiped out entire civilizations. Did you think there'd never be a price to pay?"

Something in the tenor of Flash's voice had changed. He was speaking with greater authority. Emma figured the "adversary" he'd alluded to before had assumed control of his body. There was a visible difference in his posture and in the way he phrased his pronouncements. She wondered if Flash, or Jeff, might already be gone forever, his role in this great drama finished now.

The Adversary smiled again. "Of course that's what you thought. Your boundless arrogance wouldn't have allowed room for any other possibility. But here is the truth you are about to face—your time of reckoning has come round at last."

The Dark One ceased its retreat. It exuded a calm that made Emma nervous. "Enough. I'm leaving this place. I'll deal with you another day."

It closed its eyes, screwed its face up in concentration for a long moment . . . then opened its eyes again. This time its eyes gleamed with genuine terror. A visible shudder rippled through its nude body. "No. This can't be happening. This isn't possible."

The Adversary nodded. "But it is possible. And it is happening. You see, when you believed I was defeated, that I was dead, I wasn't simply hiding. I was at work, biding my time, putting together the means to destroy you. I've accomplished that. What I'm about to unleash is the most powerful destructive force ever conceived. Already you can feel its power thrumming in this room, boxing you in, containing you. Prepare yourself to face the sum psychic total of all the suffering and anguish you've caused over the entire course of your existence. It's time to face the Storm of Souls."

The Dark One screamed. It tore at its hair, ripping bloody hanks of it out as it thrashed helplessly about in the invisible containment box. Emma finally realized what was happening. It was trapped inside Warren, unable to discorporealize itself. It raged like a cornered, rabid animal.

The Adversary's mouth opened wide and a sound like a rising, howling storm wind began to issue from it. The mouth opened still wider, stretching farther than any human mouth should have. The skin took on an elastic, stretched-out appearance, and the shape of Jeff Wheeler's head began to change, inflating to the size of a pumpkin. Then a black mist emerged from the mouth, a swirling, amorphous cloud that rose to the ceiling and spread out across the apartment. Emma shivered and scooted to the far end of the sofa. The temperature in the room dropped drastically, plunging to well below freezing level. A wind rose up, buffeting bits of paper and debris across the room. More than anything, Emma wanted to flee the apartment, but so great was her awe at this astounding sight she simply couldn't bring herself to leave. She had to see what was about to happen.

The howling sound grew louder still and the wind's fury increased to nearly that of a tropical storm. Emma held fast to the sofa, fearing she might be whipped into the air at any moment. But the wind seemed focused on the center of the room, and now it rushed upward in a tremendous blast and blew the roof of the building into the sky. Emma screamed. Zeke's mouth hung open in slack-jawed awe. The black mist coalesced to a fine point and shot toward Warren's body, entering through his open mouth and driving him up against the dining room's far wall. For a moment the mouths of the Adversary and the Dark One appeared tethered together by a black rope.

Then Emma detected flecks of white in the swirling blackness and saw the dark stream was still rushing at the Dark One. Its body was being driven up the wall. It appeared to still be conscious, but just barely—its head lolled and its arms and legs hung limp, as useless as those of a rag doll.

The wind howled again and Warren's body flew into the air, rising through the space formerly occupied by the building's roof, then high above the building, receding to a distant point in the sky. The black tether seemed to stretch forever. Emma realized something in a flash, a thing that made her gasp. The white flecks. Every once in a while she could almost make out a shape. They were faces. She was suddenly sure of it. The "Storm of Souls" alluded to by the Adversary was a literal term. This was the unleashing of every soul ever taken by the Dark One. Including those billions of humans killed in this world as well as all the countless victims from that other world.

The great Storm seemed to go on forever, but in truth the unleashing happened at a speed beyond her comprehension. The pent-up energy of all those lost souls came ripping out of Jeff Wheeler's mouth in less than ten minutes. Then the tether seemed to separate from his mouth and rise rapidly into the sky, disappearing forever within the space of a blink of an eye.

Jeff Wheeler's body fell dead to the floor, landing with a heavy thump.

Emma sat there in stunned stillness and silence for a long time, barely daring to breathe, scarcely able to comprehend the full magnitude of what she'd witnessed. Her gaze moved slowly over the living room, taking in her own nude and bloody body, Zeke Johnson's ruined hand . . .

So much blood.

So much death.

She found it difficult to believe there was anything else in the world anymore, and at last she began to cry, the tears cascading down her cheeks like water from a fountain.

One can understand how Emma felt the way she did, surrounded by so much evidence of carnage and loss.

I certainly can.

But Emma was wrong.

EPILOGUE

MY NAME IS WARREN DANIEL Hatcher, and I have been the narrator of this tale.

But how can that be? you ask.

When last you saw me, dear reader, my body had been driven high into the sky by the Storm of Souls. I couldn't possibly have survived that, right?

Wrong.

I can't pretend to understand completely everything that happened to me, but I'll tell you what I can. My last conscious memory during my time as a prisoner in my own body is from shortly after the beginning of that skyward ascent. I remember looking down at the receding apartment. I saw Emma curled up on that couch. My last thought before unconsciousness took me was of my love for her. I suppose I might have sent out a wish that she be safe, but I don't know, because that was when my time in the dark began.

When I returned to myself—and I mean that in the most literal way—I woke up sprawled on my back in the middle of 21st Avenue. I thought at first that I was dead and in hell now. But then I sat up and surveyed my surroundings. This wasn't hell, but it sure wasn't heaven, either. It was my own dead world. And I was immediately able to ascertain I wasn't far from the building where the big Good vs. Evil, Light vs. Dark, showdown went down. The Mayflower apartment building was maybe a block down the road.

Somehow, I'd been returned to earth essentially unharmed. My scalp was bleeding from where the Dark One had torn out some of my hair and I had a number of scratches all over my body, but otherwise I seemed in fair health. Not only that, but I was in true and sole possession of my faculties again. The monster that had used my body to do so many terrible things was gone. How this had transpired without blowing my physical shell into a thousand pieces, I didn't know.

Nor did I much care when my thoughts came back to Emma. Forgetting the mystery of my bizarre and inexplicable salvation for the moment, I leaped up and ran on my bare and bleeding feet toward the Mayflower. Through the courtyard and into the building, pounding breathlessly up the stairs. Then into the apartment, where Emma saw me through a veil of tears and let out a scream loud enough to shatter glass.

She thought the Dark One had come back, a natural assumption. Quite a bit of convincing was required to make her see the truth. I couldn't blame her. In her place, I guess I would've thought the same. She wanted to get far away from me. None of my earnest beseeching was working. So I finally let her leave the apartment, telling her I'd wait there for her for a few days, should she change her mind. She took off like something shot from a cannon, and believe me, I was pretty much out of faith by that point. I was sure I'd never see her again . . .

I was kind of okay with that. Not happy about it, mind you, but okay with it.

Days went by, but true to my word, I waited, hoping against hope, praying she might return. Later on that first day, Jasmine ventured into the apartment. She looked frightened at first, but then she looked into my eyes and seemed to relax.

She said, "You're back. It's really you, Warren."

I nodded. "Yeah."

And she said the last thing she ever said to me, "Okay."

Then she did something astonishing, a thing that haunts me almost more than anything else. She picked up a knife from the floor and stabbed herself through the heart. She toppled dead to the floor before I could so much as gasp. What caused her to take her own life in that moment is a mystery to me, one I can't begin to fathom. She'd survived, had endured so much, and yet, with the worst remaining threat removed from the world, she made the decision to die. Perhaps she figured it was time to go meet her husband in the afterlife. Or maybe her death was the final consequence of the Dark One's tinkering with her mind. I'm hoping for the former, of course.

Emma came back on the third day. The last time I'd seen her she'd been a mess, naked and smeared with dirt and gore. A broken thing. But in the intervening time she'd managed to clean and clothe herself.

We made eye contact, a gaze that was held for several minutes.

Then she let out a big breath and shook her head. "How?"

I knew what she meant, of course. I shook my head, too. "I don't know. I think it was part of that other one's plan somehow. It wanted me to survive. Why, I don't know. And how it pulled it off I don't know."

Emma nodded, then she sighed again. "I guess it doesn't matter. I'm just glad you're back."

I smiled. We hugged. It was hard for her in the beginning, but over time she learned to trust me again and we have managed to reclaim much of what we once had. And I'm grateful for that. Without Emma, I'm sure I could not have gone on. Without her, I would not be writing this. The prospect of being alone in this empty world is more than I could bear.

It truly is empty. I suppose there may be other survivors scattered elsewhere on the planet, but it's a big world and we may live out the rest of our lives without ever encountering them. And it's just the two of us now. Zeke slipped away one night while we were sleeping, never to be seen again. It's just as well, really. He was a damaged thing, a husk of the man he'd been, with no hope of recovery. I suspect what happened with him is similar to when ailing or elderly pack animals go off on their own to die. Maybe I'm wrong. Maybe he's still out there somewhere. But I don't think so.

In less depressing news, the world seems to be healing itself. The once numerous black rifts in the fabric of reality are disappearing. We encounter them rarely, and when we do I like to watch them for a time. I can almost see them growing smaller, the fabric of existence knitting itself back together around the edges of the blackness. And the rot long ago relinquished its grip on the land. We can grow things, drink untainted water from a stream. I can only theorize that whatever supernatural energy was used to cause these things in the first place began to burn itself out over a period of time, deprived as it was of its source.

Just about done here. I'm not sure why I wrote all this down. I know I said at the beginning I hoped it'd serve as a cautionary tale. But what I have to wonder is, a cautionary tale for who? Who will ever read this? Probably no one. Emma's made it clear she has no interest. In the end, I guess I've done it as a way to fill the time, to give me something to do. What I'll do when I've written the last word on this last page, I don't know. I could make up some stories, I guess. Become a writer of fiction again. But what's the point of that? Other than entertaining myself with fairy tales of a world unmarred by all this destruction.

One last thing. You (the theoretical, nonexistent you—hah-hah) are probably wondering how I could tell the stories of the other people I've written about in these pages. Well, that one's pretty simple. I was a prisoner of the Dark One. And when it touched their minds and absorbed the totality of their knowledge, thoughts, and emotions . . . well, so did I. And somehow I absorbed everything Flash Wheeler knew, probably a side-effect of the Storm of Souls. Which is kind of a creepy thing, I guess, but that's another of the many things I can do nothing about. They're all gone now, those poor bastards, but I thought I at least owed it to them to give them temporary life again on these pages. But now I've done my duty by them and it's time to move on.

I hope the future brings good things, I really do.

It doesn't seem likely.

But, yeah, I hope.

Why not?

What else is there?

BIO

Bryan Smith is the author of numerous novels and novellas, including *Depraved, 68 Kill, Slowly We Rot, The Killing Kind*, and *Dead End House*. He's a two-time Splatterpunk Award winner, once for best novella (*Kill For Satan!*) and once for best collection (*Dirty Rotten Hippies and Other Stories*). He is also the co-author of *Suburban Gothic*, written with Brian Keene. A film version of *68 Kill* was released in 2017. He'll have a story in the forthcoming Simon & Schuster anthology *The End of the World As We Know It: Tales of Stephen King's The Stand*. He lives in TN with his dog Mac. Signed copies of his books can be purchased at https://bryansmithhorror.bigcartel.com/

Other Grindhouse Press Titles